Paul Werner

THE BALLAD
OF THE
YARMOUTH
SIX

adventure novel

Bibliografische Informationen der Deutschen Nationalbibliothek:
Die Deutsche Nationalbibliothek verzeichnet diese Publikation
in der Deutschen Nationalbibliografie, detaillierte bibliografische
Daten sind im Internet über dnb.dnb.de abrufbar.

TWENTYSIX – Der Self-Publishing-Verlag
Eine Kooperation zwischen der Verlagsgruppe Random House
und BoD – Books on Demand

Herstellung und Verlag:
BoD – Books on Demand, Norderstedt
Umschlaggestaltung und Satz:
uc graphic, Heidelberg
Illustration: Evelyn Mantei

ISBN: 978-3-7407-5080-0

FIRST CHAPTER

1. The Wily Minx

The tiny, silvery shining fishing boat dances on the frothy crests of a confused Atlantic cross sea like a hooked swordfish desperately fighting for its life. The remaining distance to the island, whose savaged surface is gaping like a festering wound in mid-ocean, amounts to no more than half a mile. First surging breakers are literally exploding on the low-lying cliffs furthest offshore, their protective ring having only recently been overwhelmed by the devastating power of a hurricane surge.

The two tall, skinny, hollow-cheeked adolescents aboard the boat seem to have drifted into these Caribbean waters straight from the coasts of Africa. At present, they are having all the trouble in the world just to stay on their legs in the billowing waves. They had better though, since sitting down, they would lose control and more likely than not ram their boat into the belt of reefs. As if foul-tempered Poseidon was grudging them even their puny clothing, malicious squalls carrying more than just a whiff of putrefaction keep tearing away at their shoddy rags, singed by the sun and kept together but by layers of sticky salt. With reddened eyeballs, the two of them are fiercely focussed on penetrating the wet curtain of fine spray swooshing over boat and crew whenever another wave bursting with a fierce blow on the boat's bows makes the hull shudder.

The men are in dire need of a breach between the columns of green water shooting up, now here, then there, in front of their salt-burnt eyes like so many playful geysers. One of the two, standing somewhere between the bows and the primitive control column complete with lever and wheel, is desperately holding on to a piece of thin rope, whose loose end cuts deeper into the flesh of his right hand with every jolt of the boat. His mate is clutching the small wooden steering wheel, whose violent jerks threaten to dislocate or break his fingers.

Finally, they make it. Due to sheer luck rather than skill, they manage to give both Scylla and Charybdis the slip and to leave the turmoil of the raging sea behind. Their almost keelless surfboard of a boat glides into the natural haven of a shallow lagoon. Before the hull touches ground, the man at the wheel performs a brusque 180-degree turn, veering the bows into the wind, so that the boat comes to a dead halt within seconds. Then he signals his mate to kick the rusty heap of scrap-iron that serves them as an anchor overboard. While the boat is fidgeting this way and that as if only too eager to break away from this ghost of an island, the two men take up their machetes, blunted and corroded by the vitriolic air as their dull metal is, and pick up two powerful police torches in protective plastic wrapping. Then, they both shoulder knapsacks that look as if they were stitched together from motley pieces of canvas and, pulling on the anchor line once again to make sure the contraption will hold, nimbly climb overboard. Sinking into the greenish water up to their hips, they wade ashore as if on stilts.

Still breathing heavily from the effort of climbing up the sands that offer little foothold, they decide to sit and rest on the bit of beach stretching some fifty yards to the left and right of their improvised roadstead. For a magic moment, the sun, hurrying towards the horizon as if trying to catch up with the loss of time incurred by watching the manoeuvres of the two blacks, briefly immerses the beach in the soft, velvety light of the notoriously brief Caribbean dusk. The two men look out to the sea while munching some mushy crusts of bread, bits and pieces of fried fish they brought in their knapsacks together with two bottles of drinking water each. At long last, they stand up and, almost hesitatingly, muster the island they have so far been turning their backs on as if lacking the courage to face a ghoul.

In the rapidly waning daylight, the small, flat island, whose highest elevation barely bulges over the sea's surface, presents itself to them like a piece of raw flesh brutally ripped from a dying whale's huge corpse. The breath-taking stench that poisons the air stems, not from a drowned cetacean, but from the host of dead fish landed by the surge and, which, after much vain thrashing and floundering, suffocated miserably in the heat. True enough, the island never really was the most precious pearl in the string of Caribbean beads called the Lesser West Indies. Whoever went out of their way to visit it would have to be longing for time out from the hubbub of the madding tourist crowds. At this very moment, however, deprived of even its most modest natural charms, it resembles a pestilential blob that burst and turned inside out. Not so long ago, a murderous surge of gargantuan proportions swept across the low-lying, almost defenceless island flooding it, while the inexorable twister of a cyclone sheared off anything higher than two feet over the ground as if with a giant sickle. Palm trees, shrubbery, cactuses, in short, the entire local flora, sparse and tough though it was, got bent, broken, cut, uprooted and blown to high heaven. Brick and gingerbread houses, bungalows, huts, the odd colourful chapel of this or that denomination literally disintegrated, bits and pieces being scattered all over or piled into heaps of crushed wood, cardboard, and plastic. Road and traffic signs, billboards offering scarce real estate for sale were ripped from their wooden posts and concrete fixations and torn apart like so many worn sails.

The island's sole town was, to all practical purposes, destroyed, deleted from the maps. If it weren't for the lack of bomb craters, one would have attributed this state of utter annihilation to carpet bombing rather than the destructive force of nature unleashed.

Like giant feather dusters, the tussled crowns of uprooted palm trees have spread across large parts of the debris like a cloth over a corpse. A touching but pointless gesture, for there isn't much to hide. Even a look from space is likely to reveal the mercilessness with which this category four hurricane vandalized the island. What used to appear like a gleaming green leaf dancing on the cobalt blue sea has brutally been reduced to a withered water lily.

The fact that no human beings were harmed here is due to precautionary measures based on painful experience. Days before the hurricane, moving along its hardly predictable humming-top route, reached the island, local authorities ordered its hurried evacuation. To the last man and woman, its inhabitants were shipped to its partner island situated further south. Not because that one was presumed to escape the cyclone, but because it boasts a number of concrete buildings, schools and churches with hurricane-resistant basements, all of which had stood the test of prior cyclone afflictions.

Harsh administrative coercion is inevitable on such occasions since not all inhabitants will listen to the voice of reason. Nobody likes to leave their personal property behind, even if only for a few days or the odd week. After all, who knows how much of it they will find again upon their return. Money, jewellery, and other valuables of little bulk and weight the islanders, many of whom had never before left the place even for a day were obviously allowed to take with them. The rest of their belongings including a sizeable number of seriously perturbed pets they had to leave behind and hope against all hope that, this time, the raging elements would not sweep their home into the sea.

The property reluctantly left behind is an easy enough prey for looters such as these two adolescents who obviously haven't come here to offer their condolences. Yet, despite greed and avariciousness obfuscating their brains, even they are impressed by the grisly vista of this horrific scenery. Frequently looking back over their shoulders with uncouth anticipation, they cautiously approach the centre of devastation. Even the moon seems to be shrouding her face with shame. Myriads of stars, sparkling like so many ice crystals in the black void, are impassively blinking down on the righteous and villains alike. A thick cover of dark clouds restlessly chasing across the skies is approaching so fast you would think they have been lying in wait all day to be finally released like a swarm of hungry bats at the first sign of nightfall. Down South, fierce flashes of lightning are darting across the horizon.

The two looters have switched on their torches without freeing them from the semi-transparent plastic wraps. Their cones of dimmed light scurry across the sundry pieces of debris blocking their way. Where precisely public roads end and private properties start, the two of them can only guess. Here and there, they half-heartedly poke about in splintered wood, broken glass and scattered, foul-reeking rubbish with their primitive machetes. Every now and again, they stoop to pick up some promising item only to reject it after a short desultory examination. Logistics is essential. Their knapsacks being smallish and their boat anything but spacious, the men do not want to burden themselves with bulky or heavy stuff of any description.

Abandoned and left to their own devices, dogs will scupper their relatively civilised behaviour almost as fast as their respective masters. Instead of barking away as they have been taught, they will, sooner rather than later, fall back on the wolfish howling anchored in their DNA. As unimpressed as the pilferers seem by such heart-rending arias of hunger, any other, less easily identifiable sounds make them they react with both immediacy and violence. Time and time again, they freeze in mid-movement as if momentarily turned into the proverbial pillars of salt and listen in the darkness with great intensity and concentration.

The risk of some islander having dodged the evacuation measures with the express purpose of catching or killing looters and robbers such as these seems small enough to be negligible. Then again, life is full of little surprises. Take the example of one good-for-nothing, petty thief and certified wino, whose improbable story has been told and re-told in the bars of the Lesser West Indies for the last hundred-odd years. One fine day, this scallywag of a loser had, once again, been flung into the one-cell prison of Le Carbet or some such place on the island of Martinique. Nothing to it, except on that self-same day the neighbouring volcano decided to throw one of its more massive tantrums without having given fair warning. So, when this pathetic wreck of a human being had done with his post-debauch prison slumber, he had found himself, to his dismay or relief, to be practically the only survivor left in a town covered with layers upon layers of lava and smouldering ash.

And so, the possibility of this or that stoned-to-death junkie without next of kin having crawled into some obscure hole to sleep it off while the island was being evacuated can perhaps not be discarded altogether. And there is the outside chance of some competing pilferers being at it, simultaneously, as it were. On their way here, the two men have seen no other boats out at sea. But that doesn't mean a thing. Small boats lying deep in the water are hard to spot in the Atlantic swell. For the time being, though, sea gulls, dogs, rats, and cats seem to be their only competitors around. And they still have enough dead fish to feast on. Wide-open animal pupils time and again reflect the light beams of their torches like crystals of quartz in the pitch-black gallery of a diamond mine.

Every now and again, the men are startled by the grinding sound of a piece of cardboard or plywood swept across a free spot of asphalt by a sudden squall. Doors hanging askew on their creaking hinges are flapping open and shut in the wind. The far roll of thunder announcing a sluggishly approaching storm is slowly growing louder, more threatening.

Here and there the two looters stumble over animal cadavers, cats and dogs drowned or put down by their masters. Their owners probably thought they were doing their best friends a last service by shooting them instead of allowing them to be swept into the sea and torn to pieces by sharks or barracudas.

Finally, the tropical storm has reached the island and starts discharging its unfathomable quantities of water on the pilferers who are helplessly exposed to the big drops literally exploding on the bare skin of their torsos so that, soon enough, they resemble two giant poodles just returning from the shear. Forked flashes of lightning race across the night skies and lend an additional element of drama to the eerie scene. Volleys of close claps of thunder that sound as if produced by violently shaken giant slabs of sheet metal are rolling through the narrow canyons between the mounds of rubbish.

If they feel any pangs of conscience profiting from the plight of others, the two men don't show it. Then again, why should they? From their point of view, even in the best of cases, they will take no more than a dwindling portion of what their African forbears were once stripped of on the island in terms of blood, sweat and tears.

The first tenants to leave their stamp on the island, more recently belonging to the English crown, were the honourable, God-fearing brothers John and Christopher Codrington. It was they who gave their unlikely name to the island's sole settlement, a name that fits the rest of the flowery Caribbean toponymy like an insipid pair of sheep's eyeballs would fit a spicy Cajun gumbo. The commercially inclined English monarch of the time, probably Victoria the Indestructible, must have popped the corks once her very own Privy Council had managed to find two such perfect simpletons as the Codrington brothers willing to pay a handsome sum for the long-term tenancy of this utterly useless little island. To embark on a sugar cane, cotton, or banana plantation, Barbuda's marshy soil was as unfit then as it is today. And yet it soon transpired that the Codrington brothers apparently were not as feeble-minded as all that. Because the one thing the island had plenty of was unused vacant space. Which, in turn, could be exploited for the provision of the one species of raw material, without which any economically viable operation of plantations anywhere between Trinidad and Charleston, say, was not feasible - cheap labour.

Whether or not the Codringtons really did "breed" their slaves like you would cattle, as is maintained by some historians, remains a moot point. Strictly speaking, it would have sufficed for them to maintain the necessary conditions under which the black folks would obligingly multiply at the desired rhythm. What can safely be assumed, though, is that the Codrington brothers made a fortune from selling slaves on the markets of all the other islands above and below the wind.

What gave the brothers their sharp competitive edge was the fact that their slaves had been born and bred in the Caribbean and were, hence, adapted to and familiar with the local conditions, both climatic and otherwise. Because it was not least the humid heat spawning all sorts of disease and epidemics that would time and again kill off black folks who had been rounded up in some arid African region and shipped across the ocean in ships famous for their abominable squalor. They who were born on God-forsaken Barbuda, however, could be put to work on the plantations practically from an infant age, thus promising an unusually long working life. A win-win situation, in other words. Not for the blacks, of course, but for the Codringtons and their clientele.

The moment the looters seek shelter from the relentless rain under a piece of corrugated-iron roofing wedged in a slanting position, the slightly taller man stops his mate by pulling him back on his arm. Thus, immobile for a few seconds, they resemble a shiny ebony double sculpture with thin rivulets of rain water running down their body to form rapidly widening puddles at their feet.

When the pelting rain momentarily subsides, his mate, too, catches the ominous sound. A low whimpering kind of groan like that emanating from a creature breathing its last. It comes from somewhere in the heap of debris to their left. This being the direction whither they just came, they are left with a riddle. If someone is dying there, they must have overlooked him, which, even given the combined handicap of darkness and rain, seems unlikely. Very cautiously, their machetes held ready to strike, they retrace their steps.

Then, they suddenly stop with all signs of horror and the next moment assume a back to back fighting stance. An atavistic reaction planted in the DNA, perhaps, going back to the days of tribal warfare on the African plains. When there is not an attack forthcoming, they slowly relax again. The cones of light from their torches dance across the face, streaming with blood, of a white woman. Fatally injured, it would seem, she managed to crawl into the den created by two destroyed bungalows that have literally been folded into one another. Not surprising, then, that the pilferers didn't notice her first time round. Maybe she was unconscious then, anyway, and didn't produce that eerie groaning sound yet. Woken by the claps of thunder and the pelting of rain on the debris all around her, she probably woke up for a last time just now.

The looters scan the immediate neighbourhood to see whether there are more injured or walking dead anywhere. With obvious relief, they find that this is not the case. The woman has been shot at least once. Blood is trickling from a small entry wound above her right eye and, running from her forehead, nose, and chin, is dripping onto her T-shirt already tainted a darkish red. Where she comes from and how she managed to drag herself here despite her gun wound remains her secret. Sometimes the human body, frail as it may seem on the whole, is nevertheless capable of stupendous feats. The taller of the looters bends down to her and addresses her in English. Her facial expression seems to express understanding, alright, but at the same time, she is far too weak to speak. The only thing she is capable of uttering is that awful heart-rending groan of hers, soon turning into a rattling and wheezing. With great effort, she seems to be forming a word that the two blacks do not understand.

The looters hold a short sotto-voce war council. Their scarce knowledge of the human anatomy in general and the female one in particular, does not allow them to pronounce a more substantial verdict. But despite their youth, they happen to have come across dead and dying and hence recognize a goner when they see one. One way or another, they have absolutely no interest in keeping an eyewitness of their despicable activity alive. The taller one, who tried to talk to the woman a moment ago, now touches his machete and gives his mate a questioning look. His companion shakes his head. He probably knows the sad business of finishing the woman off will be assumed by nature herself. It would be far more useful to learn where the injured woman has come from and what happened to her. She doesn't look like a looter herself but doesn't really give them the impression of being a resident of Codrington either. A tourist specializing in voyages to catastrophe-stricken areas? If she was attacked here, which seems more than likely, the culprit could still be around somewhere.

As though the woman has followed the pilferers' short exchange by reading their lips, she raises her right arm and points to her left, in the general direction of the sea. The taller, more active of the pilferers, jumps on one of the heaps of debris and, by dint of a few dexterous hops, skips, and jumps manages to climb to the peak of the rubble. Once in his precarious position up there, he holds his hand horizontally against his forehead at the level of his eyebrows to form a protective shield against the endlessly pouring rain. Thus, he scans the area for whatever it was the woman intended to indicate to them – a vehicle or vessel of sorts, anything capable of throwing some light on this mystery.

And it would seem his efforts are crowned by success. When he climbs down again, he realizes the woman is dead. His mate closes her wide-open eyes with their glance turned inwards.

They leave the corpse behind in that reclining, half sitting, half lying position. There is neither time nor adequate space for a funeral. The men have come with the beginning of the ebb tide and had better be off the island again at the next high-water mark lest they have to make their way through the razor-sharp reefs at low water and doubtful light conditions. That would be foolhardy for anyone but the most experienced locals, an exclusive club which those two are not members of.

They turn their backs on the rubbish heaps and wade through the lagoon whose water reaches to just about their navels. The narrow band of shallow water is separated from the sea proper by no more than a narrow sandbank some twenty yards wide. In a matter of minutes, they have reached the beach. The rain has stopped. The storm has abated to a festival of silent summer lightning moving North. The increasing density of atmospheric layers near the horizon causes the lavish multitude of twinkling stars to thin out at about sea level. Yet enough celestial bodies remain to render the silhouette of an unlit sailing yacht just about visible against a generally dark background. Moored not far from the beach, it's bobbing in tune with the gentle night swell of the ocean.

The looters point their torches at the yacht. The light beams reach far enough for the men to realize the boat's hull is white. Now they begin to have an inkling where the woman came from. What they still don't know is who shot her and why. The yacht must have arrived sometime after the passage of the hurricane, so much is for sure. It would not have survived the way she is anchored there, without even the sorriest excuse for protection. No adequate hurricane holes have ever been reported on pancake-like Barbuda.

The fact that the yacht doesn't display anchor lights doesn't mean much at all. Passage-making crews tend to be rather willing to do just about anything to reduce energy consumption. Since the island is situated outside the more popular West Indian routes and represents little or no interest to fishing vessels, there is virtually no risk of collision for a yacht anchored here without her masthead lamp lit.

Far more remarkable, however, is the total lack of light below. Add to this the fact that the metallic clew of the genoa, partially unrolled by the tearing wind, keeps knocking against the aluminium mast in the swell without anyone getting sufficiently worked up by the noise to get up and do something about it and what you get is a thoroughly unusual, if not suspect situation. You would have to be very fast asleep, indeed, not to feel irritated by the constant bell-like toll of the clew at some stage. A modern glass-fibre carbon hull makes for a splendid resonance body amplifying even the most discrete contacts with it above or below deck more effectively than any ghetto-blaster. There is something definitely not right with this yacht, this much the two looters conclude instinctively.

Again, they hold a short pow-wow, at normal volume this time. If they want to have a closer look, they will have to swim across to the yacht and climb aboard. That could be riskier than it might seem. Whoever is aboard the boat might be responsible for the woman's death. If so, he or she will have as little interest in eye-witnesses of their doings as the two pilferers. Then again, the dead woman could have been roaming the oceans single-handedly and happen to have been robbed and shot by pirates shortly before the pilferers arrived. The pirates may have left her for dead and departed in their own vessel, carrying off what booty they may have found on the yacht. In which case the boat, in all its apparent splendour, would have to be judged as abandoned.

Without knowing their way around the complexities proffered by the law of the seas, the two of them seem to have heard of substantial fees paid by insurance companies to those who manage to salvage and bring into safe port a vessel that would otherwise clearly have been lost at sea. Always provided the vessel was insured at all and had sufficient coverage. In such cases, the fee, high as it may seem, will always represent but a fraction of the price of an adequate replacement yacht. Hence, any insurance adjuster in his right mind will be only too glad to fork out the respective amount without necessarily asking too many questions.

Such dizzying expectations way beyond what they could ever have hoped for scatters their initial qualms to the wind. Anything is better than having to act like scavengers and compete with dogs, rats and God knows what else in the race for useable rubbish. They drop their knapsacks in the sand, hang their machetes round their necks and, after a few yards' wading again, plunge headlong into the deeper, calmer part of the surf.

By the mere look of it, they have no great experience swimming, but don't really have to either. A dozen or so paddling strokes take them to the anchor chain which they cling to for a moment, huffing and puffing and spitting out salt water. Having soon recovered from the physical effort, they reflect on the boarding aspects. Groping along the immaculate, slippery hull, they find their way aft. The yacht has an overall length of some fifty-odd feet. In many Northern European marinas, that kind of size would qualify for respectful glances tainted by a touch of envy. In the Caribbean, though, anything short of, say, a hundred feet can at best claim to dory status. Suffice it to point out that many sailing yachts tied to the pier at English or Falmouth Harbours, Antigua, sport masthead and spreader lights that do not display the usual nautical white lights but proudly present the red ones normally reserved for aviation. What better way for their owners to insinuate that the sky is the limit.

At the stern, the two looters about to turn into salvagers are received by a humming and whizzing wind rotor that helps to produce electricity. Of which, to all appearances, there must be a healthy surplus on board this vessel. Several solar panels, normally also producing current, have been folded and hung over the railing like washing on a line. Either they weren't needed today, or someone folded them at sunset. Which might mean that the killing of the woman was an even much more recent event. Another piece of bad news for the men: there is no bathing ladder hanging from the transom, something that would have facilitated their boarding considerably.

The Wily Minx, one of the two men spells the yacht's peculiar name more than he reads it out. Who the hell is Willy Minx, and why is his first name spelled wrongly? As her home port, the yacht's transom reveals a place called Sark. That's another riddle for the two men. What kind of a place is that, sounding like shark? Neither of them has ever heard of it. Nor can they identify the flag she flies: a red St. Andrew's cross on white ground, the left upper box red with two gold female lions, rather thin ones, whose whip-like tails stretch across their entire, ascetic-looking backs. Colourful stuff alright, what with the emaciated lions and all, but not half as fanciful as some of the Caribbean national flags they have seen between the two of them.

Giving up on that hopeless rigmarole, the men swim to the bows again and discuss alternative boarding methods. The options are few and far between, as it would seem. One of them will have to climb up the anchor chain. That is neither easy, nor, and more important, can it be done noiselessly. On the contrary, few articles of a boat's equipment are noisier than her anchor chain, whose galvanized links will, as a rule, be forever sliding to and fro in a lip-like device made of steel. The permanent rumbling, knocking and rasping is usually loud enough to wake the dead. Silencing measures, though perfectly possible, are not always desirable, at least not for the skipper. The grating sounds of the chain, irritating as they may be, especially for the crew bunking in the forward cabin, tend to be the first warning signs of a yacht going adrift after her anchor lost its grip. Hence, many skippers, placing safety over comfort, prefer to keep this additional means of alert intact.

The taller looter, who has already proved his sense of initiative by climbing on the rubble heap next to the unfortunate woman, now puts an end to the discussion by seizing the chain and climbing up hand over hand relatively silently. Then he crawls under the railing very much like a soldier would under some barbed wire and lies flat on deck for a spell, panting and listening. The sea water dripping from his lean body forms a trickle that runs back into the ocean by way of the scupper. Down below, not a sound, so far. Up on deck, the genoa clew keeps hammering its ghastly lonesome rhythm. After a while, the man gets up and tiptoes aft, to the transom, where he takes the small plastic ladder off its fixture and folds it down the transom to provide his mate with a more comfortable means of boarding the Wily Minx.

Clasping their machetes and torches, they scuffle over the teak deck which smells of moist wood. Even in the dark, the yacht looks and smells brand new. If it weren't for that faint whiff of sweet decay in the air. The double wooden door leading down the companionway has been left wide open, as if to invite them in. The closer they come, the stronger the sickeningly sweet stench of carrion grows.

Cringing with anticipation, they stick their heads in the opening and switch on their torches. As the cones of light flit down the companionway and about the saloon, they see nothing downright untoward at first. Everything looks more or less as it should in a well-kept yacht. Except for the man in shorts and T-shirt sitting on the lavishly upholstered bunk at the far end of the wooden table. His head has fallen backwards and is now reclining on the upper rim of the backrest as if the man just fell asleep, recovering from the strain of a long Atlantic crossing. What doesn't quite fit the peaceful image is the ugly reddish-black bullet hole in his forehead, right between the eyes. No blood trickling from it any longer, the man has been dead for some hours, it would seem. What little blood has run down the back of his nose, coagulated a while ago, now forming a thick crust in his moustache. It doesn't take the verdict of an experienced coroner to realize that this man, whatever his function aboard may have been, died instantly.

Bending down low, the two looters cautiously climb down the companionway. As they start inspecting the cabins one by one, they come across two more bodies, one male, one female. They, too, seem to have been executed with a single shot to the forehead from a small-calibre firearm. The killer appears to be a stickler for precision. No killing rampage here, no hard feelings involved at all perhaps, just clinical precision coupled with a total lack of empathy. Those were neither pirates nor drug traffickers ridding themselves of awkward witnesses. The two men agree on this being rather the work of a cold-blooded and very dangerous killer, probably operating alone.

Whatever happened here can't have gone down that long ago, else the bodies would smell a lot more unpleasant and, in these latitudes, be already covered with maggots galore. If there is any animal able to pick up the scent of dead meat almost before the killing has taken place, it's the bluebottle. The killer has had just enough time to disappear unnoticed. Maybe it was the looters' sudden appearance on the island that drove him off the boat, which he might otherwise have used to sail on to Antigua or some other place. Which begged the question how he would put his retreat into practice now

Maybe he came on some other vessel? The pilferers haven't seen any, it is true. But then, they were very much focussed on navigation first, and on rummaging through the debris afterwards.

One way or another, the men are now faced with a dilemma. Either they leave the yacht and its shocking contents behind as it is, or they decide to lay claim to the salvage fee. In which latter case they would have to sail the Wily Minx down Antigua way or take her in tow. It all depends on the state of affairs in the engine room, since neither of them has ever learned to move along on sails only, and neither wants to start practicing that now.

Also, they will have to come up with a plausible story about how and where exactly they came into possession of the yacht. With a solid dose of realism fed by dim experience, it doesn't take them long to grasp that neither their presence on the island, nor the massacre on board would argue in their favour. Hence, what they need is a waterproof plan "B". For instance, they could pretend they came across an abandoned Wily Minx adrift on the ocean and took possession of her as you would of a stray horse in the prairie. Which would mean they have to get rid of the corpses first thing. Sailing along with some bloated, maggot-eaten stinking bodies aboard would, in any event, be something to be rather avoided, anyway. At least there are no traces of a fierce fight to be removed. There just hasn't been any, funny enough. The unfortunate foursome must have been caught totally unawares and taken it sitting or lying down.

Which allows the assumption that they knew their killer. Knew him and trusted him at least sufficiently for him to take easy advantage of the situation. He must be so certain of his shooting proficiency he hadn't even bothered to go after the woman the pilferers came across among the debris. He knew she wouldn't get far, fatally wounded, on a deserted island.

The two of them climb back on deck to get some fresh air and discuss the next steps. Follow the money is what they finally agree upon. Whilst one draws a deep breath as if about to go diving, and lowers himself into the saloon, the other one swims ashore once again, where the woman's body has already drawn a pack of ravenous rats. When he gets back on board, he finds his mate has disposed of the three corpses, which are now floating in the water together with the dead woman he himself contributed. Sharks and barracudas won't be long smelling the bait.

The men finally tie the genoa clew and try starting the engine. It takes three or four attempts till the starter coil catches on and cranks the engine into life. If the fuel gauge can be trusted, which, usually being the first appliance to go, it manifestly cannot, they should nevertheless have enough diesel fuel in the tank to reach Antigua. They decide to go for it and tow their own boat, whose outboard engine is that much weaker than the fifty-six horse-power Volvo Penta of the Wily Minx.

As they approach the roadstead where they left their open boat hours ago, the dawn has just spread enough daylight for them to realize with no little amazement that their own vessel has gone and is nowhere to be seen. Did it break anchor or chain and go adrift? In that case, it may have hit a reef and sunk. They look at each other questioningly and finally shrug it off. Just another detail they will have to take into consideration when spinning their yarn.

2. At Fjord's End

"Name's Kurtz, Colonel Archibald Kurtz." The man behind the wheel of a silvery grey Cherokee Longitude turns the rear-view mirror in above his head so as to make it reflect his face and gives a hearty yawn. On the whole, he appears reasonably satisfied with what he sees: the portrait of a man in his sixties staring back at him with a critical mien and a very rigid, penetrating kind of stare.

They are the dominant feature of his physiognomy, his piercing, greyish-green husky's eyes that may befit a sledge dog but, when met with in humans, tend to make everyone look the other way. Besides, on closer inspection, his nose seems a trifle too long or too wide, or maybe both. "Kurtz" turns the mirror back and looks at his watch. He has another one hundred or so miles to go on this spectacular winding rollercoaster of a scenic road. Studded as it is with hairpin bends, breath-taking falls and steep rises along the northern shore of one of the longest and most beautiful Norwegian fjords, that's going to take him another two, two and a half hours of driving. Not counting possible further breaks like the one he's just indulged in to light his first cigarette of the day.

To his right, the rays of the noon sun are doing their level best to penetrate the greenish pea soup of the fjord's calm, silent waters. They will have to hurry. In less than an hour's time, the first long shadows of the high mountain ranges rising imperviously on either side of the fjord will start darkening the surface of the water and cool it down to little above freezing point.

To the driver's left, a quick succession of dark green meadows smelling of freshly mowed grass, picturesque crofts and the odd village situated at the foot of steeply rising, gleaming wet rock faces makes for the typical fjord-country landscape. Mountain peaks covered with thick layers of snow for most of the year send their icy melt waters down into the valleys in the form of thunderous foaming cataracts hundreds of yards long. Wedged in by solid, unflinching walls of granite and gneiss, the local population, "Kurtz" muses, would stand no chance of survival in the case of a huge tsunami sweeping along the fjords of Norway's Atlantic coast.

What would it take to trigger a catastrophe like that? Not that much, in fact. A minor earthquake would probably suffice. A few tremor-like shocks might trigger a landslide of gargantuan dimensions among those seemingly rock-solid masses of stone which, in truth, are perpetually on the move. The tsunami resulting from this would obliterate all life along its path.

Hence, people living here have a lot in common with those settling next to a would-be extinct volcano that will presumably never erupt again – except when it does, one fine day. Looking at it from that angle, it's strange to see something like it has never as yet been recorded. Whenever sober, the Vikings were rather taciturn people, not exactly given to much reading or writing, it seems. But surely, a tsunami would have found its way into some saga or edda of sorts, one would wish to assume.

"Kurtz" grins and slides a CD into the car's Old-School phono system. As the music catches on, he sways to the left and to the right in tune with the rhythm: if you'll be ma bodyguard, I could be your long-lost friend…The deeper meaning of some of those pop songs remains a life-long mystery to most mortals non-addicted to pop. With all signs of boredom "Kurtz" reaches into the glove-compartment, takes out his iPad and starts frantically running the fingers of his free right hand over the screen while holding the wheel with his left. He seems unwilling to devote more attention to the admittedly sparse local traffic than absolutely necessary. The fact that he drifts onto the left-hand side of the road every now and again seems to indicate he is not all that familiar with Continental European road traffic. Be that as it may, he seems oblivious to the danger caused by the local coaches that assume the lion's share of indigenous Norwegian public transport and have a way of treating any contraflows with an air of contempt.

The fjords have for a long time been known as the favourite holiday haunt of, in particular, German tourists. Among those, teachers and pensioners with survival campers and elaborate motor homes are predominant enough to take it away. The really well-off meet on board the ludicrously expensive Hurtigruten cruise ships whose popularity, for reasons unknown, shot up in the nineteen eighties and nineties.

What are these people hoping to find here, "Kurtz" wonders as he looks around and shakes his head. A country as rugged as its population, whose provincial self-sufficiency, Hamsun-like melancholic depression and wide-spread xenophobia have all found adequate expression in Edvard Munch's extraordinary Scream.

Basically, it's another case of the hen and the egg. Was people's mentality formed by the claustrophobic set-up of those enchanted dales or did those narrow valleys attract certain kinds of melancholy, hard-drinking individuals from the very start? A bit of both, presumably.

What with their almost stagnant waters and their one-sided access to the ocean, the fjords, as opposed to the sounds, open on both sides like human guts, form peculiar blind alleys halfway between a river and a mountain lake. Like rivers, they have always served the transport of men and merchandise. Like lakes, they tend to convey the feeling of almost transcendental peace and quiet, or, on bleaker days, cause the uneasy feeling of harbouring some dark and sinister secret. Either as base jumpers or as suicide victims, not a few folks, both Norwegian and alien, ended their lives by hopping or dropping from particularly well-known mountain spots along the fjords, such as the fabulous "Pulpit".

Even at the best of times, fjords are, of course, no way near the pulsating arteries which are the large rivers of Europe and the rest of the globe. Rivers, whose meandering whims helped form our landscapes and mindscapes in war and peace. The fjords could never be that, because of their lack of shores transcending the physical and mental borders between tribes and nations. Economically speaking, their failure was a foregone conclusion if only for the lack of a viable hinterland. A vital shortcoming that turned fjords into virtual blind alleys and practically condemned the Vikings to a life at sea, forever in search of business partners further and further afield. Did they discover America? Of course they did. Did it do them any good? Not that we know of. Which doesn't mean there aren't any irrefutable successes to be marked on the bright side. One of them is linked with the name of Russia, another with that of Normandy.

"Kurtz" lets out a snorting sound and looks at his watch again. For the umpteenth time, he then looks at his iPad, which has, for some minutes now, been adorned with the portrait of a young-ish man in his mid-twenties. His somewhat complacent mien is made more easily bearable by being half hidden behind a dense mat of blond hair. Could he be gay? That's affirmative, "Kurtz" answers his own question.

"Hi there, Olaf, how's it hanging?" "Kurtz" addresses the portrait as if skyping with the blond, blue-eyed, sun-spotted latter-day Viking so completely and totally fitting the general idea of a Scandinavian. Or Aryan, for that matter.

"Kurtz" throws the iPad with the photo up onto the passenger seat and focusses on the road again, not without repeatedly taking sidelong glances at the screen as though he wants or needs to memorize Olaf's physiognomy for some future reference. Some people endowed with, or suffering from, a peculiar savant syndrome, are apparently able to remember every feature and detail of a face they may only have seen once, fleetingly, at that. "Kurtz" apparently doesn't belong in that category.

The next moment, he hits the brakes so hard that the Cherokee grinds to a brutal halt with screeching brakes and smoking tyres. Right in front of him, situated in a kind of dead-end hollow, his target location seems to be basking in the afternoon sun. That's it, your typical village at the end of the fjord, its nondescript character begging the question why in God's name anyone would take the trouble of coming here in the first place. "Kurtz" obviously has an excuse in the form of an errand to run.

He seems to have arrived somewhat earlier than feared. Deftly, he manoeuvres his Cherokee into a long-term camper and motor home parking site on the hill and places it between two manifest-ly unoccupied campers in such a way as to protect it from any inquisitive glances while having a good look at the village himself. As it points outward, it's furthermore ready for take-off any time without "Kurtz" having to turn or move it sideways first. On balance: had someone less experienced in such things devoted half a day to the search for the most appropriate parking spot to pick, they could hardly have hit upon a better spot than the one that came kind of naturally to "Kurtz" right away.

Beyond the road, the dirty grey and green waters of this arm of the fjord cutting deepest into the land keep washing over a patch of stony black shore. The somewhat bigger rocks of this former end moraine have a coat of dirty green seaweed, whose slimy tentacles indicate the state of what remains of the Atlantic tide once you are thus far removed from the ocean.

Svartdalen, the village, hardly more than a hamlet, really, is not an organically grown community with quaint but authentic wooden houses that are reminiscent of the clinker-built Viking long boats. This isn't Bryggen, either, with its stores, magazines, and workshops where leather was formed into solid mountaineering boots or iron forged into weapons and wooden poles turned into the legs of chairs and bedposts. Much rather, it's a Disneyland creation shaped on Alpine edelweiss models and stuffed with souvenir shops, cheap burger houses, Starbucks joints, run-of-the-mill restaurants and grotesquely pimped-up hotels with antler-adorned reception halls. Looking at the scenery from his vantage point on the hill, "Kurtz"

cannot help suspecting all of this phoney splendour will be dismantled at seven p.m. sharp by an underpaid mobile Pakistani worker unit to be handed on to the end of the next fjord arm, which the majority of tourists will home in on tomorrow.

"Kurtz" seems in no particular hurry. Again he gropes for the glove compartment and this time pulls out a small pair of binoculars through which he scrutinizes the flock of elderly people who happen to be taking to the road this very minute, sporting trekking gear of sorts complete with knapsacks and ski sticks. When he has seen enough, he puts back the binoculars and iPad and looks at his wristwatch.

The appointed hour of the rendezvous with Olaf appears to have come. He gets out of the Cherokee, stretches his tendons, muscles and bones and locks the door from a distance with the remote of his keys. Then he takes off his leather jacket so that his red turtle-neck jersey pullover makes him a coloured blot in an otherwise rather monochromatic landscape.

He looks around to check whether any local parking regulation might come in the way of his leaving the Cherokee to itself for a while, finds none and walks off. The village lives on bus and ship-loads of tourists. Hardly anyone gets here in their own car. Humming a tune to himself, he throws his jacket over his shoulder and continues on his way into the centre of the village. Apparently, he has a problem of sorts with his right leg, which he drags a little, so that his gait looks kind of wabbly. He stops here and there to take a look at the objects of desire displayed in this or that shop window. Finally, he enters the terrace of a café and looks around for a vacant table.

He is in luck. A young couple that has for some time been wiping away at their respective iPhone screens gets up and leaves the terrace. "Kurtz" takes possession of the table and orders a black coffee. While waiting for it, he turns his chair just enough to face both the road and the entrance of the hotel right across from the café.

The young trainee waitress has hardly had time to serve the cup of coffee with the usual footbath, when a coach stops smack in front of the hotel. Two dozen or so elderly passengers visibly plagued by the typical banes of old age such as sciatica, rheumatism and all sorts of orthopaedic ailments start leaving the coach.

"Where on earth did they go? Just to be sure to avoid the spot," "Kurtz" jokingly asks the waitress.

"Oh, they were all around thirty and fit as so many fiddles when they left this very morning," the girl answers.

"It's what our air does to people, so better take care not to breathe in too much of it."

"Kurtz" gives her a dry laugh and a wink, never losing sight of the hotel, though. Thus, when a blond young man turns round the coach all of a sudden with some aplomb, "Kurtz" immediately gets up, leaves a handful of kronor on the table and follows "Olaf" towards the far end of the village, the one opposite the campers' site on which his car is parked, that is. No doubt, this is the sun-spotted Aryan from the iPad. Maybe a year or two older, with just the suspicion of a developing embonpoint, but Olaf alright.

Dressed a little out of season with only a white cotton shirt, light blue jeans and brand-new sneakers, he doesn't look like someone hell-bent on a quick tour of the mountains. Not at this relatively late hour. More likely, he is heading for some lonely spot in the sparse grove of coniferous trees, whose first crippled specimens mark the end of the village - or its beginning, all according to which direction you happen to approach it from. In his right hand, Olaf carries a jute shopping bag dangling in tune with his firm, swift step.

"Kurtz" doesn't show himself to Olaf but keeps him on a long leash, following him from a safe distance until the man has passed the last Svartdalen houses and disappears in the grove.

It doesn't take "Kurtz" long to spot Olaf again, even though, meanwhile, the Norwegian has strayed quite a bit from the beaten path to get to the fjord's banks. In his present position, a hillock overgrown with moss and lichen shields "Olaf" from the through traffic on the road, at the same time blocking his view of everyone approaching him from that side.

He has taken off his sneakers and lets his feet dangle in the icy water while he files through a notebook of sorts. Its tattered pages indicate that the scrapbook must have accompanied him for quite some time already. Nor is this likely to be his first visit to this spot. Presumably, there have been other hot dates of the sort he is looking forward to now. Smultronstället, the secret place where the wild strawberries grow. That's what the neighbouring Swedes call a place like that. A small retreat, only known to few, a tiny little speck of Eden God allows some of us particularly well behaved to retain after the disappointing Fall from Grace, in general.

With a limp that seems to grow more perceptible by the minute, "Kurtz" now leaves the beaten path as well and, looking cagily left and right, stalks through the shrubbery towards the moss-covered hillock. Apparently, he wants to surprise "Olaf", who may not be expecting him, at least not at this time of day. As skilfully as "Kurtz" winds his way through the grove despite his handicap, he might fool even an experienced hunter or park ranger. As for "Olaf", having plunged deeply into his scrapbook, biting off a piece of the apple he took out of his bag, all he probably hears is the lapping of the curling wavelets and the rushing by of the odd motor home.

When "Kurtz" has come close enough for his purposes, he grabs under the seams of his pullover behind his back and pulls out a snub-barrelled revolver so small it almost disappears in his fist. The gun in his right hand, he pops the barrel and rotates it with the palm of his left to make sure there's a fresh round in each chamber except the first one. The purring metallic sound and the snapping of the cock have at last alerted "Olaf", who turns his head nervously and lowers his booklet. "Kurtz" is now only a few steps away from him, as he raises his gun to the height of "Olaf"'s head.

"Olaf Bergström?" he asks in the same dry, matter-of-fact voice with which a pizza-deliverer might ascertain he's found the right customer.

"Olaf" doesn't reply. He drops his notebook, jumps off the rock and makes a move towards the road. But, all things considered, that's a hopeless gesture. With a quick swerve of his gun, "Kurtz" follows the movement of his victim and fires a single shot. One shot, only. The bullet hits "Olaf" in the left temple and jerks him a step or two to the right, where he collapses and lies motionless. Blood is colouring his thick blond hair red in places like poppy growing from a field of golden rape.

"Kurtz" has to be sure of himself in more ways than one. He hasn't bothered to use a silencer, yet the relatively small calibre of what might have passed as a toy gun emits but a discrete bang. And even in the unlikely case of someone's attention having been caught by the sound, there are so many elk hunters on the loose in these parts, a solitary shot like this one scandalizes no-one.

Neither does "Kurtz" verify whether or not his victim is really stone cold dead. Instead, he pockets his gun, picks up "Olaf"'s scrapbook and, shaking his head at so much self-indulgence, drops it next to the body as if trying to make sure the blond effigy of a Viking has enough material to read while travelling to Walhalla. No traces to obliterate – there aren't any except maybe his footprints. A veteran Indian scout in the redneck backwoods of Arizona might well be able to identify the killer as a man with a limp. The Norwegian police, however, are unlikely to employ any offspring of Cochise or Geronimo. And so, with measured steps, he walks back towards Svartdalen and his fully air-conditioned Cherokee bronco.

3. Islands in the Stream

The man in the cockpit of his elderly little Westerly sailing yacht with its patriotic blue and red stripes around what must once have been an immaculately white hull lets go of the steering wheel for a moment to sip some hot tea from a Thermos which he secures in a wooden rack on the boat's steering column. The yacht is coming from the general direction of St. Peter Port, Guernsey, whose Victoria Marina it probably left an hour or so ago.

Because of their strong currents and innumerable rocks lurking above or just below the surface, the waters east of Guernsey are considered hazardous even by the locals. Yet the man in the Westerly either knows his way about or calmly places his fate in the hands of the Lord. Pleading in favour of a certain basic familiarity with the difficult local conditions is the fact that he happens to have chosen the best moment for this part of his voyage and doesn't seem to be acting with any noticeable frantic activity or unnecessary precipitation. By the look of it, he isn't particularly impressed by the region's bad karma at all.

Keeping the setting sun at his back, he profits from its warm, soft rays spreading almost horizontally, so that the man's vision is not impaired by any irritating jack-o'-lantern reflections on the restlessly billowing surface of the sea. That's a good thing, since the best possible visibility is a vital prerequisite when aiming at threading the eye of the needle between the islet of Jethou and the mere rock of Crevichon, a passage the Westerly's skipper seems ambitious enough to tackle. Excellent visibility comes as a godsend in an area like this, frequently haunted by fog and mist. While there is precious little a man can do about the weather conditions of the day, most recent large-scale charts as well as thoroughly updated tide tables are indispensable requirements any responsible skipper should see to having aboard at all times. As today's tidal data show, the rickety old Westerly is right on the money, sailing on a rising tide at halfway house.

As the saying goes, time and tide wait for no man. To ascertain the truthfulness of the former, an occasional hard look in the mirror will do. For anyone wishing to check on the veracity of the adage's latter part, the Bay of St. Malo, reaching from the spiked helmet of Mont St. Michel in the South to Cap de la Hague in the North would make a first-rate testing ground.

This is chiefly due to the topographical characteristics of this arrowhead of a gulf marking the borderline between Normandy in the East and Brittany in the West. Every time huge masses of Atlantic water are pushed north-northeast by the tide, they have no other option but to hit the natural barrier of the Cotentin peninsula, functioning like a dam in those situations. The resulting mean tidal amplitude, viz. the difference between mean high and low water marks as registered over a long period of time, reaches impressive forty-foot peaks.

For the population of the dozen or so inhabited islands, islets and rocky archipelagos scattered across the Bay like so many seeds carelessly tossed across a field by a hung-over farm hand, this is not unqualified good news.

For starters, the water in the Bay circulates regularly so that there is no pond-effect but water threatening to grow stale is hurriedly replaced and the lot, hence, clear and fresh at all times. A fact that is heartily embraced by the local marine fauna as much as, eventually, by man himself.

On the flip side, the very same tidal constellation that helps creating this natural bounty seriously thwarts man's efforts to harvest it. Since, for reasons beyond man's control, these waters have a grand total of some six hours, only, to reach their culmination point, they will have to make considerable haste, once round the Cotentin Peninsula.

Thus, tides in the Bay of St. Malo do not only reach forbidding heights, but also mind-boggling rates reminiscent of the speed of torrential mountain streams. Water moving along at around twelve knots is a navigational hazard in itself, creates unpleasant maritime spin-offs such as vortexes and counter-currents and tends to shape and re-shape the sea bed by constantly shifting sandbanks, preferably right across what used to be safe fairways only yesterday.

In some canyon-like seabed passages, the tidal currents will be further accelerated, thus becoming subsurface rapids. If and when, at the height of the tide, say, a strong wind starts rubbing the tide up the wrong way, the Bay seen from above will resemble a cauldron of boiling water.

Professional shipping gives the Bay a wide berth, anyway. Sailing yachts wishing to cruise the islands have no other choice but to lie low and wait for the best possible conditions. Even so, they should be satisfied with covering short legs that can be done on the wings of one favourable tide only. Hotspots worthy of particular attention should be approached during those brief periods the locals call the middle tide.

Some three hours after each turning of the tide, the waters in this forever rumbling bay take a short break during which they seem to be chewing the cud, ruminating on whether or not they ought to go through this entire hullabaloo one more time. That's the moment when skippers may rely on their visual alignments or "guestimates" which, in the Bay of St. Malo, largely replace both GPS and compass to this day and age. High red and white chimney north of St. Peter Port aligned with black and white chequered beacon just South of Sark would be the alignment which, crude as it may sound, is likely to take the Westerly safely through a particularly narrow passage – the one between the Scylla Jethou and the Charybdis Crevichon. A passage that, at low tide, can be crossed on foot.

That eerie places such as these, for entire centuries haunted by pirates, should nowadays be visited by evil spirits, can come as no surprise to anyone. When pirates, buccaneers and privateers went out of fashion, these cut-throats' deaths were frequently just about as spectacular as their lives had been. On top of the small but steep island of Jethou, for instance, the decaying bodies of pirates would dangle by their necks from crudely knocked-up gallows, their rags flapping in the gentle offshore breeze. The barely hidden irony in this was that Jethou island featured a huge cave, dry at all states of the tide, which, over the decades and centuries, many pirates had used as the preferred hiding place of what riches they had managed to accumulate. Hence, not a few men were hanged on top of what used to be their treasure trove.

Crevichon, on the Westerly's port side, is a totally different kettle of fish. Or of crab, rather, since, as its name suggests, it used to be a place where shellfish such as lobster, crab or shrimps was caught by the basketfuls. This would have been long before the little speck of an islet was converted into a granite quarry and layer upon layer of rock sliced off and shipped to England. The frequent blasts and hammerings probably proved too much for the noise-sensitive shellfish that emigrated to other, calmer biotopes.

Granite, as it was won all over the Bay of St. Malo, was highly appreciated everywhere as a building material that promised to last forever and a day. Apparently, the Brits used it for the steps of Westminster Abbey. The German Nazis, who got their granite slabs from the Swedes, primarily, were focussing more on everyday uses and turned the stuff into kerbstones in Berlin and other major cities, where they would soon have to stand the test of Allied bombing.

Meanwhile, the Westerly sails past one more beacon formed like a pyramid sitting on top of the rock that would otherwise only just break the surface at low tide. Moments later, the yacht turns into the wind and glides into a narrow gap of deeper water, propelled but by its own inertia. The fact this spot right beside the small island of Herm, never falls dry, makes it an ideal roadstead, or "rade", for visiting yachts.

The skipper slips the jib sheet, leaves the cockpit and walks to the mast, where he frees a tight halyard with a quick flick of his hand, so that the mainsail slides down the mast and instantly disappears almost completely in a lazy bag. Then he strides to the bows, dragging his right leg slightly but noticeably. Here, he releases the CQR anchor from its fixture and drops it into the water. While the Westerly's rattling anchor chain follows the anchor to the ground at some twenty feet below the surface, the skipper takes down the jib as well and ties it to the railing with bits of rope.

The whole manoeuvre has taken only minutes to perform and demonstrates the skipper's familiarity with his yacht. Now he sits down in the cockpit, lights a cigarette and waits for a few minutes till he can be reasonably sure that his anchor has dug in or "bitten" and is likely to hold, barring a dramatic change in the weather conditions, of which there is no sign, at present. A little later, he flips the fag end overboard and disappears below. The tide has become lively again, the water level steadily approaching today's peak. In the West, the sinking sun transforms the silhouette of St. Peter Port into the bizarre setting of a shadow theatre.

True enough, local dusks assume a more relaxed rhythm in these climes than those in the tropics. Notwithstanding, at some stage, pitch dark night will fall here, too. A thick, almost solid cloud cover prevents all but a few celestial bodies particularly close to earth from displaying their usual splendour. The man has switched on no anchor light. He probably knows that even during daytime, few yachts will stray here. The catamaran-ferry from St. Peter Port has shut up shop for the day. Besides, it doesn't use the roadstead but enters the tiny island harbour, which dries completely at low tide, so that you can free a yacht's underwater works from barnacles or even give it a new lick of anti-fouling. What you cannot do, though, is leave the place when it suits you.

As for the Westerly, it doesn't appear to have come here to undergo any such maintenance works. The chafing sound of the wooden sliding lid above the companionway announces the man's return to the cockpit. He has donned a black neoprene suit and blackened his face, thus becoming almost invisible in the dark. In his right hand, he carries a watertight plastic knapsack. Performing a three-sixty, he looks around to all sides. The blinking and flashing lights on Guernsey, Sark, and Herm seem familiar enough. Every now and again, their light intervals overlap, only to dissociate themselves again from one another in a hurry. Thus, they resemble strangers accidentally meeting in the night, briefly looking each other in the eyes, but ultimately shying away from any more intimate form of contact as if suddenly shocked by their own audacity.

On the island, the lights of Rosaire and Fisherman's Cottage are the only proof of life. The man lets down his bathing ladder and climbs in the water, which, at this time of year, must be scrotum-tightening chilly, to quote that famous Irishman's rather peculiar version of Ulysses. The skipper has turned frogman alright but doesn't really look like he wants to go either fishing or diving. With a few calm motions of his arms, he covers the small distance to the beach. As he gets out of the water on the island side, his wet neoprene suit glistens silvery like the scaly skin of a big fish that decided to take a nightly stroll on shore for once. Unnoticed, just for the heck of it. The flippers will have to go, of course. He bends down and swaps them for a pair of shoes he has taken out of his knapsack. The he shoves the flippers under the blackberry bush to his right and is on his way.

Largely concealed by the darkness, he walks on, leaning slightly forward and dragging his right leg like a runner who has just torn a calf muscle. Crossing an almost treeless meadow, he makes for a kind of manor. Every now and again, he stops, looks to his left and right and then carries on. At some stage, a seemingly big dog starts barking somewhere in the distance. There are no vehicles on Herm and the risk of someone going about on horseback at this time is small. Some never-tiring bats, noiselessly darting by like swallows of the night, are the only creatures scurrying through the humid air heavy with the scent of salty grass and rotting seaweed.

The man has arrived at the Rosy Manor, whose pink fa ade, now mercifully veiled by the darkness, probably does the manor's kinky name proud during daytime. He takes a deep breath and fumbles in his knapsack. The next moment, the lurking suspicion that he may not have come here with the purest of intentions is corroborated by the fact that he pulls out a gun. He makes the magazine drop out the butt end and checks that it's filled and ready for use. Then he pushes the magazine back and chambers a round.

Ignoring the heavy bronze door knocker, he cuts out one of the six small painted bull-glass panes that the ground floor windows are composed of. Now he sticks his arm inside and noiselessly opens the latch. Leaving the knapsack outside, he climbs over the sill. His dummy leg doesn't seem to handicap him in the least.

On closer inspection, the darkish room which he has entered in this devious manner turns out to be the manor's library, filled to the brim with preponderantly erotic literature of all times, as he confirms with a grim smile in the light of his torch. Having not enough time to sample a few specimens, the man extinguishes his torch and finds his way to the door by groping along the shelves which stretch from one end of the room to the other. He prefers this method to keeping the torch lit, presumably because its beam might give him away to an accidental outside observer. No busybody neighbour spying on the Rosy Manor. For that, the nearest houses are a little too far away. Yet, on the neighbouring island of Sark, which enjoys the reputation of an amateur astronomers' paradise, because almost all local sources of artificial light have been banned, quite a few of Sark's inhabitants are in the possession of efficient modern telescopes that are not always directed at the night skies alone.

The moment the intruder cautiously opens the library door to the corridor, he catches voices and the occasional shrill laughter from somewhere on the first floor. Quietly, unhurriedly, he walks to the landing and starts climbing the wooden stairs covered by a thick carpet. On the first floor, he stops and listens. There must be two or three persons in the adjacent room to the left. One man, presumably elderly, two women, youngish ones, if their voices are anything to go by. A conventional, if unusually high-spirited, threesome in full swing, it would seem.

The repeated volleys of shrill laughter suggest that none of the three is entirely sober at this advanced stage. Alcohol and drugs must be having a field day. The three of them are at it in what is, in all likelihood, one of the Manor's guest rooms. Their generally careless attitude allows the assumption that they are alone in the house. Which would make perfect sense, since the manor is probably only visited on rare occasions such as this one, and hence, has no resident staff.

The intruder once again checks his gun, flips the safety catch, turns the door knob and enters the room noiselessly like a shadow. It is a guest room, alright, which he has let himself into. The three merry debauchers in the spacious double bed have killed all lights except for a few small lamps above the night tables. Thus, they do not notice the man in black standing by the door. From his present position, he can calmly watch the scene like a particularly audacious Peeping Tom and, coming from the dark, give his pupils the time necessary to adapt to the glaring lights.

It is only when he suddenly takes a few steps forward that one of the two young women sets her eyes on him and cries out in a mixture of horror and surprised anger. Stark naked like her friend, she has been busy massaging an equally naked, fat, bald man lying on his back like a stranded whale presenting his less than impressive masculinity to the world at large.

Alarmed by the young woman's shriek, the other two immediately stay their interaction and, while the second woman turns round, the fat bald man raises his torso to display a sweaty forehead and face, too much bloated by liquor and, probably, cocaine, to express anything in particular.

"What the…Who the hell are you?" the fat man calls out, suddenly sobered down to some extent.

The intruder doesn't reply, but levels the barrel of his gun to the height of his victim's head. The two women have long since turned sideways and covered their faces with their hands.

"Herbert Bertrand Lamont?" the intruder asks in a level voice without bothering about the whimpering women.

The fat man wipes his brow with the back of his left arm.

"Who's asking?"

"Wrong answer," the intruder retorts coldly and pulls the trigger, just once.

The bullet hits the fat naked man in the forehead, right above the nose and catapults him back on the cushion as if knocked out by a giant fist. As sweat and blood are beginning to mingle on the cushion, the sound of two more shots is heard. Then, a dead silence fills the room.

The killer steps aside and walks towards the mirrored wall behind the bed. With a few quick blows of the butt of his gun, he breaks the glass and picks up the camera that rests in some sort of casing behind the mirror. He opens the camera and takes out an electronic chip which apparently serves as a storage device for the films secretly made during sex parties such as the one so rudely ended just now.

He drops the camera on the bed and starts sifting through the girls' handbags and the man's articles of clothing spread more or less evenly across the room. Casually thumbing through the passports, he verifies identities and nationalities as if to make sure he killed the right person. Fatsy must have been his principal target with the two women unfortunate collateral. Wrong place at the wrong time.

Still in no particular hurry, the killer leaves the room and walks down the stairs, turning a little sideways under way so as to put less strain on his dummy leg. Considering the fact that he again didn't bother to use a silencer, his must be a surprising cold-bloodedness, or disdain for the police. True, the chances of anyone having heard the shots on a nearly deserted island are perhaps insignificant but not entirely to be excluded either, one should think. One way or another, it doesn't seem worth any consideration to him.

Fittingly enough, he leaves the house by the front door like any normal visitor, picks up his knapsack, which he left under the window sill and finds his way back to the shore. As he stops for a moment on the beach, a faint ray of the Guernsey lighthouse catches his blackened face and piercing husky's eyes.

The killer picks up his flippers and swaps them for the shoes again. Then he swims to his Westerly and climbs aboard at the stern. It doesn't take him long to get back into his normal clothes and to lay out the neoprene suit in the cockpit to dry. Checking his wrist watch, he lights a cigarette and leans back on the wooden bench next to the steering column.

Shortly after the midnight hour, he stands up, starts the boar's purring engine and walks to the bows. Here, he pulls in the anchor chain hand over hand till the bow is right above the anchor, which he has then no problem lifting from the bottom of the sea, since there is next to no pressure on it from the slowly receding yacht. While the Westerly keeps drifting backwards with the engine turning in neutral, the killer allows the anchor to dangle in the water for a while so as to rid it of the lumps of mud and clay it has brought up from the bottom. Then he drops the anchor in the chain compartment and goes back into the cockpit. Very slowly, almost gently, he puts the engine into gear, veers round and heads for the St. Peter Port light on the middle tide.

Come daybreak, his yacht should be tied up safely in the Victoria marina and the slightly limping skipper making his way to the nearest breakfast diner.

SECOND CHAPTER

1. An Inspector Calls

"Stick your hands up so I can see them and don't move a muscle."

The affable Danish estate agent had warned Laura Forster one more time on the occasion of handing her the keys to her new summer bungalow. Burglaries were the bane of the Danish Seal-and riviera between Helsinore in the East and Hundested in the West. A strip of dune-lined and pinewood-hemmed coast very popular not only with well-off Danes and Germans, but also with semi-professional criminals, preponderantly of East European origin. Laura had spontaneously opted for the reed-covered wooden bungalow on the periphery of the rather fashionable commune of Gilleleje anyway. Embedded in a shadowy pinewood cove, no more than a hundred yards from the sea, the building had proved more spacious in the flesh than it had appeared on the plans Laura had studied before her first inspection visit. On top of that, it offered many of the facilities she cherished, even though, on second thoughts, much-solicited business woman that she was, she would probably never get to spend much time in it.

As a German national, she would normally not have been eligible for the purchase of real estate so close to the Danish coast. True, she had a Danish foster mother to show for, but that fact on its own would presumably not have carried enough weight with the relevant authorities. Hence, to make the transaction go down eventually, Laura had re-activated her late father's business connections with a Danish front who had been obliging enough to return some of the many favours Robert, Laura's father, had rendered him over the years.

That had been six years ago. Laura had bought the bungalow shortly after her return from Istanbul, Turkey, where she had had to snatch her adopted son Ignace from the fangs of the Snake, a cosmopolitan gangster of considerable international reputation.

Without the help of her sister Solitaire and Jeremy, the Carib aborigine who had been lucky enough to conquer Solitaire's heart of stone and become the father of their two children Bobby and Penny, Laura knew she would never have been able to bring that one off.

Once those turbulent Istanbul days were over, Laura had looked for a quantum of respite which the Danish bungalow environment seemed to offer. Her affinity to the home country of Hamlet and ham was probably due to the influence of her Danish-born foster mother Frederike, who had died all too prematurely of breast cancer. In a manner of speaking, Laura had done no more than execute part of Frederike's legacy. For years on end, Frederike had pestered her husband Robert with her intention of buying a summer bungalow near the sea. Yet time and time again, she had been frustrated by Robert's disdainful attitude towards "Uncle Tom's cabins", as he had called them with an ironic quip at Frederike's brother, whose first name happened to be Tom. As Laura had learned much later, her father had been more of a sailor at heart, and sailors and bungalows, alas, seldom make good buddies.

When, at long last, it had looked like Robert might nevertheless make friends with the idea, Frederike had already been mortally ill and died before her dream could become reality.

After six years unperturbed by burglaries, this now seemed the moment when the estate agent's words of warning had found their sad justification. Yet this man had opted for the wrong bungalow altogether, as Laura would not be slow to bring home to him. A day earlier, and his coup might have worked. But not today, when Laura had just arrived from Hamburg to spend some time in the secluded atmosphere of her bungalow. Giving the firm the slip and escaping to her private Smultronstället had become a ploy she had resorted to more and more frequently of late, whenever the everyday insanities of the job threatened to get the better of her. All the more aggravating this unabashed intrusion, the violation of her privacy. Aggravating and pointless, since there was practically nothing of particular value in the house. Which, it is true, a burglar wouldn't be able to see from outside.

The seemingly interminable ride up here from Copenhagen, where she had arrived by plane, had exhausted her. Which is why she had, upon entering the bungalow, not even bothered to switch on the light everywhere or open the windows to let the fresh sea breeze in, as she was otherwise wont to. Nor had she started the sauna or warmed up the pool but flung herself headlong on the bed in what was her only dedicated guest room. Half asleep, then, she thought she had heard sounds from the direction of the living room but had at first discarded them as a figment of her vivid imagination, like that man in the Tell-tale Heart. It was only when someone had dropped a vase or some other piece of China that was shattered to pieces on the floor with a solid clanking that she had woken to the reality of the situation and picked up the gun she always kept near her when alone in the house.

"Now turn round, very slowly," she told the burglar, expressing herself in basic English, even though her Danish was more than presentable.

"Your hands you better keep where they are and don't come any nearer. Allow me to explain: the gun I'm pointing at you is a Ruger calibre .44 Magnum. Not the kind of toy you would expect a lady to pack in her Gaultier handbag when going on a shopping spree. That said, let me assure you I have been around such calibres before and, frankly, at this distance, there wouldn't be much left of your head if I were to pull the trigger. So better don't give me a reason."

Turning slowly on his heels, the intruder finally looked her squarely in the face. Laura took a step to her left and switched on the ceiling lighting to scrutinize her opponent's features in the soft dusky glow of what had promised to be a cosy kind of evening before this idiot had turned up.

He didn't exactly look the part though. Not your run-of-the-mill burglar complete with crow bar, set of false keys and assortment of screw drivers. Instead, what she saw was a well-clad gentleman a little taller than herself, with greyish hair and a lean face marred by a virtual sewing pattern of lines. The whole was underscored by a bushy, equally grey moustache which probably made him look a little older than he really was. His lively yet at the same time cagy eyes were those of an intelligent, fully functioning sexagenarian. His correct if old-fashioned duffle coat made of some thick navy-blue lambswool, as well as his elegant black shiny lace-ups that would have attracted the admiration of a Richard Nixon, had very little in common with East European parachute silk. Much rather, the man looked as if he had done his shopping in the London Savile Row area. What she could see of his trouser legs bore the kind of crease that only a car-crushing scrap-metal press will produce. In pants like these, you could spend a week living under the bridge or on a park bench and still look reasonably well kempt. A gentleman-thief off the Cary Grant slab? Wouldn't that make for a pleasant difference, she thought.

"No offence, but to me, you appear marginally overdressed for the occasion. However, however, fashion tastes apart, who are you and what's your business in my bungalow?"

The man coughed nervously and was about to cover his mouth with his right hand. A mere polite reflex, he immediately suppressed when he heard Laura cock her gun.

"None taken. I am perfectly aware of your gun proficiency, Mrs. Forster," the intruder replied in an excellent English public school accent. The kind of clinically elaborate English that always sounds like a parody of itself. Listening to the would-be burglar, Laura couldn't help thinking of Marlon Brando playing the part of Fletcher Christian in a Bounty film of the nineteen seventies. In that movie, notoriously mumbling Brandon manages to imitate the idiom in its exalted upper-class variety to such perfection, that, most of the time, he is very hard to understand. Then again, who has ever understood Marlon Brandon, irrespective of what accent he adopts.

"How come you know my name? It's neither on the doorbell, nor on the letterbox."

That latter feature was due to a precautionary measure the estate agent had recommended. No need to rub her neighbours' noses in the scandalous fact that her bungalow was inhabited by a German, perish the thought. And since she never had letters sent here, anyway, Laura had agreed.

"True," the man replied, somewhat laconically.

"You love your privacy and are of course entitled to it. An obvious German name such as yours might cause a measure of irritation in the parish, I guess. None of my business. That said, you would probably be surprised to hear what more I know about your person, family and, shall we say, colourful life. Not counting my nail file for the moment, I am perfectly unarmed at present and certainly not out to do you in, as the jargon goes. Hence, it would be something of a relief if you could consider laying your John Wayne memorial gun down before it accidentally takes my head off, as you so rightly point out. Redskins don't attack after nightfall, everybody knows that."

"That's a load of hogwash, believe me. Redskins used to attack any time night or day if it suited them. That's what I was told in the States by people who should know, anyway."

Laura couldn't help laughing. She even started taking a liking to this upper-class version of a burglar. Notwithstanding, she held her head askew pensively as she would whenever she was in at least two minds about something. A habit she must have picked up from dogs, he sister Solitaire had often claimed. The man's English was impeccable, his manners polished, yet tinged by that wee smack of relaxed affectedness so characteristic of English colonial officers of the Sanders kind.

This eloquent duffle coat didn't by any means give her the impression of someone even vaguely dangerous, but that could be his very scam. How much easier life would be if not just some but all crooks bore the expression of their potential viciousness in their face like a birthmark or a wart. Here and now, Laura opted for a cautious compromise.

"Take off your coat and open your jacket," she told the man.

"Then lift the hem of your jacket and do a three sixty, slowly, like a male model having lately put on a touch of weight. You think you can do that for me?"

The duffle coat nodded and did as he had been told. Laura looked reassured.

"Now you lift your pant legs above your ankles."

Again, the man followed her instructions.

"Want me to take them off, too?" he then asked.

"Don't be ridiculous. I'm not interested in the colour of your underwear, just want to make sure you're not packing."

"I told you I wasn't."

Laura dropped the barrel of her gun a few inches and secured the cock with a snapping sound. Then she stuck the weapon in her belt with the barrel just above her buttocks. She was sure to be fast enough on the draw not to be rushed by an elderly duffle coat complete with ironed pants.

"We still haven't been introduced, now, have we?"

The man, visibly relieved, rose to his full height. No downright giant, properly speaking, he still beat her to it by a few inches. Which, considering Laura's walking about barefoot, at present, wasn't saying much.

"Sorry, I forgot. The name is Harry Colestron. I am, was, Chief Superintendent of the Metropolitan Police."

Laura gulped. As far as she was aware, the rank of a CS was high up the English police hierarchy and involved a pretty leading function. Metropolitan Police again was the official title of what the rest of the world knew as New Scotland Yard.

"Anyone can claim that. Any badge or other means of identification?" The alleged CS shook his head.

"Unfortunately, no. As a retired civil servant, I have no right to carry a badge. It might induce me to assume an authority that I no longer have, or so the reasoning goes. All I can offer you is an access card to the Yard's canteen. Wouldn't recommend it, though, the food's awful, I'm afraid. Even Parsifal only snarls at me whenever I take home a doggy bag instead of his favourite dog food can."

"Parsifal? You called your dog Parsifal?"

"I did, indeed. The dog and I, we're great fans of Wagner music. There are those summer nights up in Middlesex, where I live now, when Parsifal howls his way through larger parts of the Ring, my word on it."

Laura laughed again and shook her head.

"Alright, Mr. Coleman. Let's say I'm ready, mind you, provisionally ready, to accept your fine accent in lieu of a badge."

The CS smiled.

"Colestron, with respect. Why don't you just call me Harry, like the rest of mankind, including most of the Soho heavies I happened to come across in the line of duty. If I understand you correctly, I happen to have passed the shibboleth of King's English? In that case, the hilarious fees my aged parent had to cough up for my exclusive public-school education did pay off, for once. May even have saved my life, in fact."

"Okay, Harry it'll be. I'm Laura, as you probably know already. If this bungalow was standing in West Palm Beach instead of near Gilleleje, you might get carried out this very minute in a body bag. The Americans don't take trespassing as lightly as some of us Europeans do, I can assure you."

"Nor do we at the Yard," Colestron agreed.

Despite her harsh words, Laura had to grin when she heard the CS speak of his father as an "aged parent". The last time she had come across that term was when she had read Charles Dickens as a student. To this day, she had retained a soft spot for the writer and his quaint sense of humour. Had she had a dog, she would probably have called him AD, as in Artful Dodger.

"Fine. Then why don't you have a seat, Harry. Here, hand me that awful coat of yours. I take it you aren't married or else your wife recently turned blind, no disrespect. How did you come by it, incidentally? The coat, I mean, not the wife. A choice item from the Yard's evidence room?"

The CS laughed.

"Is it really all that obvious? It's Peter Sutcliffe's coat, originally. You know, the Yorkshire Ripper? I reckoned he could do without it and since it fits me like a second skin…We frequently have to slip into criminals' minds, so why not try some of their clothes, as well. Once the blood stains had come off, it looked brand new,

I thought. And no, I have never been married. A fact to which I attribute my having reached ripe old age."

Laura took the compromising piece of evidence from him, pointed at the two armchairs next to the open fireplace. Then she left the room and, after quickly going through the pockets, hung the heavy coat on the wardrobe in the corridor. Meanwhile, Colestron had positioned himself in front of the chair and waited till she had come back to the fireplace. Then they both sat down. Laura had no idea at what age British policemen are retired, but a certain orthopaedic stiffness in his movements put him at around sixty-five. Probably hadn't indulged in much sport in his life, Harry hadn't. Then again, she knew people who had and were no better off for their pains either.

"And so? I'm all ears. What was it gave you enough cause or reason to preoccupy yourself with my person and life to the extent of coming here, breaking in and ruining my china? I guess, when it comes to the point, I should be flattered. I'm no longer used to men taking such an interest in me. At around forty, a woman tends to become invisible to men, despite what desperate lengths they go to prevent that from happening, don't you think?""

Colestron chewed a little while on that one. Rightly so. A woman's age is mined territory.

"I'm terribly sorry to have destroyed your vase. I'm perfectly prepared to pay for it…"

"Oh, but you couldn't. It's priceless. A representational piece from the late Han Ming dynasty, fourth century B.C. Priceless, like I say. Unless you happen to come across it on the Gilleleje flea market on a Sunday morning, in which case you may get it for a tenner." The Chief Superintendent, who had visibly paled for a moment, now laughed out loud with relief.

"Almost had me there. Anyway, if I may pass on a choice morsel of advice: in an interrogation situation, never ask more than one question at a time, lest you give the suspect a more than welcome opportunity to drift off to some other topic. Hardened criminals will seize it, spread a smokescreen or throw you a few red herrings, that sort of thing. But no, I don't think of women around forty as invisible. Not when confronted with an attractive specimen like yourself."

He paused a second to let that one warm the cockles of Laura's heart.

"Of course, you could object that, at my age, all cats that used to look grey at night some twenty years ago suddenly start glowing in the dark, metaphorically speaking."

Laura laughed.

"I take that as a compliment, but, as a piece of advice from me, your metaphors need working on."

"Besides which I didn't break in. There was no need to. The terrace door wasn't locked."

"Okay, in view of the sage attitude of the accused and in the light of the aforementioned special circumstances, the DA is prepared to downgrade the charge to a simple trespass. Still, why?"

Colestron reflected for a moment.

"Well, here's the thing. Some colleagues handle the transition from active service to sudden retirement better than others. I myself belong to the category of the restless roamers."

"Funny. I should have thought forty or so years of almost daily exposure to mangled corpses, chasing after ghosts and diving into the unfathomable depths of human vice and viciousness were enough to make you turn your back on police work with an expression of great relief."

Colestron nodded.

"You certainly have something there. But there is habit, and there is pride. No matter how long you've been in the service, you never resign yourself to the idea someone out there might be getting away with murder. Never ever. It becomes an attitude that doesn't change or disappear with age or retirement. It's in your DNA. Some hitherto unsolved cases will haunt you to your grave, because they have become personal. And the feeling of incompletion is tantalizing not only for artists."

Laura drew a deep breath.

"Yes, I think I understand that. But what's it to do with me?"

In her thoughts, she had her virtual rap sheet flicker by: Ivan, the Russian she shot on the island of Büyük Ada. The unknown killer she had involuntarily pushed over the edge on Montserrat...He couldn't possibly know that. And even if he did, he wouldn't have come here for that. None of it would have been the Yard's business.

Colestron coughed again, a sign of embarrassment, as Laura had already noted.

"Well, to enlarge upon that in any degree of detail would take more time than you might be willing to accord me. I really don't know if I should…"

Laura brushed his qualms away.

"No, Harry. You can't come here, seriously disturb the peace and then leave again almost as discretely as you came. You have absolutely no idea what kind of absurd and by no means short cock-and-bull stories I have already been called upon to listen to, at one stage or another. One more won't make a difference. Tell you what. If you manage to get the wood in the fireplace start burning, I'll go the extra mile and brew us a tea. That should give you all the time in the world to collect your thoughts and give me an intelligible if not riveting account of the problems you are trying hard to solve. Deal?"

"You take things with a dose of irony. I like that. Deal: I'll see what I can do about the firewood. As you know, we Brits seem to have invented the open fireplace since we love our bodies sunny side up, as it were."

Laura checked the full matchbox lay on the mantelpiece and left Colestron to it. In passing, she picked up the pieces of the vase so as not to step on them later.

In the kitchen, she had to get her bearings first. An elderly Turkish woman she had once met on the booze-wagon circulating between Danish Helsinor and Swedish Hälsingborg, used to come round with her husband about once a month to look after the bungalow. They would do a little cleaning and make minor repairs whenever necessary, for a little consideration they had never asked but Laura had insisted on. Whenever this Turkish lady passed by, she would arrange and re-arrange all kitchen gear in such a manner, as to keep Laura on her toes, intellectually speaking. Whatever the philosophy behind that capricious habit of hers was, Laura hadn't complained but accepted it as a peculiar piece of idiosyncrasy. Maybe it was something that would irritate and disorientate goblins and trolls to such an extent that they would rather shun this bungalow and nestle elsewhere.

"I forgot to ask. I hope, Earl Grey with a drop or two of goat's milk is okay?" she called out as she came back into the living room balancing a tray with cups and a pot with steaming hot tea.

"Goat's milk is fine by me," Colestron laughed.

"Lends a special note to the tea. I see you are perfectly familiar with our insular beverage customs. Up in Scotland, there are more goats than people, or so they say. I'm no judge of this, never have been to Scotland, as yet, and, frankly, feel no particular urge to do so."

"Nor do I. That said, I never quite understood why a person in full command of their intellectual faculties should want to pour milk in their tea. An acquired taste better not acquired, is how I feel about it. Personally, I prefer green tea, anyway, without milk."

She put down the tray, poured the tea and placed a small bowl with biscuits in the middle. Colestron had made use of what time Laura had given him to crank up the fireplace so that the first red and yellow flames were flickering along the logs. Right away, pungent smoke started filling the room.

"The flap," Laura cried.

"You need to open the flap on the side so the smoke can get up the chimney and out, else we'll turn into smoked kippers."

The coughing CS jumped up and pulled the cast-iron flap down. Then he let himself drop in the chair again and sipped his tea.

"Have you ever heard of a gang called the Yarmouth Six?"

Laura mused on that one for a moment and then shook her head.

"No, not that I know of. What are they? No, don't tell me. A male stripper group like the Chippendales or a tight-rope circus act with men in white tights and indecently bulging crotches?"

Colestron laughed.

"Close. But no. The so-called Yarmouth Six were a gang of heavies who kept my predecessors in the Yard on their toes with a number of major crimes during the nineteen fifties, sixties, and seventies. Robberies, holdups, burglaries, production and distribution of counterfeit money, extortion, you name it, they had it. Strictly old school, though. No killings, no unnecessary violence, no drugs, not as far as we know, anyway. They used to be very well organised and always had a grip on themselves. Most of their heists had all the paraphernalia of military ops about them. Nevertheless, it took us quite a while to grasp we were dealing with one and the same gang. One with a military background, in fact."

"And there were six of them?"

"Yes. But they didn't always act all six in unison, you see. Three, four, five would operate on the scene, the other or others pull the background strings. The number involved was a function of the degree of risk and difficulty. Asymmetrical is what you would call their procedure nowadays, I suppose."

Laura nodded.

"I understand. It must have been confusing at first. But…"

"Bear with me. The really peculiar thing was that the Yarmouth Six, as they came to be nicknamed, never got caught. The respective investigations frequently ended on the rocks or just petered out. If and when the DA decided to open criminal proceedings, at all, which happened seldom enough, such proceedings were sure to be nipped in the bud shortly after. Vital pieces of evidence dissolved into thin air, witnesses changed their minds or disappeared from the planet altogether. Files got lost or smoked in somebody's pipe. Hilarious, except that the joke was on us. Needless to add, the Yarmouth Six had a whole army of first-class legal eagles who would bare their claws, spread their wings and come down hard upon the DAs."

"Why the name, Yarmouth Six?"

"Well, as it would seem, those chaps had first met in the Army, during the War. The Second World War, that is. They had been picked for a commando raid on the Channel Islands, then occupied by your fellow-countrymen. They had been trained and prepared for the job on the Isle of Wight, in a camp near the small town of Yarmouth. Hence…"

"But you just said Channel Islands…"

So I did. Funny, isn't it? The only major English island most obviously situated in the Channel should not be eligible for that title. Anyway, thing is, the Isle of Wight has some corners with steep rock faces not altogether unlike those of Sark. That was the island practically opposite, on the French side of the Channel, where the operation was to go down."

"Sark? But that's a tiny place, a kind of Hobbits' island, if I remember right. How could that ever be of any military importance at all?"

"It wasn't, actually. But that's an even longer story. I'll spare you the details. Whatever else the operation had or had not achieved, it brought the six men together. They then resuscitated their acquaintance after the war and turned to other, more remunerative areas of activity. He who learned to carry out commando raids will probably be apt and fit enough rob a bank or hold up a money transport, once he has opted for the slippery slope of crime."

"Yes, well, I can relate to that. But why is this old story still haunting you? And again, what's it to me? If it's anything to do with my father…."

"No, it isn't. Haunt is a fitting term to use in this context, since the Yarmouth Six appear to have risen from their graves again more recently. After having mysteriously kicked the bucket one by one, in the nineteen eighties, that is."

"Don't tell me. They had all developed sarcomas?"

"No. Each and every one of them fell victim to the kind of accident nobody would ever have suspected. For instance, one of them, reputed as an excellent mountaineer with long experience, fell off the North face of the Eiger, normally a walk in the park for him. Another one, known as a pundit of firearms, allegedly shot himself accidentally while cleaning his Smith and Wesson. And so on, you get the picture, I take it."

"Unlucky streaks do exist…. So, they're all…moved on?"

"All but one, yes. The sole survivor got into a bad traffic accident but lived to tell the tale. Has had to move in a wheelchair ever since, though."

"But all of that is so much water under the bridge…?"

"So we all of us at the Yard would have loved to believe. Even though some of us felt this accumulation of curious accidents a little suspect, we had put the file entitled Yarmouth Six in the bottom drawer after all this. Their case wasn't cold but frozen stiff, as it were. And then, out of the blue, we're suddenly dealing with a series of killings that started some months, half a year ago perhaps. And, strange as it may sound, guess who the chain of evidence should be pointing at if it isn't the Yarmouth Six."

"…who have been dead and gone these thirty-odd years? Did you disinter them, just to be on the safe side?"

"No, I don't think there is any need for that."

"And the one survivor is in a wheelchair. Not an asset if you're on an out-and-out killing spree, is it?"

Colestron gave a bitter laugh.

"No, I guess it isn't. Besides, as far as we can see, the survivor is a target, a potential victim rather than an offender. Again, it took us some time to realize we are probably dealing with one and the same person. The killings took place in different parts of the world and seemed unconnected and without apparent motive. It was only when we intensified our co-operation via Interpol that we noticed the killer had actually left a kind of visiting card that would no doubt have put us on his scent earlier, had the murders not been as scattered as all this."

"What visiting card?"

"He's – if it is a male, as we think it is, and if he acts alone, as we think he does – a latter-day deer hunter. You know the film with Robert de Niro and Chris Walken?"

"Yes…But I fail to see the connection with Vietnam."

"One shot only, that's De Niro's creed at the beginning of the film, which is then reflected in the bitter irony of the Russian roulette scenes at the end. Our murderer kills all his victims with a single shot to the head. Different guns, different calibres, but always only one shot."

"That's remarkable. A hired gun?"

Colestron shook his head.

"Hardly. Professionals tend to kill with three bullets to the head, to make sure. No, this bloke must have a different background. Well educated and arrogant, if you ask me. But I am no profiler."

"Motive?"

"Well, that's where we fumble in the dark. Once we had established we were getting nowhere with the killer, we focussed on the victims; that's pretty standard. Thus, we found that they are all in some way or another linked, or even related to the last remaining member of the Yarmouth Six, Sir Lucas Lamont."

Laura, who had followed Colestron's report with growing fatigue, was wide awake again all of a sudden.

"What? The Sir Lucas Lamont? Are you kidding me? I always thought of him as a staunch pillar of British society, the Messrs Zuckerberg and Soros rolled into one. And now you're telling me he used to be a gangster?"

"I didn't say that. He was never convicted of so much as shoplifting. A shrewd operator if ever there was one. Have you met him?"

"No, but his is a household name in my line of business as well. Hardly a pie that can boast not to have had one of Lamont's fingers stuck in it. And why would anyone set out on a Lamont clan pogrom?"

"That's what we don't know yet. Nor does he, or so he pretends."

"If the killer is not a professional, where has he learned to shoot like that?"

"We don't know that either. Ex-military, maybe. Even though the Army prefers rifles and machine guns and doesn't, as a rule, train people to become proficient with revolvers or pistols."

"Secret service, then?"

Possible. What is certain, though: with the snub-nosed guns he appears to use, even with his special shooting skills he will have to try and get really close to his victims; so close, in fact, he must look them in their eyes. That's something which, according to the profilers I've talked to, doesn't tally. Whoever kills people with a gun does so, among other things, because it allows him to keep his distance. A killer eager to look his dying victims in the eye would prefer a knife or a garotte. We can't make this one out. He just doesn't fit the known patterns."

"So you have to start thinking out of the box, I guess. But if the killer's motives have their roots in the history of the Yarmouth Six and has something to do with Sir Lucas, somehow, why is it the man goes at it only now? And why doesn't he pop off Sir Lucas first thing, instead of decimating his clan, first?"

"Why he started only recently, we don't know. Why he doesn't kill Sir Lucas is rather obvious: Lamont has always had a small army of bodyguards about him and hardly leaves his fortress-like mansions on Jersey and Puerto Rico. Nobody gets within a thousand yards of him without being invited. In fact, the way we're reasoning at present, the killer is taking on Lamont's clan members precisely because he can't get at the man himself. I know that sounds odd, but in this case, what doesn't."

"Puerto Rico?"

"Excuse me? Oh, yes, Sir Lucas owns some land there, a kind of hacienda north-east of San Juan. As it would seem, the locals adore him, idolize him, even, for the things he has done for them. One more reason why you would not get anywhere near him. He's got eyes and ears everywhere."

Laura whistled through her teeth.

"I see. Some act. But you still haven't told me where I come into all this."

Colestron lifted his hand and turned his palms towards Laura.

"I was just coming to that. One of the mysterious killer's more recent victims, a young lady called Solveig something or other, had a notebook on her person, well, in her handbag, actually..."

"...that had my name in it, among many others?"

Colestron shook his head.

"Not yours, no. But that of a certain Ignace F."

2. Singin' on the Train

"How did you get to know each other, after all?" Laura had asked but received no answer. Ignace had fallen asleep in his armchair. Not surprisingly so, Laura had thought, considering the amount of intercontinental travel he had undertaken during the past three days. That must have been exhausting enough. Plus the jet lag....When Laura had called him, he had no longer been at Tampa College, Florida, where he had been preparing for an important intermediate exam looming large on the horizon. Instead, he had taken the somewhat spontaneous decision to interrupt his cramming and pay his aunt Solitaire a visit on his – and her – home island of Dominica and pass a week or two in the fold of her family.

Unwind, give your brain a rest, come up for air. All fine and dandy, Laura was ready to concede. And if someone was able to make you leave the ins and outs of business administration behind, it was Sol's and Jerry's kids, Bobby, five, and Penny. three. Bobby, a true tomboy named after his grandfather on the mother's side, had started reading of late and would entertain the whole village and large parts of the island with his pranks. On market days, he would accompany his parents to the capital, Roseau, and do the tour of the different stands, shake everybody's hands and usually come away with a bagful of sweets, fruit, and what have you, which he was loath to share with his little sister.

Being as well-known on the island as the proverbial pink elephant, his parents weren't too worried whenever he disappeared in the rainforest like Mowgli in search of kind Baloo, no-nonsense Bagheera and all the rest of the Jungle Book menagerie, Sol used to resuscitate for him at bedtime.

Once or twice he had had narrow escapes from some disaster or other, but as a rule he would be picked up by some friendly neighbours who were only too familiar with Sol's reputation and, hence, were only too eager to be included in her good books. Would he break a few young ladies' hearts in the not too distant future? You bet, it was all too plainly on the cards, already now.

As was the firm assumption that the girl finding grace with Bobby's awesome mother probably wouldn't come from this planet or galaxy either.

Penny, named after her Greek grandmother on the mother's side, was a great deal more introvert, filling what little space Bobby left to her. Looking at her now, she seemed to be heading for something artistic, preferably painting. All day long she would imitate her mother, filling wads and sheets of paper with all sorts of skulduggery.

As for Solitaire, she appeared to have tasted blood during the days of the hunt for the Bullet-Proof Madonna, when she had come into contact with icon-painting. A little later, when she was already pregnant with Bobby, she had started to take up drawing herself. Clumsily at first, without much sense of structure and the harmony of colours. But she had always been a quick learner and besides had a first-rate teacher in the person of Jeremy's mother, who had placed her famous tattoos on just everybody who was somebody on Dominica.

Needless to add that Penelope's love for her grandchildren bordered on the idolatrous. Especially now that the Doc had suddenly, some would say, precipitously, died only two years ago, Penelope would have preferred to get back to the Caribbean, if only to be near her loved ones. The Doc had hardly been diagnosed with a particularly aggressive form of cancer of the blood at Salonica's university clinics when his general state of health took such a spectacular nose-dive that Laura had not even been given a chance to go to Greece and take her leave of him. That saddened her all the more since he had been a faithful loving friend ever since those chaotic days in the Caribbean, when he had turned Laura's life inside out. For all she knew, his death had left the world a poorer place.

Breeding Kangal dogs had become too much of a bother for Penelope even before the Doc's death and certainly had to be discontinued after his demise. Besides, their quarter up at Panorama had increasingly been "compacted" and gentrified, so that the new neighbours, forever closing in on them, had started complaining about the dog's frequent barking and howling.

All things considered, Penelope had overcome the Doc's decease with the help of her daughters and grandchildren faster than feared. Add to this the fact that she knew half the Salonica population by their first name, it soon became clear she would not fall into a black hole but be safely and gently caught by her social network. That said, she was no stranger to boredom and Solitaire had to mobilize her entire arsenal of convincing arguments to talk her out of a move back to the Caribbean. Maybe in so doing, she had occasionally sounded a little cold, heartless even. But she was right, Laura had thought, in pointing out to her mother that Dominica just recovering from a hurricane wasn't Guadeloupe or even the Saintes. On top of that, whenever heading for a rendezvous with folks we haven't seen for a long time, we expect them to look very much like they did when we parted company last and are, as a rule, shocked to find they've aged at more or less the same rhythm as we did. Approximately the same applied to places, give or take.

Thus, when Laura had, at long last, made contact with Ignace on Dominica, she had been relieved to find, by reading between the lines, that he hadn`t heard the news of Solveig's death, yet. Thank God for that, she had thought. Solveig having been the first great, overpowering love of his life, there was no telling what he might have done, had he got wind of her death. Anything within the wide range from suicide to murder.

According to CS Harry Colestron, it had taken quite a while for the Yard people to find out who this mysterious Ignace F. was.

"I mean sure, the name is not that frequent and points in the direction of either France or some French-speaking countries or dominions, ex-colonies. But even that doesn't really narrow it down all that much, now, does it. Hence, we had to stay on it for a week or two. Fortunately, we came across the Tampa College connection."

To send Ignace to the States had been Laura's idea, one that in a way copied her own initial career. After all, she had only been slightly older than Ignace was now when her father had insisted she should go to Florida and Louisiana. It had taken her quite a while to overcome her culture shock, but once that problem was out of the way, she had found the States...invigorating was the term she had chosen then and would choose again, now. That said, she had always kept her distance from American politics and cuisine, those being very touchy spots with most of her US friends.

"A wide-open country with a lot of narrow-minded, greedy people intellectually stuck at the level of the Old Testament, as if Christ hadn't happened." That had been Frederike's somewhat harsh verdict whenever they had discussed the US during meals. There was some truth in that, as Laura had found out herself later. Still, what remained of that old pioneer, new-ground-breaking spirit, the "just do it" kind of approach, had inspired her no end. And for someone like herself who was cut out one fine day to take over from her father and start plotting a large company such as ROLA's course through the troubled waters of the globalized and digitalized economy, the US of A proved the best if toughest school she could have hit upon. And that didn't just apply to the Big Apple or Silicon Valley, nor to the economy and finance alone.

Ignace, for his part, would never grow up to become a successful businessman, she thought. For that, he lacked business acumen and cruelty combined with a healthy sort of greed. Then again, he didn't have to slip into her shoes the way she had slipped into Robert's, willy-nilly, without ever being quite certain it had been the right thing for her to do. He had other, musical and athletic talents, which to promote and develop Laura would have the wherewithal and tolerance. What worried her was his lack of emotional self-restraint. His frequent blind frenzies to win a race, jump farther or higher than the next guy. The kind of monomaniac ambition fraught with both glory as in the case of, say, the Macedonian Alexander and doom, as in the case of, say, the Roman Nero. All the more important to let the imminent meltdown happen under controlled conditions, as far as possible.

Jeremy had flown him from Dominica to Guadeloupe, wherefrom he had taken the plane to Paris Orly without knowing what was up and why exactly his adopted mother had insisted on his immediate return to Europe. Only upon his arrival in Hamburg had Laura found it in her to break the sad news.

At first sight, Ignace seemed to digest this left hook to the liver better than Laura had feared. Yet the poker face he displayed wouldn't have fooled many women, certainly not Laura, who knew him inside out and would literally feel his temperature rising. Here and now, he had been just short of Fahrenheit 451. A wrong word, and he would surely have auto-ignited.

What complicated the situation considerably, were the circumstances of Solveig's death, awkward to say the least. Colestron had been delicate enough not to make much of it, but also outspoken enough to leave no doubt as to the nature of Solveig's presence in the bedroom of the Rosy Manor. She had obviously not been the privileged target but had come under the heading of collateral damage.

"In the wrong bed at the wrong moment, a cynic might say."

This had presented Laura with a dilemma, something she had got used to even though it always irritated her to land on her bum in that free space between two or more chairs. In the case at hand, she could let Ignace know, as gently as possible, that the first great love of his life was at least a part-time whore. If it weren't for the fact that there are things no-one can ever break gently: the end of a relationship once entered into for life, the death of a child in a stupid accident, the remaining life span of a teenager prematurely affected by some cancer or other, that sort of thing. Plus it was a matter that, if not handled with utmost sensitivity, might well put a lasting stain on the mother-son relationship as well.

Alternatively, she could keep mum on that delicate point and hold his stirrups as he was surely going to mount his white stallion. Either way, his striving at a vendetta of sorts could not be stopped, at most controlled. Better to accompany him in it and cover his back. That's why she had decided in favour of the latter option, at least for the time being.

"How and where did you meet?" Laura had repeated her question when she had realized that the tiring jetlag paradoxically wouldn't allow the dozing Ignace to fall asleep anyway. Ignace had shrugged his shoulders.

"As such things go, Mom, what can I say. The Yankees can be pretty pushy, and in Florida, they party all year round anyway, as you well know yourself, I guess. Except when another hurricane is approaching the Eastern sea board. And even then, there are those who keep on going till their BBQ takes off. Weird stuff, awesome people."

Laura had nodded encouragingly and thought of cyclone Katharina, after whose passage she had helped pick the bloated floaters off the flooded New Orleans streets. Tilt, game over.

"One of those Trump-like golf clubs buzzing with people who wouldn't recognize a birdy if it hit them in the face. Anyway, we were rather under the influence, all of us, when one of the guys, a tall Texan, whose great-grandfather had apparently helped defend the Alamo, started making a real ass of himself. Comes naturally to Texans, I guess. High, pointed fancy boots, silver buckle, huge white Stetson, the Lone Ranger himself. An ego commensurate with his father's Rancho Notorious. Anyway, he started poking fun at me because of my physiognomy, which he apparently found peculiar. The usual thing: couldn't make up your mind whether to become a white or stay a nigger and that sort of crap, pretty insulting. I had already clenched my fists and flagged the most promising points of impact on his body and face with an imaginary marker, when, all of a sudden, one of the girls I hadn't even noticed before, flung her half-filled glass of Chivas Regal in James Bowie's face. And I mean, an oak-barrel aged Chivas Regal, my word. With a casual flick of her wrist, like she did this quite frequently. The Texan with his five-hundred-dollar shirt and all was naturally upset. But hitting a woman in public is a no go in the US, even for a descendant of Jim Bowie."

He had yawned aloud and scratched his blond locks. But again, he hadn't fooled Laura. She had felt that this reminiscence of his first encounter with Solveig had got him quite a bit worked up.

"Well, that somehow put paid to the evening. We strolled along the beach a while afterwards and had a glass of beer in a bar near the WPB marina. Actually, must have been two or three glasses, 'cause at some stage, I must have said something stupid, you know, Sinatra-ish. But she didn't mind, just kissed me, on the lips, I mean."

"No tongue, though, I hope? Not at this stage?"

"Mom, you are really impossible, you know that?"

Laura sighed.

"I've been told so at times. Must be my genes on my mother's side. Anyway, carry on, tiger, you have me riveted."

"Not much to say…."

"…except that you fell hopelessly in love, but then, who cares, right."

"Yeah, you may be right there. She told me, it had just been a reflex. The thing with the glass, not the kiss. She had grown up with a younger cousin of hers who would get into all sorts of trouble regularly, so she repeatedly had to bail him out by hitting guys twice her size in the guts and…well, you know where. I guess it was her way of saying, don't get any ideas, I would have done the same thing for anyone in that situation."

"But you wouldn't be fooled, of course."

"No way. She had obviously realized right away that I was some years younger than her, but she didn't seem to mind. After that night, we started dating regularly and, well, you know…"

"No, I don't know. What is it you do these days during your rendezvous, answer your respective accrued Facebook messages or what?"

"Stop it, ya hear. I bet you were no Madonna either, in your younger days."

Laura confirmed that.

"Never have been, don't you worry, tiger. What happened then?"

"Well, when she set out for Europe, to visit some of her folks in Norway, I took her to the airport in Fort Lauderdale. We fixed an appointment end of August, at Tampa. Well, I guess, that won't happen now."

They had been silently mourning for a while. Then Laura had felt the moment had come to pop the question.

"And you're not prepared to let matters rest, I mean, let the likes of CS Colestron do their job and hunt the killer down?"

The boy hadn't blown his top, as she had feared, but had just looked her straight in the eyes.

"Would you?"

Touché, the late Doc would have said.

"The question I can't get out of my head," Ignace had carried on, "is what kind of sick person is evil enough to do a thing like that? And why?"

Laura had nodded. Like an execution, the Chief Superintendent had characterized it.

"Maybe you shouldn't read too much into it. She was an accidental eye witness and, as such, a risk for the killer. So she had to be put down."

"But whatever was she doing on that tiny island in the middle of nowhere? She had said she was on her way to Scandinavia."

"As I'm sure she was. Hers must have been a spontaneous character, as the incident with the glass of Chivas shows. So she decided to call upon a friend of a friend on Herm Island without telling you. Women do things like that, on occasion. Anyway, we're poking in the dark, here. To get a grip on it, I guess we'll have to dig a little deeper into the matters of the Yarmouth Six, do a bit of modern archaeology, as it were. Their history is like the seventh book of the Apocalypse. And the key to that rests with Sir Lucas. I guess I'll have to have a little one on one with him on the subject."

"On Puerto Rico?"

"No, Harry, the CS, that is, was kind enough to let me know that Lamont is in the habit of spending a few of his remaining days on the island of Jersey every year so far. And lo and behold, this is the very week. I think I'm gonna profit from the occasion. I smell fun."

"I'll come with you, of course."

"No you won't."

It was the last thing Laura could risk at that stage. The odds of Sir Lucas making nasty remarks on the subject of Solveig and the cause of her presence at the Rosy Manor were high, to say the least.

"Sorry, tiger, but that's adult stuff. Besides, you have travelled enough of late. Get some rest and watch out for those Santa Ana troops. For starters, I have no idea whether or not the man is prepared to meet me at all. Maybe he is loath to be questioned about the past, under present circumstances. I for one couldn't blame him if he was. But if he is, the presence of a charming woman might put his mind at ease and loosen his tongue. I'll mobilize all my magic reserves bottled up for years now and make him talk. No offence, but your presence might be an irritant, make him feel awkward, shifty, if you see what I mean."

This exchange had gone on for a little while longer, but in the end, Ignace had seen reason and agreed to let Laura go to Jersey alone. The relatively difficult modalities of travel by plane, train, boat, and car were perhaps conducive to sweeten the pill for him.

Now, sitting in the Bistro compartment of the Paris-St. Malo TGV, sipping her hot black coffee and recalling the details of their conversation, her self-imposed mission started taking on downright surreal features. How come that, following her natural urge to help, she regularly landed herself in such deep shit? Properly speaking, she was much too busy for this kind of time-consuming journey to Jersey – now, when her presence in Hamburg was well-nigh imperative. The German IRS would soon descend upon ROLA for a bit of humourless ransacking of business and tax files. It would be the first audit since she had come into office, what, six years ago. She had that from reliable sources embedded deeply in the IRS structures. Snitches, as Robert used to call them, who formed part of her father's more unsavoury legacy portions.

As if that wasn't enough, ROLA's request for a short-term large-scale investment loan was held up in the loop somewhere for reasons unknown. The firm needed the cash for the financing of an unfriendly takeover – grow or go, that was one of the more important laws of free market economy, laws a globally active player such as ROLA wasn't free to ignore.

As it seemed, the whole thing hinged on some quarrel about the evaluation of this or that unmovable ROLA asset. My foot, Laura thought. The truth of the matter, of that she was convinced, was that someone higher up the food chain down-thumbed the project for some reason or other. An important shareholder of the bank perhaps, who had speculated against the deal going down, who knows?

The real trouble with a situation like that, a loan in limbo, that is, was its potentially defamatory effect. Business was, among other things, applied psychology. Facts were silver, expectations gold. In an atmosphere of hectic stock-exchange speculation, any rumours, any hearsay could and would be detrimental. If word got round that ROLA was still waiting for a loan slow in forthcoming, the news would spawn all sorts of more or less oblique hints as to the company's present liquidity. And once that came under flak fire, it was good night, Eileen. Even if and when such rumours turned out as completely unfounded shortly afterwards, the irreparable damage would have been done.

For all of those reasons, she should really have stayed in Hamburg. And would have, too, presumably, had it not been for the urge to help her son. Or, on second thoughts, was it perhaps nothing to do with Ignace, Solveig, and all the rest of it? Was she perhaps rather going off at a tangent and only too happy to plunge into some crazy adventure, once again, to assume the role of Tarzan's Jane? Of course not, perish the thought. She sipped on her coffee again, that somehow withstood the laws of thermodynamics by refusing to grow colder.

Heinz Marquardt, her most loyal, most reliable colleague, had promised to take care of things while she was away. He was used to doing just that. Their first encounters went back to the days when she had not been sure at all what to do about the firm and her future role in it. Ever since, they had travelled down a great deal of bumpy roads together. If somebody was able to find out who blocked the loan, it was Marquardt, her one-man secret service.

Sometimes she wondered. Would he have killed for her, had she asked him to? Probably depended on the circumstances. Given the right conditions and motives, the killer in all of us will raise his ugly head.

And so she had taken the plane to Paris, where she had stepped onto the TGV taking her to St. Malo. A trip almost as long as Paris – Marseille, in fact, as she had ascertained by dint of the timetable.

She looked out if the window absent-mindedly. Outside, the rolling French coastal countryside passed by peacefully, as if it had never even heard of D-Day. The clickety-clack of the TGV wheels of steel on the glistening steel rails sounded like the percussion part of the Goodman / Guthrie song called the City of New Orleans. One of her favourite songs of her adolescent years, even though some of the text had remained a riddle to her. Good Morning, America / how are you; say, don't you know me, I'm your native son....She started humming the melody and found her first impression confirmed. The rhythm fitted perfectly into that of the wheels. Had Goodman perhaps composed the song on the train, like the Bee Gees are said to have dreamed up their Jive Walking while going from the Florida Keys to Miami, suddenly starting a-humming and a-knocking in tune with the peculiar rhythm of the car tyres bumping over the expansion joints between the slabs of concrete forming that particular bit of Florida freeway's macadam?

Not a stupid twist to have a train describe and comment on its own journey. Soon, however, Laura ran out of text and let the City of New Orleans rumble on without her.

Meeting Sir Lucas Lamont was not an easy proposition. On Laura's behest, Marquardt had moved heaven and earth for Laura to be granted an audience at his Jersey manor. The man probably spent his days in a coffin and only came forth at sunset. On the other hand, he could hardly be blamed for his reclusive lifestyle, considering that the number of his clan's people was being reduced dramatically at a rapid rate and his brother shot only a few weeks ago. The impacts were coming ever closer.

"Well, alright then. One hour flat, and not a minute more," he had at last conceded.

"The lady on her own, at my place. No camera, no recordings." Or so his private secretary had transmitted Lamont's conditions. Laura had accepted them right away; what else could she have done? This entire rigmarole of a journey for a meagre hour's interview? Then again, he was Chingachgook, the real article. Nobody else around to give first-hand information on the ways of the Mohican. This outstanding authenticity alone justified the effort, after all.

Laura suddenly felt she was under observation from a man two tables further down the carriage. He made every effort to appear casual and absorbed by some booklet he was holding up. But Laura knew from experience she could rely on her instincts. And they told her, the man had an eye on her. A secret admirer or an agent? Maybe not only Lamont himself, but everyone who approached him was under some sort of observation? If secret admirers, in her case, were a thing of the past and could safely be ruled out, the latter hypothesis must of needs apply. Soon, if her sudden unwarranted outbreaks of sweat were anything to go by, Laura would soon enter her menopause. No, that train had long left the station. Ignace was more than likely to remain her only child. So what? The boy was clever, gifted, affectionate. That was more than many a mother could have said about her biological son or daughter. Seen from that angle, she could have fared worse. And whether or not she would be able to tolerate a man about the house at this stage, letting his socks lie about everywhere and urinating standing up, she wasn't sure at all. Mental rigidity caused by old age creeps upon us long before its physical equivalent makes itself felt. A man alone is in bad company, the saying goes. What about a woman, then? If she was ruthlessly honest, for once, she had trouble being in her own company most of the time.

She didn't give the man with his silly booklet any more thought, gulped down her coffee and made her way back to her seat. Of course, she felt pity for Ignace. On the other hand, cynical as it sounded at first, this fate the girl had suffered, a fate that no-one would have wished for her, might, after all, be more easily supportable for Ignace than having to battle with the truth about Solveig. Nothing in life was so devoid of hope it couldn't somehow be turned into something good or useful. That's what the late Doc had taught her. Hence, it had to be right. She looked at her watch. Provided the train didn't pick up more delays, they should be entering St. Malo main station in two hours' time precisely.

3. The Malvins

Seen from the sea, St. Malo had a dismissive, even vaguely hostile air about it. That was exactly the kind of impression its founders had intended the town and harbour to instil. The mere view of this old centre of town, protruding into the sea like the figurehead of a huge ship was meant to keep uninvited guests at bay, and did.

Laura sat shivering outside on the narrow, wind-swept quarterdeck of the Condor Express, a Catamaran-ferry to St. Helier, Jersey. While trying to warm her hands on the plastic mug of hot tea, she was admiring the fast receding panorama of the Brittany port. She had spent the night in a small but neat hotel situated intra muros, viz. inside the wall which surrounds the old part of town. The hotel bore the quizzical name of Quic en grogne, which, translated with a finger twist of poetic licence, came across as may he kiss my ass. A motto fitting beautifully to both Laura's and the hotel owner's present disposition, even though, originally, it had rather been intended to express the generally defiant attitude of the Malvins. That's what the town's inhabitants took considerable pride in being called. Like the rest of the population, the proprietress considered herself neither French nor Breton, but Malvin. Laura had talked to her for a while and understood her to have lost her husband to the sea not so long ago and, being thus brutally thrown back on her own devices, had opened the hotel without really having any prior experience of this line of trade.

"A man's got to live on something, and so does a woman," she had declared and gracefully accepted Laura's emphatic words of moral support. Laura had promised her to go the extra mile and, once back in Hamburg, make what publicity she possibly could for the place. She felt both the hotel's resolute owner and its promising name deserved no less.

"Where did you spend the weekend, then? Not in the Kiss my Ass again, did you?"

She was sure it would make a kill in certain less uptight Hamburg circles.

The spirit of spite could be felt in each and every one of the town's pores, its cobbled streets and alleys as well as in their cafés, which were really pubs. There was no doubting its glorious past, even though the fifty-thousand soul town had to be rebuilt from scratch after it had been virtually obliterated by carpet bombing. Allied carpet bombing, that is, not German, for once. The commanding officer of the German occupation forces had liked it so much here he had insisted both obstinately and pointlessly on staying and offering resistance instead of capitulating to the vastly superior Allied forces. Thus, he had ultimately provoked the bombing.

Upon hearing the adjectival name "Malvins", Laura had immediately associated it with the Falkland Islands, that God-forsaken archipelago in the South Atlantic, to this day proudly flying the Union Jack. During the reign of the Iron Lady, aka Margaret Thatcher, they had become a casus belli poisoning Anglo-Argentinian relations. When Argentine forces had started beleaguering the islands they called the Malvinas, at the beginning of the nineteen eighties, Lady Thatcher had not hesitated for a moment and sent a sizeable British fleet complete with aircraft carrier and SAS troops down South, in the general direction of Cape Horn. It had been a campaign in the spirit of the nineteenth, rather than the twentieth century and had borne all the hallmarks of the Crimean War, with a marginally better result for the Brits, though.

Laura had always taken the term Malvinas for the Spanish equivalent of the Falklands – which it was, albeit once removed, as it were. Because originally, it was neither the Spaniards, nor the Argentinians that had come up with that name. Instead, it had been derived from the St. Malo fishermen and sheep farmers who, incredible as it may sound, were the first to settle here, a long way from home. Which seemed all the more peculiar as they had a fair number of islands waiting right beyond the horizon. Except those islands belonged to the local Norman noblemen and warlords and, hence, were of little use to them.

The Malvinas having no strategic or economic value to speak of, the Battle of the Falklands, sold as a number one patriotic duty, had essentially been a welcome opportunity for the Iron Lady to avert public attention from her largely debatable home policy moves, to wit, the crushing of parts of the English trade union movement.

The last detail of the town that kept sticking out for a while longer than the rest was the needle-like steeple of the impressive cathedral. Meanwhile, Laura felt frozen solid. She got up and toddled towards the restaurant. At this time of year, the ferry was fairly empty. Eight or so decades ago, the shuttle traffic between the islands and the French Brittany coast must have been a good deal more brisk, in fact, probably even bordering on the chaotic. What with the German troops advancing a lot faster than hoped for, many civilians from the Northern regions of France, a lot of Jews among them, had fled to ports such as St, Malo, to get from there on to the islands and, hopefully, to Britain. Not few of the refugees got stuck on the islands, though, some missing the last boats, others held back deliberately because, as aliens, they might well turn out to be German lice in the British fur. Others again, such as the several hundred Irishmen residing here more or less permanently, to help with harvests and all sorts of occasional jobs, would have been happy enough to stay. As nationals of a neutral country, they didn't have much to fear from the Germans, or so they reckoned. Why would they want to return to the bleak poverty and hopelessness they had escape by hopping across the Channel? Alas, they weren't allowed to stay, but were shipped off to England, where they were stuck in internment camps.

Such administrative absurdities were rampant. Then again, taking a step back and looking at the chaos administrative authorities are likely to cause at the outbreak of even the tiniest civilian crisis in times of peace, the system couldn't reasonably be expected to work any better under the additional stress of war and occupation.

As a child, Laura had once accompanied her father on a brief visit to the Channel Islands, both Jersey and Guernsey, in fact.

She couldn't remember all that much, only that they had been pleasantly surprised by the conviviality they met with here. There must still have been not so few islanders holding grudges against Germans, no doubt. But either they hadn't come across any, or those they had met had swallowed their occupation-induced susceptibilities. Behind his usually rather sullen and rugged façade, her father Robert would hide a surprisingly engaging nature that allowed him to "grow on people", as he put it. Yes, he did have something of a fisher of men. The true nature of his business with the islanders had escaped Laura at the time. Today, however, she wondered what on earth he had been looking for in these remote parts. Probably something uncouth, that much you could always safely assume.

Something she clearly did recall, though, was that Jersey had had a decidedly French atmosphere about it, complete with mushy croissant and doll's bath-tubs filled with milky brown coffee. Later, a lot later, that is, she had learned with interest that all of these islands used to belong to the French Normans. Some of their "Northmen" or Viking forbears had apparently felt bored, stuck as they were in the far recesses of their fjords. During their frequent raids south, they couldn't help coming across these islands profiting from the closeness of the Gulf Stream waters. Delighted with what they saw, they had settled both here and on the adjacent Continental coast. It was they, too, who gave the islands their names, whose precise meaning was unfortunately lost in translation. What seemed fairly reliable historical stock-in-trade was the final –(n)ey syllable, also met with in the Orkneys, for instance, as well as in, say, Norderney, which is a corrupted reflex of Scandinavian for island, viz. ö(ya)..

Left-hand driving, fish 'n chips, and old age pensioners weren't the only features following in the wake of the unfriendly British take-over. Next to tourism and miniature agriculture, offshore banking became the islands' third and most important pillar of their economy. Letter-box companies sprang up everywhere like mushrooms, especially on Sark, which counts way more virtual enterprises than inhabitants.

Aiding and abetting that kind of development on the islands was their hopelessly antiquated, discombobulated constitutional status. Unlike, say, the Isle of Wight, they are not part and parcel of the UK, not by a very long chalk. Nor are they crown colonies like, say, the Isle of Man. Strictly speaking, they count among the personal belongings of the respective English monarchs. And what they do with them is nobody's business.

Heinz Marquardt had called Laura the night before. As it would seem, he had managed to catch the amorous eye of the secretary to the bank's head of industrial credit department. It had something vaguely seedy about it, no doubt, but time being of the essence, they had to set scruples aside.

"Patience, Laura, patience: give me a few more days, and I'm in. What? No, in the files, not in the lady. I have been in and out of her for the last three days, or nights, no offence. No need to waste time. You know perfectly well I will stop at nothing to serve my company's interest, self-sacrifice included."

"Don't pull a tendon, though, tiger. Meanwhile, what about the Dutch, can we hold out on them a little longer?"

"The Dutch" was short for the logistics company ROLA was hoping to swallow before either the Chinese, Russians, or Arabs did. That's what the loan was ultimately for. Of course, they had so far been holding their cards close to their chest but couldn't continue doing so forever. Any time now, somebody was likely to call their bluff. Should the shit hit the fan and the deal go South, well, Laura's position in the company, the prestige and respect she had managed to obtain at no small pains over the years, might go out the window.

Marquardt had promised to keep Laura posted continuously. Actually, she had thrown a bit of a tantrum in frustration, when Marquardt had finally hung up. Banging her mobile against the wall, she had cursed so loud and blasphemously that even the piratical spectres of the past still haunting the hotel must have turned away blushing.

"Madame? Everything okay with you?" the worried owner, alarmed by the unholy racket, had come up to enquire.

"Okay? Okay? No, not really. In fact, I have hardly ever been further away from okay than tonight."

The proprietress had then invited her to a glass or two of Calvados, which had had a soothing effect on Laura. Unfortunately, it had come with a headache tasting faintly of apple in the morning, which is why she had placed herself at the stern of the ferry to breathe some fresh air and get rid of the pulsating ache.

Fortunately, she had Marquardt on her side. With uncharacteristic loyalty, rarely met with on the corridors of power of either ROLA, Whitehall, or the Vatican, for that matter, he had remained her staunch number one supporter. But even he was neither omnipresent nor omnipotential. So, what had to happen now was relatively clear: they had to smoke out their secret opponent operating in the dark, for one thing, and she had to find the killer of the Lamont dynasty, for another. Upon reflection, the one looked as unlikely a cause as the other. Suddenly, the ferry brusquely slowed down with a jerk and, turning from a surfing to a displacing vessel, sunk her bows deeper in the water. They had reached the port of St. Helier. Laura had not yet cleared the gangway when she began to feel like the ferry had not just carried her the thirty-odd miles from St. Malo to Jersey but had crossed the Atlantic and put her ashore in the Caribbean. The pleasantly milder climate, the decorative palm trees here and there, as well as the town's generally Mediterranean air seemed to bear no relationship to the island's objectively verifiable geographic position. She had read somewhere that some of the less educated and perhaps land-locked German occupation soldiers had, upon their arrival here, mistaken the islands for bits and pieces of the African coast. She had found that hilariously stupid. But, revisiting the concept from where she stood now, it did no longer seem all that unlikely to her. Some of those soldiers later had occasion, as part of Rommel's El Alamain divisions, to realize at their cost what the African coasts really did look and feel like.

Still a little shaky from the voyage as well as from the aftermath of the Calvados, Laura squeezed into a taxi and gave the driver the details of Lamont's posh Jersey abode called the Golden Manor.

The names of places and shops whizzing by did more often than not sound more French than English, with a leaning towards the ridiculously pompous. A tailor's workshop, for instance, was apparently run by a Bob Le Sueur, Esquire. Laura briefly wondered whether she would feel tempted to take advantage of the services of a tailor calling himself "Sweating Bob".

Hard as the Jersey inhabitants had obviously tried to preserve the island's French ways, they had not been able or willing to beat that bane of road traffic, the English left-hand drive. The Germans on their part had of course put their boot down and switched traffic on the islands to the Continental-Germanic mode for the duration of the occupation. Given the narrow roads in conjunction with the complexities of local topography as well as the lack of driving experience on the part of many islanders, this innovation had inevitably led to a number of rather hair-raising accidents. As Laura had found on the occasion of her Red Chapel adventure on the island of Cyprus, switching from one system to the other, is not as hard as some would make it appear. Not, at any rate, as long as you're cruising along blithely and carefree. The crunch comes with a sudden crisis situation forcing you to react as it were viscerally. It was in such unexpected predicaments that you tended instinctively to turn the wheel to the wrong side.

At first sight, the Golden Manor looked just as much of a Fort Knox replica as did Lamont's private Puerto Rican fortress he had jokingly called his Hacienda del Suerte. It reminded Laura, who had seen photos of it, of a boat whose hull had been constructed of solid armour plating and then baptized the Little Butterfly.

The external wall round this Jersey estate of Lamont's consisted of locally won grey granite. It was guarded by alien-looking small but sturdy green men Sir Lucas had probably flown in from the Caribbean. How they had managed to obtain permits for the heavy arsenal they carried around with them remained Lamont's secret. It gave Laura a first inkling of the kind of influence the man wielded with the powers that be. The taxi driver stopped at the cast-iron double-door gate.

One of the two burly guards positioned here bent down to look inside the car through the pane that Laura slid down eventually. She gave him her name and showed him the print-out of Lamont's secretary's mail confirming the invitation.

"Sir Arthur is expecting me, I believe."

Meanwhile, the other guard had examined the car's undercarriage with a mirror at the end of a long selfie-stick, slowly doing the tour once round the entire taxi.

"Wait here, please," the one who had looked inside asked them, when the first inspection was over. He turned sideways and started conferring over his slim headphone with someone probably sitting in the building's centre of operations stuffed with screens and phones. After some toing and froing, which Laura wasn't able to follow, the guard turned towards them again and, opening the gate, told them to drive up to the flight of steps leading to the manor's heavy principal wooden door.

The driver did as he had been told. When he arrived at the foot of the steps, two more armed bodyguards appeared on the top steps. Laura was in two minds as to whether or not she should ask the taxi driver to wait for her. An hour wasn't much to her. It might be for the driver, though, who had perhaps other fish to fry in the meantime. So, she decided against it, paid the man and walked up the granite steps. Fortunately, the driver had been prepared to accept Euros. Laura had forgotten to obtain pound sterling and the local monopoly money was only accepted as legal tender on the islands and in Gotham City. Some parts of the two-storey building's façade were overgrown with ivy, which softened the overall fortress impression and even lent it a mildly enchanted air. One of the bodyguards frisked Laura for weapons a little more thoroughly than she would have wished, while the other was looking on with a broad grin. Then they rifled through her travel bag, an all-leather affair bearing her father's initials, RF, a bag that had rendered both him and Laura excellent service over the decades. Laura positively loathed this kind of procedure that was all too reminiscent of a visit in former Alcatraz. But she saw no alternative to submitting to it. She had by now gone through too much to just walk off empty-handed, just because of some idiosyncratic reflex.

When he had finally ascertained that Laura didn't pack any potentially lethal weapons, the one bodyguard gave the other a nod, whereupon his colleague opened one wing of the door and waved her through.

"Welcome to Karen Hall," Laura murmured, as she stepped inside. Hopefully, the Golden Manor's owner didn't have Goering's massive proportions. Laura had seen a portrait of him in her Who's Who, but that must have dated back to the years immediately following upon the end of WW II and, hence, gave little or no idea of what he might look like now. More recent photos of the man just didn't seem to exist. Fair enough, she thought, as long as the man himself did.

In the foyer, she was met by an inscrutable-looking butler, who took her coat and travel bag, both of which he passed on to a maid with a facial expression that seemed to recommend the triggering of immediate de-contamination procedures. Then, the butler asked her to follow him up the marble stairs covered with a thick carpet that muffled the sounds of their steps. In passing, Laura took a casual look at the portraits of what presumably were the present or former owner's forebears, all of them seemingly staring back at Laura with unconcealed curiosity. If the Who's Who had got his date of birth right, it couldn't be long until Sir Lucas completed this bizarre gallery of pretentious mug shots.

The upper landing of the marble flight of stairs was stylishly framed by bronze statues of both Artemis and Apollo in the nude. Apollo's behind appeared to be glistening a mite brighter than that of Artemis. Was Sir Lucas gay? The Who's Who, at any rate, had remained silent on the subject. The butler led her to the right, to the two wings of another wooden door. This one was adorned by all sorts of carvings reminiscent of wine-drinking Dionysos in the midst of naked ladies dancing hand in hand with one another. When the butler announced her with an unexpectedly booming voice, Laura started and looked around. In the dim twilight of what seemed to be the manor's principal dining hall, she discovered no-one who might have profited from the butler's stentorian announcement at first. So, she waited until the butler had left and closed the door behind him. Then she took a closer look around. She hated to be kept waiting albeit only for a few minutes. Besides, she had no idea how Lamont intended to count the measly sixty minutes he had granted her. If the clock was ticking already, there would hardly remain enough time for more than shaking hands plus some small talk.

She passed the palm of her left hand across the smooth surface of the seemingly endless table that was framed by two rows of twelve uncomfortable-looking chairs. At the far end, she discovered one more portrait, for some reason or other hanging way lower than the rest. Suddenly, the portrait moved its eyebrows and started talking. Was she hallucinating from the after-effects of the Calvados? She didn't understand what the man was saying to her, which was due, partly to his apparently feeble, wheezing voice, partly to Laura's total absorption by the bizarre situation she had found herself in.

Thus, it took her quite a while to realize she was actually being welcomed by none other than the man in the flesh, even though there was much less of him than Laura had had reason to expect. A tiny figure with delicate features, to say the least, sitting in a wheelchair. Which was why Laura, half blinded by the twilight, hadn't noticed him before. A dwarfish figure with a sparse crown of grey hair and the sunken face of a very old person who should probably have joined his forebears ages ago but, for reasons of his own, stubbornly refused to do so. When she followed his invitation to come closer, she perceived him as a broken wreck of a man with dead-fish eyes probably suffering from cataracts. In fact, Laura thought, if the killer saw him like that, a tattering, possibly half demented old-timer in a wheelchair, he would probably call off his vendetta as perfectly meaningless. By the look of it, Sir Lucas had long since crossed the threshold beyond which life, rather than death, becomes a man's scourge. Then again, first impressions can be deceptive. Maybe, under that mask of old-age frailty, there lurked a tough old gangster, someone who like a snake, would lure his victims into some kind of hypnotic stupor, only to dig his fangs into them at the moment they least suspected it. Laura decided to be on her guard.

"Mrs Forster?" Lamont called out her name for the third or fourth time. Laura pulled herself together and nodded.

"A good day to you, Sir Lucas. Sorry, I was a little overpowered by the splendour of your manor. Thanks a lot for receiving me, I appreciate it."

"As well you ought to," the old man croaked a little pertly, she found.

"I don't usually indulge in interviews, as you were probably told, but….."

He waved her even closer and offered her the chair on his left. The end of the table was laid for two. When she sat down, Sir Lucas lifted a monocle that had hung on a silver chain by his side and looked her up and down with the unmitigated curiosity of a biologist looking at a new species of Galapagos beetle. Laura didn't flinch from his stare and regretted not having brought a monocle, as well. Two one-eyed jacks staring at one another with grotesquely blown-up pupils would have been fun.

"You will have to excuse me for not getting up to meet you comme il faut, but my legs…an unfortunate car accident, decades ago. What can I say, old age's a drag, let me assure you…"

"Not at all. I'm the one who has to offer her excuses for prevailing on you so shortly after your lamentable loss…"

The old man looked puzzled for a moment.

"Loss? What loss? Ah, you're referring to my brother's demise, are you? For a terrible moment there I thought you were insinuating one of my financial interests had gone belly up. Well, as far as my brother, half-brother, actually, is concerned, I repeatedly warned him and told him to get himself a host of bodyguards the way I did. I mean, it's not as if he couldn't afford it. But no, he preferred being in the company of whores. Had it coming, I guess. No, if there's a loss that really got to me, it's that of my two sisters."

"I didn't know your sisters had been shot too," Laura declared. If the truth be told, she had had no idea Lamont had any sisters in the first place. She must send a note to the editors of Who's Who.

"No, they weren't. Abigail and Emma, both a little younger than myself, became the unfortunate victims of a freak accident. The two of them used to go to Switzerland at least once a year, with their respective husbands and kids, to do some skiing and stuff. Had two boys each. Most of the time, they rented a chalet somewhere – Grindelwald, I believe. Expensive haunt."

"What happened?"

"One day, their husbands and sons were out skiing and the girls, my sisters, that is, decided to take it easy and do some serious chatting and drinking. So, they sat down outside, in a kind of porch swing, mostly consisting of metal parts, of course. Far off, a storm was brewing, as will happen in the mountains. Even though it was still miles away, a flash of lightning came literally out of the blue and killed them on the spot. Meteorologists later explained to us that storms are largely incalculable events and that lightning can advance the storm cell proper by several miles. A fluke, one that killed my sisters. Heavens."

He paused as if still battling with the memories after all those years.

"A bit like you coming from nowhere, hopefully not to strike me down. What is it you are hoping to get from me?"

"Well, as you may know, my son, adopted son, Ignace, used to be a close friend of…"

"…this girl Solveig, yes, so I heard. But still I don't get it. You want to start a private investigation? What for? Because of a whore's untimely death?"

Laura's voice suddenly gained in acuity.

"I must ask you to watch your language, Sir Lucas. Solveig may have been a prostitute – who am I to judge or condemn. But my son was in love with her and that makes her special, to him as well as to me. Hence, I will not tolerate your…"

"Alright, Mrs Forster. Point taken, you may dismount again. I understand and excuse me for calling a spade a spade. Why don't you sit down again, so we can continue our conversation as the two mature adults we are. Well, myself a great deal more than you."

"No offence, but you remind me of my mother, adopted mother, in fact. She always claimed that men grow up but never mature."

Lamont gave the short croak of a laugh that could also have been a cough.

"That may well be so, except I would be a bad judge of it. Who else was adopted in your family?"

"You don't really want to know."

"Maybe not. I just hate to have to apologize. At my age, you feel apologetic for most of the time. For a host of reasons not under your control. Most of all, because you have the nerve to be still alive although the world at large began to look upon you as a write-off some twenty years ago already. And there you still are, unabashed, as if you were entitled to immortality. People can stand others being richer than they are. They can also stand others who get older than most of them could ever hope to. But people who are both better off and, in all likelihood, longer lived, that's what takes the biscuit. Folks' looks have that murderous glint in them when looking at you. In antiquity, there were communities, island ones, mostly, who expected people that had reached a certain age and were no longer productive in any sense of the term to commit suicide so as not to become a burden for the rest. We are more civilized, more humane, but, notwithstanding, the basic concept still forms part of our DNA, I guess."

"But you don't look it, I mean…."

"Oh yes, thanks for the flowers, but I think I do. The last thing standing between myself and a merciful bullet in the head is the hope of looking the killer of my next of kin in the eyes, one day. Preferably the day I turn my knife in his guts and watch him die. Ironic, isn't it? A killer that keeps me alive. I devoted a substantial part of my considerable fortune to the catching of that deeply disturbed individual and any of his possible instigators. I've already put a small army of bounty hunters on him. To no avail, so far. Still, it's more promising than putting my money on the law. What makes you think you'll be more successful than all the rest of them out there?"

Laura shrugged her shoulders.

"I happen to have caught other weirdos before and…sense I may be the one to nail this one too." Lamont fell silent for a moment.

"Anyway. I thought you might be hungry and thirsty after the long pilgrimage here. So, I had Harold, my butler, prepare a bite and a sip for you. I hope you'll appreciate our cooking.

Personally, I find our British cuisine a trifle insipid, but since I don't eat much these days, anyway…A cucumber sandwich does it for me, you know. The great culinary legacy of the British Empire. It's the cockroach among the smørrebrøds of this world, you know. Even a nuclear holocaust will not harm it – our indestructible cucumber sandwich."

He laughed about his own crack.

"Which, unfortunately, doesn't apply to me. If I am to believe my greedy doctors, who write bills faster than you can pronounce the word prescriptions, my next glass of alcohol could be my last. Well, there are worse ways to go, aren't there? Which brings us back to the topic, I believe."

He picked up the small bell in front of him and shook the life out of it, whereupon the door behind him flew open and two maids set Laura's snack and Lamont's sandwich on the table under the supervision of the inevitable Harold.

While Laura was making hearty forays into the salads and cold cuts, the old man watched her with envy. When she had downed her first glass of water and sampled the Riesling d'Alsace sur le lis, Lamont sighed and picked up his sandwich as if it was exhibit one in a murder trial.

"Well, I guess we don't have much time left, better get cracking then."

THIRD CHAPTER

1. Double Jeopardy

"…that said, I still fail to grasp why my fellow-countrymen insisted on bombing the island ports when they could actually have landed here without so much as firing a shot. Seems particularly evil and cruel to me."

Laura was chewing on the last piece of roast beef and gulped down the remaining drops of wine.

"Can I get you some more…? No? Well, I'm glad you liked it. Now, even though I have no interest in defending the Nazis, I think when it comes to the subject of the Channel Islands' occupation, one has to grant them mitigating circumstances. You're right, of course, to point at the de-militarisation of the islands that had taken place shortly before the first German troops arrived in Cherbourg. Even today, however, some islanders hold almost more of a grudge against the Brits than against the Germans because of what they have always considered a let-down of historic proportions. Try and put yourself in their position. On one side, the Krauts are approaching at great speed. On the other, the Brits are leaving even faster, throwing the islanders to the wolves. Incidentally, this grudge of theirs received fresh sustenance when Margaret Thatcher sent British troops to the Falkland Islands in 1982. Could you blame the people on Guernsey, Jersey, Sark, or Alderney for looking on with a quantum of bitterness? I think not."

"I still see no reason for the Nazis to drop bombs on the islands."

"I'll be coming to that. Even though, for historical reasons, the islanders' loyalties were divided between France and Britain, they had, at the latest after the fall of France, been looking for Britain to bail them out. When it became clear to them that this wouldn't happen, they felt betrayed and abandoned, as indeed they were. The Brits for their part, one has to remember, were still shell-shocked from the disastrous outcome of their Dunkirk adventure and felt they could not afford to commit both men and material to the defence of islands which were of no strategic military importance whatsoever for them. Being within uncomfortable reach of your Heinkel's and Junker's, the Channel Islands simply could not be held for any length of time. Hence, better keep all of your forces ready for the defence of Britain herself, whose invasion seemed imminent. As for the Germans, on the other hand, and here is my answer to your question, they had absolutely no knowledge of the islands' demilitarisation, and that's a fact."

"You really mean to say they hadn't been told or couldn't have guessed?"

"Neither, nor. You see, the British, loath as they were to let the Germans know the islands were there for the taking, had hoped for their enemy to think along the same strategic lines as they did and to come to the conclusion that they might as well leave the useless bunch of islands be. What they should have seen but lamentably overlooked, however, was that the Nazis thought in entirely different categories. Already on their way up to government, they had learned the intrinsic value of propaganda and made abundant use of it. When it came to swaying reticent masses of people and bring them to heel, nothing could replace propaganda: a truism that was even more powerful in times of war, of course. Thus. the occupation of an albeit tiny morsel of would-be British territory was an unparalleled propaganda coup the Nazis could not possibly sneeze at. Even today, I can see the big banner on the front page of the Völkische Beobachter: This morning, German troops set foot on British soil."

"Even so, they must surely have carried out preparatory aerial recon that would have shown no trace of British forces of any description on the isles?"

"Wow! I can see I'm talking to an expert here. You're right, the Germans did do their homework. But the recon planes of the period, it must be remembered, used to fly at relatively great heights, to escape flak fire. Also, the photographic material used for such purposes, though state of the art then, wasn't any way near our present days' high-resolution zillion-pixel stuff that will show the colour of your eyes on a shot taken from the ISS. If it had been, the Germans would not have been fooled by the dummy planes, tanks and canon the Allies placed all around the English South coast shortly before D-day. In other words: whenever you discovered an enemy's artillery pieces on the photos, for instance, you could be vaguely certain they were really there. Unfortunately, the opposite didn't necessarily apply. Maybe your enemy had just been clever enough in camouflaging his canons and troops and decided not to interfere with your recon planes either, so as not to give their positions away at an early stage."

"And so…"

"And so, in June 1940, some forty-five people in both St. Peter Port and St. Helier got killed absolutely pointlessly."

Laura mused a little on that one.

"Wait a second. But the inhabitants could have waved white flags or something to indicate no-one would offer resistance?"

Lamont nodded.

"I'm sure they would have done, had they been told that the Germans hadn't been told. You see, that's where the ultimate letdown comes in. The Brits had not told the Germans and had let the islanders under the impression that, being on demilitarised ground, they had nothing to fear. There can be no excuse for that, it was plain treason committed by the British High Command with the purpose of poisoning German-islanders' occupational relations, hardly ever harmonious, anyway, even more from the word go."

Laura nodded again.

"Food for thought, indeed. I for one would not put it past the politicians…. What happened next?"

"Well, if my fellow countrymen had really been as ruthless as to speculate on the bombing directing public aggravation on the Germans, they had another think coming. Instead, the islanders' grudge against what they conceived of as the Great British Let-Down reached new, unprecedented peaks, so that the British

Government hastened to inform the Germans of the true situation via the American ambassador in Berlin. Hence, no more bombing or strafing, no more victims here, for a while."

Laura scratched her head.

"Why is it, not many more of the, what, one hundred thousand inhabitants had left the islands before?"

"Sixty thousand, actually. Today you might be right, it's probably more like a hundred thousand, indeed. Depends a little on how and who you count, as always with these things. That being said, you have to try and open the curtain wide on the full picture as it presented itself then. Shipping people by the thousands and tens of thousands, male and female, young and old, fit and frail, across a Channel, already teeming with German U-boats? In what? The Dunkirk experience couldn't be repeated, obviously. Besides, like I say, by circumventing the French Maginot Line, the Germans were advancing much more quickly than anyone on the Allied side had counted on, so that a solid dose of panic was to be felt everywhere. Rapidly knocked up admin structures soon crumbled under the stress of the logistic paraphernalia of evacuation, the lot was in tatters. But even if the transport side of things had functioned relatively smoothly, where would all those islanders shipped to England have gone to? The bombing of London and other British cities was pending. Once that started, thousands of homeless Brits would join both the refugees from the European continent and the Channel Islanders. There were not enough structures to receive, register, accommodate and feed everyone."

Lamont shook his head disapprovingly.

"Hence, many of the islanders, on arriving in Britain, may have regretted not having stayed here," Lamont continued

"Strange as it may sound today, not all the islanders even understood enough English to grasp what was happening to them. People who had never left their homes for any length of time at all, suddenly found themselves lodged somewhere in the wider Manchester area or in Scottish-speaking Glasgow, sooty, gloomy industrial centres the likes of which they had so far only heard of, if that. More often than not, they lacked the material and moral comfort of their husbands, wives, of next of kin. Once a ship lying in St. Peter Port or St. Helier was declared full up, it would slip its moorings and make for England, irrespective of whether or not couples were separated or families torn apart. Even if, say, the wife or mother managed to get on a later vessel, the defective reception procedures would cause her to spend months in search of her husband and children."

He gave a deep sigh and leaned backwards in his chair as if his back was giving him intense pain, which it might have been.

"And that wasn't the end of it, either. Historians and sociologists of all sorts had made us believe that small, insular communities such as ours that had been forged over the open fires of mutual affection and seasoned by the pangs of isolation had reached a degree of natural solidarity that would resist pressure of any kind. Well, how wrong can you be? The Germans hadn't even set foot on any of the islands when this would-be unflinching solidarity was seen melting away faster than the proverbial snowball in hell. Islanders who were bound for England had packed their stuff and made for the harbour, leaving their houses largely unlocked. Chances were, or so they must have reasoned, that German military command would requisition a number of houses, preferably empty ones, anyway, to lodge their rank and file. When they found the door unlocked, they wouldn't have to kick it down and create more damage than necessary. If and when it so happened that the family in question did not get aboard the ship that day, they would of course go home to get some rest and maybe try again next morning. Yet, lo and behold, when they arrived at what had been their home, they would find their house looted, stripped of all pieces of furniture, the wooden panelling sometimes ripped off the walls and carpets or even linoleum floor covering removed. A wrecked ship visited by beachcombers could hardly have looked more heart-rending than a home thus ravaged – not by the enemy, mind, but by neighbours these people had grown up with and whose kids used to play with theirs. Moral decay, in other words, was accompanying, if not preceding, material disintegration. That was arguably the greatest, most shocking let-down of them all. Collaboration with the enemy, as was later suggested, may or may not have taken place, on occasion. Looting by friends and neighbours did take place without the shadow of a doubt. It's an ugly blot that will not disappear from the records in a hurry."

Laura looked at her watch. The granted hour's interview must soon come to an end, she feared. So far, she had learned nothing from the old man that promised to be of any help in her search for the killer. She felt she had to make hay.

"And what about the Yarmouth Six, where do they come in?"

Lamont had plunged into thoughts of his own and seemed not to hear her question.

"Who? What? Oh, the Yarmouth Six. Well, I suppose you could say they were the result of a collective bad conscience on the part of the Brits. From day one of their occupation, Winston Churchill, who had allegedly opposed the decision to demilitarise the islands, made it his business to have ever new commando raids planned and executed. Pin-prick strategy is what they called it: a handful of men would land on this or that island, check its respective defence installations, establish contact with the locals, capture or kill the odd German. Such was the general idea. A military fig-leaf barely apt to hide the private parts of betrayal. Well, it didn't take the military high command long to realize that, unfortunately, most of the pricks happened to be on our side. Nobody having any experience to speak of with such delicate ops, they would come out as something put on stage by the Marx brothers. First-rate slapstick material, I assure you. If and when, on a very quiet night, you would hear resounding volleys of laughter roll across the Channel, you knew that another covert operation had hilariously failed. There were organizational trip wires everywhere. For instance, our chaps of course had to be put off close to the respective island coast by submarines or small landing craft. The last mile or so would frequently have to be covered by a canoe or collapsible kayak. In one case, the respective operation didn't get off the ground, because, on boarding the submarine, and only then, it was noted that the canoe in question wasn't quite collapsible enough to fit through the tower's hatch. Surprise! In another case, the ship that was to take the raiders of the lost ark to Sark missed the island altogether in the dark. I mean, Sark's a flea shit on the chart, you blink twice and pass it by. What had happened was, the ship's hull had been wrapped in coils of live electric wire. This ingenious contraption helped avoid German magnetic mines alright. Unfortunately, by the same token, it also made the magnetic compass go haywire. Surprise again! In yet another case, the landing party managed to step onto the right beaches. They even happened to establish contact with a local, who then turned out to be probably the respective island's last speaker of one of those hilarious Norman-French dialects once flourishing there. So whatever he may have been in a mood to impart in the way of information would have been lost in translation."

Laura couldn't help laughing at the old man's dry humour. A pity the Doc had died. He would have loved to hear stuff like that.

"Even if the locals our men bumped into had more sense and a better command of English than this one, they would as a rule not relish such unexpected encounters and rarely give away more than the time of day for fear of German reprisals, which were quite severe. If the raiders survived, they would soon go back, whilst the locals had to go on living with the Germans. Like I say, I for one can't blame them. Probably, the Germans were quite disappointed when, for some weeks or months, no commando raid took place and they had to make do with one or the other of those Leni Riefenstahl films Hitler loved no end."

He was shuddering in his wheelchair as if the memory of all this caused him physical disgust.

"Not that the Krauts themselves were total strangers to slapstick performances. How could they be, with a Rumpelstiltskin like Hitler as their Fuehrer. Once, a successful British commando landed on the Casquets, a dangerous rock formation some twelve nautical miles west of Alderney. The rocks bear an important lighthouse which was then guarded by a dozen or so Germans. When the Brits entered their enemies' quarters at the dead of night, for a moment there, they must have thought they had raided the Cage aux Folles or the Moulin Rouge, by mistake, because most of the German soldiers wore hair nets. Hair nets! My word. Probably shaved their legs as well, they did. That said, the lighthouse, of course, was not to be held for more than a few days. Then the Germans re-possessed it, hair nets and all. Speaking of which."

The old man put on his monocle and looked at his watch, a Rolex so big it further dwarfed his already rather thin wrist.

"Unless I'm mistaken, our little rendezvous is already coming to an end, alas. But I like you. You have excellent manners and are a good listener. Allow me to submit a proposal I hope you will not find indecent. If you so wish, you may stay. I'll have tea and coffee served in the library, where we can continue our little powwow."

Even though Laura had the impression this was going more along the lines of a monologue, she didn't have to think twice. Secretly, she had actually hoped for a prolongation. A good thing she hadn't asked the taxi man to wait for her.

"That's exceedingly kind of you. I think I'll accept your offer with pleasure."

Lamont rang the bell again. While the maids were clearing the table, the butler rolled his master into the library, where someone by the name of Harold had lit the fireplace.

As the flames were licking up and down the softly crackling logs, their light was darting across the neat array of richly-bound books of all shapes and sizes behind Lamont's crouched figure. Laura wondered whether that was a thoroughly studied effect or something that just happened and somehow crowned this magic session with a man who knew how to drag the past from the shadows of oblivion.

"Excellent," Lamont croaked after they had both installed themselves in the armchairs, the landlord with Harold's help, obviously. While Sir Lucas asked for an espresso, Laura, who had had some rather miserable coffees on the train and on the ferry, stayed with the tea.

"Where was I?" Lamont asked.

"A little downstream of the Marx Brothers," Laura replied with a smile.

"Right, thanks. Well, at the time our little group was formed, in March '43, the experience accrued in the meantime did go a long way to improving the performance of our commando raids, of course. Most of the teething troubles had been overcome. Then again, the other side had not exactly remained idle either. Largely contributing to a continuous sense of alert was the fact that the Gods of War turned away from the Germans, many of whom began to see the writing on the wall. The debacle at Kursk on top of the Stalingrad fiasco was deeply depressing, as was the turn of the tide in submarine warfare largely due to breaking the Enigma spell. Then there was the appearance of Americans on the European theatres of war. That put paid to Hitler's original far-reaching ambitions and caused the Fuehrer ultimately to switch from attack to self-defence.

The one major defence element remaining to the Germans beset by enemies on all sides was the Siegfried Line, as we used to call the string of innumerable defence works stretching from The Hammer in Norway to Cadiz in Atlantic Spain. Its southwest corner was to be formed by the Channel Islands, which suddenly seemed to assume a surprising strategic importance. Since the Fuehrer, in glaring contrast to the majority of his generals, seemed deeply convinced the Allied forces, and in particular the British, would attribute a very high priority to the re-conquest of the islands, albeit as a matter of prestige, that could not and must not happen.

"But the original, almost casual abandonment of the islands by the British ought to have taught him a lesson, one should think."

"Well, it was the same phenomenon again, only in reverse, this time. Hitler thought the Brits were thinking in the same propaganda categories as himself, where, in fact, they were guided by military strategy alone. That said, as far as the islands were removed from the rest of Europe, they were not totally protected from the winds of change. What with German morale beginning to show the first cracks, their initially polite and correct relationship with the locals suffered the consequences. The fact that the Nazis had deported two thousand islanders the year before and had rounded up the few Jews still living on the islands hadn't exactly helped either. The most obvious sign of the relationship coming apart at the seams was the ominous appearance on the scene of the SS. More and more soldiers and workers, volunteers as well as forced labourers, had to share ever depleting stocks of food. The conversion of the islands, especially of Alderney, into regular fortresses abounding with guns and cannon of every description by Organisation Todt swallowed up hundreds of thousands of tons of material and tied down men later ruefully missed in the defence of Normandy."

Harold served coffee and tea in person, a definite privilege, Laura thought. Maybe she ought to have one of those well-educated, discrete and housebroken penguins in her Hamburg home.

"In view of this slightly changed backdrop, the commando raid pin pricks, far from being the laughing stock of some years ago, now rose to the status of grist for Hitler's mill in that they seemed to confirm his view. Being taken seriously came with a price-tag, though. German guards and posts everywhere on the island's coasts were on their toes from now on. If and when you succeeded in breaching that first ring of artillery-backed forward defence, the almost total wall-to-wall mining of both the coastal waters, the beaches, and, in many cases, the adjacent ground increasingly turned such raids into suicide missions. Several of our mates had already been torn to pieces by mines, others shot dead while swimming helplessly in the water."

Lamont sipped his espresso and sloshed it round in his mouth as if he was cleaning his dentures with it.

"Add to this, if you wish, the increasingly hostile attitude of the locals who even started making representations in the House of Commons for this illegal mounting of commando raids on officially demilitarised territory to stop. What you get is a climate not exactly conducive to successful covert ops. And, saying that, I haven't even made mention of the cherry on the cake's icing.

According to Hitler's so-called Night-and-Fog decree, any members of such commando operations caught alive were to be court-martialled and shot unceremoniously. No prisoners taken."

"And yet…" Laura involuntarily threw in.

"Like you say. Or, as H.G. Wells, who I greatly admire, so deftly put it in his War of the Worlds: Ogilvy, the astronomer, claims the chances of anything coming from Mars are a million to one – but still they come…"

2. The Citadel

"The target of our operation Sea Leopard was the island of Sark.

In tune with the archipelago at large, Sark has a ragtag past as a notorious pirate den, something that you wouldn't suspect in view of its present-day almost ostentatiously contemplative peacefulness. Spruce, well-kept gardens and enchanted coves can very well conceal the fact that plenty of Sark's erstwhile inhabitants were vicious cut-throats, more often than not ending their natural lives on the gallows of Jethou, so as to be in full view of their home isle. Despite many shared features, there was one aspect in which Sark differed from neighbouring Guernsey, Jersey, or Alderney. Its Bailiff, called Seigneur, the constitutional head of the island, in other words, was a noble person by the name of Hathaway, Dame Sybil Hathaway. The lady in question being a direct descendant of one of the most dreaded one-eyed jacks, a bloke called Carteret, her family's rise to nobility status must have followed rather devious paths, I suspect. Then again, Drake did it, so why shouldn't the Hathaways."

Look who's calling the kettle black, Laura thought but preferred not to lend a voice to such heretical doubts. The old man seemed to read her thoughts, though, and grinned a toothless grin that might have befitted the grim reaper himself, only with dentures, of course.

"You are wondering, how I came by mine? Well, suffice to say that I wasn't born with the proverbial silver spoon in my mouth. Besides, I honestly couldn't give a hoot. Titles such as these are the uncovered drafts of any monarchy."

"But I always thought the noblesse oblige principle was still very much en vogue in Britain."

Lamont laughed his croaky laugh.

"Is that so? Personally, I feel obliged to nothing in particular, to tell the truth. Even though I got some foundations of social denomination up and running, which are involved in all sorts of re-socialisation projects. But who hasn't, that's beside the point. Let's get back to Sark. The second important aspect in which Sark begged to differ from its neighbours was the surprisingly low number of people who had left the island during the evacuation weeks. Almost everybody had stayed. It would seem that this was due to the extraordinary influence Dame Hathaway wielded on Sark. A strong-willed lady of Wagnerian stature, who, as opposed to many of her three or four hundred loyal subjects, had travelled abroad a lot with her American-born husband. The two of them had repeatedly been to Germany, where she at any rate and had been imbued the Germanic culture, including the language, of course. Without going as far as to call her blindly Germanophile, she probably knew, or thought she did, the Germans to be more civilized and on the whole less ghoulish than their more recent reputation. Don't be silly, she must have told her people, and let them come, I'll deal with them, you'll see. From today's point of view, that attitude would seem a trifle naive. But you know what – by and large she proved right, funny enough. German males seem to like the Valkyrie type of woman. She was the dominatrix of Sark and German officers would stand in line to get their bare asses spanked. Well, I'm joking. Or maybe not, who knows."

"Female intuition and charm, I prefer to think. The Nazis didn't know what they were up against."

"Quite. What turned the tables, here, were the pointless deportations of island residents who weren't born and bred here but had taken up a fixed abode here late in their lives, mostly as pensioners. A German retribution measure aiming at, first and foremost, World War I veterans such as Dame Hathaway's husband, who had retired to the Channel Islands.

Harold entered noiselessly to check all was fine and whether either host or guest had any further requests, which they hadn't. So, he piled a few more logs on the fire and beat his retreat as silently as he had sneaked in.

"The most important thing for us with regard to the raid was the details of the topography. The two-part island of Sark being vested with a series of steep coastal cliffs, it is well-nigh inaccessible from the sea in many places. A feature that went a long way towards pleasing the resident pirates, obviously. For our purposes, it was a rather more mixed blessing. The good news was that a coast of that kind is hard to protect by an unbroken ring of mines. The bad news: to get onto the island at such more or less unmined spots, we would have to do some serious climbing. Translated into layman's terms, it meant we had Hobson's choice of either getting blown up on a beach or smashed to pieces at the foot of some cliff. That's how we saw it at the time, anyway."

"Who's we? Who were your mates and where did they come from?"

"All but my own self were juvenile offenders, Borstal boys, as we called them, doing time in Portland's Verne Citadel, on the other side of the Channel. English penal law being strictly no frills, you can go to jail for a substantial number of years at, say, the age of twelve and be given a life sentence at age fourteen. I'm exaggerating, but not much. Even our American friends treat juvenile offenders with more lenience, and that's saying a lot."

"I know that has a long tradition in your country. In the eighteenth century, a little boy who had nicked a silk handkerchief from a lady in the streets of London would be hanged unceremoniously."

"Quite, and probably deserved to. Anyway, these lads were young but tough, hardened from back-breaking work in the Admiralty quarry next door, whose granite blocks had served to build the Citadel, ironically enough. Original concept, don't you think: come and build your own prison."

"And dig your own grave while you're at it. What were the selection criteria?"

"Origin, for one thing, any special talents for another. I was the only real volunteer, a young lieutenant more or less straight from Lakehurst. I had ogled at the allegedly soft assignment of a group of radar operators' superior officer at the Sumburgh Head station, up Shetland way. That was an important installation at the time. Whenever the German Heinkel bomber fleets crossed over from Norway to attack our Scapa Flow Naval Base in the Orkneys, they would have to come close enough to the Shetlands to be caught out by our radar devices at Sumburgh, basic as they were, and reported to our Spitfire squadrons standing by. Have you ever been to the Shetlands?"

Laura shook her head.

"Neither had I, then. When I saw the place for the first time, I started having second thoughts about my choice of venue, right away. A raw place with no flora to speak of. No trees, no bushes, no shrubbery or hedges. Just moss, grass and lichen. A Martian landscape, only green instead of red, but just as monotonous. Fortunately, the meteorological conditions hide the lot under thick fog cover most of the time. The Sumburgh radar station is situated next to a major lighthouse of the area with a giant fog horn operated by a steam engine strong enough to propel the Titanic. Hence, what with fog being the prevalent meteorological feature of the place, anyone working round there is sure to come away deaf as a door post after only a fortnight. Even the capital Lerwick, which we used to call Airwick, wasn't much to write home about. It grew around a Victorian fort from which the garrison's artillery blokes used to shoot at seals with their cannon out of sheer boredom. Under such adverse circumstances, you may understand, I rather opted out. It took me some time to pull the necessary strings, but Sark being my birthplace, that's what brought me to operation Sea Leopard, eventually."

He picked up his monocle and absent-mindedly wiped it clean with a napkin. He probably hadn't spoken as much in one go for years, Laura thought, so it had to exhaust him. On the other hand, he seemed to enjoy it and Laura was determined to profit as much as she possibly could.

"How had they got on to me? Well, someone in the Mixed Operations central must have been just about as bored as I was and thumbed through the files with all candidates' personal data. Thus, he came across my being born and partly raised on Sark. That My father, another World War I veteran and model soldier if ever there was one, had been dumped there at the time of my birth. Must have spent a great deal of his time making babies, the old geezer. Well, can't blame him. What else was there to do but cut back rose bushes and procreate. I myself left the island again aged thirteen. The thought I might have passed my puberty there among sheep and goats makes me break out in a cold sweat even today. Well, enough of me. Three of the other six blokes also came from the islands, none from Sark, though."

He fell silent for a moment again..

"Am I too long-winded? Would you rather scram before I finally reach cruising speed?"

"No way," Laura protested.

"On the other hand, I hate to abuse your hospitality. That said, if I count correctly, you were the Yarmouth Seven, then?"

"You are very welcome to abuse to your heart's delight. If it weren't for you, I might have spent another day drowning in self-pity and, who knows, finally have put that bullet in my head, after all. So, you might flatter yourself you're performing a bit of rejuvenating geriatric care. As for the dichotomy of six versus seven, I'll return to that a little later in the saga, so bear with me. On balance, anyway, three of the boys had only heard talk of the Channel Islands but never got anywhere nearer than the Citadel. Yet, despite their youth, they were impressive specialists in different disciplines that would stand us in good stead during the operation. Those of us, who, like myself, had no special gifts to offer, were trained in one specialty or other. Thus, they turned me into a proper powder monkey, as the Americans called it. After only four weeks, I was able to dig out German T-mines, defuse them and fabricate IED's myself from virtually anything."

He licked his dry lips and looked for some water. Laura poured him a glass and gave it to him.

"Thanks. There was Jimmy McDuff, a sinewy small Scot from Stornoway on the Outer Hebrides, a lad we nicknamed Haggis. He was a mountaineering freak already known by the climbing community in many parts of the world. Would have conquered the K2 by then, I'm sure, had he not done his occasional stints in the Citadel. That's what hampered his climber's progress. His anatomy was such as to locate his centre of gravity smack in the middle, which I was told was a considerable advantage with mountaineering. Had a good sense of humour, too, and would rock any pub on a Friday night. His acts were always entertaining, even though we barely understood what he was saying with that Scottish accent of his. An acquired taste, like the dish."

"What dish? Oh, you mean haggis? I only tasted it once and quite liked it."

"As long as you don't know what it's made of. His task was to help us up the cliff of the island we only called by the code-name of The Citadel, borrowed from Verne, of course. It fulfilled the secrecy requirement and gave the boys a sense of homeliness, strangely enough."

He stopped again, sipped a little water and passed the palm of his left hand over his brow as if clearing his brain for the next pageant.

"Joe Brady, then, a lean, tall Londoner with an Irish father. Which is why called him Hooch. He was a hard-drinking radio operator, one of a threatened species who were still familiar with the ancient Morse code. Which was a vital asset because it might help us communicate noiselessly with one of our submarines or minesweepers waiting off the coast to pick us up again. All we would need was a lamp at night or a small mirror during daytime. For the purposes of voice radio services, he was of limited use, though, because of his peculiar mixture of Irish and Cockney, which we got used to after a while, but which an outsider would have given up on before long. What with Haggis and Hooch on our party, people on Sark would suspect we came from Mars, which was just as well. Hooch could not only handle but build a radio from scratch if need be. Had done so at Verne already. Very good swimmer, too, Hooch was."

Again, he fell silent for a moment, no doubt passing the figure of the man before his half-closed eyes.

"Stocky, black curled Ronny Goldsmith was a Portsmouth man who couldn't conceal his Jewish ancestry. Jibed and sneered at as a kike from his earliest childhood, he had learned to defend himself and hold his own at what he called his colleges, the rough-and-tumble Naval pubs of Nelson's town. Neither fastidious, nor squeamish, he would put to good use what happened to be available: fists, knife, bottles, glasses, telephone directories, chairs, you name it. Listening to him, you could come away with the impression most objects of daily use had really been invented with a view to self-defence. He was our karate kid, in a manner of speaking. None of us had dared put a tag on him. Scarface would probably have headed a short list, with Rocky a close second. You wouldn't want to pick a fight with somebody like him. I never heard him threaten anyone, but, once he ran out of arguments, he would hit his opponent once very hard and that would then be the end of that. What made him special in my eyes was that he had no problem accepting defeat. If and when he ran into somebody even stronger or shrewder, more cruel than himself, which I guess must have happened pretty seldom, all told, he respected that and didn't resort to anything downright perfidious like pulling a gun or knife. Not if his opponent hadn't. Thus, even though he had probably never even heard of Queensbury, he stuck to a code of honour not unlike the Marquess'."

He sipped some water again.

"Keith Donovan had been born and bred on Guernsey. Later, his parents had moved to Bristol, where young master Keith had experienced problems adapting to the language and Welsh-bait mentality. He, too, was a good mountaineer. Not quite as daring and devoted as Haggis, but better looking and a little taller too. Like Haggis, he had a handshake like a vice. Had to, what with free climbing and all the rest of it. His role was to support Haggis and take care of logistics, you know, odds and ends department. We called him Brain, because he would keep his calm in any crisis situation, coolly reflect on the options and usually come up with a feasible solution. At his age and with his motley background, that was a rare gift."

Laura sampled her port and smacked her lips.

"Next was Kenneth Langtree, who we could not but nickname Lily, of course. Which he didn't mind. He was a Jersey man, of rather slender build and, well, camp I believe is the term. Not gay, I mean, not that we would have noticed, anyway. Who knows, he may actually have been related to the famous actress four or five times removed. On small, isolated islands such as ours, incest is always an option. Lily was a very polite young man who, it has to be admitted, had found himself a little too frequently on the wrong side of the law for comfort. But he had always listened and watched court proceedings attentively, thus building up a sizeable thesaurus of legal sciolism that might, at a pinch, have qualified him for a lunch or two at the Bar, you know, another one of those quaint traditions of ours. He was not to be our solicitor, of course, but our soft-spoken, infinitely capable armourer. The firearm he hadn't yet handled wasn't on the market. He could compose a workable submachine gun from such items as a clothes hanger, mattress springs and a corkscrew, or very nearly. Besides, he was always accessible, only too glad to explain in great detail why this pistol risked jamming or that revolver would notoriously shoot high, and so on. Incredible bloke, Lily. And what a shot! Would take a fly's right eye out at ten yards."

The old man shook his head in admiration. Lily, so much was pretty obvious, must have been his favourite of the Wild Bunch.

"Last but not least, there was Peter Collins. Born on Guernsey, but later a Liverpudlian by choice. He liked to pass himself off as a footballer but had apparently never made a major team, as yet. To begin with, he seemed almost as weird to us as Ronny had done. You know, the Rocky Balboa from Portsmouth I just told you about. The notable difference between them being that Peter would never hit anyone but knife them. That was his thing, knives, which he handled like you and I would a pencil. He would open a spring knife unseen and throw it the James Coburn way, you know, not downwards from above, but vice versa. That was his show piece and we didn't get tired asking him to do it again and again. But he could also rip open someone's gizzard in a split second, cut their throats before they even knew it. Had never been convicted for murder but claimed to have killed at least six in gang wars. We came to call him Gooey by dint of his strange obsession with animal or human entrails as would pop out of a slit stomach. He could really enlarge on that unappetizing subject at night, by way of a bedtime story, when you were trying to conjure up details of the female anatomy rather than dream of a pig's innards. A real sentimental soul, Gooey was."

"And what about you? Didn't you have a nickname, a handle?" Lamont smiled.

"I sure did. The blokes would call me Luke the Duke. And I don't mind telling you that I was rather proud of it."

"Duke, like that terrier of John Wayne's?"

"Terrier my foot. Like the man himself! Anyway. The Verne inmates eligible for the job had been given the choice either of volunteering for the Army and joining Operation Sea Leopard, or rotting away in the Citadel cracking rocks for the remainder of the war. Most of the lads had declined the opportunity to commit suicide and gone back to their respective cells. The six blokes I told you about preferred to swap their prison stripes for Army trappings. Incidentally, at that stage, for secrecy reasons, nobody had told either me or them the true nature of the operation in any detail. Still, we were all fairly convinced it wouldn't be a walk in the park. Not with that kind of expertise requested.

I myself was less than enthusiastic about the prospect of leading these guys. I had absolutely no experience and, as a young, no doubt arrogant officer, probably represented the kind of authority these men had come to hate most. How would I fare with social misfits and natural born killers such as Gooey or Ronny? Well, I may flatter myself unduly here, but I think I may say that I managed, bit by bit, step by step, to rise in their esteem and finally even to win their trust and respect. How did I do it? By following a co-officer's advice and literally wringing all sorts of perks and small privileges for them from the Army's more than reluctant administration. Also, I stepped in whenever the non-coms immediately responsible for our training on the Isle of Wight started cracking wise-ass jokes at my men's expense. My natural organisational talent helped too, I guess. The ill-fitting rags we had received were soon swapped for proper, presentable uniforms, our museum carbines for shiny tommy guns as inspected and marginally improved upon by Lily, of course. The food was getting better after a while, the bunks that hadn't seen new mattresses in years, suddenly resembled real beds put to excellent use during the organized visits of NAAFI wenches from near-by Portsmouth, some of whom Ronny still knew by name from his former life.

"And why Yarmouth?"

"Why not Yarmouth? It's situated right around the corner from Verne and more or less opposite the Channel Islands. Besides, the coastal cliffs around the Needles' area offered ample opportunities for practicing and improving our mountaineering skills. And, finally, the unassuming little village of Yarmouth was hardly the kind of place that would distract us from our training with its rich offering of pubs and clubs, if you see what I mean. That said, we came to like the neighbourhood. More so, as, in the course of our six-week training period in the camp right next to the town, we happened to become local heroes. The folks at Yarmouth would watch us climb, mock fight, swim, shoot, the whole shenanigans. Nothing compared to a modern Seal's training that literally kills recruits off, but state of the art in 1943. The one moment we managed to soften the hearts of even the most reticent islanders was when Hooch, who, like I said, was an excellent swimmer, saved a little local girl's life. Susan, that was her name, had been fooling around the railing door near the Lymington ferry's stern. The grown-ups' attention had been absorbed by the small port of Yarmouth approaching, so nobody had paid attention to Susan, a pretty blond three-year-old. Thus, when the railing door suddenly swung open and she went over the side, immediately falling into shock in the icy water of the Solent without so much as screaming, she was as good as dead. Fortunately, she had that guardian angel on duty called Hooch. He happened to have observed the accident and didn't hesitated a second to jump in and go after her. When he arrived at the spot where she had fallen in, she had already disappeared, but, as he told us later, Hooch managed to dive and grasp her by her blond hair, pulling her up to the surface. A piece of heroics that would have made the tabloids in peace time. Except that, with half the world at war, both heroics and mock-heroics were on an inflationary rise. But for the locals, Hooch and, by extrapolation, all seven of us, were definitely idols from then on."

"What was the object and purpose of operation Sea Lion, then?"

"Sea Leopard. Well, like I said, we had no idea, except that it would involve climbing, fighting and maybe swimming. Details were to be handed out the day we went aboard the submarine that was to take us across the Channel. That way, none of us had an opportunity to shoot off their mouths accidentally in the pub or while in bed with a whore. Well, I say, time's flying. When's your ferry leaving?"

Laura, too, looked at her watch.

"If I remember correctly, fifty minutes ago, actually. I have no idea when the next…"

"I presume you brought your toothbrush?" Lamont interrupted her.

Laura looked at him nonplussed.

"Well, of course. I had to spend the night at the hotel in St. Malo…"

"Which one was that?"

"Kiss my ass."

"Beg pardon?"

"That's what it was called. Quic en grogne, in French."

"I see. Never heard of it. Might I suggest you stay for the night and take the first boat tomorrow morning. How does that grab you?"

Laura shrugged her shoulders.

"Well, I had intended to take the night train to Paris, actually. But if it's no major inconvenience for you…"

Lamont shook his head.

"It's not, I assure you. It's been some time since I last spent a night with a woman of your class under the same roof."

While Laura was musing on the portent of that one, he rang for the butler again.

"Harold, Mrs. Forster will be our guest for the night. Do see to it that the blue room is prepared for her, will you? And we'll be needing some supper, of course. Thanks, Harold, you're a true treasure of a butler and I bet you know it, too."

Harold gave no sign of appreciation or approval at being called a darling but nodded gravely.

"Very well, Sir Lucas. Will that be all for the time…?"

The old man thanked him again and waited till the butler had closed the door behind himself.

"Don't know what I'd do without him. Loyal old soul. Jersey man if ever there was one. Normally, we converse in the old patois, but that would be impolite in your presence. They'll have to bury him with me, I'm afraid, since even in the other world beyond, hopefully freed from this wheelchair of mine, I would need his services."

Again, his croaky laugh resounded through the library.

"Came the day when it was all going to fall into place. We were handed our camouflage fatigues, arms and ammunition and all the rest of it. They drove us to the Ryde Sands and transferred us to Portsmouth. Here, with hearts sinking, we went aboard the Sunfish, a submarine of the S class. S as in shit, let me tell you. None of us had ever set foot on a submarine and the Sunfish had been announced to us as a pre-war model. By God, they had omitted to tell us what war it was they had been referring to. It looked as if its parts had been fetched from the Lambeth Imperial War Museum, American Civil War department. Speak of claustrophobia. This thing was not a floating, but a diving coffin. It stank of diesel fuel, oil, sweat, faeces, and the inevitable bangers and eggs and bacon sizzling in the tiny galley, as it seemed, at all times. It was hell afloat. Hot tubes oozing boiling water and steam everywhere, rusty, dripping valves that looked like they might give up on the water pressure any moment and allow the sea right in. The bulkheads you had to negotiate to get from one compartment to the other were low, round and narrow. The regular crew would hop, skip and jump through them like a group of trained chimps, but we either hit our heads or our shins or, better even, got our toes caught so that we were dumped onto the other side like so many sacks of frigging flour. The berths were harder and narrower than prison bunks, I was assured by my men who were experts in the matter, after all. The rule was two men for one berth, one crew member sleeping while the other was on watch. Or guzzled eggs and bacon with bangers. There were no cots for us. We had to stand or sit around, trying not to be in everybody's way. Most of the time, somebody was shouting orders and announcements in a funny Naval lingo incomprehensible to us. Come to think of it, had the Sunfish started sinking all of a sudden, we would probably have been the last to be told. I felt like a tourist on a Chinese no-frills cruiser trying to make out whether the vely honoulable passengers were being invited to a ball or asked to abandon ship. I have no idea how men can survive in those steel coffins for weeks on end: submerged, with rapidly dwindling oxygen resources, no fresh air, attacks of claustrophobia and fear of depths, good night, Eileen."

He shuddered visibly at the mere memory of it.

"And now, at long last, we were to be let into the details of our mission plan. Apparently, we were to land on Sark at Dixcart Bay, not far from the so-called Coupée. That's the narrow but high isthmus connecting the larger Northern part of the island with the much smaller Southern bit. Dixcart Bay was a high, steep place well-nigh inaccessible from the sea. That's why nobody would expect us there, or so we hoped. It would befall Haggis and Brain to get us up the cliffs called Noir Bais, somehow. At night, in the dark, of course, not to make it too easy. Once arrived up there more dead than alive, we were to pass through the minefield that had already claimed some of our predecessors' limbs and lives. Were we to survive that, too, against all odds, as it were, we were to take a good look around, identify any German gun and machine gun emplacements, establish contact with the locals, squeeze them for what pieces of information they held and kill a few German soldiers, if the situation lent itself to that. Afterwards, we were to disappear as ghost-like as we had come. Child's play, really."

Lamont fumbled in his jacket pocket and pulled out a mangled pack of Marlboroughs.

"Would you mind if I...."

Laura shook her head. She, who had frequently sat through the Doc's pipe sessions, would hardly be affected by a little cigarette smoke.

"Strictly against the Toubib's orders, of course. But doesn't that somehow lie in the paradox nature of old age? We're all of us hell-bent on prolonging our lives no matter what. Why is it we so monomaniacally insist on witnessing our own decay?"

Laura smiled. She liked hearing someone talk of a Toubib. It brought back memories of the Doc, Ti Martin, the Caribbean.

"Cynical, the whole thing."

"What? Life?"

"That too. No, I'm talking of our raid. At the time, I felt we had a big sign hanging round our necks saying Here come the expendables, Give them a hand, if you will."

He drew the smoke deep into his lungs but then seemed strangely loathe to let it go again. Laura was already beginning to ask herself whether, over the years, the old man had grown other orifices for the purposes of discrete used air disposal, when he continued talking, wrapping every word in a thin veil of smoke.

"The voyage through the Eastern Solent and across the channel was carried out in the surfaced mode, visible, in other words. The Sunfish had Asdic, a predecessor of sonar, if you like, but no radar, strangely enough. Any of the German fast patrol boats regularly scurrying through the Channel waters could have launched a torpedo at us any moment. When we closed in on Alderney, the Sunfish went sub-surface, and continued at periscope depth, running on its electric engine. For a moment there, I thought the thing would be diving and diving and never be able to stop till we hit rock bottom. A natural reaction on the part of a submarine novice, I suppose. But the laughing crew wasn't slow in explaining to us that diving was nothing downright extravagant for a submarine. I knew that, of course, but on the one hand, ever since man crawled on land and took to lung breathing, there is something deep inside us that warns us of going beneath the water's surface. And besides, I for one didn't trust the Sunfish from here to the door and was afraid it might, if not sink, then break apart. That was nonsense, of course, but some of the submarine features set me a-thinking. S class boats still had magnetic compasses, we were told. Which meant, among other things, that, in order not to cause any compass disturbance or excess deviation, the periscopes had to be bronze ones. For stability reasons, these periscopes had to be a good deal shorter than the German ones made of steel. The Nazi U-boats preferred gyro compasses, which cannot be influenced by magnetism of any kind. Thus, for the Sunfish travelling at ten knots at periscope depth meant that, even submerged, it couldn't go deep and would be easier to spot than desirable. Also, staying close beneath the surface meant we got our fill of the sea's rough motions in a stretch of water which probably boasts some of the most unpleasant swell patterns world-wide. Add to this the stench I already described and the rarefied air, and what you get is a Yarmouth seven puking their hearts out. No big deal on an ordinary vessel. You hang half your torso over the railing and let go. On a submerged submarine, though, things are a trifle more difficult. I don't suppose the captain of the Sunfish could be blamed for not surfacing for no better reason than to allow some landlubber commandos to retch overboard. I spare you the details and limit myself to my final remark that, ever since, my guts start revolting as soon as somebody mentions the two words sun and fish in one and the same sentence."

3. The Treasure Trove

"We slid through the Alderney Race like a canoe across the Colorado rapids," Lamont carried on and made a gesture with his right hand that was to illustrate the speed and elegance of the motion.

"The sudden acceleration was making itself clearly felt even under the surface. In later years, I had a similar experience only once, on a friend's yacht: coming from the north coast of Cuba and heading towards Miami, we were suddenly picked up by the deep blue Gulf Stream waters, and whoosh, off we were. But the Alderney Race is faster, though a lot shorter, obviously."

He squeezed his monocle in and pulled out a pen. Then he sketched a rough plan on the yellow cloth of the side table.

"After another two hours' silent running, we were cautiously approaching the rock-infested surf around the coasts of Sark. The Sunfish broke surface like a dolphin gasping for air. The skipper waited till we had launched the dinghy and installed ourselves in it and then ordered to quickly dive again. The tidal current ran as calculated, so that we didn't even have to paddle, but just to keep course in order to reach the designated spot. At night in Dixcart Bay, the steep island rock was looking even more forbidding than we had anticipated it, literally towering above us like an insurmountable solid wall. Later, they erected a hotel there, I believe. Anyway, seen from an ant's perspective, it seemed like the North face of the Eiger, at least. For a moment there, I thought that, fooled by the dark, we might have come to the wrong place, after all. Shit like that had happened before. The chief cause of the Gallipoli campaign's lamentable failure in World War I, for instance, was that the Anzac troops had been set ashore a bay too early by the blundering Navy. Thus, our boys, mostly Australians and New Zealanders, of course, had to climb the almost vertical face of a huge dune that offered them little or foothold. Can you imagine: climbing with soaking uniforms, boots filled with water, and their guns and equipment dragging them down. The Turks sitting on top of the dune hugging their machine guns obviously had a field day. Churchill, whose political career had almost been curtailed by the fiasco, nevertheless called it a successful operation. The boozing prick, excuse my language. And that mistaken landing had happened during daytime. But, unlikely as it seemed, we finally had to look the stark truth in the eyes. Believe it or not, we had come to the right Dixcart Bay, indeed. Here and there, a faint light flickered on the heights to our left and right. Shouldn't have, not during curfew. So maybe they were not lamps, but stars, impossible to tell from where we were standing. The dinghy's extravaganzas had led to some of us having renewed fits of nausea. I asked them politely to keep their retching roars down. Something, incidentally, I myself have never been able to. Have you? I always admire people who can throw up in a plane without even their immediate neighbours noticing. Whenever I get sick, rarely enough, fortunately, I have to break into such a lion's roar, next thing you know, everybody on the plane has to join in. It's highly catching, puking is. But I am straying again. On a silent night like that, with us being surrounded on three sides by granite walls, our roar would have carried all the way to St. Peter Port, I'm sure, and mobilized the Germans to the last man. But what could I do? Or rather, what could they do? The retching reflex lingers on for quite a while as if the stomach was too dumb to realize the cause has been removed."

He chuckled and stuck the pen back in his pocket.

"I guess you have no problem figuring what we looked like when we finally felt solid ground under our feet. Our fatigues looking – and smelling – like the inside of so many second-hand barf bags, soaked with water and sweat, one or two pants reeking of shit and urine, as well. The legend of the Zombie Six about to be hammered in granite, you might say."

He laughed and lit another Marlborough. Or was that a joint? Laura found the old man fascinating, if his habits a trifle icky.

"Having said that, the worst was still to come. There was the flaming rock face to be climbed. Some three hundred almost vertical feet, along a surface that looked as smooth as if it had just been given a fresh lick of whitewash. Not even a gecko in his right mind would have seriously considered an ascent. Not surprising the Germans wouldn't bother to place any guards here. Our two mountaineers were the first to tackle the rock. Amazing, how they managed to spot the smallest fissures and tiniest gaps in what seemed a well-nigh unbroken surface to a layman. One by one, they fastened their hooks and spikes, ran their ropes through them and made their way up. Once on top, they would support and secure our somewhat clumsier efforts till all seven of us had reached the ledge and we rolled on our backs, exhausted and beaten, panting for air with finger-tips hurting like hell and lungs on fire. Without the renewed generous dose of Pervitin, we wouldn't have managed, I don't think. N-Methyl-amphetamine or crystal meth, basically, the stuff that large parts of the war effort depended on. Haggis and Brain had recovered much more quickly and begun to hoist up our guns and equipment. For me, this was the toughest physical effort I had ever experienced so far. And considering my present state of physical fitness, I think the record will remain unbroken. A six-foot dive under the ground is all I will able to deliver."

As if to accelerate the procedure alluded to, he took a deep drag and again kept the smoke inside as long as humanly possible.

"Then we picked ourselves up and ever so apprehensively started tackling the minefield. Lily did his stint as our mine dog. We were all connected to one another by a thin rope, not unlike we had been on the rock face only minutes before. Walking single file, with sufficient distance between one another so a detonating mine wouldn't blow all seven of us to high heaven, at once, we tiptoed along. What helped was our knowledge of the German mine-laying pattern: three staggered rows, roughly two yards' distance between the mines of one row, one yard between the rows, such were the Wehrmacht instructions, and they usually stuck to it. We were lucky. Nothing happened. Being second in line, I thought I had stepped on a mine at one stage, and had already said a very short last prayer, when I realized it was only an empty can with a German label that some squaddie must have dropped here carelessly. Labskaus is what the label said. I had no idea what that was, but never forgot the curious word and later tried the dish on occasion of a visit to Northern Germany. You are from Hamburg, aren't you? Do you like Labskaus? Horrible stuff, I found. A bit like haggis that has already passed through the digestive channels once and smells of gastric acid with a wee tinge of fish aroma. But a lot more beneficial than a mine detonating on an empty stomach. When we could be sure of having passed the ring of fire, as it were, we hurried on towards the southern part of Sark, which, on land, you can only reach by passing the Coupée. The present-day asphalt road with its guardrails left and right didn't exist at the time. It was first constructed after the war, by German POW's. Till the moment that happened, in 1945, kids or frail old-timers who wanted to cross the Coupée in bad weather conditions were advised to go down on all fours lest they be blown over the edge by a sudden squall. As a child, I had been taught about the sudden acceleration of gas and liquid flows caused by abruptly narrowing profiles. The teacher had quoted a simple rhyme: Bernoulli saves a pulley. Bingo. Verse tends to have this mnemonic effect used not only at school, incidentally. There were times when even sailing directions were handed down in rhymed form. Imagine an island, whose eastern coast is fraught with dangerous cliffs. The sailing directions would then say something like, Watch out for the East, 'cause there lurks the beast, or something to the tune. Easy to retain for a lifetime of sailing."

Laura smiled and thought of Solitaire. What with her passion for rhyming slang, she would have liked this part.

"Right. That night, we were in luck. No German guard in sight and even the wind had abated. All that was left was a soft breeze carrying a bunch of noiselessly zig-zagging bats to their hunting grounds. Swallows of the night is what I call them. You literally had to pinch yourself in the bum to realize you weren't strolling in Kew Gardens but roaming an island occupied by the enemy. Even though I hadn't visited Sark for the previous five or six years, I had no problem getting my bearings and leading my little platoon to the building which, according to our sources, housed the German garrison headquarters. Which is probably a rather pompous term to use in the context of the tiny island. But you have to remember that, in 1943, there were more Germans than locals on some of the islands. Certainly on Alderney, which had been almost totally evacuated, but also on Sark. That night, you wouldn't have noticed that, however. Not with the gingerbread houses, the spruce gardens, the tomb-like flower beds, the gravel paths and all the rest of it. Hence, the headquarters had been established in a traditional pub or rather inn, called the Hart and Weasel. Apart from the length of rose bushes and the chessboard cut of lawns, there was not an awful lot to administer on Sark, I bet. And if and when the proverbial sack of rice did slump to the floor, well, there was always the Valkyrie, Dame Sybil Hathaway to turn to. If proof had been needed that the Sark folks had picked the right person for the job of Seigneur, the years of occupation provided ample evidence to go by. Even the Germans are said to have consulted her on Sark's domestic issues. Had they but listened to her, D-day wouldn't have gone the way it did."

He ground out his half-spent cigarette, picked up his pen and drew a sketchy plan of the Hart and Weasel's "headquarters."

"We thought it strange, to begin with, that neither Hart nor Weasel seemed to be mounting the guard here. Were we about to knock on the wrong door? Had the headquarters been moved somewhere else, meanwhile, or simply faded out of existence? But no. We were just about to surround the building when a German soldier emerged from the shadow of the neighbouring house. He must have had a pee, smoked a cigarette or paid some neighbouring lady a courtesy visit. Fraternising was frowned upon by the Nazis as well as by the local men, at least. Another one of those funny misnomers, don't you think. Calls to mind, my mind, anyway, some gay rendezvous of two monks, when, in fact, we're talking of jolly good intercourse between German soldiers and local women, whom we used to jeer at as jerrybags. Heavily frowned upon, like I say, but looked at through our fingers. Usually rather breathless affairs, hastily consumed at night in the shadow of this or that pub. Leaving your post when on watch duty, though, would invariably land you in trouble, big time. The Germans would give any offenders as short a shrift as ours did. The fact that the unsuspecting squaddie hadn't noticed us lying flat-bellied in the grass practically right in front of him was probably due to the combined effect of our blackened faces and his blurred vision. Obviously, he hadn't counted on a raid such as ours and was probably cursing his bad luck, again to have drawn the short straw and, consequently, having to take on what is commonly known as the dog watch in the ghostly hours between midnight and four a.m. Not least because of our raid, the Krauts would later become much more careful. And even more numerous. But at that very moment, at the dead of night, another British raid on the Hobbit central must have seemed as likely to them as an attack from the planet Mars."

Easily comprehensible, Laura thought. Mounting guard day in, day out, for no earthly purpose must have had a deadening effect.

"Gooey finished the German off noiselessly with a clean cut of his throat with almost surgical precision. Hooch and I were the first to enter the unlocked Hart and Weasel, Brain bringing up the rear."

As he spoke, he pointed at a narrow rectangle apparently representing the front door.

"We stalked along the corridor, guns and knives at the ready, and listened at each door with a stethoscope to pick up snoring and other sounds and guess at the number of soldiers asleep there. As far as we could make out, there were two dormitories with nor more than a handful of soldiers each. We opened them one by one and dispatched the Germans in their sleep. I know that sounds cruel, but if you imagine the different kinds of deaths soldiers are likely to sustain in an all-out war, a quick flick of the knife probably ranks among the less painful ones."

"Maybe not cruel, but heartless."

"Well, it didn't come that naturally to us as it sounds, Gooey excluded. I had never killed anyone before, nor had most of the lads. We had counted on it happening, obviously. It was part of our remit, so to speak. But nothing can ever prepare you for the experience."

"I know," Laura said calmly. Lamont looked surprised.

"You do?"

"I shot a man not that long ago." Laura replied. And pushed another one over the cliff, she added to herself.

"Did you now? I say. Well, with due respect, shooting a man is one thing, sticking a knife in his chest quite another. The sound of a blade entering and exiting human flesh is unique. No-one who has ever heard it is likely to ever forget it again. Some serial killers developed a real addiction to it, or so they say."

"Notwithstanding. Not much heroics in butchering defence-less people asleep."

"I never claimed there was, did I?"

He stopped and looked absent-mindedly at Laura as if waiting for her absolution.

"Thus, like I say, a vital portion of our mission had already been accomplished. But there was more to come. We had spared one of the Germans, so we could interrogate him and maybe extract some valuable pieces of information. But time was running out. Any moment now, an MP patrol might pass by and wonder where the hell the guard had gone. The run-of-the-mill squad-dies appear to live in constant fear of their MP with those silver dog tags. Made them look like latter-day Roman centurions. And they knew why, because those guys were merciless and made it a habit to appear where and when you expected them least."

"To always keep everybody on their toes, I suppose. Some-thing like that might focus my staff's attention too. Have to give it some thought," Laura commented half in jest.

"Could be helpful," Lamont agreed.

"But then something strange happened. Something that threw us off the track of what had, until then, been a raid running smoothly as if on rails. Actually, with hindsight, what happened was to change our lives forever. I had only scant prior knowledge of German but had been given an opportunity to widen my vo-cabulary in the framework of our training at Yarmouth. Military terms, primarily. Officer's ranks, guns, standard military proce-dures, that sort of thing. But this soldier we were interrogating, expressed himself not so much in standard terms but was babbling away nervously, gushing forth words in a dialect I had never heard before. Thus, the man was as incomprehensible to us as Haggis or Hooch would have been to Germans with but a smattering of English, Scottish, and Cockney. When we realized that the interrogation wasn't going to lead anywhere, we were about to kill our sole prisoner and be done with it. But the frenzied bloke kept pointing up skyward all the time. At first, we thought he wanted to remind us of the Almighty watching over all of us. But then he made signs we should follow him, which we finally did. Otto, as we called him for simplicity's sake, led us up the stairs to the second floor. There, he let us into an improvised office dominated by a massive desk and a portrait of the Fuehrer on the wall behind it. Of course, we smelled a rat. Gooey's razor-sharp blade never left the man's throat. Otto went to the wall and took off Hitler's portrait. Not without saluting it apologetically first, I kid you not. What emerged behind the Fuehrer was a safe. We looked at each other with a degree of perplexity. What with all the different specialities assembled in our platoon – no-one back there at Yarmouth had thought of including a yegg, just to be on the safe side, if you excuse the pun. Before joining the Verne crowd, some of the lads had had the occasional contact with experienced safers. But they had usually just blown the things up, a technique that wasn't really open to us then and there."

"If I remember your CV right, you managed to fill that knowledge gap later."

"No comment. Anyway. The German's plan was becoming increasingly clear. He was going to try and buy himself a few more years with the contents of that safe. He went to the desk and came up with a thick file. Thumbing through it with jittery hands, he suddenly hit the page where the safe lock's combination had been jotted down. Great sticklers for order, the Germans. As we opened the safe, a whole treasure trove of rough diamonds, jewellery and banknotes literally fell into our lap. The latter ones all counterfeit, as we were to learn later. Operation Bernhard. The Germans had rounded up some of Europe's most skilful forgers, locked them up in their Sachsenhausen concentration camp and forced them to produce counterfeit pound sterling to be circulated in Britain, where they would cause havoc and revolt. And God knows, those people had made an excellent job of it. Imagine the odds: thickness and texture of the paper, printing ink, water mark, signatures, the whole caboodle. Thought to be impossible by most specialists. And yet, they had done it and, without knowing it, we were looking at some of their masterpieces. Our eyes must have glowed in the dark like those of predators observing the last few steps of their prey. For a moment or two, I guess we clean forgot that the contents of that safe didn't exactly belong to us but would have to be handed over to the Army on our return. I may be flattering myself again, but I think I was the only one to keep his cool, telling the boys to pack the stuff into one of the knapsacks we had seen in the dormitories below. That's what they did. But when we talked about it years later, there wasn't one who would have denied that, from that very moment, all they had been able to focus on, was that damn treasure trove and the question how they could possibly manage to smuggle that past the Army.

Lamont smiled at the memory of his greed that hadn't really left him after that.

"A treasure worthy of a former centre of piracy. Where did it come from?""

"Excellent question. Not from pirates, so much was for sure. I mean, even in the years of war and occupation the folks on Sark were not exactly destitute. Didn't float in tanks of money like Donald Duck's uncle either. As for more likely sources, they would have been anybody's guess. The black market looking a likely candidate. What with the dwindling resources of food and objects of daily use from toothbrushes to saucepans, black-market business was brisk. Diamonds and jewellery were the preferred forms of legal tender. Hence, we were possibly looking at some black-market proceeds assembled by some locals and subsequently sequestered by the Germans. But that would have thrown a spanner in the works of barter, whose impeccable function was becoming increasingly important not only for the locals, but for the Germans, as well. So why hack off the branch you happen to sit on? One of the objects found among the jewellery was a red cross on a red ribbon. Something its owner had probably worn round his neck at some stage. That was what took us on a totally different scent. At first sight, you would have thought a peculiar version of the German order of the Iron Cross – maybe meant for heroic medics or God knows who. Then, Hooch voiced the coy opinion it might have belonged to a freemason. That sounded a little far-fetched but was all but impossible. None of us was able to refute his theory, anyway. Freemasons love secrecy, as we all know and stick to their fellow-sectarians. If that's what was on your mind, an island such Guernsey or Jersey would afford you all the privacy you and your like-minded friends might be looking for. Which is probably why Jersey, in particular, had been teeming with them in times of peace. The Nazis, for their part, hated freemasons. Along with the Jews and Jesuits, Ludendorff had already blamed the freemasons for the German defeat in the First World War."

"But, surely, a freemason wouldn't hawk his cross, now, would he?" Laura interjected.

"Certainly not. But his wife or other next of kin might, once the original owner had died. Admittedly, Jews and freemasons make strange bedfellows, at first sight, although they do share their contempt for Christianity. Historically speaking, the Jews were not allowed to occupy higher administrative or government posts in many European countries, dukedoms, city-states and what have you. The Nazis held that the freemasons, having a fair share in what we would nowadays call the deep state, had frequently acted as stirrup holders for the Jews, secretly facilitating their discrete ascent to some form of power. Which I believe is doubtful. What with their loan and credit policy, the Jews used to hold so many influential people by the short and curly they probably wouldn't need the assistance of the freemasons to pull a few strings here and there."

"How many Jews were there on the islands?"

"Maybe two score, all told. What cannot but strike the neutral observer with regard to them is the fact that, when the Germans requested all Jews to be registered, the local administrations were only too eager to oblige. Whereas they showed themselves a lot more hesitant when the Germans asked them to do the same thing with the freemasons. Even more peculiarly, the Germans themselves did nothing much to put more pressure on them. Despite Hitler's repeated reminders, no local freemasons were ever rounded up or harmed in any way, as far as we know."

"Orders lost in translation?"

"Or so it would seem. Obviously, the chain of command between Berlin and the Channel Islands via Paris and St. Malo was long and twisted, so that a certain shrinkage was to be expected. Besides, as from 1941, the beginning of the rather ill-fated operation Barbarossa, Hitler was preoccupied with progress on the Eastern front rather than allowing himself to be bothered with such trifles on some crummy Western islands. Still, for German commanding officers repeatedly to turn a deaf ear and blind eye to Hitler's instructions was risky and required guts. You would need a strong enough motivation, one should think. You wouldn't stick your head out like that, unless…"

"…unless what?"

"Well, looking at the German officers surfing in on the first wave of occupation, what strikes the naked eye is the number of such men who either belonged to the nobility or were intellectuals who shared its high standards of honour. Old-school gentlemen, you might say, for whom the loud-mouthed parvenu Nazis, whose leading figures were all petty bourgeois types, must have made uneasy company. What tied them together, for the duration of the war, or almost, was the common longing to blot out the disgrace of the World War I defeat. It's not an accident that Hitler's would-be assassin was a Count, don't you think?"

He squeezed his monocle into his right eye, perhaps to verify that Laura was still wide awake.

"With regard to most aspects of military and civilian life on the islands, officers such as Colonel Albrecht Lanz, the first CIC of the occupation troops, must have been more or less permanently at odds with the likes of Hitler, Goebbels, or Himmler, for that matter. Lanz, a graduate of Heidelberg University, was a doctor of both law and philosophy, an erudite, considerate officer and gentleman who probably knew both Greek and Latin, but, alas, no English. Small matter. On the contrary, with that kind of background, he conferred the patriotic message that German, and not English, was the language that you needed to learn if you were to forge yourself a future on the islands. Despite his Prussian sense of military discipline and civil law and order, he always saw to it that the locals' everyday life wasn't interfered with more than absolutely necessary. And I dare say he went the extra mile by entering into a number of amorous relationships with local women. Who would want to throw the first stone is all I say. Whenever he presented himself in the nude on horseback, along the not yet mine-studded beaches of St. Helier, at the crack of dawn, he could be sure to draw furtive female glances that admired the physique of both his stallion called Satan, and himself. Be that as it may, the presence of men such as Lanz on the Channel Islands was no mere accident either. Presumably, the Nazis wished to demonstrate to the English, who were next on the to-do list, that, very much in Dame Sybil Hathaway's line of thinking, the Germans weren't half as bad as their unfortunate reputation: Look at our officers. Would you buy second-hand cars from them? Of course you would, and rightly so. Well, the invasion of Britain didn't happen. And to the extent that the general war situation for the Germans went from bad to worse, the quality of military staff sent to the Channel Islands would be commensurate with that decline. The obvious peak of that negative trend being the arrival of SS troops in the archipelago."

"No more Mr Nice Guy?"

"Exactly. Hence, my presumption would be that Lanz and his colleagues were indeed freemasons themselves, men who tried to help their Channel Island brethren out by disregarding Hitler's orders. The freemasons' assets, however, could not be let off as easily as their owners. To leave that totally unscathed would, from the Nazis' point of view, have added injury to injustice. From the very beginning of their rise to power, the Nazis, forever cash-strapped to keep their propaganda and war machineries well oiled, had had the international community of executors and debt-collectors breathing down their necks. That's why, wherever they went, whatever country they attacked or occupied, they would always have dogs with them that would sniff down what stray assets there were for the taking. In the case at hand, it's possible the Wehrmacht had skimmed off a symbolic portion of the freemasons' total assets and allowed the remainder to be declared the fiscal property of Jersey's and Guernsey's respective parliaments. With that, the Germans would, at least for the time being, be able to pretend they had no further access to those coffers. Measures like these could only be taken with the knowledge and, at least, tacit assent of Lanz & Co. How the result of this financial haircut could have ended up in the Sark headquarter's safe, your guess is as good as mine. To find out, wasn't a priority for us then. All we knew was that, come what may, this treasure trove was to be ours. We had risked our lives coming to this bloody island, and this was to be our reward."

FOURTH CHAPTER

1. The Cave

"To wrap things up, we tied and gagged Otto and left him lying in the office. How did he explain the gutted safe to his superiors I wonder? If you ask me, I wouldn't have believed a word of what he would have told me and had him shot right away."

After having had dinner, Lamont and Laura were now back in the library. Laura had profited from the short intermission and taken a look at her room. Not the most luxurious set-up she had been exposed to, but not less comfortable than her room at the Quic en grogne either.

The old man had slipped into a jade-green silk dressing gown and looked like a chocolate wrapped in shiny paper. For her part, Laura hadn't changed but stuck to her blouse-and-jeans leisurewear. She had asked Harold to pour her a glass of Italian claret. Lamont was taking sips of a very old ruby-red port that had matured in oak barrels probably even a day or two older than himself. The fire had been kindled again. In short, the stage had been prepared for the next instalment of the seven-men drama on Sark.

"Now, we wanted to escape like a bunch of bank robbers who know full well that the Sweeney is going to pull up in front of the building any minute now. As a matter of fact, they were already waiting for us outside. So, when we came down the stairs and were about to step into the open, they opened fire. Fortunately, the Germans hadn't packed their dreaded Schmeisser submachine guns. If they had, it would have been curtains for us, of that I am dead sure. With their carbines, they could only tickle but not crush us with their superior fire power."

Laura's head began to swim at the first whiff of the claret. She felt she would now have been in the mood for some serious tomfoolery but sensed that nothing like that would be forthcoming. Not with Lamont continuing to ride his wheel chair down memory lane.

"We did a hasty about turn and gave the German squaddies a good shoot-out for their money, literally. The night was waning fast and we knew that we had to evaporate before dawn broke and the enemy would have the double advantage of daylight and reinforcements. Besides, if we lost more time, we would risk missing the bloody Sunfish, which was to pick us up again where she had left us. And so, we decided to go for it and try out the surprise factor. Our attempt at breaking the spell by scampering out a back door worked out fine, quite surprisingly. We created a thick smoke screen and ran as fast as we possibly could. Lily and Gooey were shot during the sortie, one in the leg, the other in the arm, but we couldn't really do anything about that then and there except help Gooey to hobble along."

Laura thought she must get some bottles of this claret as soon as she got home.

"In the treacherous light of dawn, you don't know who and what you're looking and shooting at. I'll bet you a tenner the Germans shot one or two of their own in the process. Anyway, we ran for our lives, back to the Coupée, into the minefield above Dixcart Bay. This gave us a small advantage because we had strapped the rope that had connected us on our way inland, to the ground like an Ariadne's thread, so that we knew which route would be open to us. Thus, we were able to go over the ledge and rope ourselves down to the rubber dinghy still where we had left it. Except now, it was floating. We had come at low tide. By now, high tide was in full swing, which meant the water level was rising and tons of water pushing against the rock. To get back to the Sunfish, waiting for us half a mile out at sea, we now had to paddle like mad. Which is a lot easier said than done. But for any group of people to paddle rhythmically, applying just about the same amount of force on both sides of the thing, is difficult even under normal circumstances and proved impossible under the present one, despite all our training. If and when you don't paddle straight, however, you obviously go in circles with a dinghy, which has no keel and practically no constructive stability to speak of."

He took a sip of port, clicked his tongue appreciatively and shrugged his shoulders.

"We had thought of almost everything except our possibly having such difficulties getting back to the submarine. Meanwhile, the Germans, too, had reached the minefield and were driven on by their officers, whose hoarse voices carried all the way to us down there. Of course, we had taken the precaution of picking up our Ariadne's thread. Two, three detonations signalled to us the enemy was getting a dose of his own poison. But at some stage, they had reached the ledge and furiously opened up on us. We were hovering somewhere between a rock and a hard place with bullets whizzing all around us. The Krauts even started firing at the Sunfish. What good is a submarine riddled by bullets, I was just asking myself when Lily caught a second slug, this time in the shoulder. More and more bullets were raining down on us, some of them puncturing the dinghy's inflated chambers, which, consequently, started losing air rapidly. I was lying curled up like a hedgehog in the dinghy's stern. Haggis and Hooch also caught bullets. Operation Sea Leopard threatened to end in a shambles. But if you can rely on something in St. Malo Bay, at least at this time of year, it's fog. A sudden bank of mist arriving out of nowhere hid us from the Germans and thus saved our skin. Unfortunately, it also hid us from the bloody Sunfish. The submarine's crew started whistling and shouting so we might home in on them. But under fog conditions, you lose not only all visual, but also a great deal of your acoustic orientation. The dinghy, by this time reduced to a giant floating pancake, got into a minor vortex, turned around its own axis a few times and left us at a complete loss as for the precise direction to follow. Finally, with the Germans still firing away merrily and blindly, the hissing sound of air escaping from the chambers petered out altogether and the dinghy lost the measly remainder of its erstwhile buoyancy. We dropped our weapons and rid ourselves of what other equipment there was left, with the notable exception of the knapsack containing our treasure trove. This was now carried by Gooey bleeding profusely from his leg wound. Then, we all went over the side, in a manner of speaking."

At this juncture, he was blowing air through his lips, almost closed as they were, as if to render a true-to-life impersonation of what had happened to the dinghy out there. Then he shuddered.

"I have never frozen like that in my life. By now, our boys on the Sunfish had probably realized that they couldn't help us but had to try and save their own skins before the first German battery would receive its firing co-ordinates. Hence, they must have dived and started on the homeward leg. As for us floating in the water, we were immediately picked up by the lively tide. Where it was going to take us, we had no way of knowing. Maybe straight back to Dixcart Bay and the Germans, who had finally stopped wasting bullets. We clung together and formed a ring, as we had learned during our training. Life vests would have been a useful asset now. But during the raid, they would have been a cumbersome burden. And to strap them on afterwards, in Dixcart Bay, we would not have had sufficient time. We knew from experience that these old-fashioned contraptions had a tendency of getting their straps and buckles more easily entangled than a woman's bra, so you usually ended up nearly strangling yourself, especially when under stress.

"But all of you did know to swim, didn't you?"

"Oh yes, that had been something our Yarmouth instructors had tested with great devotion. Because, you see, already during one of the first raids, some of the lads had drowned in relatively easy reach of the coast, even though, when recruited, they had claimed to be good swimmers."

"Who would do a thing like that, practically committing suicide?"

"God knows. Maybe they had been motivated by an overdose of patriotic ambition. Or maybe they had told the truth, but not taken into consideration that it is one thing to do a few leisurely lanes in an Olympic pool, but quite another to survive in a rough sea. Anyway, from that day on, the men's alleged swimming proficiencies were never taken as read any more but exposed to realistic conditions. People still drowned on occasion, but only under conditions no Olympic champion was likely to have survived either."

He lifted his glass and looked at Laura with grotesquely enlarged and distorted ruby-red eyes.

"Strange, our brain literally waylays us with curious associations, don't you think? Mine seemed to have been patiently waiting for an occasion like this to remind me of some unfortunate islander's story that did little or nothing to cheer me up under the conditions. There was this Guernsey fisherman, whose story I first heard when I was, what, maybe six years old. He had stood out to sea in his little boat to do his day's fishing, when his outboard flunked. It's what outboards do best, make a pest of themselves. And since the man wasn't able to repair it then and there and had no radio set either, with which he could have asked for help, the only thing he could do was sit down and leave the rest to the tide. When he passed by Alderney, through the Race, he was seen waving by some locals. But since he was too far out to make himself heard, the islanders, not reputed for their intellectual achievements, anyway, waved back and silently wished him God speed. In the afternoon, the man in his still powerless boat came back by the Race. Again, he flailed his arms and again, the Alderney half-wits waved back at him. Thus, the poor fisherman had to live, not once, but several times through the frustration of neither reaching Guernsey, because for that, the tide would turn too early, nor attracting the Alderney lifeboat people's attention. After having done his bizarre voyage some three or four times, night and day, someone luckily picked him up. Was my brain insinuating the same thing might happen to us now, in the immediate future, only without a boat and presumably as bloated corpses?"

Laura suppressed a yawn. The old man's yarn was beginning to strain her patience.

"But we were in luck again. The tidal current was getting weaker all the time, and the fog bank lifted or dissolved, whatever it is fog banks do. Hardly able to peep through our salt-crusted eyelids, we saw another cliff-studded part of Sark coast bobbing up and down in front of us. I actually recognized this bit as being situated close to the southernmost cape of the island. The tide had veered just about enough to the South-West, to dump us in lee-ward of the Germans who were probably still roaming the place in search of us, the British Schweinehunde. Almost frozen stiff, with four of us very nearly bleeding to death, we were watching some indistinct figures dashing to and fro along the coastline to our right. Impossible to tell whether it was locals or the Germans. Either way, I knew it to be well-nigh impossible to discover a human being floating in the sea even in normal swell conditions at a relatively short distance. With the naked eye, only a fish eagle will be capable of that, not least because of its favourable vantage point. Which goes a long way towards explaining the high number of men and women gone overboard that are only found dead, if at all, even though SAR measures may have been triggered almost immediately. All you have is this darkish needle-pin of the person's head in a sea producing all sorts of light reflexes. Well, in this case, it worked in our favour. We succeeded in clutching to a few rocks and eventually crawled ashore like mudfish using their gills as a means of propulsion. To our left, a small, rotund and rather high rock towered some sixty feet above us. I recognized it as something the locals call Moie de Brennière. Most of these maritime hallmarks still go by their quaint old Norman-French names. Anyway, for the time being, we seemed safe enough, al-right. All of us that is, except Gooey. Either he was, after all, not such a good swimmer as he had appeared on the Isle of Wight. Or else, and more likely perhaps, his knapsack unduly restrained his mobility. Or perhaps his heart showed the first signs of wear and tear in the cold, I don't know. At any rate, he suddenly raised his arms and started shouting for help, clearly in extremis. When I say he shouted, that's of course a bit of an exaggeration. His mouth wide open, he looked grotesquely like Edvard Munch's Cry, but his parched throat would not yield much more than a desperate croaking sound. Yet even that could have been enough to set the Germans on our trail again. So, knackered as we all were, some-one had to do something about it. If Gooey drowned, our treas-ure would follow him into the deep. I hope I'm not sounding too cynical in admitting that this, too, was a consideration at that moment. Hooch would have been the first choice, but having been shot at least once, with the corresponding loss of blood, his part devolved unto me. Despite my physical and mental exhaustion, I slid back into the ice-cold water to fish for Gooey who had gone under, meanwhile. At least, the water here was crystal clear. Up in the heavily churned waters of the Channel, I would probably have looked for the man in vain, what with the clouds of sediment and sand in permanent turmoil. To this day, I remember my surprise seeing how deep the water was so close to the coastal rocks. I got a hand on the knapsack and tried to pull Gooey to the surface, but that was impossible. I mean, the man was all but slender, dressed in his combat fatigues and heavy boots. He went down like a rock and felt slippery all over, too. At last, all I had to show for my efforts was that damn knapsack, while Gooey sank to the bottom with arms wide spread and eyes wide open. His eyes, expressing surprise more than horror, have followed me about all these decades. I mean, I had done what I could, and nobody ever did blame me either. But still, I can't forget that kind of other-worldly look he had on his face as if to say, well, if this is death by drowning, I'll take it. That's how I read it then, anyway."

"One broke his neck and then there were only six...."

Lamont nodded.

"Quite. Upon reflection, we six little Indians weren't that much better off than Gooey. Of course, we were alive and even felt rich in a manner of speaking. But neither the money nor the jewellery or the diamonds would buy us food or drinking water. And exposed as we were, they would find us rather sooner than later. We needed a hideout first thing, some place where we could rest, attend to our wounds and discuss where to go from here. I myself hadn't been shot, but the sharp edges of the rocks had torn the crumpled and soaked skin off my fingers, hands, and knees. None of us had come out of this unscathed. I seemed to remember there was a cave somewhere near the cape. That would do as a preliminary hideout. But I see your glass is empty. May I..."

He rang for Harold, who appeared right away and poured more wine and port. Laura briefly hesitated. Probably, she should have stopped drinking, but then, it would appear impolite to let Sir Lucas sup on his own like some lonesome old wino.

"By that time, the Germans had probably written us off as drowned. Notwithstanding, they would be on the lookout for our bodies washed up on a beach somewhere. Fortunately, they had no dogs to sniff us out. Together with any felines, horses, donkeys, pigs, rabbits and other more or less domestic fauna, canines had long since ended their career in somebody's saucepan, either local or German. The generalized food shortage on the islands had reached such worrying dimensions that whatever vaguely edible-looking creature got caught was turned into a soup, a stew, a ragout, or a meatball of sorts. A year or so later, with capitulation only months away and no more supplies reaching the islands, people even took to eating grass, tree bark, worms and seagulls. Have you ever tried the meat of a seagull? It's ironic, in a way, that the one marine bird that could be said to live primarily on its proximity to humans refuses to return the favour by being practically unappetizing."

Laura felt her flesh creep at the mere thought of eating seagulls.

"But then, what with all those French genes in their blood, Jersey men ought to be used to frog's legs, for example. I always thought French cuisine followed the motto, if it moves, eat it?"

Lamont emitted some hoarse sounds that could have expressed anything from disgust to glee. Laura decided to take it for the latter.

"There's probably some truth in that. But anyway. At nightfall, we felt a little safer, had provisionally bandaged our wounds with strips of uniform and recovered from our worst pains and bruises, both physical and mental. The gunshot wounds were hard to take care of without any disinfectants, proper bandages and other basic stuff you would find in any medical kit. Ours was resting on the bottom of the sea, next to Gooey, as it were. Fortunately, none of us had a slug to be dug out of his body, all wounds being through-and-throughs. Hungry, thirsty, brow-beaten and generally down and out, we started discussing what to do next. Not that we felt particularly enterprising or were overpowered by the number of options available to us. To surrender to the Germans would have been suicide. After all, we had just killed eight of their mates and thus aroused their understandable wrath. As regular soldiers in uniform, though tattered uniforms, we should, according to international martial law, have been treated as combatants and taken prisoners. But, what with Hitler's Night-and-Fog decree, we were convinced the Germans would stand us up against the nearest wall and shoot us. So that was no feasible solution. The odds of the Sunfish or some other vessel coming to look for us appeared forbidding. Our radio set was lost, so there could only be visual communication. And even in case someone back there on the British coast was convinced we were still alive, well, when push comes to shove, six men pull less weight than an albeit ramshackle old submarine. No, we had to start from the assumption that we were on our own and had to hide, lie in wait of a boat, anything that floated and would, courtesy of the tide, carry us north in a sort of island-hopping manner. Of course, we knew the Germans had strictly forbidden any unauthorized boat traffic among the islands whatsoever. Besides, Creux Harbour, Sark's only sorry excuse for a port, had not been given its curious name for nothing. Creux being the French word for a small hole or, in a figurative sense, a feeling somewhere between growing appetite and wolfish hunger. Creux Harbour was all of that, a hole blown in the rock to form something between a sizeable bath-tub and a very little port basin. Accessible only by way of a short tunnel, it was easy to guard and practically impossible to sneak into, or out of. Worse, I'd say, because there was no vantage point on the island from which you could have caught so much as a glimpse of what vessels were possibly tied up there at any given time. Add to this the fact that the south coast of England is a solid seventy nautical miles away from Sark, and you will realize that our chances of getting there alive, somehow, were a million to one, or worse. Then again, what other options were there?"

"What did you do with the treasure?"

"Well, hiding something was no problem. Both Sark and nearby Jethou island are literally riddled with caves of all sizes. Over the millennia, rain and salt water wash away the softer, chalky layers of stone, thus wrecking the static equilibrium of the rock formations. Sooner or later, big slabs will then fall off and leave cavities all over the place. When we were kids, we used to roam these caves and feel like pirates returning from successful buccaneering raids. Our treasures were a little more modest then, of course: flat pebbles looking like doubloons, rusty pieces of scrap iron that would stand in for muskets or other items of a pirate's arsenal. The tricky thing about many of these caves, though, was that they were situated around the level of what the sailors call the chart datum. All according to what charts you happen to consult, that could be the level of mean low water springs or that of the lowest astronomical tide ever recorded. In simpler terms, many caves such as ours risked getting flooded and if you didn't leave in good time, you risked getting caught, drowned or suffocated."

"Why astronomical tide?" Laura asked. The Doc as her nautical mentor had forgotten to tell her about that. Presumably, because it was of less consequence in the Caribbean than here.

"The expression refers to the fact that not only the moon, but also the sun and other planets have a certain push-pull effect on our oceans, especially whenever two or more planets are in conjunction with one another or the sun. Minute variations, hardly comparable with the force of the moon, of course, which comes away as number one because of its proximity alone. Which is why other seafaring nations ignore it altogether and stick to the mean value of low water marks as observed over the decades. That's what they take as their reference level or chart datum. The Brits ruling the sea, however, go that little bit further and reassure sailors that, no matter what – Venus in conjunction with Mars, moon, and sun, abnormally high atmospheric pressure and your wife having her monthly period – the minimum depths indicated by Admiralty charts can always be counted on. Excessive, some would call it, but there you are. In some things, we tend to be even more pedantic than the Germans."

He groped for his monocle and looked at Laura as if to verify she had understood his little excursion into the fascinating realm of tides.

"One way or another, for the reasons explained, not all caves on Sark were safe places as such, not at high water."

He dropped his monocle, sipped some port and clicked his tongue again.

"I vaguely remembered a cave which remained dry at any state of the tide, or almost. But it was situated on the other, western side of the cape to whose east we had landed. To limp and climb there, six people single file, would have caused unwanted attention. There was even an outside chance the Germans had found out about that cave and were waiting for us to turn up there since it would have been such a natural choice. Hence, it was better to split and leave it to each and every one of us to find his way out. I hesitated for a while to submit that proposal, since it seemed to run counter to all we had learned during our training sessions: stay together at all times, take help, hope and encouragement from your mates, and so on and so forth. Those were the rules of procedure for dispersed combat groups that had been separated from the rest of their troops during a campaign. And I'm sure they were helpful and correct as far as they went. Our situation being very special, however, unusual and maybe even devious means of conduct were called for. I was convinced the others would come round to my way of thinking sooner or later, and bided my time."

Lamont lifted his water glass.

"Drinking water was the most urgent problem. Our tongues stuck to our palates like they had been glued there by the salty sea water. After all we had gone through during the past few hours, our throats were parched and felt like cheese graters. Fortunately, it soon started raining as if by special appointment. We all lay down on our backs and opened wide, greedily swallowing the rain water drop by drop. Those of us who had been shot in this or that part of their anatomy were able to cool their wounds with sweet water. It helped us through the next few hours. Without food, the human body survives a week, perhaps two, all according to your general state of fitness and existing body fat. Without water, you are dead in seventy hours, no matter what. Whichever way you looked at it, we had to split and pull through somehow. As I had foreseen, it didn't take long for the lads to wrap their minds round that. Only one question left: what was to be done with the treasure?"

The old man appeared to be getting tired. He closed his eyes for a moment, then opened them again in a startled manner like a soldier who had been caught dozing off on his watch.

"I suggested hiding the treasure in one of the smaller holes that surrounded us on all sides. We would stuff the knapsack there, cover it with rocks and pebbles so that it could not be found that easily, nor be carried away by some particularly atrocious tide. Whoever was to come back here first after the war would take the lot, according to the finders-keepers principle. That should have been sufficient motivation for all of us not to go dying in the crazy war. The lads hesitated, as was to be expected. What if several of us were to survive but one just happened to arrive, say, an hour later than the other? I appealed to their gambling spirit. There was nothing to it but winner takes all. In a round of poker, you get no points for coming in second, now, do you? The one bloke who happened to return first would be the lucky devil to take home the jackpot. If he was prepared to split with whoever else was left of the platoon, fine. But that would be his free and independent decision."

Again, his eyelids became heavy as lead. He yawned like a lion in his cage.

"I beg your pardon. My old shell of a body is demanding its portion of sleep. Patience, my friend," he added, patting his stomach, "you'll soon get plenty of that, but don't let me hear any complaints then, ya hear?"

"And so you split?"

"Yes. But not without practising what was to become a fixed ritual with us years later. We took each other's hands and formed the magic circle. Then, we swore an oath to do our worst to beat the Grim Reaper to it and survive this goddamn war no matter what the odds. Once peace would return to Europe and the world, we would get together again and use both our innate talents and our newly-gained proficiencies and experience to our own profit. Society and the nation owed us, or so we felt, and we were determined to collect. The world would be hearing from us. In a way, we were merely whistling in the dark, I suppose. The enormity of what lay ahead of us had not really sunk in yet. How could it? Still, in retrospect, I guess that, on that day, as the crack of dawn projected our rugged shadows on the cave's walls, the gang that was to be known and feared as the Yarmouth Six was born."

2. The List

Laura looked at her watch with sleepy eyes. Half past four in the morning. Was it some unusual sound that had woken her up or was it the pressure on her bladder making itself felt at this unearthly hour? Supported by a throbbing headache that smacked of Italian claret? Either way, it took her a while to gather where she was in the first place.

"The manor's interior has been covered almost entirely with wood, as you already had occasion to note," Lamont had warned her.

"A lively building material which somehow never quite settles, it would seem. Instead, it extends and shrinks again; it arches, develops rifts and cracks and is generally on the move, as it were. Hence, don't be surprised if things go snap, crackle and pop during the night. Ghosts, on the other hand, you're not likely to meet, I don't think. They are as strictly off limits in the manor as are dogs or pets of any size or description."

Laura switched on a light and freed herself of the thick duvet which, even though praised as light and fluffy by the maid, was beginning to feel like a menhir Obelix had dragged onto her place of eternal rest.

Probably mistaking the manor for a hotel in a state of light inebriety, she had forgotten to enquire about the location of the toilets before turning in. To go out now on the crackling corridors like a somnambulist, at the risk of accidentally getting shot by one or the other of Lamont's bodyguards seemed a little dramatic an ending. There must be other ways.

Looking round for an appropriate vessel, she discovered nothing that would have pressed itself upon her as a substitute chamber pot. Finally, two flower pots with a species of geranium moved up on the short list. If shit was good for crops, urine couldn't be that bad for flowers now, could it? Changing the pH-value of the soil, it might lend a new colour to the blossoms. So what? Or were they bearded begonia instead? With a deep sigh, Laura slipped on her jeans, pushed the seams of her nightgown down into the belt and stepped on the corridor, noiselessly like a thief profiting from the wee hours of the morning. A latter-day Danielle Foussard climbing the Nice rooftops in her duel against Cary Grant. Talking of which. There was something slightly alien about Cary Grant, she had always felt. Another of those one-face actors Hollywood seemed to breed, his hair a solid block of God knows what. A doubtful gypsum figure the men in black would have taken out no questions asked.

Outside, all was quiet. Were there any CCTV cameras about, hidden in the panels, maybe? Now, where would a nineteenth-century interior architect have placed the toilets? If he had actually wasted a thought on such pedestrian items, at all. Urban legends came to her mind that told of entire skyscrapers which had to be pulled down again because, in their frenzy for modernisation and steel-and-glass streamlining, their architects had forgotten to install toilets.

Two doors further on, there was a thin shimmer of light protruding from the doorsill. Could have been the landlord's private chamber. Could have been anything, in fact. But whoever lived in there seemed to be up, so why not take a chance before she peed in her pants.

Ever so gently, so as not to wake the whole house, she knocked on the door. When there was no answer, she knocked a little harder. Again, no reaction. Not that she had noticed in the course of the afternoon and evening, but maybe Lamont was as deaf as a post and had just been clever enough to hide his hearing aid. As soon as he was alone, he would put it aside and not hear the knocking, obviously. Bugger it. She pressed the handle down and entered.

It was the landlord's private quarters alright, there could be no doubt about that. Lamont himself was sort of crouched in a tall swivel office chair, naked. The man, not the chair. His back was turned to the door and he must have been reading till he had fallen asleep God knows when. The office lamp with its stylish jade-green cover was the only source of light in the room. Further back in the darker recesses of the room Laura thought she could distinguish a bed and Lamont's wheelchair. How had he managed to get to the desk without it? Never mind, she told herself. As it seemed, this was Lamont's combined study and bedroom, arranged to suit his habits and needs. Speaking of which. The toilets should not be that far away, all things told. Unless Lamont used chamber pots.

"I'm terribly sorry, Sir Lucas," she stammered, "but I happened to see your light. And the thing is, I'm desperate for a rest room, you see, so I thought I might…."

Lamont didn't react. Either he had fallen into a coma or had passed away. She didn't finish the thought. The old man suddenly coughed and gasped as if someone was strangling him in his dreams. His head, albeit connected to the neck, rolled onto his left shoulder, where it came to rest. So he wasn't dead, after all, the last surviving member of the Yarmouth Six, but rather in a limbo hard to define with any degree of precision. Maybe this was his normal routine, some act he unwittingly played out night after night, wondering whence his neck ached in the mornings.

Laura came closer to the desk and peeped round the chair to get a better look of Sir Lucas – Luke the Duke with the little fluke. Laura couldn't help chuckling about her own excursion into Solitaire's realm of silly rhymes. If Harold or someone entered the room now, she would have had a lot of explaining to do.

Lamont was naked alright, but otherwise unharmed, as it seemed. Maybe he had got out of bed, haunted by some chimera of the past that had caught up with him. How he had reached the desk would remain his secret. Probably crawled on all fours. Then he had picked up a file, thumbed through it and fallen asleep again. Perhaps this long walk down memory lane in Laura's company had sapped more energy than hit the eye at first. The three or four glasses of port might have played a collusive role in this intrigue and flattened him out with a delayed detonation sort of effect.

In his left hand that he had supported on the desk, he held a thin file that was opened at about the middle. Laura knew full well she was badly trespassing but could not help herself.

Very cautiously, feeling the old man's breath on her cheek, she approached further, picked up a pen and started turning the pages. Inquisitiveness is the most important driving force of any detective, Conan Doyle once said. Or was it E.A. Poe? No matter. So far, she felt she had not heard anything from Sir Lucas that might have moved her any closer to Solveig's killer. To go back to Hamburg totally empty-handed would have been shameful. Not with the troublesome, time-consuming route here. She hadn't brought her glasses, but what she saw on the pages of the file made her whistle through her teeth despite herself.

Very carefully and gently, she wrought the file from Lamont's gouty, liver-spot studded hand, closed it and, sticking it under her arm, beat a discreet retreat.

When she was back in her room, she lay down on the bed and, putting on her glasses, began to read the document. Being almost totally absorbed by what she had found, she had clean forgotten about the toilet but was soon reminded of that involuntary omission by her bladder. With another sigh, she looked across the room at the two flower pots...

On the face of it, Lamont's file looked very much like a hit list. On closer scrutiny, though, it turned out more like a research paper on the Yarmouth Six and anyone who had ever been close to them. Names, dates, short CV's, past or present employment, postal and web addresses complete with phone numbers. Had Laura not been on Jersey, but, say, on the East German island of Rügen, instead, she might have mistaken this collection for the files of the Staatssicherheit or ex-secret service of the former GDR. What made them stand out from those, however, was the blatant lack of any indications as to political adherences and sexual proclivities. This was no Kompromat, as the Russians would call it, no compromising material that could serve blackmailing purposes or at any rate be made to surface at the appropriate moment to destroy a person's reputation. This was much more harmless, even though, it would seem, established with an all the more astounding assiduity.

Laura needed a copy of this register that would save her a lot of time-consuming research work of her own. She seized her mobile, got up and straightened out the file's pages one by one under her night table lamp to get a better result. The quality of the photos would probably leave a lot to be desired, nevertheless, but could perhaps be improved upon with the help of photoshop apps. It took her about half an hour to shoot the twenty pages. Now all she had to do was put the file back into Lamont's hand.

What if he had woken up, meanwhile, wondering where his list was at? Impudence wins, wasn't that what they said? She slipped into the fluffy dressing gown that hung outside on her cupboard and stepped out into the corridor, once again. Down on the ground floor things were livening up, it would seem. Maybe the kitchen staff was making first preparations for breakfast. With fast mincing steps Laura approached Lamont's room and already had her fingers on the door handle, when she heard Harold's unmistakable voice right behind her.

"Anything I can fix, M'am?"

Caught in the act, Laura thought, slipped the handle and turned round with the brightest of smiles. Before Harold could recover from her surprise charm attack, she had already pressed Lamont's file upon him.

"Good morning Harold. Sir Lucas was kind enough to leave this with me for perusal last night. Would you be so kind as to return it to him at your earliest opportunity? I would highly appreciate it, thanks a lot. And, incidentally, where are the rest rooms in this gorgeous manor, just in case…?"

Harold pointed at a door near the end of the corridor and explained the details. When he turned round again, Laura had already disappeared into her room.

Coming down to the dining hall for breakfast about two hours later, freshly made up and in excellent spirits, she was wondering whether, meanwhile, Harold had told Sir Lucas about his strange encounter with Laura and the files. If so, the old man didn't let it show in any way at all but immediately fell into the chatting mode.

Laura knew about the encouraging tongue-loosening effect she had on people in general and men in particular. An effect she had found confirmed here, once again. Her mere sustained presence in interrogation rooms, she felt, would probably result in an avalanche of confessions on the part of even the most monosyllabic of suspects.

"A real shame you couldn't stay for a few days longer. I enjoyed your company no end, I really did," he said politely while gnawing on a slice of buttered toast like a toothless cowboy on a piece of his saddle.

"Keeps reminding me of the hardtack we got on HMS Sunfish at the time. Hardtack with a tuna paste which I wouldn't be able to pop down the hatch if it was the last thing to eat on earth. But of course, in 1940, and under the circumstances....As long as the rumbling stomach was silenced for a while."

"Hardtack reminds me of Treasure Island and Moby Dick," Laura commented apologetically.

"But I've never tasted it myself."

"Don't start. It's not worth the effort."

"Some time later you will have to let me hear the continuation of that story of the Yarmouth Six," Laura insisted and got a grateful look from Lamont who probably feared that he had laid it on a little too thick the night before.

"But now I have to return to Hamburg on the double, unfortunately. Maybe another occasion will present itself, who knows. Like the man said, life is full of little surprises. Do you ever grace the Continent with your presence, albeit fleeting as it may be?"

The old man laughed.

"...the lobster asked the jellyfish? If you're talking of the European continent, well, I try hard to avoid it. Too much red tape, crummy parochial mentalities, makes even a midget like myself feel like a giant visiting the Lilliputians, if you see what I mean. During the brief spells I spend on the island, while Harold is taking stock of this and that, attending business, I mean, I fancy myself in the role of England's last lighthouse keeper watching the horizon. I like that expression, watching the horizon. What for? Any chance of it disappearing of a sudden?"

He held his breath for a moment and wiped the remaining crumbs of hardtack off his fingers.

"An honest if melancholy way of making your living, lighthouse keeping, don't you think?"

Laura readily admitted that, so far, she hadn't given it much thought.

"Of course not. Incidentally, have there ever been female lighthouse keepers?"

"I once read about a woman in Spain...."

"Well, either way, it took a degree of physical and mental resilience. Two, three, or four weeks in a row alone out there on isolated, wind-swept rock formations such as the Casquets or the Fastnet must have worked your nervous system, while. banana-shaped bunks would work your discs, at night. If a gale lasted for weeks, which it could during North Atlantic winters, there would be no food supplies, no communication perhaps. Just the eternal howling of the storm and the thundering of the sea that would send earthquake-like shock waves up the tower, wrap it in spray and make its residential parts sway like a punch-drunk boxer in the ring. And all the while the keeper would be on porridge and hardtack."

"Were they always alone?"

"No, sometimes two keepers would share the boredom and isolation. Which could be less of a blessing than one should think. Imagine the two of them not getting along all that well and one of them having an accident – slipping and falling down the stairs, breaking his neck, for instance. The suspicion of foul play hovering over the lighthouse like a cloud, the surviving part did well to live with a corpse around the house until such time as the relief came and took the stiff to the nearest morgue. Such cases weren't exactly rampant, but they did occur and would eventually lead to lighthouses being manned and monitored by three or even four keepers. As for lightships, they would even have an entire crew of six or seven aboard. Had to, since, once they broke their anchor chain in heavy weather or became one with the heavy ice floes on the loose, any lightship thus going adrift had to be considered a normal vessel en route to be operated by a crew of able-bodied sailors. Horrific things, lightships. Got constantly bumped into in fog and sunk with many losses of life. Imagine yourself standing on deck of a lightship in thick fog. As you're lighting your last fag of the day just before turning in, you suddenly see these huge knife-sharp bows of a liner materialize out of nowhere and bear down upon you at high speed. The steam whistle blowing would be the last thing you heard in this life. Hallucinating stuff, don't you think?"

He fumbled in the pocket of his jade-coloured dressing gown and pulled out his mangled pack of Marlboroughs.

"Speaking of which. Tonight I dreamed a fairy had paid me a visit and tenderly stroked my hand."

Well, Laura thought, as long as it's only the hand. Was the old man pulling her leg or was her bad conscience causing her to imagine things?

"Would you be so kind as to call me a taxi, please. I really ought to be on that first ferry to get back to Hamburg in time. I'll take the TGV to Paris and fly back from there."

"That's the thing about islands. Like attractive women, they may seem virtually unattainable to begin with, till such time as you suddenly find you are stuck with them.

Laura laughed.

"I didn't hear that. Politically as incorrect as you can possibly get, you should be ashamed of yourself."

The old man gave her a wry smile that expressed anything but pangs of remorse.

"You may think of your return trip as cumbersome alright. But spare a thought for the unfortunate islanders, two thousand of them, who were deported and interned in those Southern German camps such as Biberach and Bad Wurzach. Must have spent a whole week in those uncomfortable, smelly railroad carriages. No service, no bistro, nothing but the eternal rat-tat-tat of the rails."

"Did all of them return after the war?"

"Not all, no. Some women fell in love with German men, frequently invalids of the war, and stayed. But those cases were few and far between."

He lit his cigarette that could have stood in as a corkscrew. " Materially speaking, our people fared much better in the camps than many of those who were allowed to stay on the islands. The internment camps were not run by the SS, as were concentration camps such as Auschwitz, Bergen Belsen and the like, but by the German police. And out there in the country, there was always food of some sort or another. They even organised festivals and carnivals in the camps. Normal, everyday German folly ruled okay, no offence. Nevertheless, the situation was unstable, the peacefulness deceptive in that a trifling offence could land you in one of the places of no return. For years, the fear of such punishments or reprisals must have choked the internees' occasional spells of mirth and pleasure."

He rang for Harold, who, for once, took a little longer than usual to appear.

"I suggest you get out the Bentley and take Mrs Forster to the ferry terminal in St. Helier. Do you have a reservation? No? Harold, see to it, if you will. And stop over at the pharmacist on your way back. Once again, I've run out of anti-depressives. In half an hour, would that be okay with you?"

Laura nodded.

"Thanks a lot. You're being very kind. To be honest, I had come here to ask you for your opinion on the most recent murders. But somehow, we never got round to that, did we?"

"No, we didn't. Instead, you had to sit through hours and hours of the Saga of the Yarmouth Six. I'm terribly sorry, but, then again, when it comes to the point, I probably don't know much more about the killings than you have probably learned already. We're all just conjecturing. Should you, in the course of your investigations, succeed in throwing more light on this entire affair, I should be awfully indebted for any useful piece of information apt to unveil the killer's identity."

Laura smiled even though she didn't believe for a moment that Sir Lucas was quite as ignorant as he pretended. Not now that she had found his list.

"Paradoxically, the legend of the Yarmouth Six appears to begin at the very moment you decided to split up." Lamont smiled.

"That's true, I suppose. I've never as yet seen it from that angle."

After breakfast, Laura packed her few belongings, bade the landlord farewell and followed in Harold's wake. The butler guided her past the bodyguards down the stairs to a waiting R-type Bentley with the winged "B" on the bonnet.

"Year of construction 1952," Harold murmured.

"I hadn't thought you were that old," Laura teased him. But he seemed impervious to such flippancies.

"Any chance of abducting you? I could do with a butler of your class."

"I'm afraid not," Harold politely replied.

"But if you're really interested, I can give you the address of an excellent London butler school with, on an average, three or four first-rate graduates per annum. Obviously, they don't come cheap, but then, money doesn't seem a subject worth mentioning with you."

"I'm making ends meet, thank you very much. But those graduates, they wouldn't have your class, I'm sure."

Harold seemed flattered.

"They would certainly lack one of the most valuable assets of our profession – experience. Besides, enjoying the privilege of serving gentlemen such as Sir Lucas would request certain proficiencies you couldn't acquire at a school. I am his secretary, bodyguard, and sometimes his confessor."

Laura laughed aloud.

"Sounds like a full-time job to me alright."

"With regular unpaid overtime, yes, M'am, quite."

Laura was about to profit from the half-jocular atmosphere she quite unexpectedly had managed to establish with Harold to bring up the subject of the purloined files. But then she decided against it. Any further mention of the incident would sound like a lame excuse to the butler. Better keep her stiff upper lip and pretend nothing untoward had happened. As long as he made no bones of it...

When they breezed into the harbour, the Condor Express was tearing at her mooring lines as if only too eager to get going. Laura said goodbye to Harold, took out her reservation at the ticket desk and stepped aboard. She had only just had sat down in the restaurant for a second helping of breakfast when her mobile rang. Without her glasses she couldn't decipher the caller's number on the display. She did notice, though, that it wasn't either Ignace or Marquardt.

"Mrs. Forster?"

Laura recognized the Chief Superintendent's voice.

"Hello, Dirty Harry, what can I do you for?"

"Hi Laura, where are you? In Hamburg?"

"Not by a long chalk, no. I'm on a ferry boat from St. Helier to St. Malo. I fear this phone connection might prove wobbly since we're bound to fall into one of those dead zones. I'm only mentioning it in case we are suddenly cut off. No fault of mine."

"I understand. Don't want to keep you, anyway. Listen, why don't you give me a call at this number as soon as you are back in civilization? I wish you God speed."

Laura thanked him and hung up. Were there any more murder victims? She couldn't help thinking back to her so-called Dirty Dozen, the twelve men and women that had formed per privileged think tank during the first few years of her ROLA leadership. They had advised her in all business and many private matters and had, among other things, contributed largely to the success of her Istanbul adventure, some six or seven years ago. Their analytic thinking and crowd intelligence would come in very nicely now that the entire Yarmouth affair didn't make more sense to her than it had done before her visit, list or no list. Why had the cops not identified the killer yet, seeing that he appeared to leave no end of traces behind?

"The point where fiction and the reality of criminal investigations part company most spectacularly is with the time factor," the Chief Super had told her.

"As long as murder or manslaughter isn't based on the degeneration of personal relationships, which, fortunately enough, it frequently is, investigations can run over years and decades before they sometimes come to fruition. The famous-infamous twenty-four hours are largely a myth. If the murderer and his victim were in any way close, we normally need less than that to catch the killer. If they aren't, we usually need a lot more time than that. With others again, we have to sit it out and wait for forensic science to break hitherto uncharted ground, thus enabling us to tackle cold cases with new instruments. Always hoping that vital pieces of evidence haven't dissolved into thin air by then."

From the TGV, Laura called the Chief and gave him a short report on her visit to Lamont, holding back on the little detail of the list, though.

"Yes, you're right," the Chief replied, "Lamont tends to wander off at a tangent unless you harness him in. Be that as it may. I take it you remember the fourfold murder off Barbuda? Precisely, on the Wily Minx. Very mysterious case that. The colleagues on Antigua had one more heart-to-heart with the two black gentlemen who claimed to have hit upon the abandoned yacht out there on the open ocean. Their story didn't seem to hold water if you will excuse the pun. Well, turns out they had found the Wily Minx off Barbuda with four bodies, not three bodies on it. A fourth victim, a woman, had somehow managed to crawl ashore, despite her mortal wound. Before she died, she had tried to tell them something the two of them had not understood then and could only guess at later."

"Yes? So?"

"Well, what she seems to have said was two words – the boxer. Make any sense to you?"

Laura mused a while on that.

"'fraid not, no."

"In her situation, the woman may just have been hallucinating."

"Could be. But I don't think so. She had that one shot at leaving a very important clue as to the identity of her killer. She couldn't possibly allow herself a hit and miss. Believe me, I happen to have lived through a similar situation and not taken enough notice then. And almost came to regret it."

"You may be right there. Anyway, what speaks in favour of your thesis is a note we found in the scrapbook of Norwegian Olaf Bergström. Another victim of the killer, he was carrying that thing around when he got shot. Olaf seems to have been sexually very active, I mean, for a Norwegian, anyway. Attended blind dates a lot, it would seem. The kind arranged by the usual suspects on the internet – portals and chat rooms where interested parties confer with fancy wrestling tags such as the Stavanger stallion or the Bergen Bull. Well, one of those appears to have called himself the Boxer. Could be coincidence, except...."

"Except the police don't believe in coincidences, now, do they?"

3. For a Pocketful of Marbles

"Which boils down to saying that, all things considered, your trip was as futile as could be."

Ignace sat at the piano back in Laura's Hamburg villa, strumming away the same handful of melodies over and over. Laura's report hadn't seemed to interest him beyond a polite minimum of attention and the odd question. He was quite obviously still miffed about having been left behind on that occasion.

"I wouldn't quite put it that way," Laura replied with a certain pertness in her voice and triumphantly pulled out a hard copy of Lamont's photographed list Marquardt had produced for her the night of her return from Jersey.

"What's that then?" Ignace asked, still not really excited about Laura's summary.

She explained it to him and placed the pages on the music stand right in front of his eyes.

"It's a list I came across at Lamont's. It will greatly facilitate our task. What struck me during my first superficial perusal is the fact already mentioned by the Chief that none of the Yarmouth Six died in his bed, quietly and peacefully. With the notable exception of Lamont himself, everybody fell victim to some accident or another. Not just any old accident, either, mind you."

"What do you mean?"

"Each and every mishap looks very much like an ironic comment on the respective victim's way of life. For instance, Hooch drowned in the Canal du Midi, during a holiday, even though, according to Lamont, he was an excellent swimmer. Lily shot himself accidentally cleaning his gun. Again, according to Lamont, he was a great expert at firearms. Haggis, the best mountaineer of the lot, fell off a cliff of the lowest category, usually recommended to rank beginners. Ronny was beaten to death during a row between some Hell's Angels and rival Bandidos. Brain was knocked over by a truck. Well, this last one lacks a little imagination. I mean, such a spate of bad luck is unlikely, to say the least. Somebody must have pulled a few strings, had the lads liquidated one by one. All but Luke the Duke, who escaped with grave injuries nailing him to a wheelchair to this day. You know what? I'm afraid we'll have to work our way through the list to unveil the darker secrets of that gang. Our boxer is an avenger-type killer. But what or who is he avenging? And why now and not some twenty or thirty years ago? Is he the same person who killed the other members of the gang? Hardly, he would be too old now to be going on a renewed killing spree. Question upon question... We'll need a lot of patience and imagination. I know you can do imagination, but can you do patience?"

Ignace shrugged his shoulders.

"Guess I'll have to. Whatever it takes to find the bastard and put him in the ground."

Laura was about to reply when the phone rang. She took the call and put her hand on Ignace' shoulder.

"Could you stop your gig for a moment. This is important for me."

Then she concentrated on the conversation with Marquardt, who gave her a short summary of what initiatives he had taken with respect to the loan business.

"What's that you're saying? Lamont? Are you sure about this? I can't believe it. You would think he would have breathed the odd word on the matter during my visit to Jersey. Okay, he may hold a majority share in the bank without even being aware of it, as it were. Much of his business is apparently done by his butler, or so he told me. Bradshaw Logistics form part of his group. But still...I mean, is it possible someone is using him as a front without his knowledge? The old cynic pretends he is totally unimpressed by events, but, chances are, his head is swimming with suspicions, intrigues, all sorts of shit, pardon my French. On top of that, he is forgetful, with respect to some aspects of his life whereas others stand out as if they happened yesterday. That's the impression I got talking to him. Or rather, his talking to me. Do me a favour and stay on the ball, if you please. It's do or die for me. Can I count on you?" Marquardt laughed.

"You don't really want me to reply to that, do you?"

Maybe not, Laura agreed. A few more polite exchanges and Marquardt hung up.

If only she had known about this before she had gone to Jersey. There, she could have discussed it with Lamont in person. To call him now would be a second best. Business transactions as delicate as this one need to be discussed man to man or man to woman, whatever. On the phone, it would be all too easy for him to fob her off. There, too, she needed more precise information she could use as leverage, or maybe a decoy, something apt to make Lamont lower his defences and come on out in the open. The list, maybe!

"Ignace, from the business point of view, I'm running the shareholders' gauntlet at present. Meaning I have no time to study the list. How about you take care of that side of things? You know, run through the list and see what you come up with, if anything."

"A boxer?"

"Excuse me?"

"You were talking of the killer as the boxer a few moments ago."

"Was I? Really? Ah, yes, you haven't heard that one yet." She told him about the telephone conversation she had had with the Chief.

"The Boxer?" Ignace' span of attention seemed spent. He started strumming again, to all appearances not an iota wiser for his money.

"You got to dig in, tiger. Investigations are frequently arduous, time-consuming stuff. I'm sure the solution is hiding somewhere in that list, peeping at us and laughing at our dim-wittedness. Besides which, we have to discuss your eventual return to the States. There's an exam waiting for you, remember? Solveig's murderer may still roam the place for quite a while and you can't just blow it all to high heaven just like that. I'm sure Solveig wouldn't have wanted this either."

Ignace nodded and kept on playing. It was his way of dealing with stress, Laura knew. She had become accustomed to this, even though sometimes, the strumming sometimes got the better of her, so she had to leave and take a walk.

"What's that you're playing?" she asked Ignace.

"What? This?"

He repeated some tunes and chords of what he had last played.

"Yes, what is that, it sounds familiar, but I can't put my finger on it."

"It's a Paul Simon song," Ignace replied without stopping.

Of course, Laura thought. Now she recognized it as what it was – a song called The Boxer.

"You think…?"

"No idea. Just a thought I was toying with."

"What's it with that song, then? What's it about, really?" "Properly speaking, one of the most bizarre songs of pop history."

"Why's that?"

"For many reasons. Basically, it's a premature baby that was never given a chance to finish its nine months' period in the mother's womb, as it were. A freak song, something that should never even have made the producers' offices. Probably wouldn't have either, had it not come from the famous Paul Simon. Imbalanced, piecemeal, with all sorts of structural shortcomings, and yet another bloody hit."

"So? Why so critical?"

"Simple: the song must have been knocked together in a hurry. Nothing fits, nothing works. A real shambles, if you ask me. For starters, some versions have a stanza more than others. Which doesn't really matter because the extra stanza is nothing to write home about, anyway. More seriously: while all other stanzas tell the boxer's story from his perspective, the last stanza talks of the boxer as he. An unmotivated change of perspective, in other words. And the décor changes inexplicably: whereas we were following the boxer through the bitterly cold and cruel New York streets all the time, at the end, we suddenly see him in a clearing. What clearing? Why are we suddenly in the woods? Makes no sense. What follows is that interminable la-la-la which was originally supposed to be filled with text later. Except that Simon couldn't think of any. That said, the plot suits the spirit of the epoch, the seventies, recalling, as it does, Harry Nilsson's

Midnight Cowboy as much as Glen Campbell's Rhinestone Cowboy, for instance. The respective protagonists are down-and-outs who missed the train called The American Dream. They were left on the platform penniless and try to make a living by doting on the only thing left to them – their body. The rhinestone man dreams of rodeo triumphs, yet we sense some steer's going to break his bones. The Midnight Cowboy sells his dick for a dollar and the Boxer, well, he is already past it. They all live or used to live for an pocketful of marbles such are promises."

Laura whistled through her teeth..

"I'm impressed, Professor Forster. Reminds me of Hemingway's short story about a boxer who is facing a fight that, if he loses it, may easily turn out his last. All he thinks he needs to win is something as banal as a steak that will give him the necessary strength. Only trouble being, he can't afford one. Anyway, edifying as our little discussion may be, what's it got to do with the killer?"

"I don't know. We might be looking at a central part of his personality, something that allows us to profile him. Let's assume for a moment it's his favourite song, one he would be humming or whistling while he is preparing to shoot his next victim. Sounds bizarre to us, but if serial killers' brains worked as everybody else's, they wouldn't be what they are, I guess. He may identify himself with that type of loser, even draw a queer sort of moral force from that underdog narrative. All raw conjecture, of course."

Laura was truly impressed. The boy could be right. Either way, things weren't getting easier. Instead of a person who was, or had been, a boxer, they would then have to look for someone who went in for pop songs and appeared particularly fond of Paul Simon ballads, because he identified himself with its protagonists.

"Someone who is roaming the land as a humming and singing terminator?"

"Rubbish. But maybe it's the musical expression of the one would-be noble mission of his otherwise miserable, thoroughly messed-up life. He is the boxer, hell-bent on plying steely fate into the shape he wants."

Laura shrugged her shoulders.

"Maybe. At all events, I think we have to take the unfortunate woman's hint on Barbuda seriously. I have been in a situation not totally unlike the one presumably prevailing on the Wily Minx at the time of the four-fold murder."

"You mean, on the Yellow Dancer?"

"No, on Cyprus, at the battle of the Red Chapel, when I was almost certain you had got killed. It was raining bullets from all sides. In the end, Süleyman the Silent bought a fatal slug or two and, while breathing his last, tried hard to leave me a hint as to your whereabouts. Not for my sake or yours, mind. He must have felt betrayed by the Snake and wanted to get back at him. At times like that, you aren't lying, you aren't leaving any red herrings behind, I don't think. And there is no time for lengthy descriptions. Hence, you have to ask yourself, in a flash, as it were, what would be the one hint apt to give the killer away? On that background, I'm almost certain we're not going to find any boxers on Lamont's list."

She yawned heartily.

"However, be that as it may, I think I'll have to turn in. We'll talk in the morning, okay?"

She slid off the couch and was just about to shut down the computer, when a discrete ping of a sound announced the advent of electronic mail. She hesitated for a second but, having an uncouth presentiment, opened her mailbox, anyway.

It was a mail from the Chief Super. True to his promise, he sent her a copy of some very old interrogation protocols dating back to the nineteen seventies. The persons strapped to the grill were the Messrs Jimmy McDuff and Joey Grady aka Haggis and Hooch. They had been picked up by the Sweeney and were helping the police – a term Laura had always loved as the epitome of British understatement – with regard to a bank job in Liverpool, gone down in 1974. Provided with that basic information, Laura snapped her laptop shut, kissed her prodigious son of pop and climbed up to her bedroom like mountaineering ace Gerlinde Kaltenbrunner running out of oxygen only steps away from the summit of K2.

When she had removed her make-up and put on her night Paco Raban moisturizer, she yawned again heartily, stretching all fours on her double bed, which she had been using solo for more years than she would have cared to count. Maybe she should change that part of the décor and get a single bed, soon. A large one that might, at a pinch, sleep two. If there was something she decidedly didn't need, it was a constant reminder of her present single parent status.

The laptop seemed to be calling her name. She tried to ignore it for a while like a young mother pretending not to hear her baby cry at four in the morning. But, as always, her curiosity prevailed.

Hooch and Haggis had been caught red-handed, it would seem. Something that didn't happen often whenever the Yarmouth Six were involved. Of course, they had no idea what the police were talking about. Their presence in the bank late at night, well, yes, it might seem a little odd, suspect, even, but then, the nature of their business allowing for no delays….and so on and so forth. The usual game of snakes and ladders, with loaded dice.

Irrespective of how clear and self-explanatory things might seem, hardened criminals such as these were masters of invention, perfectly capable of adapting their narrative to the respective progress in their opposite numbers' investigations. And whenever they did run out of ideas, for once, their lawyers would step in and fill whatever gaps had opened. Not an easy job, police work. Never mind how hilarious the suspects' subterfuges, the cops would have to disprove it, first, every time, and produce evidence that proved beyond the shadow of a doubt that things could not have happened as described by the criminal. That was hard and time-consuming enough at the present state of forensic science. Back in the nineteen seventies, the odds working against the police must have been forbidding.

Haggis and Hooch were supposed to have made a major nightly withdrawal from the Liverpool branch of the Northern England Savings Bank, NESB. As it seemed, their escape route had accidentally been blocked by a truck, something they could not possibly have foreseen nor reckoned with at that hour. Plus the Sweeney had been at the scene of the crime faster than expected, for once. Either way, they had been nicked.

Neither of them had offered any resistance to their arrest. Nor were they armed – a fact that tended to soften the hearts of any juries and judges. Speaking in favour of immediate honourable release, as it were, must have been the fact that no spoils of the crime were found on them either. How on earth they had managed to have the money evaporate betwixt cup and lip, God alone knew. And even He may have scratched His head.

At some stage during the proceedings, which, as was all too often the case with the Yarmouth Six, would amount strictly to nothing, Harry Colestron, who had been a young inspector then, had started paying the talkative half-Irishman Hooch regular visits in his cell. They would sit there, light a cigarette, sip their tea and talk about this or that, friendly-like. To begin with, the cop had intended to lure Hooch onto thin ice, make him compromise himself. It had not taken him long, however, to acknowledge that such attempts were still-born. Talkative as he may have been, Hooch had a built-in jaw-lock mechanism that would snap shut whenever he smelled a rat from afar.

By then, the young inspector had started taking a real interest in Hooch, as a personality, that is. Tasted blood. His stories about the war years and the time immediately after fascinated him. And so, he kept on chatting with the man, making notes that he would afterwards transform into regular protocols. Not for any legal purposes, of course, but with a view to maybe writing a book about it later, much later, when retirement would not be a far-off chimera, but a very concrete proposition. Those were the texts he had copied and scanned, so that he could let Laura have them shaped into any convenient format.

Laura skidded over the first ten or so pages rather perfunctorily, since they dealt with much of what she had already learned from Lamont. The really interesting part started with that moment in the cave when they had decided to split up and try to muddle through individually.

We were hesitating to accept the Duke's proposal, since it ran counter to everything we had been told by our drill sergeants. But when all was said and done, we had to agree with him. Luke the Duke was the first to split. After all, he was unhurt, familiar with local customs and conditions and generally inventive. If someone was going to make it, it was the Duke. I had hoped he would take me with him, but that he refused offhand. When I say alone, I mean alone, was all he balled at me. He was probably right there, too. A man alone might be able to slip into some rathole or other and lie in hiding for a while. Two's a liability, three's company, as they say. Don't you worry, he added, as he kissed the treasure trove goodbye. Nothing lasts forever, not even wars. This one will soon be over, if I am any judge. The Huns will soon be at the end of their tether, mark my words.

Laura skipped a few pages again.

Alright, but carrying on separately was easier said than done. We were stuck on the smallest permanently inhabited island of the archipelago. So where do you go to escape the Germans, avoid the locals, and try not to stumble over one of your mates? As for myself, I saw the sea as the only possible way out. I was a good swimmer. Maybe not with quite as much stamina as Gooey, but thanks to my Irish roots, endowed with a solid portion of trust in the Lord and His mysterious ways. My gunshot wound and bruises from the contact with the rocks we had landed on hurt like hell and limited my mobility on land. One more reason to focus on the sea. If I could get hold of a beam or other piece of solid wood, I might be able to catch the four o'clock tide to St. Peter Port. Or have the current take me to the French coast, which wasn't that far off to the East. With hindsight, I would probably have been frozen stiff by the time I ever got there, but I saw no other option then, anyway.

And God knows I was lucky. Only a few hours after the others had left the cave one by one, I got my eyes on this trunk drifting close to the coastline. A piece of tree with roots sticking up in the air. Westward-ho, as it seemed. There it was, my ticket to Guernsey. So, I jumped into the water and paddled to the stump. The thing was squidgy like a slab of soap, let me tell you. I had hoped I could sit on it, but no way. Every time I tried to mount it like a bronco, it would roll and I would slide back in the water. And so, after a while, I just clung to the roots for dear life, at the same time hiding from any German sniper who might otherwise have spotted and targeted me. I quickly drifted away from Sark, well aware that I could not last long in the ice-cold water, certainly not all the way to Guernsey.

What can I say? I was lucky one more time in that a favourable little counter-current carried me to that small islet West of Sark, a place called Brecqhou, as I was to learn much later. Seen from where I was floating, it seemed to host no German military emplacements. More precisely, it looked devoid of any population whatsoever. Which was all the more peculiar, as the islet was dominated by a miniature castle of a manor, standing on a hillock, in the middle of nowhere, as if it had drifted here on a high-water spring very much in the same manner as I had.

I couldn't tell why, but, somehow, I sensed this two-storey brick building in Victorian style with its alcoves and fancy arches to be uninhabited for the time being. Nonetheless, I decided that discretion was the better part of valour. I let the tree trunk drift on and swam ashore. I soon found a small cave in which I cuddled up like a bear cub whose mother had been shot while hunting for food. I must have fallen asleep there and then, exhausted and cold as I was. Hours later, when I woke, I looked around for something edible. But the only thing I came across was a piece of rag-tag woollen blanket probably alive with lice. But this was no time to be fastidious. At least something to keep me warm for a little while.

Even though the wind didn't hit me as squarely in the face as it had done on Sark, to call the place cosy would have been an exaggeration. But I seemed reasonably safe, nobody around to spot me or take pot shots at me. Lighting a fire was not on the cards since I had neither matches nor a lighter. And whatever pieces of soaked twigs or branches I would find here were unlikely to yield a spark, irrespective of how long you rubbed them. In view of my generally miserable situation, all of my limbs hurting with every one of my movements, the temptation to sneak into the little castle seemingly empty, soon lost all its initial provisos. I mean, what could possibly happen? Even if it had been none other than Count Dracula's place, I'm sure the two of us would have got along just fine. What with him sleeping during daytime and myself during the nights, we would not have got into each other's way.

And so, I waited till nightfall and observed the area with great attention. There was no light anywhere around the house. I closed in from the rear. The nearer I came, the more unreal the manor seemed to me, especially now, in the dark. If it had suddenly disappeared in the ground or vanished into thin air, I probably would not have been all that surprised. Never before or since have I felt that I was in such an eerie, other-worldly situation.

Yet the castle didn't vanish or shrink back from my sudden cold touch. Arriving at the back door, I shook it carefully at first, then more and more violently. But it wouldn't budge. Hence, I resorted to plan B, smashed in a window pane and let myself in that way.

This is how I penetrated into the manor's dark and silent interior. If somebody did live here, they hadn't noticed my intrusion. My heart racing, I started to examine the ground floor rooms one by one. The air was moist and stuffy, as if the shaggy owner had just left the building. The rooms were mostly empty. What pieces of furniture remained had been hidden under huge linen covers to protect them from dust. Any moment now, I expected one of the covers to be torn aside with a flurry and the irate owner plunge forth. Of course, nothing of the sort happened.

Then, armed with a bit more self-confidence, I walked up the creaking staircase and continued my systematic examination on the first floor. The same thing – empty rooms, ghostly silence and stuffy, humid air. Where the blazes was the kitchen? Must have overlooked it. Or could it be in the basement? Hardly. A kitchen needs to be well ventilated. Now that I was really sure I was alone in the house, I was growing bolder. Even started humming a tune or two, shouted after the lazy bones of butler – imagine the lark if one had answered my stupid call at that very moment.

Then I found the kitchen. A great disappointment. Pots and pans galore and all the shenanigans to cook a meal, but not so much as a piece of hardtack, let alone meat or fish, nothing. That was critical because it meant I couldn't stay here for long, sit the war out, as it were, and chew the linen. Maybe the Duke was right and the German war machine would come to a grinding halt, soon alright, but not soon enough for me not to be starved to death by then. My bones would be rotting away in this Heartbreak Hotel of a manor. On the bright side, the water supply hadn't been cut off. Neither had the electricity. But that was of little avail, since lighting a lamp at night would have been tantamount to shooting a gun to catch the Germans' attention.

I picked a room for myself right next to the kitchen, one of the few that still had beds, freed the mattress from its cover and slipped under the thin linen. It smelled of the freshly deceased Queen Victoria's dead body, but, again, beggars can't be choosers. Besides, I always had been a fan of Queen Vicky's. Thus, from hell's forecourt on Sark, I had performed a rogue's progress to Purgatory's Business Lounge on an island whose name later reminded me of the sound Swedish hunters use to make to attract male elks. I must have fallen asleep in a jiffy. I still know what it was I dreamed: I was having dinner at O'Leary's in the Kensington area. Jacket potatoes, lamb chops, sugar peas and tiny carrots, the lot washed down with a bottle of Chablis.

Laura's eyelids could no longer resist the relentless forces of gravity. This last part of Hooch's memories she could well relate to, even though lamb prepared the Irish way was not exactly her thing. Already deep in Morpheus' arms, she just managed to close her laptop, leaving Hooch to his miniature castle on a Brecqhou teeming with elks.

FIFTH CHAPTER

1. The Left Arm of the Lord

And let the games begin...The ROLA tax audit was on in earnest. A five-predator team from the Hamburg IRS branch office had descended upon the headquarters at the crack of dawn like paratroopers and demanded to be given access to all records of the past four centuries, digital as well as analogue. In order not to make it appear all too obvious that the day of the raid had been leaked by an approachable inside source, all respective EOLA staff involved had been instructed to show themselves duly surprised and to take their time when searching for the requested records. They had already been sorted out weeks ago, of course, but the IRS didn't know that. Suspect, perhaps, but that was all. Under the prevailing circumstances, the Monday morning routine conference with Laura, Heinz Marquardt and all heads of departments had been shortened, accordingly. For the duration of the audit, the ROLA tanker would be sailing at dead ahead. About noon, Laura called home to see whether Ignace was still on the ground or had taken off on his own. Once she had been reassured on that score, she had interrogated Marquardt about the bank loan and learned that, for the time being, there was no news on that front.

At his specific demand, she had given her collaborator of the month, as she used to call him jokingly, a short outline of the convoluted history that surrounded the Yarmouth Six murders and tried to render her impression of Sir Lucas Lamont. Marquardt had taken it all in and promised to keep his eyes peeled and ears clean at all times.

In the afternoon, when the sun hesitatingly started peeping through the Hamburg cloud cover, Laura strolled down to her favourite café on the Alster city lakes. Here, she sat down, ordered her cappuccino and opened her laptop. As she quickly ascertained with a thin smile of relief, Hooch was still where she had last left him, in his castle on the islet of Brecqhou.

In the course of several days, I was attending my gun wound, what with bandage material abounding in the house. My stomach gnarling away from hunger, I would watch the complicated rhythm of the tide from the first floor of the manor – without ever opening the shutters, of course. To try and bring off another stunt like the one that had brought me here would be risky. Guernsey was still far away, too far for swimming or drifting. But the prospect of staying marooned on the islet like a latter-day Robinson Crusoe without food or my man Friday for company didn't carry much appeal either. All the crabs, mussels, cockles and limpets in the world wouldn't be enough for that perspective to gain in attraction. Even though I would have occasion to cook them, at least. Meanwhile, hunger and cold made me hallucinate, I suppose. I kept dreaming I was Ulysses caught in Calypso's comfortable den, where I was kept prisoner by the jealous nymph who resembled Queen Vicky more and more by the day. I should have been so lucky! If I didn't somehow manage to get off the islet, the old or new owner of the miniature castle would come across my skeleton in a couple of years' time and get a headache trying to piece the odds and ends of my unlikely story together. Well, Fate herself intervened to free me from my invisible chains. It must have been at dusk of the fourth day, I think, when something rather bulky was washed up on the little piece of beach where I, too, had landed. From my observation post on the first floor, it looked like a human body. I waited till nightfall and then sneaked down to the beach. It was a human body, alright, though there didn't seem to be much left of him. In the dark, I first mistook him for a British Naval officer killed in action, nibbled at, found largely indigestible and then thrown up here by the cruel sea. Close, but no cigar, is all I say. When I looked him over as best I could with no light other than that of a measly half-moon, I realized I was dealing with a naval reverend occupying the rank of a lieutenant. As gnawed at and bloated as he was, he must have floated in the water long enough for a number of fish to have tried his more appetizing parts. His eyeballs had gone, probably eaten by seagulls. From his entrails, an eel long as a common viper emerged. The man's right arm had been ripped off, presumably by some shrapnel. The rest of the man had been burnt badly. He must have been dead when falling into the water. Impossible to tell on what ship he had served when the Almighty's impervious call had suddenly rung in his burnt ears. But since only bigger units would afford the luxury of a padre of their own, it had to be something between a frigate and a battleship. Judging from the sorry state of his carcass, whatever man-of-war he had served on could safely be assumed to lie at the bottom of the Channel.

Suddenly, I had an idea. I undressed the body, peeling off large flakes of his skin burnt by fire and softened by sea water in the process. Disgusting stuff, I know, but if and when you're desperate enough…Anyway, I then slipped into his torn and tattered uniform, and may the Good Lord be praised. At least, this servant of the Lord had his name stitched into his shirt collar. According to this, I was about to slip into the Reverend Bert Calhoun's skin, may he rest in peace. Had his uniform still been intact, it would have been a size or two too large for me. He must have been a rather tallish, strong man, apt to carry more than a bible and crucifix. But now that his bloody mangled rags were clinging to me, they fitted me fine. A more attentive observer might have wondered why my jacket lacked a sleeve, while my right arm was still intact, or why the whole uniform was much gorier than the relatively small wounds I had sustained during our raid seemed to justify. I obviously had to dream up some sufficiently dramatic story of trying to keep my seriously wounded crew mates alive in the water, covering myself with their blood while a shark was taking off my sleeve. Sharks were not a permanent fixture in the Channel, it is true, but, being by their nature inquisitive creatures, one or two of them had been spotted by fishermen. Hopefully, I would rouse more pity than suspicion.

Laura was slurping her cappuccino, shuddering. To slip into the clothes of a mutilated corpse would take a degree of callousness few men would possess. Or desperation. All things considered, this man Hooch must have been a rather shrewd and audacious operator.

Paradoxically, a corpse would be my ticket back into the realm of the living. It fleetingly reminded me of the Count of Monte Cristo, even though he only slipped into the dead man's shroud, not skin. All I had to do now was make myself noticed by someone on Sark. This I promptly did in the morning, when I walked up and down the islet like a heron with ruffled feathers. It didn't take long for a German T-boat to show up. It must have come from St. Peter Port, since it could hardly have fitted into Creux Harbour. I only just had time enough to hide the half-naked reverend behind some rocks. His skeleton may still be lying there, for all I know. Somebody ought to inform his family, his next of kin, I mean. If he had any.

The Germans zoomed in with the usual panache, producing a bow wave like a huge surfboard. Two of the crew came wading ashore, holding their rifles over their heads. I immediately held up my crucifix as if putting the Devil in his place and gave them my blessings the way I had seen the Verne reverend do it, calling the Germans my sons, which clearly made them feel awkward but mildly respectful. They took me to the boat, helped me aboard and rushed back towards Guernsey. Naval staff of any description or nationality have a sense of belonging to what you might call the International Fellowship of the Sea. A certain feeling of brotherhood in the face of the Beast, if you see what I mean. But in 1943, even that was at an all-time low with the Germans. The lieutenant in charge of the T-boat immediately started drilling me. I replied whenever I could and took to re-blessing them all round whenever I couldn't. The captain was unwittingly providing me with the cues. Had I served on the Charybdis, he asked me. At first, I thought he had somehow got wind of my Calypso dream scenarios and was pulling my leg by resorting to Homer. But how could he possibly have known? I replied with a heart-rending sob he apparently took for a yes.

Later, much later, I learned that, some days before that, HMS Charybdis had been sunk in the Channel some miles north of the islands by German T-class boats such as this one. Operation Tunnel had seen no light at the end, it would seem. Not unlike the victims of the Battle of Jutland, during the First World War, who had been washed ashore on the west Swedish skerries, the corpses of, all in all, twenty-one officers and crew of the British light cruiser had ended up on the beaches, by then heavily mined, of both Guernsey and Jersey. The reverend Bert Calhoun, in whose skin and uniform I now stuck, would have been number twenty-two. Seen from that angle, we were dealing with a plain miracle. Who dares maintain the Almighty isn't looking after His own, when a reverend such as Bert managed to survive on the wings of the tide? I just hoped no next of Bertie's kin would get their eyes on a newspaper picture of the reverend and wonder what had happened to the man to make him look so entirely different from the person he had been. But that was unlikely on two grounds. First, miracles and acts of heroism were almost commonplace in those days. Had to be, you see, to keep morale up. And second, local papers would only reach the British Isles by dint of the tidal currents, with great delay and in a sorry state, too, so they would not even be fit to wrap dead fish in them.

Laura leaned back in her chair and let the sunrays caress her cheeks. Yes, she remembered that story of the Battle of Jutland. One victim on the German side had been a certain Johann Wilhelm Kinau, who had given himself the bizarre pen name of Gorch Fock. To bury his body as well as those of his mates, all washed up on the grey and red granite rocks of the Swedish West coast skerries near Gothenburg, must have been a tough job alright. A good and fitting thing dynamite had been a Swedish invention. Some years later, Gorch had been exhumed and his mortal shell been taken back to the green grass of home.

Understandably, all Guernsey was up in arms as we cruised into St. Peter Port. The Germans, it must be noted, had buried the twenty-one victims of the Charybdis with all military honours, no small matter in the somewhat heated atmosphere of 1943. On the contrary. Berlin had finally had enough of the pussy, soft-footed military leadership on the Channel Islands and had sent in bullies from the SS Totenkopf Division. Those men weren't kidding. The locals, for their part, had transformed the burial ceremony into a silent but nevertheless impressive mass-demonstration of unity and solidarity. Imagine me barging into this unholy mess like a nose-diving bird dog crash-landing among a flock of floating ducks. Of course, everyone wanted to catch a glimpse of this one-sleeve Johnny-come-lately, unlikely survivor and reverend rolled into one. Given more time, the locals would have brought me photos of their defunct relatives and asked me to bless them. The Germans, though, weren't all that happy. Probably feared my magic rescue might be given more symbolic meaning than appropriate. If only they had an inkling of how right they were on that score. For them, the war was going from bad to worse. The general food situation on the islands was degenerating by the hour. And whenever soldiers or officers went on leave to come up for air in their respective homey environment, they invariably found those places were no longer there, but had been replaced by heaps of scorched rubble and skeleton façades by Allied bombers. The Americans would fly during daytime, so as to make sure they hit the industrial or communication centres marked on their maps. Harris' Lancasters would be satisfied with following at night, because laying out bomb carpets required no precision to speak of.

The question of why carry on fighting in the face of inevitable defeat and humiliation must have pressed itself on more and more Germans, both military and civilian. On the bright side, many have felt it was better to starve to death on the islands than to freeze to death somewhere along the Eastern front lines.

The long and the short of it: even though I should have been treated as a POW, the Huns sent me to Alderney. There, I was stuck into a labour camp the Germans had baptized Borkum, after a Frisian North Sea island that may or may not have presented topographical similarities with Alderney. For an uninformed observer, the name probably carried a whiff of sun, fun, and the Strength-through-Joy movement, as indeed it was supposed to. That it was all but this, the name Alderney as such amply guaranteed. Strictly speaking, I didn't know the island at all, but our Yarmouth camp drill NCO's ominous stories about it were enough to turn my stomach when I heard its name pronounced.

Laura looked at the lake, whose surface was just rippled by a squall. The sky was getting dark. The sun kept staring down at the town as if verifying exactly how it had presented itself when he had last shone on it. Laura ordered another cup of coffee and a mineral water. Listening or reading, she had noticed on other occasions, already, made her almost as thirsty as talking.

Situated at the Northern end of the archipelago, Alderney is closer to the French mainland than to any of its neighbouring islands, nominally belonging to the same archipelago. Small, bordering on the bald, it doesn't really lend itself to agriculture but, when it comes to making a living for the inhabitants, looks out at the sea. It wasn't for nothing, I suspect, that next to nobody on Alderney seems to have hesitated when offered the chance to leave the island behind during the evacuation operations. Whatever was waiting for them on the other side of the Channel could hardly be worse that what they had left. Thus, of the island's five hundred or so people only an insignificant eighteen had remained on Alderney. All members of one and the same family, called Pope, believe it or not. Eighteen next of kin, ring a bell? No offence, but incest was the curse of all small islands and other isolated spots round the globe. The smaller the island, the closer the blood relationship. I suspect there is, or was, a correlation there somewhere. Has anyone bothered to check it out? Of course not. Whatever. While the Pope family were probably busy clearing their neighbours' abandoned houses of anything that represented any value at all, the Germans did what Germans are best at, building camps. And they weren't joking either. As small as the island is, with its three by one and a half, the Germans nevertheless managed to place no less than four camps here. You've got to hand it to them, when they mean business, they put their heart into it. All four of them were outposts of Hamburg-Neuengamme concentration camp, I was told later. One of them was called Borkum, like I said. The other three had also been baptized after German North Sea islands: Norderney, Helgoland, and Sylt. Even though very much alike in structure and lay-out, there were remarkable differences between them as for the composition of the inmates.

Borkum was a normal work camp housing hundreds of mostly volunteer nationals of West European states that had been occupied by the Germans, such as Holland, Belgium, France and the like. Helgoland was used to accommodate mostly East European Untermenschen or sub-human species, as the Nazis insisted on calling them, brought here very much against their will. Norderney was almost exclusively reserved for the Jews, mostly East European ones. Which led to the paradoxical situation of local Jews being deported to Continental camps and Continental Jews being ferried to Alderney in droves.

Finally, there was Sylt. This was the one to be avoided. It was a camp erected for the express purpose of punishment and extermination. Anyone who happened to make themselves unpopular in any of the other camps would be transferred here. And, in most cases, never be seen or heard of again. This entire hassle was deemed necessary by the Nazis to turn Alderney into an impregnable fortress. Maybe Hitler should have stopped and asked himself at some stage towards the end of the war what earthly purpose a fortress served that no-one had the intention of taking. In modern commercial terms you might say the Nazis had at great pains put out a product for which there was absolutely no demand in the market.

Laura laughed. She had to think of Idéfix, the dog of Gaul clan-chief Asterix. Why was it no-one had ever come up with a Hitler Comic? The man with his stupid little moustache seemed absolutely ideal for something like that. There was always Art Spiegelman's Maus, of course. But that was a gloomy concentration-camp comic clearly emulating, in a frightfully shocking way, Walt Disney's Mickey. No, something in a lighter vein, a Hitler with Idéfix instead of Blondie at his feet, quarrelling about some item of household expense with Eva Braun. The research alone could be a killer, though.

Hard to imagine, for those who hadn't seen it with their own eyes, what quantities of dynamite, steel, and cement the men of

Organisation Todt had to take to the islands at Hitler's behest. In the build-up to D-day, Alderney and the other Channel Islands must under no circumstances fall to the enemy. Those ill-fated clods of would-be British soil in the Channel approaches had to be defended against the expected onslaught of the British troops. An onslaught that never was to be. Had he bothered to take a look at the history books every now and then, Hitler would no doubt have learned that the Channel Islands had already once been ignored by a major campaign event. When the ships of the mighty Spanish Armada, that is, had been on their way to the coasts of Britain, in 1588, they had veered to starboard at about the Casquets, leaving Alderney untouched, even though bonfires from that island are said to have announced the Armada's impending arrival to members of the British Admiralty such as Drake, Frobisher and others. Or so I was told in the Borkum camp by a Belgian who we came to call the Professor, 'cause he seemed to know just about everything. Peculiar man. Wasn't really fit for the hard toil on bunkers, tunnels, and casemates and killed himself some time later by deliberately stepping on a mine. Most men thought it to have been an accident, but I saw him do it, and I'm sure he did it deliberately, with a smile on his face.

That manifest lack of interest in the Channel Islands clearly documented in their annals wasn't going to fool Hitler, or so he thought. Alderney as the advance post had to be transformed into a fortress, end of story. And I had been lucky enough to become part of this aspect of the German war effort. Well, then again, better working my guts out on Alderney than being executed on Sark or starving to death on Brecqhou. Or so I thought. The following months taught me a lesson I shall never forget, one that would make me wish, on some occasions, I had stayed in my castle and quietly hanged myself."

2. The Overcoat

"Hello Ignace, how are you doing? Have you been able to squeeze anything out of the list? Any leads at all?"

The boy sounded in unexpectedly good humour. That looked promising enough then, Laura thought.

"I...I don't know, can't see a clear pattern yet."

"How so, dear Watson?"

"Well, we started from the assumption that either the killer or his principal has personal motives for the murders. Motives rooted in past of the Yarmouth Six, did we not?"

"I believe we did, yes."

"Well, if the accidents that killed off the entire gang with the exception of Lamont weren't really acts of God, as they say, the descendants of all five would have reason enough to go for the instigator's jugular. And that could be Sir Lucas. Why then are we dealing with one killer only? And why has that single killer become active only now? We seem to be overlooking something all the time. Something important that keeps eluding us, don't you think?"

"Either that or our knowledge is simply too sketchy as yet. Something I came to think of is whether we might perhaps be dealing with a Laughing Policeman."

"A what? What are you talking about?"

"Just an idea. When I was your age or thereabouts, I loved to read the whodunits by the Swedish couple Maj Sjöwall und Per Wahlöö. As far as I can see, they are the founders of what later became a popular branch of its own, the Swedish crime novel. Sjöwall and Wahlöö's books all take place in their home town of Stockholm, their protagonist being inspector Martin Beck. What they really are is social criticism in the guise of detective novels. They make damn good reading and carry the smell of the late sixties – a time of departure, decampment, discovery of new horizons, promiscuity, the films of Ingmar Bergmann and all that jazz. Anyway, even the titles of their novels were well worth the price of the paperbacks. In the Laughing Policeman, a seemingly crazy man shoots a dozen passengers in a bus. Just like that, indiscriminately. In actual fact, he was after only one of the passengers but shot twelve of them anyway to dissimulate both the true target and his motives which would otherwise have led the police straight to him in no time at all."

"I understand. Yes, sounds a bit laboured perhaps, but why not? But I don't think it applies to our boxer. No, he seems to kill systematically, and means it every time. Why? Because he feels safe. His motive rests entirely in the dark and as long as that's the case, he knows he has nothing to fear."

"Well, in that case you may be right, and we're failing to see the forest for the trees."

"That's got to be it. The solution is not on the list. If it were, Lamont would probably have found it long time ago. It's got to have something to do with what the list is not telling us. Are you sure, by the way, that Lamont doesn't know you had access to his list?"

"You…you think he passed the list on to me deliberately? That's ridiculous. How was he to know I would get up in the wee hours to pay him a visit in the nude?"

"I beg your pardon?

"Well, he was in the nude, not me, of course."

"You scared me there, for a moment. But no, that's not what I mean. The somnambulant part was happenchance, naturally. His butler must have told him about the list, though. The fact that he pretended not to be in the know when you had breakfast with him in the morning seems to indicate that he had thought about it and found it expedient for you to keep the list."

"Why?"

"For several reasons. I think we may assume he has read the list over and over again many times, finally giving up on it. When you came along and nicked it, he may have thought, yeah, why not let her have a shot at it. Maybe she'll see something I didn't."

"In that case, he could have just handed me the list."

"That would have been a little ostentatious. Maybe, he just wants the list to keep you occupied largely in vain, waste your time and distract you from the true motives he may vaguely suspect, I don't know."

Laura wasn't convinced. She had hardly hung up on Ignace when her mobile rang again.

"Hello Chief Superintendent. What's it this time? More copies?"

Harry Colestron let out a deep sigh.

"Wish 'twere, Laura, wish 'twere. No, we have yet another murder case on our hands, well, not I, the colleagues, actually. This time, it occurred right at your front door, so to speak, on the island of Helgoland. The German police contacted the Yard about the body of a man carrying a British passport. His corpse was floating at the foot of one of those giant pillar-like red rocks that remain of the island…"

"…thanks to British bombing exercises, yes. Funny, I haven't yet heard anything about it on the news. But people do fall off those cliffs every now and again…"

"I'm sure they do. Others jump. But few shoot themselves a bullet in the head before jumping or falling, I guess."

"I see. Shot at close range?"

"Point blank, this time."

Laura chewed on it for a moment. It sounded very much like the Boxer. But why pick Helgoland? Was he trying to convey a message? If so, for whom?

"What's the victim's relationship with…you know?"

"A certain Jamie Brenson, a nephew of Lamont's. I thought I might as well let you know so you're abreast with what's going on."

"I appreciate it, Chief, even though I would be lying if I said it makes things that much clearer. On the contrary, it's all getting more and more blurred, the deeper you penetrate."

"That's normal. The moment will come when it falls into place, trust me."

Laura thanked the CS once more and hung up. Helgoland? Strange coincidence. Only hours after she had read about the Alderney camp of that name. Was somebody telling her to leave off, stop digging in other people's past? Possible, but unlikely. Most of the spectres we see in the woods bear the contours we give them. Better stick to what evidence there was. She groped for her laptop and started looking for the text that concerned Haggis, the mountaineering Scot. His motivation for spinning his yarn was different from that of Hooch. Haggis had been interrogated about, among other things, the nature of his relationship to a certain Frenchman by the name of Gaston Samuelsson, who the French police suspected of dealing in goods from the Yarmouth Six. Apparently, there were letters suggesting Haggis and this Gaston had been close, at one stage. So we were, Haggis had replied and had told the Chief the amazing story of his escape from Sark and how he had made Gaston's acquaintance. Maybe his version of things would shed new light on the Yarmouth Six and yield the decisive clue the list so stubbornly kept to itself.

Again, she had to do some considerable forward scrolling till she got to the part where it was beginning to be interesting.

After we had decided to each go our own ways, I didn't wait long but followed right in the Duke's wake, so to speak. Not without first having hugged Hooch, Joe, Lily, and Brain for what might have been the last time, for all I knew then. Then, I clambered out of the cave. My objective and only hope was Creux Harbour. Sure, it was well guarded and even if, and that was a huge if, I managed to give the Germans the slip, I had no idea what awaited me in that little font of a harbour, if anything. But since I could neither fly nor swim for any considerable duration, I saw no other way. Creux Harbour is situated on the East coast of the northern, bigger part of Sark. Beyond the Coupée, in other words. The sky was clouded, that was good. I sneaked along the coast, trying to avoid even the faintest of sounds. When I reached the Coupée, I hid and waited to see whether the coast would remain as clear as it seemed right now.

A good thing I had not just carried on regardless. Two stout Germans appeared as it were out of nowhere and started pacing up and down, their guns slung over their shoulders. Their marching back and forth had something absolutely unnervingly monotonous. The only way for me to clear them was to try and cross the Coupée by climbing along the rock face hand over hand, without any rope to secure my fall should I slip or lose my grip. Mind-boggling stuff, even for a trained mountaineer such as myself, let me tell you. The moment I felt it was dark enough, I slid over the edge like a snake and groped for the first best foothold. Normally, free climbing is not necessarily my thing. I always considered those blokes show-offs and braggarts. A human being is no gecko. Try and free-climb Everest, dummies, is what I used to say. And now here I was doing it myself. Well, it wasn't exactly Everest alright, but a tough proposition, nevertheless. Plus, I had been shot in the shoulder. At each and every one of my movements, tiny as they were, pangs of pain would flash through my body as if someone had touched me with a live wire. But I soon learned to use the pain to my own profit. I kept telling myself it would keep me on edge, get me through this, eventually. Once I had found a reasonable foothold, I started moving sideways like one of those famous chamois goats on the Cingino dam in the Piemonte area of Italy. Only, they have a cleft hoof that enables them to walk straight and I don't think they have heard of fear of heights either. I had to proceed sideways, like in a chess castling manoeuvre.

If you think that was a feat, wait for it. There's more to come. When I was about half way across, I heard one of the guards approach the ledge. He had to take a leak – fortunately not more – and did so peeing right over the ledge, straight onto me. Unwittingly, of course. What was I to do but wait and take it on my stride. He must have had a bladder the size of a cow's udder, I swear. Maybe he was a diabetic. They have to drink all the time and, hence, pee all the time as well. Discover me he would not, of that I was sure. Few people have the nerve to come that close to a sheer drop like that. A little squall, and you're a goner.

It must have taken the greater part of an hour till I reached the other side and could climb up to the level of the path.

At the same time, a fog bank came drifting in from the East. The lukewarm offshore breeze from Cotentin made contact with the surface of the cold Channel waters and, bingo, we were in the fog before we could say Jack Robinson. I cursed my luck. Had the fog descended a couple of hours earlier, I could have passed the two German guards no problem at all. Might even have killed them and taken their guns. But I didn't know when the next shift was due, so that could have become awkward.

Laura shuddered again. The cold-bloodedness with which this man Haggis had conquered the vertical rock deserved respect. Whoever had selected guys like him or Hooch for the Sea Leopard job knew his business. Laura would have hired him as a staff manager for ROLA no questions asked.

On my way to the harbour, I almost stumbled into a German machine gun nest. But the time I had spent at sea and later in the cave had sharpened my olfactory senses to a degree that even the stink of urine on my clothes couldn't quite neutralize. Sounds maybe improbable, but is a fact, nevertheless. A few hours at sea will make you perceive typical land scents with greater acuity. Thus, when I suddenly caught a whiff of cigarette smoke mixing with the smell of the moist grass all around, I knew there had to be Germans lying in hiding somewhere. Fortunately, the breeze had brought their scent to me and not vice versa. Tobacco had become a rare commodity on the islands by 1943. So rare, it had risen to the status of legal tender on the black market. The locals had long since taken to smoking all sorts of dried and ground leaves and herbs. As long as there were bibles around, they had used the wafer-thin paper to roll their tobacco-substitutes, thus inhaling the word of the Lord. Later, they would use anything that promised to turn into smoke. Thus, if someone still smoked tobacco, it had to be Germans. If they didn't smoke it themselves, they used it to barter food from the secret stashes that farmers will always keep somewhere. The peasants would then either barter tools and stuff to replace their worn-down farm implements or try and buy favours from this or that administrative outpost known for its leaning to corruption.

Hence, I was on my guard. I lay down flat on the sands of the shore that fortunately boasted a few dune-like humps. The fog had lifted again, and yet it took me a while to spot the burning cigarette in the dark. That, incidentally, was proof of poor professionalism. A good soldier always covers the glow of his cigarette with whatever comes to hand, precisely not to give away his position. Then, one of the two Germans squatting next to the machine gun rose from the ground and walked towards me. My heart missed a few beats. How could he have discovered me? And, if he had, why didn't he just shoot me? But he positioned himself a yard or two away from me, flicked the glowing fag end towards me and unbuttoned the fly of his pants. I already feared for the worst, but he, too, only had to pee. Straight on me, of course, the second time round. Had to be my special day. I took it as a lucky charm, anyway, and calmly waited till he finished the procedure with a thundering fart of the garlic species. While he was returning to his mate, I crawled backwards flat-bellied in the general direction of the sea. It smelled of herring and seaweed. Strange, I thought, as if I had had no other things to worry about. Back on the Hebrides, the Atlantic Ocean smells of salt in winter and of seaweed in summer, but never of herring. The ports such as Stornoway yes, of course, especially during the herring season, but not the sea.

When I suddenly hit my foot against something solid, fright made my body twitch as if I had received an electric shock. I thought I had touched a mine. Which was illogical, because a mine wouldn't have stuck out for everyone to notice and if it had, it would have blown me to bits already. But you don't think logically in moments like that. In fact, you don't think at all. Very slowly and cautiously I tried to turn round without moving my foot or even twitching my big toe. Lying right behind me was not a mine, but a tiny kind of life raft. The sort Lancaster bombers sometimes carried in case they had to crash-land on water or bail out over the sea. The thing was in a pathetic state. The tarpaulin rooftop had been ripped off and half the air in the chambers had gone. It must have been floating round the islands for some time already, with or without a dead pilot in it, to begin with. Nobody in his right mind would risk a walk across the minefield beach to pick up this wreck of a raft. For me, however, it might serve a purpose, provided it carried my weight. I didn't think for long, not with the first cracks of dawn hard on my heels. Ever so carefully, I pushed the raft back into the mild surf with my feet, never taking my eyes off the spot where I knew the German MG nest to be. Then, I rolled myself with my stomach first onto the raft, hugging it like a dear old friend. Lo and behold, it did carry my weight. Not without groaning, but, eventually, resigning to the sheer force of my will, I imagine. Perhaps it didn't have a hole but a slowly leaking valve, for instance. In which case it might still be good enough to take me off Sark and towards either Guernsey or the Continent. A paddle would have come in handy, I suppose, but for the time being, I couldn't care less. All I had to do was put my chips on the right tidal current. Slowly turning about itself like an Arctic ice floe, the raft with its stowaway drifted further and further away from the Sark coast. Fortunately, the raft's rubber skin hadn't been painted signal red or a rape yellow, like the modern ones, but was a military olive. That must have been the result of a compromise: for search and rescue operations such a colour would clearly be detrimental. But then, it would remain invisible for the enemy, too, that way.

I could hardly believe my luck. What were the odds of my hitting upon this sorry excuse for a raft at the very moment my life depended on it? One to a billion? It didn't contain any bottles with drinking water, nor any foodstuffs that would keep a ditched pilot alive for a week or so out there in the middle of the Atlantic or Pacific Oceans. But I wasn't heading from, say, Dakar to Recife either, but only from Sark to bloody Guernsey. Under the circumstances.

Time and time again, the waves would wash over the raft and threaten to rip it out of my hands. So I had to be on my guard and not fall asleep. After a number of vain attempts, I managed to tie myself to the thing with my belt. Better lose my pants than the raft. That helped. I don't think it could really have gone down, but I had to preserve a minimum of manoeuvrability. The general direction was okay, as far as I could judge. The sea remained calm. As long as no coastal battery picked me up and decided to use the raft for a bit of target practice, nothing much could happen to me. Unless I was to pass Guernsey by altogether, and head for the Casquets. Out there, far from civilisation and within easy reach of German rifles, I would hate to end my life.

Laura leaned back in her chair. Thus, as the saying goes, one man's loss was another man's gain. Modern life rafts like the one on Yellow Dancer used to have a tent-like roof to protect castaways from the seething sun and etching froth. Also, they carry drinking water, astronaut food, and all sorts of useful accessories such as a knife, angling hook, flares and rockets as well as signalling mirrors. So they were relatively liveable vessels, as long as you could harness in the inevitable bouts of sea-sickness these things would cause by their uncontrollable bobbing up and down, with the occasional roll-over thrown in.

The crossing soon became more and more eerie. Not being able to sit, lie or let alone stand, I had to change position every quarter of an hour or so. Lying on my stomach, I threatened to drown the moment I fell asleep from sheer exhaustion. Lying on my back, I risked getting blinded by the sun and hacked at by the seagulls. Each and every self-respecting wave would sweep right over me and give me the momentary feeling of drowning. Besides, I was slowly freezing to death, shivering and quivering all over most of the time. That way, I drifted round the north cape of Sark towards Guernsey. When daylight broke, I must have been somewhere between the two islands. It was to become a sunshiny day, like in the song. I must have started hallucinating from thirst. But I forced myself to hold on, using my pain as a stimulant, like I had done back at the Coupée. I even took to hitting my gunshot wound with my fist to keep me from drowsing off into the other world. The treasure kept me going, as well. I was going to survive, no matter what, and go get that knapsack.

Laura bit her lips at the thought that, during her passage from St. Malo to St. Helier, she had complained the coffee had been too thin for her taste. It's all a matter of perspective.

Soon it grew cold and dark again. My swollen fingers felt more and more spongy. Maybe I was being transmogrified into a creature of the deep? For the first time since my departure from Sark, it started raining. I lay on my back, trying to catch every drop, as we had done in the cave. What with the rain, I could be reasonably sure there would be no gales. Rain kind of beats down the wind.

At long last, I, nevertheless, must have dozed off. Because, at the next crack of dawn, I was woken up by a grinding sound. My feet felt firm ground again. The next thing I knew was that the raft literally propelled me, spat me out into the Guernsey surf. A few paddling motions took me ashore, where I lay on the beach like a stranded whale. Exposed to the cold, the human body, in its desperate effort to preserve its core temperature, focusses exclusively on vital organs such as heart, liver, kidneys, lungs, and leaves the extremities to fend for themselves. Hence, my legs and arms were absolutely numb and unfit for use. It must have lasted an hour for me to be able to get up and toddle on across the beach. Nobody appeared to have noticed me as yet. And once again, I managed to dodge the mines with the unwitting assuredness of a somnambulist. The Lord Almighty must have plans for me was all I thought. Why else would He have bailed me out so often during the past two days? Curfewed St. Peter Port to my right looked dark and gloomy like a latter-day necropolis. As long as I kept roaming the place dressed in my uniform, or what was left of it, I had to avoid any contact with both the Germans and the locals. The latter might denounce me, the former would shoot me.

And so, I hastened on, picking the odd cart track and farm lane past long flights of high brick walls overgrown with ivy. There were plenty of hothouses with tomatoes still a poisonous green. I dimly remembered unripe tomatoes to be no good for the human organism but was so hungry I just couldn't resist and gobbled down a handful of them. Tomatoes need a lot of water, that much I knew. Hence, there had to be taps and tubes around. And there was. I guess I downed half a bucket in one go. Soon I felt my stomach swelling like a balloon. Green tomatoes and water make good bedfellows on a patch, but less so in a man's tummy.

I barely managed to free myself of my pants, whose legs had apparently decided to stick to my skin forever, when I already felt the evil-smelling shits running down my thighs.

I had to wash and get some new clothes somehow, somewhere, quick. I looked around, but there weren't many houses to choose from. Here and there, a small lamp or candles were lit and showed me the place was inhabited. At last, I chose a small, isolated dark brick house that looked dark and deserted. Cautiously, I approached. There was no light or sound from inside. The front door stood wide open. That should perhaps have roused my suspicion. Then again, many families had left the islands without bothering to lock the door after them. I entered the place. The first thing that hit me was the sickeningly sweet stench of decay. If you ever get a whiff of that, you're unlikely to forget it. Almost like the smell of shit I myself brought to the party. I fought my nausea and searched the house's interior for anything of practical use to me. In the bedroom, I hit upon the source of that stench of death. A man and a woman, roughly the same age, probably the couple who owned the house, were lying peacefully on the bed. Had they not been fully dressed, both of them, you would have thought they were asleep. I didn't lose any time with a closer examination. Much less so as I spotted the first maggots at play already. There was no need for forensics. All too obviously, the husband, who still held the gun in his hand, had first shot his wife and then himself. The woman held on to a framed photograph that showed a group of people, probably the couple and their children and grandchildren.

That was the second warning I disregarded. Like I say, at such moments, you don't think straight. I washed as best I could and helped myself to the moth-eaten rags the two of them had still hanging in their clothes cupboard. Because of the darkness, I had to grope for the clothes as it were blindfolded. Finally, I felt a very thin kind of overcoat, more like smocks, which I hastily slipped into.

As far as food goes, there was but one measly slice of mouldy bread which I chewed on while walking towards the town. It was still early and barely dawn, but there were amazingly many people about, I thought. Mostly girls and women. I was soon enough to find out why. Long queues were building up in front of almost all shops that still bothered to open. What exactly they were selling, nobody seemed to care, since anything is of use to him or her who has nothing. It reminded me of the jokes Russians used to crack during the times of the socialist economy: No, I'm sorry, but here we have no bread. No meat would be across the road. At any rate, the queues round the harbour area were so long already that by the time those further back would reach the shop's threshold, whatever it was that had been for sale would then surely be sold out. Not least the Germans would take care of that. Wherever they appeared, they would shove everybody aside and march right into the shop. I believe that made them more unpopular with the locals than the deportation measures. People for whom queuing up with patience and discipline at bus or tram stops or in front of a shop, for that matter, serves as a model case of civilisation and a symbol of solidarity cannot but despise such boorish behaviour.

Hogwash, all of it, if you ask me. No other nation, with the possible exception of the Indians, has developed such a keen sense of intricate class differentiation as the English have.

Class consciousness is in our DNA, I'm sure. Two Englishmen accidentally encountering one another somewhere in a train compartment, say, will almost automatically try to place each other in the respective class slot. There's a whole panoply of criteria for them to go by, the most important one being language, of course.

But at the bus station we suddenly turn into a classless society? A big myth if ever there was one. Try pull the other one, is what I say, it's got bells on it.

Anyway. When I stopped, now in broad daylight, to catch a glimpse of the goods in one of the shops that seemed particularly much solicited, I saw a little girl pull her mother's coat sleeve, at the same time pointing at me with her index finger. Look, mom, she cried, the man's wearing his coat inside out.

Only now did I realize the girl was right. Understandably, I had been so much in a hurry to leave the house of death that I had not noticed I had put on the coat or smocks the wrong way.

And since its material was so thin and threadbare, I had not become aware of it on my way here either. Had I taken the trouble to button it up, it would of course have struck me. But we're all slaves of our habits. I once knew a bloke who couldn't be bothered to tie his boot laces, most of the time. As for myself, I hardly ever button my coats. Buying them a number or two too small, as a rule, buttoning them makes me feel like I'm wearing a strait jacket.

Not to stand out like a sore thumb any longer, I hastily took the coat off and put it on again the right way. To be on the safe side, I looked myself over in the shop's dusty, half-blind window. On the face of it, I quite liked what I saw: a handsome young lad, a little emaciated and dishevelled, yes, but not without a certain panache. The only really embarrassing feature that kind of blotted the overall favourable impression was the yellow Star of David with the red J in it perfunctorily sewn onto the coat's left lapel.

3. Gaston de Lyon

Laura pushed her laptop aside for a moment. Then she pushed her hands against both temples and started rubbing them in a circular movement. How many of those incredible stories had the war given rise to? Who would ever be able to relate them all? Somehow, she felt cheap, rummaging like that in other people's past. What she was looking at here were the quintessential confessions of a man who might have passed himself off as a true war hero but preferred, or so it seemed, to stick to the truth and nothing but the truth, sordid as it might seem, at times. That attitude deserved her respect.

I'll spare you the gory details of my arrest and the ensuing interrogations by the Gestapo, who had kept a low profile initially, but, over the years, had come more and more to the fore and, in close co-operation with the SS, was clearly in charge of things on the islands by 1943.

I could of course have come clean and told them I wasn't a Jew but a British soldier. Which, in view of my not being circumcised, they would probably have believed. But that would only have pushed me from the frying pan into the fire by leading to my immediate execution. Jews weren't executed but deported to the camps on the Continent, where they would either be gassed or killed by work, the slow way. Not a tempting prospect either, but one which bought me a little time I might be able to use to my profit.

The question of my circumcision seemed to nonplus them for a while. But I explained it away by telling them my parents had read the writing on the wall at an early stage and decided I should not be circumcised so that, if I ever fell into the hands of professed Jew-haters, I might all the more easily escape. In the end, what prevailed was their disbelief in someone who wasn't a Jew deliberately pretending to be one. That seemed so desperately dim-witted that they finally started believing me. The Nazis' motto anyway being better kill an Aryan too many by mistake than let a single Jew escape.

Hence, I convinced them that I was none other than the unfortunate David Goldberg, who had pre-empted his deportation and assassination in the gas chambers by committing suicide.

Strictly speaking, there was no need to take local Jews to Auschwitz or similar destinations. After all, I had heard of camps on Alderney that would probably have served the same purpose. But bureaucracy yields bizarre results, at the best of times, which those weren't. For the Germans, even Armageddon couldn't go down without the appropriate forms having been filled in and the necessary stamps and signatures applied.

To begin with, I was taken to Braye Harbour, Alderney. There, I was ferried, together with several hundred forced labourers, who seemed to fare even worse than I did, onto one of the floating coffins that still occasionally sailed to Cherbourg. Since, during their short voyage to the Cotentin peninsula, those ships were accompanied by men-of-war, the risk of getting caught out by British submarines or bomber planes, as soon as they left harbour, was ever present. So, they would preferably sail at night, and, to the extent possible, in heavy weather. This was the case with the motor vessel Franka, which took us aboard at Braye Harbour. Together with another cargo ship of very much the same build and desolate state of repair, she slipped her moorings at nightfall. There was a jolly gale blowing from the northeast that had already sent thundering spray and froth over the Braye Harbour breakwater all day. What followed was perfectly predictable. We had barely cleared the harbour entrance when both ships were pushed onto the coastal rocks by the furious sea. Both hulls sprang substantial leaks immediately, so that tons of water rushed into the hold and lower decks. Fortunately, we couldn't sink, because both ships sat wedged in on the rocks, only a stone's throw from the island coast. We were down in the hold already half filled with water and thought the Germans would help us get out. Well, they couldn't be bothered. Maybe the idea was to have a maximum of us perish, so there would be fewer mouths to feed.

Not that we got much to eat, to begin with. But the conditions down there were atrocious and quickly got worse. At high water, the sea would tickle our navels, at low water, our ankles. When the gale abated after a few days, the Germans coolly inspected the damage done and decided the carcasses, once botched up again, were still good for a few voyages. You have to hand it to them, engineering and repair are right up their alley.

Down in the hold, we were left to our own devices, in a manner of speaking. Every now and again, the Germans threw us bits and pieces of food as you would throw bananas to a cage full of chimps. Drinking water was dispersed with the help of thick naval hoses. How we managed to catch the water was our business. Many of us just pushed their way through to the artificial waterfall and opened wide. There were no toilets. They placed two or three oil barrels at our disposal. You know, the ones the folks on Trinidad and Tobago use for producing their steel drum music. Those were to be our latrines. Obviously, it wouldn't take long for the barrels to be filled to the brim, so they would spill over with any movement of the hull. Folks didn't even make it to the barrels but let go where they stood or crouched. Thus, our piss and shit would mix with the sea water and the whole brownish soup slosh about our legs day and night. It was a life in the cesspit, you might say. On the bright side, though: since the hold's covers were kept open most of the time, the stink was just about bearable. The price for that privilege: it was cold as hell. At night, we would huddle close to one another like emperor penguins on King George Island, just to share what little was left of our bodily warmth.

Not surprisingly, under the circumstances, people would die, drop dead like flies – freeze to death, drown, suffer from heart attacks or all sorts of epidemics; in short, they would die every which way imaginable. Heads would go under in the brown soup like those of feeding ducks and not come up again. Until such times as the Germans deigned to hoist a few days' or maybe a week's new corpses on deck with long ropes, they would be floating among us. As we could hear from the impact noises, the corpses were promptly expedited overboard.

How long were we stuck down there? I don't know. Two weeks, a month? You lose all sense of time, because it suddenly doesn't matter any longer. There came the moment when the Germans had some-how put that floating Humpty Dumpty of Franka together again well enough for her to take another shot at the crossing to Cher-bourg. The vacancies left by those who hadn't survived the waiting period were filled with other camp inmates. Mostly East-Europe-ans, who didn't understand a word of English and whose languages we, for our part, didn't understand. Whatever the circumstances, the lack of communication tends to make it all worse.

Laura's mobile rang. Heinz Marquardt gave her a short report on the progress of the tax audit so far. He had personally seen to it that the records contained minor informational gaps and break points that were time-consuming to deal with and would hope-fully incite the IRS people to strain the gnats Marquardt had fly by them while they would be swallowing the camels he had cam-ouflaged as cows.

"And what does it look like at the bank?" Laura asked.

"I'll be going for the jugular tonight," Marquardt replied. If things run the way I want them to, I'll be back with more encour-aging news tomorrow, I hope."

"Well, you had better, Heinz, you really had better. Go get them, tiger. No prisoners."

"No prisoners."

Laura hung up and gave a sigh. What it was the bank lady found so irresistibly sexy about Heinz Marquardt definitely es-caped her. He must possess hidden talents that he was unlikely ever to reveal to Laura. Never mind that, as long as the loan was finally released. She went back to Haggis, recently converted to Judaism.

When we arrived in Cherbourg, our guards didn't even have to make an effort to chase us out of Franka's hold. Most of us literally fell down the gangway by ourselves or were carried off, wedged into the stampede of the ghoulish figures appearing on the quay. I don't think the port, in its long history, had ever witnessed a scene as surreal as this one. The bulk of my companions in misery were hounded to the right, only a few privileged ones to the left, myself among them. The reason for this difference in treatment soon became obvious. In the Nazi food chain, Jews were situated somewhere rock bottom, beneath even the East European Untermenschen. And, once again, the German sense of order prevailing, Jewish scum had to travel in the company of Jewish scum.

As for my co-victims, most of them had already been lined up on the rails facing the ruins of what had once been the proud Cherbourg railroad station. Some still wore their yellow stars, others had lost them in the general turmoil. Two bulky German soldiers extended a less than jovial invitation to me with the butts of their carbines, one of those invitations I couldn't possibly turn down. So, I hurried to get in line with the rest of the travelling party opposite a freight train, whose wooden carriages seemed to have been used for the transport of animals, until very recently. Which would explain the decidedly porky whiff that hung in the air. Somebody blew a whistle, whereupon the soldiers opened the sliding doors. Now, there are not only scents, but also sounds that will haunt you for the rest of your life. Every time you hear them or something deceptively similar, you start breaking sweat and have to pull yourself together not to panic. For me, it's that grating sound of the Franka's punctured steel hull scraping across the rocks, back and forth, with the current and the waves that does it for me. And this shuffling of the sliding doors that would end in a big thump when the doors had reached the end of their rails. You hear them slide and wait for the thump. You know it's going to come and still start and shudder when it does. I don't think I could ever live in Japan, where they seem to favour sliding doors everywhere for lack of space.

Laura could relate to that remark of Haggis'. In her case, it was the rattling of old-fashioned letter boxes she found hard to take. That and the peculiarly wailing sound certain kinds of elevators will produce when getting under way. She had sat next to one of those once, aeons ago, as a child, on the hospital floor outside her mother Frederike's room. It was a soft yet pervasive sound she had later noticed with other elevators and always associated with death. A strange idea, Death coming by elevator, since his feet are killing him?

Then, we were herded into the carriages. Since I had been standing in front, I was one of the first to board. Shots began to ring out left, right and centre. Some of the desperate people thought they could profit from the general commotion and, crawling under the carriages, somehow scramble to freedom. Of course, the Germans, who had long experience and routine with such transports by 1943, had placed guards on the other side of the train as well, guards who now took pot shots at the would-be escapees.

That said, not few of those who did as they were told and climbed into the carriages would soon wish to have been among those left dead on the rails. More and more people were filling our carriage. You know the feeling: you're standing in a crowded lift at Harrod's and think: one more person, now, and the bottom's going to fall out. Fortunately, I don't suffer from claustrophobia. Others who apparently did started shouting hysterically. At long last, the maximum quantity had been reached. The doors slid back, thumped, and the solid padlocks clicked shut. Again, there was a whistle, this time much longer, and the train rumbled into gear.

'How far does your reservation go then?' somebody behind my back I couldn't even see asked me in the polite, matter-of-fact voice you would expect from a British Rail ticket collector. I twisted my head like a chameleon with some difficulty and turned my neck so I could take a look at the joker. He was a small guy, roughly my age and, as far as I could make out, dressed in clothes whose upper parts looked as if they had been picked from various Oxfam drop-outs without special attention to style, cut and colour compatibility. The way he was grinning at me with a three-mile gap in his upper teeth, I quite liked the fellow.

Actually, I was hoping to go to Biarritz and do some swimming, you know, work on my tan while sipping a few cocktails, I answered. What about you, then? The guy laughed.

In that case, I have bad news for you, mon cher, he said. 'Cause today, exceptionally, we won't be stopping over at Biarritz'.

Are you quite sure of that? I asked him. He nodded with a mock-apologetic shrug of his shoulders.

Well, if that is so, I request to talk to your superior, immediately. My travel agency on Guernsey clearly gave me to understand that I could get off the train at Biarritz.

The little guy laughed again and presented himself as a Gaston Samuelsson, from Lyon.

From my early childhood, everybody just calls me Gaston de Lyon, so why don't you?

He seemed to find that funny. So, I laughed without really knowing about what.

Doesn't sound all that Jewish to me, Gaston Samuelsson, I ventured an opinion.

He nodded gravely.

Try and make that clear to the Germans. I can't put my finger on it, but I have that creeping suspicion my circumcision is pleading against me being a goi.

I see. I mean, not quite. What's it got to do with Japanese fish?

Gaston literally roared with laughter.

No, that's kois you're thinking of. Goi is what we Jews call the small global community of non-Jews.

I felt I had manoeuvred myself into a predicament here. If I presented myself to him as David Rosenberg, he could have taken that as presumptious and offensive. No matter how hallucinating the circumstances, a goi such as myself should not impersonate a Jew. That was adding insult to injury. On the other hand, what did I know about him? For all his obliging, affable attitude, he might have been an informer trying to save his skin by selling the Nazis somebody else's.

And so, I told him my name was David Goldberg.

Well, well, doesn't sound that Jewish to me either, he laughed.

Well, not without a circumcision it doesn't, I thought.

The ice was thus broken. As my spine would soon be, unless I created myself a little more ball room, as it were. Bulk cargo such as wheat, barley, or human beings, moved up and down or to and fro in a ship's hold or a freight train carriage, will invariably lose volume, that's a law of nature. In the days of tall ships, the phenomenon used to lead to dangerous heeling or even capsizing of sailing ships carrying, say, wheat or barley. As solid as the cargo may have seemed when the ship had set out to sea – after a while, what with the air bubbles between the individual grains dissolving and the total volume shrinking, accordingly, the cargo would find room enough to shift to the side the sailing vessel was heeling to already. In that precarious situation, one big squall would make the vessel capsize. The answer to that was compartmentalisation of the hold.

As for our train, at least it didn't heel and wouldn't sink, so much was for sure. And the reduced volume helped some of us to, well, not exactly make ourselves comfortable, but find spots and niches to fill, stretch a leg, rest our torsos against the carriage walls.

The floor had been covered with a thin layer of straw reeking of the pigs that had probably been the last animal passengers. To deport Jews to the extermination camps in trains that used to serve for the transport of pigs, among other things, had the taste of deliberate humiliation, although, personally, I'm not sure the Germans were even alive to the irony of it. Germans like to be sarcastic, scathingly satirical. Pussy-footed irony tends to be lost on them.

Speaking of which. Toilets didn't exist here either. We all had to relieve ourselves between two low bales of hay stuck in a corner of the carriage. After all I had lived through on Franka, this came close to a rolling holiday camp. It was less so for others. Especially women and girls found it degrading and many of them cried, while others again seemed pretty hardened. A lot of these people, young or old, had been brutally separated from their friends and next of kin without knowing whether or not they would ever see them again, which made for an even more depressing overall atmosphere. As a practicing Christian, you may at least derive solace from the thought of soon being re-united with your families again, in Paradise. For many Jews, even orthodox ones, however, there is no life after death, as Gaston explained to me. Hence, he who is loved by Jehovah can expect to be rewarded in this life, instead of having to wait for the next. Hence, to end like this, being taken to annihilation like cattle to the slaughterhouse, must have something of a double whammy, as it were. The Germans kill you and Jehovah doesn't seem to care.

Laura leaned back again. She had never as yet seen it that way. This man Haggis was no fool either, it would seem. Not so surprising, then, that the Yarmouth Six had had such a remarkable gangster career. In a different epoch, they might have been successful bankers or real estate agents. Gangsters, again, of course, but with a bourgeois front and high reputation.

The train was rolling along. Not very fast, to judge by the regular, drowsy clickety-clack, but with that dogged persistence of passage-making. The heat in the almost hermetically closed carriage was stifling, even though it must have been rather cold outside. The only air duct was a narrow gap above the door's right side. To catch a glimpse of the outside world, one normal-sized person had to climb on somebody's shoulders. Since that was too difficult in the long run, a particularly tall man declared himself ready to carry a boy who would then give us regular reports of what he saw gliding by. Since his vocabulary was limited, we had to ask him to enlarge on this or that detail every now and again: the shape of trees, the approximate size of villages, the width of rivers, that sort of thing. After a while, the lad got the hang of it.

There were stops, alright, but almost exclusively dictated by technical requirements and always out there in the middle of nowhere. The German civilian population should not be disturbed, least of all moved, by the sight of our dreadful misery, I guess. At least the dead would be pulled from the carriages and raw potatoes, bread and some water distributed among the living, on such occasions. Then, the train would move on.

The monotonous rattle of the wheels had a strong soporific effect on me so that I dozed on and off, most of the time. Gaston had been a teacher in Lyon, or so he had told me. It sounded true enough, since he was pretty knowledgeable, besides having a surprisingly tenacious character, full of that will to survive. His young wife had died of tuberculosis years ago. They had no children; there had hardly been time for that, he said. The Germans had caught him in the act of trying to become a member of the

Résistance, which, as he assured me, wasn't all that easy as a Jew. The man who had allegedly wished to recruit him had turned out to be a Vichy spy.

Gaston seemed an okay guy, so, after a while, I decided to tell him the truth about myself. I gave him the briefest of accounts of what had happened to me from the Yarmouth days to the Sark raid and the circumstances of my capture in St. Peter Port. The latter made him laugh aloud.

Well, yes. Life presents you with gifts more poisoned than those of the Achaeans, right? Take this trip of ours into the blue. Any idea where we might be?

I shook my head.

Your guess is as good as mine. Perhaps somewhere near the Polish-German border, provided our general direction is still East.

Gaston nodded.

That's what I think. If so, the camps can't be that far away, any longer. I don't know how you feel about it, but I need some fresh air, honestly. Besides, the food in this train sucks. As does everything else. So why don't we hop off?

I must have looked at him rather dumbfounded.

With pleasure, count me in. How, though?

Two options that I can see. Either we try to jump the guards on the occasion of our next stop. Fat chance. The Germans have all the experience in the world with transports such as ours. So they know stops to be critical and will be prepared. I would be in their place.

And plan B?

Gaston pointed downwards and brushed the straw aside.

We open up the bottom and drop on the rails. I've heard of people who seem to have managed. Highly risky, of course. We'll have to wait till the train goes uphill, slowing down somewhat. And even then, the odds of getting killed or maimed are such as to make it a suicide mission. You don't drop quite straight or can't flatten yourself sufficiently quickly, and good night, Eileen. The trick, or so it would seem, is to get your feet down first and let them drag over the sleepers a few seconds, before you let go of the floorboards. Anyway, you still in?

I nodded. My enthusiasm had cooled somewhat, but what did I have to lose.

We didn't waste any more time, either, but went at it right away. With our bare fingers, we started scratching off the wood around the rusty nails so we could pull the things out at some stage. Others began taking an interest in what we were doing and asked to join us. One man had a self-made knife of sorts he had hidden from the Germans. That helped a lot. Still, it lasted an eternity till the first nail came out. We hailed it with great relish. Soon after, the first floorboard came off. Another round of cheers. Thus, we already had more fresh air. But looking down on the sleepers rushing past like the steps of a crazy escalator was a sobering sight. We put our fear behind us and continued scratching, pulling, and lifting. More floor boards came off. Finally, we had made a hole wide enough for a slender person to squeeze through. Slender was no problem on that train, not with most of the passengers not having had solid food for weeks on end. Still, you had to squeeze, no easy slipping through. Had we not been pressed for time, we would have widened the gap first, but Gaston, who had become master of ceremonies, decided against it.

It's now or never. Who's going to bail out first? he asked.

The man with the self-made knife raised his hand.

Okay, fine, Gaston agreed.

I suggest we wait for the next uphill passage. Should there be none in the course of the next half hour, we'll do it anyway. By the time we stop again, it might be too late. The Germans may discover the gap in the floor boards or somebody may give us away for an extra slice of bread. No disrespect, but I've seen it happen. So have most of you, I'm sure. The Germans will declare it sabotage and execute us as casually as they break wind. Remember: as soon as your feet touch ground, count to five and then let go. Mazel tov. We have no idea as to where we are exactly. Therefore, I suggest the survivors stick together and try and muddle through in unison. We may be able to join the Polish resistance movement. They don't like Jews all that much, but, with any luck, they hate the Germans more.

He looked at his watch. How had he managed to keep that, I wondered.

After Mordechai, – that was the guy with the knife – it will be the goi's turn.

So that was me.

Then I'll go and whoever else feels like it will be welcome. The piece of good news at the end: we're not expecting any rain out there today.

Laura could hardly believe it. To jump off a train was risky enough. To let yourself drop under a rolling train, suicide. It could work alright, theoretically speaking. But it didn't take much – a brake hose hanging a bit low, some minor bump between the rails or the least bit of clumsiness with limbs lame and numb from the long journey – and that would be it.

Some fifteen, twenty minutes later, the train started slowing down. We were going uphill. Not a very steep climb, by any means, but just enough for our purposes. Gaston gave us an encouraging nod. Mordechai squeezed his lower legs through the gap and sat there for a few seconds, collecting himself. Or saying his prayers, I don't know which. Then, he squeezed his thighs and behind through and was only hanging by his arms and elbows for the briefest of moments. Then he was gone as if someone had plucked him by the legs from underneath the train. We were stupefied. Why hadn't he stuck to procedure and counted to five before letting go? This wasn't the time for idle speculation.

I came next. I emulated Mordechai's initial approach, let my feet down, first, then my shanks and thighs. The moment my feet touched the ground, I understood what had happened to Mordechai. The sleepers ripped off my shoes and tore at my speed-bumping heels like mad. The soles of my feet were cut open by the pointed gravel between the rails and sleepers. I had barely counted to three when I was no longer capable of holding myself with my arms still resting on the floorboards. I dropped down. The back of my head hit the gravel and my legs seemed hell-bent on overtaking me. Then, I didn't feel anything any longer for a while. When I opened my eyes again, Gaston was kneeling above me.

Welcome to Poland, my goi friend. I already checked you for major damages and am glad to report there are none. The gun wound is of earlier origin, I expect. You'll keep on suffering from a headache for some time to come, I'm afraid, but that, too, will pass. Your back is tattooed by all sorts of bruises and stuff, but nothing broken that I could feel. What you need now, my goi friend, is the loving care of a Polish partisan woman. They do accept women, I take it. But be warned, the Poles are sturdy Catholics. Your newly-acquired Jewish wisdom might not pull much weight with them. Either way, we ought to get going before someone notices our absence.

Aching all over and hardly able to focus, I tried to raise my torso from the gravel. There was no more sign of the train. No sign of Mordechai and his knife either. Gaston sadly shook his head.

No, goi, I'm afraid we are all on our own. Mordechai didn't make it and the others…well, failure of nerve, I guess.

I got up and we took to the maquis, as the French say. Several hours passed till we happened to come across some sort of village in that deserted area. Its town sign bore the name of Brzezinka and confirmed we were in Poland. Who but a Pole would have been able to pronounce that name.

I'll spare you the ins and outs of our moving in ever narrowing circles for days. At one stage, we had just been about to show up at the Auschwitz camp, by mistake as it were. We had no idea we were that close to it. Fortunately, a patrolling partisan platoon stopped us and took us with them. Wouldn't that have been a lark for the SS: two dumb Jews risking their lives by dropping out of the bottom of a train only to waltz into the camp later by mistake. Thigh-slapping material.

We stayed with the resistance movement till the end of the war in the East. Then, we had to try and stay ahead of the fast-approaching Red Army. To us, it felt a bit like escaping into a tunnel with a pack of wolves on our heels, only to run into a herd of wild boar forcing us to do a one-eighty in mid-tunnel. What little Polish I learned I forgot again later, except very basic stuff such as cienkuje barzo, thanks a lot.

So that's how I made the acquaintance of Gaston Samuelsson aka Gaston de Lyon. As far as I know, he went back to his native town, but didn't take up teaching again. Did he take to selling stolen goods? I don't know. Wouldn't blame him, though, if he tried to get his pound of flesh. A man's got to make a living somehow and the war didn't just destroy buildings but moral values as well. What I do know is, he probably saved my life, the life of a goi, that is, inadvertently turned into a son of David. You'll never hear a bad word about Gaston or his Jewish brothers and sisters from me. Not ever. And now, leave me to my memories, if you please.

SIXTH CHAPTER

1. Road to Salvation

Laura's fingers literally dug into the Boeing 737's arm rests. Gibraltar International, or so she had learned in a recent TV feature, counts among the five most dangerous airports worldwide. Not the most natural choice for someone suffering from aerophobia, or fear of flying, anyway. The short runway cutting right through the narrow isthmus that connects the Rock to the Spanish town of La Linea de Concepcion started in the East only yards away from the sea and ended in the West only yards away from Algeceira Bay. And as if that wasn't enough to make her hair stand on end, it was crossed by a heavily frequented four-lane thoroughfare. This road serves as the only access for the large alien army of mostly Spanish workers without whose daily contribution neither hotels nor restaurants on Gibraltar could be run half as smoothly as they were. Understandably, traffic tended to be brisk at all hours of the day, reaching mind-boggling peaks during mornings and evenings.

Which is not to say that the road remained open during the touch-downs and take-offs of planes, of course. But the risk of some wise ass testing his luck with a sudden last-minute dash past the barriers and across the tarmac like a jack rabbit was always very real. Better not think about it.

Laura had met with Ignace and Heinz Marquardt at the brand new Elbphilharmonie concert hall the night before. It had taken her a while to spot the two of them in the foyer of the rather vast complex. While Marquardt had dressed up for the occasion, Ignace would easily have passed as a relief usher. The boy obviously loved his comfort. By way of punishment, she had embraced him and kissed him on both cheeks, something she knew he hated. She didn't care. If he really didn't like it, she thought, he should not have allowed himself to be adopted by someone as emphatic as herself. The owner of Marquardt's most recent female scalp under his belt had stood him up, in a manner of speaking, cancelled the nightly rendezvous because she had to work overtime in the bank. Upon hearing about that, Laura, who had excellent connections in the Hamburg theatrical and concert community, had invited him to the Elbphilharmonie, instead, so that he could relax, come up for air, whatever. Which applied to herself, too, incidentally. Robert, her late father, had introduced her to the world of classical music. And much as she had loathed listening to Beethoven's symphonies on records and CD's, the combined effect of hearing and seeing music in the making had fascinated her from the very start. Ever since, she had been a regular fan of concerts more than operas, it is true, but no disparagist of either. That night, the NDR Elbphilharmonie-Orchestra under the exceptional leadership of conductor-maestro Zubin Mehta had promised a regular treat. Laura had been very much looking forward to some entertaining hours without audits, loans, one-armed corpses and lonely ghost trains rolling through war-swept landscapes on a moonless night.

"How are the investigations coming on then, Watson?" she had asked Ignace.

"Dragging their feet, somewhat, I'm afraid," he had replied.

"Maybe the best approach would be to wait till the last members of the Lamont Clan have been eliminated. The last man standing must of needs be the killer."

"Expedient, I'll grant, but not exactly the classical method recommended by the Auguste Dupins und Hercule Poirots of this world," Marquardt had objected.

"Brain apparently was the only one possessing some degree of musical talent and interest." Ignace had put forward.

Laura had already forgotten which of the six men that was.

"Keith Donovan, the Welshman," Ignace had refreshed her memory.

"Used to be responsible for logistics, among other things. Seems to have played trumpet and sax, at some time or other."

Laura hadn't seen what that had to do with anything. Then she remembered the Boxer. Ignace seemed to think that, maybe, the

Welshman's musical genes might have passed on to one or the other of his descendants. Perfectly possible, of course. But a bit of a long shot.

"There's a granddaughter of Donovan's in Gibraltar. Seems to have made a fortune in the real estate business so she was able to retire at the age of forty. Not a bad idea, come to think of it."

Laura had asked Ignace to contact the lady in question. Which Ignace had promptly done and even managed to make her agree to an interview at the Rock.

"But time is of the essence," she had added.

"The day after tomorrow, I'll be in Marrakesh, Morocco. I have a small estate in the making there and would like to have it finished, soon. Trouble is, you have to check these Moroccans all the time. Turn your back on them and nothing much gets done, see."

They had arranged to meet at an Indian restaurant in the marina situated beneath the town's Southern gate.

Laura's tummy performed another somersault. The Boeing literally dropped out of the sky as abruptly as if it had fallen into an air pocket and almost slammed its wheels onto the tarmac. Then, it came to a brutal stop and turned almost like a car in an Alpine hair-pin bend. Ignace was stroking Laura's hand.

"Everything alright, grandma, we did it, we'll live. You may now open your eyes again."

The taxi was threading its way through the pile-ups between the Rock and the Bay with great pain. The daily toing and froing on noisy stinking mopeds was the price locals and tourists alike had to pay for getting the all-round service they expected.

Gillian Donovan was already waiting for them at the India Star restaurant next to a marina that looked rather empty at this time of year. The yachties who wanted to cross the Atlantic from here had long since left and those who were heading for the Med had not yet arrived, Gillian explained.

She was a resolute lady pushing fifty, in fact. A little stocky, with an old-fashioned hairdo and lively brown eyes that signalled the lady was no push-over. To frighten this lady, you had to bring friends, lots of them. Not surprisingly so. To succeed in the real estate business as a woman, in this crowded environment where a square meter of living space came at a small fortune, she must have been able and willing to use not just her elbows but had presumably presented her whole arsenal.

After a short exchange of polite small talk, Gillian came to the point immediately, as could be expected of her.

"What is it you want me to tell you?" she asked while Laura and Ignace were ordering their food and drinks. Gillian had told the waitress she had just made close friends with their variety of Bourbon on ice, and would stick to it, for the time being.

In a few words, Laura told her about the motive of her preoccupation with the Yarmouth Six, mentioning neither her meeting with Sir Lucas, nor the preliminary results of their investigations. Which was all the easier, as there practically weren't any results worthwhile noting.

"I really don't know whether or not I can help you there." Gillian wrinkled her forehead from the effort of thinking.

"Those people from the Yard have approached me on several occasions. But what could I tell them? I really haven't a clue who is acting the serial killer and why. He doesn't like Sir Lucas, so much can be said. Some time or other, he will don the mask of the Red Death and gate-crash Lamont's seemingly eternal ball. Until then…Nobody escapes their fate. You do know the story of Death in Samaria, now, don't you? Well, to me, Lamont seems like a latter-day version of Ali, the old servant. Confronted with death on Jersey, he now jumps on his master's fastest horse to escape to Puerto Rico. Only to find on his arrival that Death is expecting him there already. In fact, Lamont's name has been in his notebook all that while, with place, date, and time of the day."

"Nice oriental fairy tale," Laura agreed. Gillian shook her head.

"Not oriental at all, really. It's a short story by Somerset Maugham, if my memory serves me right. But before the Grim Reaper takes the three of us away, what is it you were expecting of me?"

"Well, we have been able to follow Brain, your grandfather, that is, all the way to that cave on Sark. Do you happen to know what became of him afterwards? I mean, how did he get off the island?"

"With great difficulty, obviously. Being much too young at the time of his untimely demise, I was never privileged enough to have heard his story from the horse's mouth, as it were. But he left his eldest daughter, my mother, in other words, a stack of letters he had written her and she had kept and collected. They did that then, in those antediluvian days, write letters, I mean. When my mother had a stroke and became a nursing case, those letters, with loads of photos and other memorabilia, fell into my lap.

She paused and waited for the meal to be served. As for herself, low-carb liquid lunches like this one seemed to suit her fine.

"I took the trouble of reading those letters, on and off, so I have a vague memory of what was going on at the time. After the cave, you say? Well, I guess you'd rather have him tell you all about that. But since he's no longer around and my mother passed on recently, I'm afraid you'll have to make do with me. And I'm a fairly chaotic kind of seanachie, so be warned. Anyway, as far as I remember, he pushed off and left that cave in the company of Harry Langley."

"Lily?" Gillian laughed.

"Exactly. Lily's Brain, that's what Keith used to call the pair of them in his letters. The two of them became inseparable. Some sort of kinship of souls, I gather. They must have wandered around for a while without knowing what to do with themselves. Lily had been shot twice and barely managed to limp along. Which was one more reason for Brain, who had come out largely unscathed, to agree to stay with him. They had no idea how to get to Guernsey first and then maybe onto the Continent. So, they hid in a barn where they found bits and pieces of animal feed they chewed on. The farmer who owned the little holding soon found them. My grandfather was afraid the farmer would hand them over to the Germans. An option the man may actually have considered, initially. German reprisals for harbouring and concealing enemy commandos were getting harsher all the time. If you didn't deliver them, your neighbour might. In a small community like that, you can't keep things secret for long, can you? Here's to your good health."

She lifted her glass and brought out a toast.

"To a long and happy life…"

"I'll drink to that," Laura, who found the toast more than fitting after that landing, agreed.

"Where was I? The farmer, right. Well, he proved an exception in that he hid the two young Brits in his house. His wife had apparently left him recently, before the occupation, and gone back to the North of England whence she had originally come. There were no children. Thus, the two of them, Lily and his Brain, hung out there for a week or so, till they had overcome their pain and cold and had gathered fresh forces. Then it was high time to change location. Question was: how?"

She took another swig of Bourbon and downed it like a Canadian grizzly wrestler. Laura half expected her to blow a purple belch at her next. But she didn't.

"In one of the cupboards, my grandfather had come across two black uniforms packed in protective sack-like cloths. Uniforms he had by way of a first reflex thought belonged to the SS. The farmer had laughed aloud and explained what they really were. His wife and he himself, he said, had both belonged to the SA, as he called it. And those were their uniforms."

She raised her empty glass and sought to catch the waiter's eye, which she finally did.

"SA?" my grandfather had asked, with some apprehension. He must have felt like the young boxer, who, relieved at the news that his fight against Johnny Liston had been cancelled, had swallowed hard upon hearing that the right honourable Gerge Foreman had agreed to jump in, I imagine.

"I always thought they wore only brown uniforms," he had asked a little coyly.

The farmer had laughed and hurried to explain that this SA was none other than the Salvation Army. His wife and himself used to wear them during parades and other festive occasions. And since those had become scarce, more recently, they had wrapped them in protective covers before hanging them in the cupboard."

Laura couldn't help smiling as she tried to image the scene with the farmer and his two confused guests.

"As it turned out, the farmer and his wife had not been just ordinary recruits of the Lord, but had belonged to the CI's number one SA brass band. And there was more to come: one of the rare parades of the corps through the streets of St. Helier on the occasion of William Booth's birthday or the anniversary of his death, I forget which, happened to be imminent. Both being the founding father of the SA movement."

"And the Germans would let that happen?"

"Oh yes. Well, you know your fellow countrymen. Anything for a decent march or parade with umph-ta-ta and rat-ta-tang, never mind the occasion. And this SA was unarmed, to boot. Unless you belong to the rapidly dwindling group of people who believe that the word cuts deeper than the sword. Plus the Nazis themselves always professed a certain propensity for the socially disadvantaged, did they not. And black uniforms, well, they were just up their little alley, I guess. Even though these carried but one S on their lapels. It's the gesture that counts."

"Now, which of the two, Lily or Brain, had the brilliant idea to somehow misappropriate those uniforms and use them for their own devious purposes, I don't know. My money would be on my grandfather. After all, he played the trumpet and would have no problem adapting to the chanda-rapta-boom of the Salvation Army. Emaciated Lily risked looking a little grotesque in the uniform of the farmer's eloped wife, but that had to be as it was. Together, Brain and Lily would jump aboard the boat that was to take the Sark SA brassband members, five in all, to Guernsey the very next morning. The extraordinary ferry traffic had been okay'ed by the Germans and should therefore be safe for the two Brits."

The waiter placed a fresh glass of golden-brown Bourbon in front of Gillian, who nodded appreciatively.

"Lily's jacket was a little too wide, apparently, and my grandfather's uniform pants had to be kept in place with braces, so as not to end up on his knees all the time. But for the rest, the two of them looked a treat. The farmer, whose name I don't remember, or do I? Jack something or other. Anyway, he presented Brain with his trumpet, a World War I version that looked like it had been in the thick of fighting since time immemorial. Lily got the wife's C flute. Not that he would have been able to produce so much as a single straight note, but again, the Germans wouldn't know that. Cheers."

She downed a swig of the blessed stuff, shook her torso as if she had just been forced to swallow a particularly bitter kind of medicine, and carried on.

"So, the next morning, Lily and Brain, dressed in SA attire, marched to Creux Harbour with, I imagine, their hearts in their mouths. Because this was a critical moment. Had the other three members of the brass band, who had never seen those two before, so much as looked perturbed or confused, the hoax might have ended there and then. But as it happened, the others barely batted an eyelid and welcomed Brain and Lily in their midst as if they had known them for a lifetime already. By the way, watching the two of you munching away merrily, I kind of feel a little hungry again, myself."

She waved for the waiter again and ordered a chicken vindaloo, the kind that requires asbestos-lined guts. Laura began to understand why this granddaughter of the trumpet-playing Brain seemed a little hefty round the hips, at her estimated age, anyway. She might be paying lip service to low-carb food and drink, but, once again, the flesh had proved weak, it would seem.

"Thus, the passage to St. Peter Port must have gone smoothly. But who should welcome them on the quay but an officer of the SS waving a bunch of papers at them. As the five soldiers of the Lord went ashore, the officer with the skull-emblem on his cap must have eyed them with the innate lack of trust common to his species. He probably smelled a rat but couldn't as yet figure which of the five he might have to hand over to the Gestapo. He asked all of them their names, addresses, dates of birth and so on and compared the data with those on his check list. My grandfather gave the farmer's name as his own, with the details the man had given him. Lily was the odd man out. That wasn't good. In fact, my grandfather wrote that, at this point, he had almost been willing to throw in the towel and hand over his trumpet as a sign of capitulation. As it turned out, that would have been a rash thing to do. Because, you see, Lily was no Brain, but no downright fool either. He had in a way foreseen this predicament as one scenario they might be confronted with and had dreamed up some cock-and-bull story to deal with it. He told the SS man, the farmer's wife had eloped and gone back to England, which was no more than the bare truth. The young lady who used to replace her in the band, had died of TB only recently. When approached by the band leader, he, Lily, had agreed to act as a stop gap for the single occasion of this commemorative parade but, what with all those turbulences, had clean forgotten his ID on Sark. The obligation to carry ID on your person at all times had been one of the first things the Germans had introduced on the islands. Anyone who was caught without ID was liable to a year or more in prison. Hence, normally, the SS man would have had Lily arrested right away and confiscated his flute. But as it seems, he was a firm admirer of the incomparable actress-cum-courtesan, the one and only Jersey Lily."

The vindaloo chicken arrived together with some rice. Gillian tasted the meat and nodded approvingly.

Harry Langtree? the SS officer had asked with an air of manifest disbelief, almost dropping his check list.

Not related to….you know…?

Lily had immediately sensed this German's Achilles' heel and shot his first arrow.

Absolutely, he had confirmed in the safe knowledge that, in a place such as Jersey, everyone would at some stage become related to everyone else. It was all a question of how far you were prepared to climb up and down the pedigree.

She was my great aunt on my mother's side, he had added unabashed.

If you're interested, I could let you have a look at the photos, letters, and other memorabilia I have back there on Sark, on occasion, I mean. He had held up the bait. And, believe it or not, the

German had bought it. Had they not stood there in full view of the public, he might have taken Lily up on his word. As it was, he had to exercise the kind of arrogant detachment expected of his office. And so, he severely reprimanded Lily for the lack of ID, at the same time giving him to understand that he might pay him a visit on Sark soon."

Laura had seen old photos of Lily Langtree and found her an exceptionally beautiful woman even by modern standards. She would no doubt have made a killing in present-day Hollywood. Seen from that angle, the SS officer could hardly be blamed for what he probably would have characterized as leniency.

"Before Lily could start dripping blood from his wounds again, the five Sark SA members went up to the church, where they mingled with their mates from other islands and finally filled the ranks of their band. Following upon the occupation in 1940, the exchanges between individual regional sections of the Salvation Army had been less intensive than its adherents would have wished for. Which meant, among other things, that new faces popping up here and there would be accepted as something quite normal. As could be expected, all Brain needed, on the musical side of things, was a quick look at the notes. Lily, again, was a more complicated case. He pretended to have fallen during the ferry passage, thus hurting his fingers to a point that would make his active participation impossible. Now, between you and me, what's one bloody flute more or less in a brass band? A bee lacking in the hive, I'd say. The leader told Lily to just hold the flute and pretend he was playing. His colleagues to the left and right would compensate by blowing all the more loudly. Your good health."

She proposed another toast.

Laura was fleetingly wondering whether the lack of a C flute would be noticed in a symphony orchestra gig. Probably not. If it played off-key, yes. But for the rest it would take an afficionado with the keenness of hearing usually attributed to bats, only, to notice such nuances, she suspected.

"The parade seems to have gone alright, even though the Army of the Lord may not have won over new recruits that day.

Not with that C flute lacking. After the event, my grandfather and Lily had hoped for a drink, I mean a beer, something they hadn't tasted for a while. But they had forgotten what company they were in. If there's something the soldiers of the Salvation Army hold in even lower esteem than the Devil Himself, it's alcohol, of course. When Lily and Brain had finally got their mind round that, they took a hasty leave of their companions and lingered around the harbour of St. Sampson's. Here, they had noticed a ship waiting for the first throes of the ebb tide to head for St. Malo. Presumably, they had all sorts of offenders on board who were to be taken to either the Paris Cherche-Midi prison or the even less popular Caen jailhouse. That was Lily's and Brain's ticket. All they had to do now was get aboard unnoticed. Again, I guess it had been my grandfather who had this crazy idea. You want to hear it or want me to shut up?"

2. Gefillte Fish

"Don't you dare stop now," Laura protested. Gillian reminded her more and more of Solitaire. Minus the girth, of course. Once all this rigmarole over, she had to pay the woman a visit in Morocco.

"Not that you got us hooked on your grandfather's story, we want to hear the end of it, and if it's the last thing we do, eh, tiger?"

Ignace looked a mite less convinced but was polite enough to sing from the hymn book.

"Absolutely. Do carry on."

"Alright then, it's your burial. Here's the thing: during the exchange that had taken place between Lily and the SS officer some hour before, my grandfather had been musing on the surprising parallels between the two uniforms. The black colour and the respective S or SS-emblems had struck him. When they were out of German hearing, my grandfather had detailed Lily his audacious plan. They would look for a tailor ready and willing to make a few but essential alterations to the Salvation Army uniform so that Brain could impersonate an SS agent on a secret mission that consisted essentially in taking a dangerous British spy, impersonated by none other than Lily, to St. Malo and from there to Paris where he would no doubt be tortured and interrogated at the Paris Gestapo headquarters. As you can easily imagine, Lily's reception of the plan fell a little short of being downright enthusiastic. Not that he was totally against it. No, he would just have preferred to swap parts, so that he would do the SS agent and Brain the spy. Trouble was, as my grandfather didn't dally to point out, that Lily didn't speak any German. My grandfather, on the other hand, boasted a reasonable smattering of the language of Goethe and Schiller. Enough to bark simple orders in German anyway. Because, you see, he had grown up in a quarter of town where many German-born Jews had settled even before the first war. He had played with their kids and become a sort of mascot of the hood, sometimes eating dinner with the Rosenbergs or spending the night at the Goldsteins, you know, that sort of thing. The kind of Yiddish German he had learned there would, as a matter of course, have been adorned with all sorts of kasher words and exhortations. Apart from that, by 1943, the dwindling ranks of the SS had increasingly been filled up with other than German nationals, fanatics of Nazi racist ideology and shameless opportunists who were hoping for personal privileges. There were Poles, Finns, Ukrainians, men from the Baltic nations and what have you. Their German had to be reasonable but was, as a rule, a long cry from perfect or even accent-free. Apart from many military expressions, they would master basic abuse such as Judensau or dreckiger Untermensch. My grandfather's somewhat dodgy German would, hence, raise no eyebrows. Not, as long as he didn't wish an SS colleague mazel tov, that is. Trouble was that Yiddish expressions formed part of his linguistic DNA, you see. I suspect that, most of the time, he didn't even know exactly what they meant. We tend to learn languages by imitation, don't we? On occasion, that hits back at us."

Laura and Ignace both had enough experience in the area to nodd understandingly.

"At long last, Lily allowed himself to be convinced by reason. The pair was then looking for a suitable tailor's in the St. Sampson area. That was no problem since the few tailors that still functioned had all long since specialised in the repair of German uniforms. A fact that was not just due to a military obsession with anything spruce, proper, and shining, but had its chief cause in the fact that, by 1943, the two kinds of supplies that would still reach the islands were cement and forced labour. Which, inevitably, led to most uniforms becoming more and more decrepit and threadbare. And since most officers and men had but one set with them, two at the very most, tailors used to be busy round the clock. There was even a point when uniform buttons tended to replace tobacco or chocolate as hard black-market currency. Add to this the general food shortage that increasingly beset people, it is clear that their clothes and uniforms began to look like they had been handed down to them by their elder siblings. Again, the tailors would have to come in and do their best, taking off surplus fabric and tunic here, there, and everywhere. To begin with, the owner of the tailor shop Brain and Lily addressed themselves to just shook his head in disbelief when he heard about the plan. Its feasibility depended to a large part on the few minor retouches my grandfather had in mind. The scandalized fakir on the pin cushion was to convert the small red patches on the lapels into black ones, with a double – instead of single – S on each side. The Salvation Army S bore little or no similarity to the stylized double flashes of lightning of the SS original, but never mind that. At a superficial glance in the dusk soon to be expected, they might at a pinch be mistaken for the real thing. The SA motto, Blood and Fire, would come across even more convincingly than the corresponding motto of the SS, My Honour is Loyalty, which would not look totally out of place on the wall of a Doberman-breeders' club house. And, lastly, most of the Germans had spent so much time on the islands they could not possibly be abreast of all of the most recent uniform fashion frills that had meanwhile cut a dash or two on the Obersalzberg. Relations between members of the Wehrmacht and those of the SS, never brilliant at the best of times, had deteriorated further, so that no Army officer would take a second look at an SS uniform, checking it for possible deficiencies. Hence, the only species Brain and Lily, once slipped into their prospective roles, had to avoid at all cost were members of the true SS."

Gillian, who had dug into the chicken and rice, was starting to sweat, not so much from the heat as from the spicy dish.

"What, in the informed opinion of the tailor, my grandfather would desperately need if the hoax was to succeed was a uniform cap, a pair of jackboots and, if at all possible, one of those camp tapered SS overcoats, a definite must for the enterprising young SS man of today, as he appears to have put it so deftly. And so, the improbable pair now dressed in civilian rags the tailor had lent them for the duration of his work on the uniform, paced up and down St. Sampson in search of a possible source. They finally hit upon a pub that was frequented primarily by Germans, and, among them, preponderantly by the SS, as it would seem.

The simple reason for this was the fact that this pub was still serving genuine beer, whereas what came out of the spigots of other public houses on the islands was offensive substitutes won from God knows what parts of local botany. The two of them had hardly entered the public house in question when a booming yet slurred, barely articulating voice cried out: Over here, Lily Langtree! What with the murky light in the room, it took them a while to identify the caller, who turned out to be none other than the SS officer who had received them at St. Peter Port this very morning and was now knocking it back in the company of three or four colleagues. With some apprehension, Lily and Brain approached their table and let themselves be presented to the SS officer's company. Especially Lily must have felt like a proper circus clown. The man from the harbour seemed to be the highest in rank of the five and explained to the others the vague nature of Lily's alleged relationship with the ex-courtesan turned actress, or vice versa. A CV not altogether unlike that of Dutchwoman Mata Hari, incidentally. So that is how my grandfather and Lily got their beer, after all. When the SS people asked them whether they wanted something solid to eat, as well, it literally slipped out of my starved grandfather's mouth: yes, with pleasure. Some gefillte fish would be great. I suspect he had been dreaming of that for quite a few days already. It used to be the Shabbat classic that he had tasted umpteen times during his childhood. Now, during the past days with the Sark farmer, the idea must have taken possession of that part of his brain which had food supply written all over it, so that when the Germans had asked, it had popped out like a conditioned reflex.

For a short eternity, the place was so silent you could have heard the proverbial pin drop. Suddenly, the SS officer from the harbour started laughing. The others first looked at him, puzzled, then followed his example. All laughed and laughed, shook their heads and slapped their thighs. As soon as the laughter was about to subside for a moment, someone would shout gefillte fish and again, everybody just guffawed and roared with laughter. I wonder what Heinrich Himmler, being a notoriously humourless person, would have made of the scene. Lily, at any rate, had peed in his, or rather, the tailor's pants. My grandfather's heart must have missed a few beats too. They both thanked them for the beer and pretended they had the Sark ferry to catch. They left the pub in a hurry but took the time to lift one of the SS uniform caps complete with skull, as well as a coat from the rack at the entrance. All the while, the Germans were having yet another fit of laughter and didn't pay enough attention to notice they were being robbed. Probably, the mere idea of someone having the guts to steal parts of their clothing wouldn't have occurred to them anyway.

Meanwhile, back at St. Sampson's, which was Guernsey's industrial harbour, the one from where all the granite won on the island would be shipped to England, the tailor had finished his work on the uniform jacket. The only thing missing now were the jackboots. Now, what I said about the tailors applied, to an even greater extent, to the local cobblers too. Shoes and boots always have a hard time in the military context. Marching, parading, carrying out manoeuvres in all kinds of terrain, soon left traces on the soles and heels of soldiers' footwear. Leather, on the other hand, had been in short supply from the start of the occupation and so, cobblers had to make shift and do what they could. Stacks of boots would crowd their workshops to capacity. As Brain and Lily took leave of the tailor, my grandfather promised to return after the war to pay the bill they had incurred. But the man just raised his hands, saying he felt adequately rewarded with the thought of them having pulled one over on the Germans. Then, he gave them the address of a cobbler who he felt was reliable enough and saw them off into the night that had fallen over the harbour by then. Brain and Lily found the cobbler's alright. The man had apparently gone to bed, already, so they had to ring the doorbell. The locals would always turn in early, at the time. What else was there to do? Radio sets had been confiscated by the Germans. To read, you needed light, which was a no-go during curfew. Cinemas and theatres had been closed for good. Thus, you had Hobson's choice between heavy-hearted sex or listening to your own gnarling stomach. Just as well to go to bed, curl up under your itchy, matted blanket and dream of liberation day just around the corner. The cobbler was upset, of course, since nightly visitors as a rule meant trouble. And Brain, it must be remembered, was already wearing his mock SS gear, minus the boots. Opening his door with trembling hands, he let the two men in and only calmed down when Brain told him what they were on about and who had sent them. He lit a candle and let my grandfather pick a pair of jackboots that fitted and were still relatively presentable at first sight. Theft was a wide-spread phenomenon, had to be, it always flourishes in any kind of scarcity economy. To function smoothly, the black market had to be regularly provided with saleable goods. Which reminds me. I notice you're running dry. Waiter!"

Laura, who already felt slightly under the influence, made a lamely defensive gesture which Gillian either didn't notice or chose to ignore.

"So, finally, my grandfather had his gear together. Time to put it to the litmus test. They hurried down to the quay, where the crew of the ship they had chosen for their purposes were about to cast off the land hawsers. The crowd of pale, emaciated and barely dressed prisoners and forced labourers who had found no room in the hold and were, hence, sitting or standing on deck, half hanging over the railing like so much washing to dry, were guarded by only a few soldiers. There was no sudden revolt to be expected from those human wrecks, and even if they had turned against their guards and overpowered them, where would they go from there? Hence, two visibly bored officers seemed all the Germans had thought necessary to set aside to supervise the operation. The prisoners on deck risked freezing to death the moment the ship stood out to sea, exposing its passengers to the vile Northerlies. Those in the hold risked being blown up or drowning in case a bomb or torpedo found its way to them. My grandfather had picked up a piece of rope on their way down to the harbour and tied Lily's hands behind his back for a surplus of authenticity. Arriving at the gangway, they were immediately stopped by a soldier who saluted wearily first, and then requested to see some papers. Brain had expected that to happen, of course, and had prepared a major piece of bollocks, which, to the uninformed observer, must have sounded not totally unlike the famous Paprikaschnitzel tantrum that Charlie Chaplin throws in The Great Dictator. Hitler's German must have sounded rather bizarre to many Germans, even then, let alone now, of course?"

Laura nodded.

"Well, that's always been one of the greatest mysteries of the Third Reich for me. His Austrian German would sound peculiar to us in many instances, like you say. In his studied tirades, he would mix up his prepositions, every now and again, and gesticulate like Rumpelstiltskin. His writing has neither rhyme nor reason but is a hotchpotch expression of idiosyncratic ideological and racist leanings. How a man of such relative illiteracy managed to become the Pied Piper of a nation that had been a model of cultural creativeness as well as scientific prowess escapes me to this very day. I just don't understand it, I'm afraid."

"Well, whatever. My grandfather's Chaplin-inspired bollocks, incomprehensible as it probably was, left the soldier with the deep overall impression Brain had hoped to create: what in flaming hell he was thinking of, asking him for papers. Would he ask the Fuehrer to kindly present his ID? This was a top-secret Night-and-Fog operation which demanded no bloody paperwork. If such documents fell into the enemy's hands by any chance, the lives of hundreds of German secret agents would be at stake. Had he never heard of the Enigma disaster? And where were his superiors hiding anyway? You get the picture... The next in command, who had followed much of the exchange from the bridge, wasn't slow in presenting himself on the gangway. Now, you have to remember that, at high water, said gangway would lie more or less horizontal and would, hence, be easy to cross either way. But at low water, the thing had such a slope it resembles a chute for pigs' carcasses more than anything. And so, while Brain and Lily zoomed past the confused soldier, to climb up the gangway, the officer in charge came more or less sliding down at them in a rather ridiculous posture, which put him at a disadvantage. All Brain and Lily had to do was side-step him and let him tumble down the slope. By the time he had picked himself up again, and knocked the dust off his uniform, Brain and Lily had already gained the high ground. From up there, Brain flung some more abuse at the two Germans: perhaps they would prefer to help the bloody Soviets with their railroad projects in the Far East? Well, that could easily be arranged. A single phone call would do, and so on and so forth. Getting sent to the Eastern front was the one thing all members of the German occupation forces feared more than anything. The mere mention of it would strike terror in the hearts of even the bravest of them. And while he was ranting and raving like the Fuehrer himself, Brain would slap Lily round the ears every now and again, for good measure, as it were. There would be no more talk of papers, of course. On the contrary, Brain and Lily were hurriedly attributed a cabin normally occupied by the two officers. Without thanking the Germans with more than a gracious nod, Brain took possession of the place and installed himself and Lily in their quarters. Here, the matter of unnecessary slapping seems to have come up as a subject to be heatedly discussed during most of the passage. I say, cheers!"

Another toast followed. Laura tried to pull herself together and think clearly. The fact that Brain had slapped Lily about must have been painful and humiliating. But not serious enough reason for later vendettas. On the whole, then, this meeting with Gillian, pleasant as it was, risked not yielding any clues either. All the more reason to enjoy the company of both Ignace and Gillian, now that she had come all the way to Gibraltar anyway.

"That said, the passage to St. Malo seems to have been rougher than the weather conditions at their departure from St. Sampson had given cause to suspect. On the bright side: in weather like that, the ship would be less exposed to bombers or submarines. Lancasters returning from the flattening of German cities made it a habit to drop any explosive left-overs over the wider Channel area for fear the plane might otherwise blow up during a possible crash-landing. Once the ship had arrived in St. Malo, Brain and Lily had had no problem disappearing without a trace in the bedlam of hundreds of zombies going ashore and guards having to herd them onto trains or lorries. My grandfather got rid of his compromising uniform in a dark archway, swapping it for the clothes he had found in the cabin. Then, the two of them hid in a fishing boat till its owner succeeded in bringing them together with the local Résistance. My grandmother, I'm proud to say, was French."

So that was where her lively disposition stemmed from, Laura thought.

"I hope I have been of some service in some way…"

"Absolutely. That was more than we could ever have hoped for. What an excellent memory you got there."

A lot less, though, she secretly added, than we would have needed to be getting on with things. Better change the subject.

"Doesn't it mean a lot of stress selling real estate here on the Rock, where living space is so scarce?"

Gillian only laughed.

"Stressful? Maybe. But rewarding. The more restricted the availability, the higher the price. The higher the price, the more substantial the commission. Well, you know all about that. But, seriously, if you're interested in acquiring an apartment or office-complex because of the favourable tax climate, no income and very little corporation tax, I might be able to point you to some attractive locations."

"Where? Underground?"

"If you prefer…Lying in wait for the Germans who would never get here, the Brits drilled a whole system of tunnels and bunkers into the Rock so that you might speak of a town underneath the town. You've got to go take a look, really impressive. The Germans had hoped Franco, whose behind they had bailed out during the Spanish Civil War, would return the favour by letting them pass through his country so that they could take Gibraltar. But Franco's reckoning was another. By refusing the Germans that crucial passage, he hoped the Brits would show themselves grateful enough to hand Gibraltar back to the Spaniards. How wrong can you be? Once the British lion has put his paw on a piece of land, be it Gibraltar or the Falklands, it will not let go of it for love nor money. I'll drink to that."

3. The Toad

"Another blank, then?" Laura commented on their flight back to London.

"I don't know about you, but I feel my conviction dwindling. Somehow, I no longer believe we'll ever be able to create that breakthrough and shed the necessary new light on all of this mess. I mean, you can't say we haven't tried, now, can you? But we seem to be getting nowhere."

Ignace was holding Lamont's list on his knees but seemed to be looking right through it somehow.

"I think you're being too pessimistic, mom. In my humble opinion, we are even hard on the killer's heels but don't realize it, because we keep looking the wrong way. If we're not on our guard, we'll be stepping on the snake's tail without being aware we were following it all the time. That's when we risk getting bitten."

Laura could not follow his logic.

"What are you driving at?" Ignace shook his curly head.

"I wish I knew. It seems to me we're looking at the dark sky, searching for a black hole, by its nature invisible."

"The sky being the list?"

"Yes, the bloody list with its six major planets."

"So what do you suggest?"

"Like I say, the black hole as such is invisible. What do astronomers do when searching for one they suspect exists somewhere out there in some obscure neck of the universe?"

"You got me there."

"Well, I'm not an astronomer either, obviously, not even a fledgeling one. But I think what they do is look for anomalies in the orbital wanderings of the planets closest to the spot where they suspect the black hole – the one perhaps almost imperceptible erratic movement most likely to have been caused by the gravitational force wielded on the planet by the black hole. That's when you know approximately where it must be and can even compute its approximate size, which needs to be commensurate with the tractive force it can muster. Laura laughed.

"But that's how astronomers go about it," Ignace protested.

"Okay, I believe you, Han Solo. But what's it got to do with our list and the Boxer? If I understand your metaphor correctly, you think our killer or the Black Hole, as he will be known as henceforth, is linked to the Yarmouth Six alright, but has no immediate relation to any of the persons on the list and…, what?"

"In whatever we already did and possibly will learn about the Yarmouth Six, we'll have to be on the look-out for some odd detail, perhaps only a strange aside, whatever, that will point us in the direction of the Boxer. We may not immediately recognize or even understand it. But it's got to be there."

"Provision of deduced evidence, a highly speculative method. Besides, we only have one more possible witness left, don't we?

"Yes. Ronny Goldsmith, from Portsmouth. The Achilles of the group." Laura laughed.

"Well, then let's hope he's going to present us with the one vulnerable spot of the gang, it's Achilles' heel. If he doesn't…."

"We'll have to start all over again. Problem: he has practically no descendants. A son, who disappeared in the Australian Outback somewhen during the nineteen eighties."

"Probably eaten by a croc or bitten by a taipan, torn to bits by a great white or electrocuted by a sea wasp, take your pick. A good place to die, Australia. What I'm wondering is, how can anyone live there?"

"Yeah, well, the Goldsmith clan is probably doomed, one way or another. If it hasn't already died out. The only grandchild that crops up on Lamont's list used to live on Martinique."

"Used to? That doesn't sound too good."

"It isn't, not for him, not for us. He was killed in a shoot-out between two competing drug gangs, more than a year ago, actually. So, we won't have to look for him, I guess."

"Now you seem a little rash. People rarely vanish entirely without trace. Not if they can help it. We may frequently get that impression, because we didn't find anything or didn't even bother to look. In our perfectly justified indignation about the world having the nerve to just carry on regardless after our decease, most of us have that desire to leave something or other behind, a proof of life, if you will. You know what. I'll contact Solitaire and ask her to activate her Martinique connections. It may turn out to be another blank alright. But he's our last chance, I guess. And if there's anything at all, Sol and those guys on Martinique will find it, you can rely on that. What about the Australian's wife?"

"He was a Brit, never married. The guy on Martinique was born out of wedlock."

"Age?"

"Who?"

"The grandson, stupid, the grandson."

"Twenty-five at the time of his death."

"Old enough to have been around girls. Somebody close to him, anyway."

"Somebody who he told the story of his pugnacious grandad to?"

"Go on, ridicule me."

She formed a cup with both hands and held them to her mouth, "I am only your mother."

"Okay, sorry, Darth Mader. But what do you expect from Sol in this context?"

"No idea, tiger, just a hunch. In his fear of drowning, a man will hold on to anything – a snake, if need be. Sol's my snake. Don't you go tell her. What's the guy's name?"

"Jean-Baptiste Renard, aka Le Crapaud."

"Really? The toad? His CV reads more like that of a Crapule."

"No, Le Crapaud. Isn't that what they call the…"

"…inhabitants of Jersey, yes. Maybe there's a link there somewhere. I doubt it. In case the Toad left anything but sticky, poisonous slime behind, Sol's people at Fort-de-France will track it down, that you can bet your mock-astronomer's ass on."

They both fell silent for a while, each plunged into their own thoughts. Finally, Laura seized her son's arm.

"But this is the last bullet, Master Ignace. If we miss again, you'll find yourself back in Florida the very next day. Read my lips: Florida, US of A. No point in blowing your career at this stage. Some crimes are solved only after many years have gone by. Simply because new methods of forensic analysis have been discovered or somebody decided to come clean at long last on his or her death-bed. We really cannot wait that long. Seriously, promise me that. We worked our way through the list in good faith and, common-place as it may sound, life does go on, elsewhere."

"Alright," Ignace agreed and squeezed her hand.

Laura kept watching him from the corner of her eye. Convinced wasn't the adjective she would have chosen to describe Ignace' present state of mind.

From her Hamburg office, she phoned Solitaire. After the sisters had gossiped for a while about Jerry, Solitaire's husband, as well as about their two kids, Bobby and Penny, Laura gave Solitaire a brief account of their investigations into Solveig's murder. The matter being downright confusing, anyway, she left out a lot of less salient detail and came to her request.

"Get it?" Solitaire asked back.

"Do I get it? No, I'm afraid not. Sounds like a God-awful mess you've lost yourself in again. Do you do it deliberately, and if so, why? To punish yourself? I can't make you out, sis, I really can't. Just let me know what you want me to do."

Laura told her about Jean-Baptiste, the Martinique Toad.

"I may be getting carried away there by my hunting instincts, but I refuse to believe people vanish without a trace, see? He must have left something behind, a little more than just his footprints."

Solitaire laughed.

"Well, I guess he left his fingerprints as well. I hate to contradict you. But ask some folks in Tijuana or Medellin, they have seen whole armies of people disappear without trace. But alright, I'll see what I can do. I'll get in touch. When do we see each other again? Bobby and Penny keep pestering me about Aunt Laura…"

"I like the sound of that. How's the boy doing, anyway?"

"Keeps hanging in this or that palm tree, helping with the co-conut harvest. Bobby and Ignace, that would be the real terror of the Caribbean…" Laura laughed.

"You could be right there. But apart from that, I might soon have more free time on my hands than I might care for. So, I could travel and visit my next of kin in Greece and the Caribbean, let's wait and see."

She sketched the rough outlines of her negotiations with the bank and the repercussions they might produce with regard to her leading position in the firm.

"Well, you had better not fuck it up then, hadn't you? Anyway, you'll always be welcome here, you know that. Jerry can teach you to fly a plane, so you can do some serious island hopping or be a drug carrier for Theo."

"Me pilot a plane? That'll be the day. Theo? Is he still alive?"

"So they keep telling me. His subscription must still be valid. But he's getting old, doesn't fly to Kingston town that frequently any more. Guess Brigitte has left him for a younger guy, the kind of thing women will do if and when not properly looked after."

"Did he ever discover Ti Martin's recent grave on his premises at all?"

"If so, he never mentioned it. He's a man who has seen a lot in his lifetime. You can't expect him to pay undue attention to a fresh grave appearing smack on his golf course. Anyway, I had better look for Bobby before he takes the next liana to town. Like I said, I'll be in touch. Kisses and hugs all round and do take care. You seem to be dealing with a really mean raptor there."

As always when talking to her sister, Laura hated to hang up. Her thoughts went back to Dominica. Life on the island wasn't carefree, far from it, at the best of times. Now, so shortly after the passage of the hurricane, it was downright cumbersome. Still, the problems there had a different, more immediately palpable quality which made them more easily bearable somehow.

As if on cue, Marquardt entered her office without knocking. He was the only one to enjoy that privilege.

"What's up, Heinz?"

"Hi Laura. Good to see you back again. I tried my level best, I honestly did, but we're not making any headway. I think you will have to have another heart to heart with Sir Lucas. The bank people pretend they are still checking a few details. Rubbish, of course. It all seems to hinge on Lamont."

"And the Dutch, what's their attitude?"

"They keep turning the price screw. So would I, in their place. For us, it's a double whammy: our goodwill is systematically undervalued, their goodwill systematically jazzed up. Like I say, another one on one with Lamont could work wonders. You might even consider...."

„Consider what?" Marquardt started stuttering. Laura dropped her pen, looked up from her papers and pretended she didn't know what exactly he was talking about.

"Yes, you were saying?"

Marquardt shrugged his shoulders and smiled sheepishly.

"Well, since I seem to be at the end of my tether charm-wise, maybe it's your turn now to deploy yours."

Laura shook her head disapprovingly.

"Heinz, you disappoint me there. The man is ninety-odd years old. An OD of Viagra's going to DOA him. And for me to lie naked under the corpse of a very old trooper who didn't smell all that good while he was alive is not my idea of a killer weekend. Sorry, Heinz. I am prepared to go the extra mile for the well-being of the firm, you know that, but there are limits to self-sacrifice."

Marquardt had hardly left when her mobile rang again.

"Sol? Forgot something?"

"Not that I know of." It was the Chief's voice.

"Hallo again Laura. I take it you've just been talking to your sister now. Right, none of my business, I agree. It looks like someone may have been watching you getting into contact with Gillian Donovan at Gibraltar, though. May I make so bold as to enquire about any possible fruits of that conversation? Concerning the case at hand, I mean?"

"You may, Chief, you're welcome to. On balance, nothing that would get us so much as a step further, unfortunately. A very pleasant person, though, Gillian."

Colestron fell silent for an ominous moment. Laura didn't like it.

"Anything wrong? You're not telling me....No!"

The Chief Superintendent gave a nervous cough which bode evil.

"All we know is that she hopped on the Casablanca ferry shortly after having lunched with you and Ignace. Trouble is, she hasn't arrived there as yet. Not that we know of. Under any other circumstances, we probably wouldn't worry all that much. But in view of the context…"

"And she couldn't have jumped ship unnoticed at Tangiers?"

"The CC cameras in the harbour would have picked her up there, I guess."

Laura felt thunderstruck. She remembered the story of Death having an appointment with Ali in Samaria and she felt sick at the thought that Gillian unwittingly might have predicted her own end.

"The Gibraltar Straits have peculiar currents. Anyone who falls overboard during a passage has next to no chance of survival, as is amply proven by the number of North African illegal migrants who lost their lives trying to cross it in unfit craft. Which is why a Maghreb politician once called the Straits Morocco's largest graveyard. Sorry I have to be the harbinger of sad tidings. You're sure though, there's nothing you would want to share with us?"

"Yes, dead sure. Except that this Yarmouth business has now become a little more personal for me too, now."

"Yes, I can understand that. Nevertheless, you should keep your distance and leave the work to us, my colleagues, that is. It could be a mere coincidence. In the real estate business, you easily make yourself enemies: people squeezed out of their homes to be upgraded and resold, for instance. Or jealous competitors. It's all mafia structures, you know."

"That may be so. A word of advice from me too: you better hurry to catch the killer, 'cause if and when the Forster sisters lay their hands on him, he can kiss his chances of remission goodbye."

SEVENTH CHAPTER

1. Betty Boop

The small package from Roseau, Dominica, which Solitaire had announced by phone, arrived a few days later via courier. Solitaire had been as good as her word and contacted some people on Martinique who had looked around the seedy harbour quarters of Fort-de-France. Not the police. They would have needed to trigger a time-consuming process of obtaining a search warrant, possibly several. Which would have incurred lots of unwelcome questions. No, such things were better dealt with inhouse, so to speak.

It turned out the Toad had of late hung out in one of the miserable wooden hovels that made up the town's less salubrious outskirts. Its warped walls and rusty corrugated-iron roof had not seen fresh paint in decades. Inside a saggy, worn-out splotchy mattress whose original colour was a matter of conjecture. The lot complete with used syringes, empty pizza and burger boxes, three or four empty rum bottles and half a dozen mangled beer cans. What in God's name was anyone to find in this gargantuan mess? No self-respecting mongrel would have spent more time here than it took to knock up a bitch.

Yet first impressions can be fallacious. When Sol's people slit the mattress, what should come to the fore, next to a handful of green bucks, but a kind of scrapbook which, even though it looked in a sorry state, promised fresh information. Its cover was lacking altogether and most of its pages had been tanned by the Caribbean sun and marbleized by uncountable spilled cups, mugs, and glasses filled with beverages of all colours of the rainbow. The writing was tiny, with the lines so close to one another you needed a good pair of binoculars to keep them apart. Not surprisingly, therefore, it had taken Solitaire quite some time to realize what a true gem the Martinique guys had presented her with. It was a primitive scrapbook or "journal" put together by

Ronny Goldsmith in clumsy handwriting and simple language. What objective he had pursued with that, how the scrapbook had found its way to the Toad and why the latter had bothered to sit on it over all those years, were questions that had to remain unanswered for the time being. Pecuniary interests were hardly at play. For third parties, Ronnie's notes represented no value at all. Even a historian working on the subject of either the Channel Islands or the Yarmouth Six would presumably not have deigned to thumb through that sort of material. What they represented for Laura and Ignace would remain to be seen.

Laura asked her secretary to scan the lot so she could download and work them over in order to make the text more easily accessible. For someone who knew how to use his fists, Ronny had a surprisingly small, almost childish, no-frills handwriting. His way of expressing himself was simple, but to the point. If there had ever been something of a foreword, it seemed irretrievably lost, because, together with the cover, some of the initial pages had been ripped out.

Here again, Laura had to feel her way through to the moment when Operation Sea Leopard had to be considered at least a partial failure. What followed didn't seem to differ dramatically from the other versions she had read or heard so far. Frustrating news for the hobby astronomer, she thought.

After the dinghy had given up, we floated in the ice-cold water for a while. The fog that suddenly sprang up hid us from the Germans, but also from the Sunfish. We were stiff with the cold to a man. If the tide hadn't pushed us on the rocks so quickly, I don't think we would have lasted a quarter of an hour longer.

As we crawled ashore on all fours, I looked back at the Duke. He was swimming towards the cliffs. Paddling rather, like a dog. I reached out for him with my left arm while clinging to a rock with my right. He was just about to seize it, when Gooey started shouting, croaking, rather. He was about to drown, funny enough. His shouting for help was muffled by the water every time his mouth went under the surface in a wave. But what noise he did make was not only heart-rending for us but could also be sufficient to catch the Germans' attention. Gooey being the best swimmer of the lot, I didn't understand what problems he had to keep above the surface. The knapsack on his back didn't exactly help, of course, but even so…. Maybe he had suffered a sudden heart attack, God knows.

Laura took off her glasses, cleaned them and enlarged the writing yet some more notches.

I was about to jump off the cliffs again to lend Gooey a helping hand. But the Duke gestured for me to stay where I was and paddled back to Gooey, who was only yards away from him. The fog was lifting again at that moment, but it remained kind of hazy. Which is why I could not really see exactly what happened out there. I'm pretty sure the Duke was trying his level best to pull Gooey up yet the man must have been at the end of his physical tether, and Gooey in boots, fatigues, and with the knapsack must have been pretty heavy. Like I say, I couldn't quite make out the details because of the haze. The Duke suddenly had Gooey's knapsack in his right arm while paddling towards us with his left. Gooey had gone under. I looked at the others. Everybody was lying on the rocks half dead, their faces either down or towards the shore.

Laura asked to be brought another coffee and kept gazing at the screen. It was a strange account, she thought. She couldn't put her finger on it, but it read like it had a sub-text Ronny hadn't cared to spell out. Why stress the fact that it was still very hazy? Did he suspect foul play? And if so, why didn't he say so? She dropped the spoon with which she had been busy stirring her coffee, sort of absent-mindedly. That was it! That was the "anomaly" they had been looking for. It had to be. If Luke the Duke, instead of pulling Gooey to the surface, had pushed him down beneath it, as Ronny seemed to insinuate, that would be a motive for whoever made it his business to revenge Gooey. But how would the killer know? Not from Ronny's scrapbook, that was for sure. And yet, as he noted himself, Ronny would have been the only witness. The blob in the orbit was there alright, but the black hole itself remained elusive. Maybe there was more to come.

I know it may sound odd, but thoughts were racing round my head at that moment. I realized I would probably fare best pretending I hadn't noticed anything untoward. Because, in fact, I hadn't. To split up our group by putting forward possibly unfounded accusations would have helped no-one. At the same time, however, I decided to watch my back whenever the Duke was around. I may have been an indiscriminate bully, but he might be a stone-cold killer.

What followed were notes of the discussions on the subject of staying together versus splitting up. Ronny had apparently felt secretly observed by the Duke. Lamont probably wanted to know what Ronny had seen and whether or not he was likely to snitch. If Lamont was what Ronny took him for, he would try and not leave open ends, at any rate, so that Ronny did well to watch his back.

I left the cave after the Duke, but before the others. At night, like a common thief, I arrived at the Coupée. The guards there were up in arms, no idea why. Maybe they had discovered traces of the Duke having given them the slip. For me, the Coupée would be off limits. Besides, I was afraid they might strew even more mines. I mean, getting killed by a bullet is one thing. But getting your legs ripped off and then bleeding to death is a shitty way to go. Hence, I turned on my heels and made for the few houses that formed the village. Here, I lay down flat on my belly next to a hothouse full of flowers. Excited Germans were dashing to and fro in a flurry for a while, pushed this way and that by their nervous officers. I mean, these people hadn't seen an enemy soldier in years. So, when there was talk of a raid, it must really have looked like a dress-rehearsal for D-day for them. But soon, all fell quiet again. I even managed to doze off for a couple of hours. During daytime, next day, I kept watching the one-storey building next to the hothouse. It appeared to be occupied by a single person. A woman around thirty, chubby, rustic, but by no means ugly, with a pair of boobs that made my fingers twitch. When I had ascertained beyond a shadow of a doubt that no Germans had taken up quarter with her, I sneaked to the door as noiselessly as humanly possible. It was only when I felt the pointed prongs of a pitchfork in my backside that I realized I had underestimated the Lady's watchfulness. As it turned out, she had already noticed me at the hothouse but not reacted in any way because she had counted on my disappearing again sooner or later. Yet when I moved on her house, she had felt the time had come to intervene.

Laura smiled. The episode reminded her of her first encounter with Harry Colestron at the Gillileje summer bungalow. Would she have acted as courageously as this lady under comparable circumstances? Probably, but without the pitchfork.

I explained to the woman who I was, where I came from and what business I had on Sark. She must have believed me because she dropped her pitchfork and asked me in like a hunch-backed relative on a surprise visit who had just been blown in on the ferry. She proved a real lady, pitchfork or not. She hid me away in the house, gave me a slice of bread, water, some own-grown vegetables and potatoes. Then, she directed me to the sofa as my bed. Dead tired as I was, I tried it out immediately. It proved too small even for me, so I had to curl up like a tomcat. But it worked. I slept like a log for hours on end.

Laura's mobile rang. Ignace wanted to make a lunch appointment with her, but Laura was too keen on reading the rest of Ronny's story.

"You were right, you know. I think I found the anomaly we talked about. The black hole is there, somewhere, definitely. Let's discuss it tonight, shall we."

Ignace would have preferred to come to her office there and then, but Laura wished to read it all to the end herself, first. A touch of egotism, perhaps, but justifiable, she felt. Ignace would get it straight from her mouth later.

We took a definite liking to each other, Betty and I. Fell in love, if you prefer. Before we knew it, we had established a daily routine and lived together as if we had never done anything else. During daytime, I would stay in the house, do the invisible man stunt. After nightfall, I would help her in the vegetable garden.

Outside, I would move about only at night, always alone and, most of the time, in pieces of Betty' clothing, so that any inquisitive neighbours might mistake me for her at some distance. Minus the boobs, of course. I would no longer sleep on the couch but in her double bed, glued to her voluptuous body for some animal warmth. Her sex was of the barn floor kind. No frills, no extras, as generously offered by the French whores that came to visit us at our Yarmouth camp every now and again with the permission of our elders and betters, of course. But that didn't matter. Communication between us was easy and pleasant. I never learned Betty Boop's age, nor her real family name, incidentally. That she must be quite a few years older than myself, of that there was no doubt, considering her collection of wrinkles in the right places. But despite the difference in age, we seemed to be getting on just fine.

Till that fateful morning when the Germans surrounded the house and hammered at the front door. I realized the game was up and came out with my arms raised above my head. There had been no gun in the house that I knew of, anyway. And even if it had, there was absolutely nothing to be gained from a gory shoot-out.

During much of the days and weeks to come, I obviously kept wondering who it was had given us away. Some jealous neighbour, perhaps, who had looked through my camouflage and sold us to the Germans for a pocketful of coins, as it were. Things like that happened all the time. Why would folks on the islands be better than the rest of us? But the longer I thought about it, the more convinced I was of the probability that Betty herself had called in the Germans. Which would explain why nothing happened to her that I could see. They had left her alone, untouched. Obviously, that kind of let-down infuriated me. If at least I could have understood it. Maybe she was married and afraid her husband, fighting at some Western front, might come home unexpectedly. She could have told me and I would have left. After the war, I wanted to pay her a last visit and ask her what had got into her then. But what the hell. Water under the bridge. Why should I shame her and cause her problems? What would that have given me other than destroying the memory of a few wonderful weeks we had had together anyway?

When the Germans had beaten me up and taken me back to St. Peter Port tied on all fours like a wild boar shot outside of the hunting season, I still thought differently about that. I had just had time enough to don my uniform rags. Thus, I could at least demand to be treated as a POW. But that soon proved naive. Even without Hitler's Night-and-Fog decree, the Germans were not willing to treat that mad British dog as a combatant. Why they hadn't just stood me up against the wall of Betty's house and shot me in full view of the owner, I don't know. Maybe they thought that an execution squad or some improvised gallows would be too lenient for a bastard like myself. Much better watch him die slowly from exhaustion, starvation, and daily beatings. And you have to hand it to them, what followed didn't fall far from their expectations.

By and large, Laura thought, Ronny had found a fluid, almost elegant style of writing. The sentences, if they got a little long-winded at times, never lost clarity. His vocabulary wasn't exactly rich. For that, he would have to have read a lot more than he had probably ever had occasion to. All of this proved that some considerable time span must have elapsed between individual passages, which were unfortunately not dated. Whatever Ronny had done meanwhile, he had apparently not just wasted his time but reflected on what had happened to him and tried to tie some of the odds and ends together.

2. The Ship

When it comes to strikingly unique features among the Channel Islands, not only Sark, but also Alderney has something to show for itself. Geographically speaking, it is situated closer to the French coast than to any of its neighbouring islands. True to Oscar Wilde's quip that he who is despised does well to look despising, small, insignificant Alderney seems to turn its back on the likes of Guernsey, Jersey, Sark and the others quite deliberately. Looking at Alderney from above, you may probably have reason to ask yourself whether you're dealing with an island, at all, or rather with a cleverly disguised ship. Her lack of any vegetation to speak of as well as the three dreaded races that surround her – Swinge in the North, Screech in the South and the Ras d'Aurigny, as the French call it, in the East - seem to transform her into a vessel heading West on the rising tide and East at the falling one.

Add to this the fact that, irrespective of where exactly you may place yourself in the open on Alderney, you will never lose sight of the sea even for a moment. Which makes you feel you're facing not so much the topography of an island as the decks of a sizeable ship. Not surprisingly then, many of the Soviet forced labourers at home in the endless recesses of birchwood Russia beyond the Ural, folks in no way familiar with the ocean, are said to have had the impression, upon their arrival on Alderney, to have been trans-shipped from one floating coffin onto another.

To this day, Braye Harbour does little or nothing to confirm Alderney's alleged island character. How could it, never having been much more than a grand project of Victorian engineering cut back to its present pedestrian size by the combined forces of nature and the economy. The only thing that protects the harbour from the devastating onslaught of the Atlantic rollers hammering at Alderney's doors at all times is the island's long breakwater. Impressive as it may seem at first sight, it's a kind of concrete giant resting on feet of clay. Crumbling away under the perpetual rush of the sea, it tends to spring leaks and breaches that have to be stopped time and time again.

One of the Guernsey men who had been arrested, indicted for sabotage and sent to Sylt labour camp, where I was privileged to make his acquaintance, told me an interesting anecdote about Alderney. In fact, it was a kind of sailing instruction he had received when he had decided to earn his living as a fisherman age eighteen or thereabouts, he said.

Now, it must be said that this was long before radar, GPS and fish finders became standard equipment on even the smallest of fishing vessels. Hence, whenever you got caught by one of the fogbanks suddenly forming in the Bay, you had a serious problem of orientation. Fishermen then, it must also be remembered, were busy, most of the time, preparing their gear, bringing out or hauling in their nets and all the rest of it. In other words, they didn't have much time to plot courses, do their dead reckoning, to define their exact position, in other words. So, they were prone to getting caught out by fog, apparently one of the eeriest experiences you can have at sea, not made more pleasant by your knowledge of the proximity of granite rocks and reefs all around you. From one moment to the next, you are blindfolded, so your other senses must take over – ears and nose, primarily. Skin, even.

A tall ship called Padua on its way to fetch wheat from Australia, that Guernsey man told me, once passed an iceberg in the roaring forties or screaming fifties in dense fog. A life-threatening situation. The crew, pricking their ears and spreading their nasal wings, heard the sea birds on the berg, felt the temperature drop dramatically for a moment, even smelled the remnants of the fish that had served the marine fowl for lunch, but never laid their eyes on the thing. At other times you may approach the massive rock of an island such the Shetlands or Fair Isle and only find it take shape the moment you can virtually touch its rock faces with your outstretched arms.

Anyway. Whenever caught by fog on your way north to the fishing grounds of the Channel, this man was told by an older, vastly more experienced colleague, don't panic. Just continue on your compass course till you suddenly see what looks like the contours of the huge hull of a ship take shape in front of you.

That'll be the island of Alderney. That's where you want to turn sharply to starboard.

I found that Guernsey man downright fascinating. I hope he survived Sylt and lived a happy life ever after. According to what he said then, at Sylt camp, we were on a ship of the dead. In their eager pursuit of transforming the entire archipelago, and, in particular, Alderney, into floating fortresses, the Germans, spurred on by their monomaniac Fuehrer, seem to have felt a like similarity of the island to a battleship. That's probably why, when it came to installing heavy artillery batteries here, they automatically fell back on such cannon as had been dismounted from captured and laid-up enemy men-of-war. It must have been a natural choice. Thus, the biggest single artillery piece to be found on Alderney was a Russian calibre 305 millimetres ship's cannon I'll call Crazy Ivan for simplicity's sake. This was not your run-of-the-mill piece, mind you. Before even getting to Alderney, Crazy Ivan had already completed an odyssey liable to illustrate the lesser absurdities of war. It originated from a Russian ship of the line captured by the Germans during the First World War and handed over as a gift to the representatives of the ailing Osman Empire, who chose to station it at Izmir.

What with the Osman Empire going under for good, soon after, Crazy Ivan somehow made its way to Belarus, where the French seem to have picked it up and intermediately stored it at a Tunisian harbour. When the Second World War broke out, guns suddenly were in great demand again, obviously. The two Scandinavian countries Finland and Norway, devoid of any gun production of their own and notoriously short of cash to boot, expressed their interest in purchasing Crazy Ivan. Swedish Karlskrona with its renowned Bofors gun company would, of course, have been a more natural choice than France, let alone Tunisia. But, alas, the devious Swedes had declared themselves neutral. Besides, Bofors were specialised in smaller-calibre rapid-fire cannon as used in modern mobile marine warfare, whereas their Scandinavian neighbours felt they needed big-calibre long-range cannon to be deployed in defensive stationary coastal batteries, firing one shot per hour, so to speak.

The Finns were lucky in that, not Crazy Ivan, but some other canon arrived safely and in time. Which meant that the Russians, during their Karelia campaign, found themselves fired at from coastal batteries built by Russian engineers, with canon stemming from Russian ships. The boom must have sounded vaguely familiar to them.

As might have been suspected, the cargo ship transporting Crazy Ivan to Norway, never arrived at its destination. It was captured by the Germans and the guns mounted on the Channel Islands, with Crazy Ivan taking the uncontested lead on Alderney. In other words, in the course of a quarter century or thereabouts, the thing had been shipped round half the globe without ever firing so much as a single shot in anger.

It takes more than one canon to make a fortress. Alderney was to receive ever more batteries, flak, MG nests, fire control centres and so on, the lot connected by an intricate system of tunnels and bunkers, soldiers' quarters, magazines, even underground field hospitals.

To put those ambitious plans into practice, the Germans needed labour, lots of it. Which is why they had erected no less than four camps on an island that measures roughly two miles by three, land miles, that is. These four camps had been named after German North Sea islands: Borkum, Norderney, Helgoland, and Sylt. These islands had for many decades been German holiday favourites and would, to the uninformed German observer, evoke pleasant images of sunny days by the sea. For the miserable labourers on Alderney such as myself, they became household names of horror.

As comparable as their respective size and structure must seem, their target groups were different. All of them were closed shop, though, in a manner of speaking.

If you were lucky enough to get to Borkum camp, your odds of survival were just about even. The men lodging here were mostly nationals of such West European countries as the Nazis had overrun during the first months of the war already: Dutch, Belgians, Frenchmen, together with some Spanish members of the opposition against the Franco regime. There were even volunteers who preferred working here for a pittance to sitting at home penniless. All a matter of perspective, I guess. Others again had been sent here because they had committed minor offences which could not be classified as sabotage by any stretch of the imagination. Because sabotage invariably carried a death sentence.

Hence, a motley crowd that didn't exactly lead the life of Riley, but got along somehow, and, with any luck at all, stayed alive.

The composition of the Norderney population was more homogeneous in that it housed preponderantly East Europeans: Russians, Ukrainians, Belarusians, Poles, and so on. They were considered second or third-class human beings by the Nazis. To even get into contact with them was difficult. At first sight, they seemed to form a kind of linguistic-ethnic monolith, as they should, most of them coming from what came later to be called the Eastern Block. As soon as you bothered to take a closer look, you noticed, however, that they, too, had their own little hierarchies, with Russians resenting being called comrades by the wrong socialist neighbour. And so, Russians, more equal than the rest of the lot, would stick to Russians, Ukrainians to Ukrainians, and so forth. Such structures were hard to penetrate not only for linguistic and cultural reasons, but also because of the all-pervading lack of trust. Deep-rooted distrust and fear of spies and snitches had become part of their DNA long before they had even come to Alderney. The situation there being what it was, such Stalinist characteristics of the cement people became strengthened, if anything. Cement people, incidentally, was a nickname not only for the East Europeans, but for more or less all of us. This was due to the fine layer of that sticky stuff being permanently embedded in every pore of our bodies, so that, after only a week in the camp, we would look like an army of skeletons dipped in cement.

Inner, mental homogeneity was perhaps even greater at Helgoland. That was the camp reserved for Jews, generally. Not Jews from the islands, but, again, largely from Eastern Europe. On the Nazi scale of disdain, those people ranked rock bottom. Survival here was not necessarily on the cards, but still a vague hope.

Not so at Sylt. If, at Norderney and Helgoland, you were slowly dying, at Sylt you were a dead man walking. Whereas the other three camps so to speak fulfilled logistic purposes and could somehow be considered stones in the great puzzle of albeit pointless fortification works, Sylt had but one perverted mission, and that was to break, not granite rocks, but human beings. Which is why, after an initial phase of Wehrmacht administration, it soon came to be run by the SS, the experts on death and annihilation. The only thing that set Sylt off from death camps such as Auschwitz or Bergen-Belsen was the lack of gas chambers and crematoria. Neither was needed here. Men would be killed through excessive physical exertion accompanied by simultaneous chronic starvation and the refusal of access to medical help of any kind. If that failed in rare cases of particularly resilient individuals, the guards – not German, by the way – would resort to beating them with whip-like batons and sticks till they breathed their last. Such terminal punishment could be administered on the smallest of pretexts.

Hence, there were corpses galore on Alderney. At first, they had at least been buried in the sands at low tide. Later, they were just chucked into the sea. Such rustic corpse disposals, it has to said in defence of the Germans, were none of their invention but had long been commonplace in the whole North Sea area and beyond. The grinding movement of the sands at the bottom of the sea, induced by the interplay of strong tidal currents, counter currents, and vortexes, was used for burial purposes in many coastal regions. Corpses once disposed of in that manner were gone for good and would never come to the surface again or be washed ashore as if refusing their sad fate. Having had ample occasion to watch such practices on Alderney, I rarely eat fish and never touch eel.

Who were the unfortunate inmates of the Sylt camp? Well, the Nazis would probably summarily have characterized them as scum. To put it a little less crudely, it could be anyone, irrespective of nationality, creed, or age, who had had the misfortune of catching the Germans' attention: by looking askance at a guard at the wrong moment, or by allegedly not pulling their weight at work, by being rebellious enough to ask for some crumbs of bread or by simply being denounced as a saboteur by someone who wanted to get hold of your blanket. Anything could serve as a pretext and there would be neither investigation nor mercy. You confessed to what you hadn't done and were beaten to death or didn't confess and were beaten to death anyway.

Thus, with a bit of imagination, Sylt could be said to have a supporting function in that it stood out as a permanent threat and stimulant to perform as best you could and never show any weakness, which, for people at the very end of their physical and mental tether, is a lot to ask for.

There were many common criminals as well as political prisoners, who might for instance have distributed leaflets with defeatist slogans back home or criticised the Fuehrer in the presence of the wrong friends and so on. If nothing else seemed to work, sabotage would. It was a proper one-size-fits-all sort of crime. At times of war, there's practically nothing that cannot be ultimately classified as sabotage, viz. as something liable to harm the war effort, even if it is only the theft of a stupid paper clip. It goes to show that if law weds power, their baby will be called ideology.

If this particular constellation at Sylt camp had so much as one advantage, it was the fact that here, to a larger extent than in the other camps, perhaps, you would, time and time again, run into clever, erudite people whose company I kept whenever possible. And for as long as possible, because most of them would only last a few weeks there, if that.

If someone asked me to describe the situation at Sylt camp, I guess I wouldn't know with which of the appalling grievances to start. With the accommodation unfit for human beings, the life-threatening, backbreaking work, the systematic malnutrition, the recurring bouts of epidemics, the nerve-racking parasite infestations, or the regular beatings? I am no Dante, not enough of a magician of words to describe the everyday horror of this hell in a way that might come anywhere close to reality. Which is why I can relate to the taciturnity or even speechlessness of ex-concentration camp prisoners who are asked to give an account of their agonies to a jury in court or a wider TV public. You look into those eyes full of expectation and faces full of sympathy and, at the same time, you know instinctively: irrespective of what I may or may not say, I will not reach these people. Whoever hasn't been through that hell himself or herself will not be able to fathom this kaleidoscope of evil.

Each and every day of grey hopelessness is like the one before. All night long, you keep listening to the wind whistle as it squeezes through the cracks and crannies between the wooden boards of the crudely knocked-up shack. No matter how tight you wrap your flimsy, threadbare blanket, held together by dirt and co-inhabited by all sorts of vermin round your skinny body, it will refuse to warm you. Any time now, you know you will be roused from your wooden bunk in the wee hours of the morning. Your back aches from another night on bare boards without a mattress. In fact, your entire body hurts, itches, and smarts. Sometimes, you're given the sorry excuse of a breakfast in the form of a piece of stale bread with a mug of thin coffee substitute. At other times, not even that. As you raise your head and look around you, grey, sunken faces with hollow dead caverns are staring back at you, greedily eyeing the last bit of bread you're trying to munch with your gums. They are vampires just risen from their graves and as yet uncertain what the day will have in store for them. Well, gentlemen, the options are few and far between, I fear. Their ludicrous grey costumes, tailor-made from empty sacks of cement, the only item there is no shortage of, hang about their bodies like wrappings threatening to fall apart any minute. The undead are in luck: it seems like we're heading for another of those clouded skies over the Channel which the sun's rays will not succeed in penetrating. No risk of vampires being burnt to a crisp at the first contact with sunlight, then. Not today.

As dead as their eyes are, as toothless are their mouths. Teeth are not just for chewing. They give a face shape and dignity. Some may have fallen victims to scurvy. Most, however, were knocked out by the guards or other prisoners in fights over some crumbs of bread.

Breakfast over and done with, the march to one or other of innumerable building sites all around the island starts. As short as the distance may be on a given day, the march is sheer torture for those of us who have no shoes. And that means most of us. Russians, Ukrainians, Kazakhs, Mongols and others were in the habit of walking about with rags instead of shoes on their feet, even in winter. The others, myself included, had to learn first, how to wrap them so they didn't fall off right away, and how to stuff them with straw or grass so they keep the warmth, for a few hours at least. To begin with, some of us did have shoes alright. But they got either stolen or soon fell apart. Then, for days, your feet would look like raw chunks of bloody meat. It's a good cure against sweaty feet, but not necessarily against athlete's foot which, if untreated, has a propensity to spread all over your body. One way or another: whoever falls by the wayside gets beaten till he either stands up again or stays down forever.

Everywhere on the island, groups of workers and forced labourers would dig, hammer or blast holes in the ground and surface rock or help construct this or that piece of observation tower, dragon's teeth or other forms of anti-tank barriers. The Sylt crowd would have the privilege of being deployed at the most dangerous hotspots, mostly in tunnels or bunkers, hence, preferably underground. Most of the island underground consisting of granite, blasting operations were our daily bread. The decisive questions were when and where the next detonation would take place. The Germans displayed their special sort of Schadenfreude humour by not telling us at all or telling us so late we had to run for our lives. Not to make it too easy, they would indicate a direction and say a word of warning, in German. Most of us not understanding the language, we wouldn't know whether the direction they indicated was the one for us to run or the one from where the blast would come.

We may be forgiven for not sharing this odd sense of humour. Most of the Germans spoke enough English to deal on the black market. Here on Alderney, they suddenly seemed to forget it all.

Blasts were not all. Many of the tunnels had been lined with concrete at the beginning. The further you penetrated into the ground, the less support for the walls and roof of the tunnels there would be so that, time and again, you had whole sections collapsing, burying workers under tons of granite. For lack of suitable containers, the spoil from the tunnels would be filled into empty cement sacks to be carried out by workers, whose shoulders and backs were bloody from the pointed slabs and pieces of stone that would press through the sacks, which, on top of that, frequently tore.

The air in the deeper recesses of the tunnels and many of the bunkers was so low on oxygen we often could but crawl on all fours and gasp for air. There were no filter masks, of course. Anyone handling cement would inhale the stuff and sustain silicosis, sooner or later. Which was less dramatic than it sounds, since most candidates died of other causes before it would have been silicosis' turn to have a go.

When working on the construction side of things, building an observation tower, for instance, you had to watch your head. More often than not, material and equipment to be hoisted would be secured rather sloppily. Hence, many men were smashed by bits of timber, blocks, or large concrete slabs.

The concept of lunch breaks did exist. Their primary function, however, seemed to consist in reminding us of our nagging hunger rather than assuaging it by letting us have a square meal. That's the impression you had when staring at your bowl filled with a kind of watery soup so thin you could always see the bottom. There's no carb like low carb.

Late in the evening, often enough at dark, we would be marched back to the camp. Again, men would collapse and be beaten ruthlessly, mercilessly. On the bright side: if they lived, they would now have the night to recover and go back to work the following morning. Anyone not getting up from his bunk at the Réveil would, as a rule, not be seen again, ever.

The double sleepers had been knocked up with raw timber and looked like oversized orange crates. Most coffins are more comfortable to lie in, I suspect. No mattress, just a few handfuls of straw, at best, and blankets that were frequently stolen by your mates. Whenever you complained about the theft, the guards would treat you with heavy irony and ask, for instance, why you had not stitched your name into the thing. If there was a life-form of sorts that thrived in the camp and will always think back to Sylt with great melancholy, it's the fleas and lice. All of us had been bitten from tip to toe. Herds of those malicious parasites would welcome us as it were, tail-wagging in bed. They seemed to know full well from experience that we would be too exhausted to raise as much as a finger in defiance.

Speaking of parasites. No group of people of whatever kind or denomination can possibly fare so ill, materially speaking, as not to engage in quarrels about possession. That's what the guy sleeping in the bunk beneath mine told me one night. Intelligent man, Belgian, had for many years been a GP in Flanders, ait seemed. The Germans had arrested and deported him because they suspected him of poisoning cattle. Anyway. The greed for material possession is the strongest driving force of man's doings, maybe second only to the urge to propagate. Which, when it comes to the point, is frequently but a form of the craving for possession. Nothing more sexually stimulating than the conclusion of a decent business deal, or so they say. It's not a question of the absolute value of objects, by no means. Nothing is ever so totally useless and trashy that no-one in his right mind would deign to take possession of it: a piece of stale bread hard as granite, foot rags, bits and pieces of clothing, blankets, almost bald, bristle-less brushes, never mind what – as long as it is mine. If possession is theft, he used to say, thieves serve a nobler kind of justice by punishing the owner for his anti-social behaviour. All a question of perspective. The alleged universal prevalence of law he called another form of opium for the people.

The really funny thing is many of my fellow prisoners came from societies that condemned private ownership for ideological reasons. And yet, they all stole and sometimes even killed for items that, under normal circumstances, you would not look at twice, things that had no immediate survival function either.

How quixotic or blockheaded that guy Karl Marx must have been not to realize that man defines himself by his possessions, his ownership. If you take that away, the world will eventually stop turning. That was my impression and experience from the lower decks of that ship of the dead called Alderney.

3. The Fox and Ferret

"And how did the six of them come together again after the war, all told?" Ignace asked after a while of silent amazement. He seemed to find hard to digest what Laura had told him about Ronny and his Sylt tribulations. Which wasn't surprising, since Laura herself couldn't hide that it was something that had touched her deeply.

"Well, as I have been able to make out, so far, Lamont tracked them down and picked them up one by one and formed them into a team again. That may seem odd to us today, but at the time, what with the clocks set back to zero, with half the world lying in ruins and the next war already looming large over the horizon, many folks were without orientation or perspective. You could presumably consider yourself lucky to be accepted as a member of this or that group, or gang, little matter. None of the six had either a wife or kids yet. Yes, I think I can relate to that."

"But they had nothing in common, any longer."

"Not more, not less, that is, than they had ever had, I presume. Besides, even if it is true what they say that every war year counts double with regard to your life-span, they hadn't been separated all that long, after all. And, like I say, without any next of kin, they were free to do as they pleased. I guess they felt society owed them something and they were determined to come and collect. It was a way of turning some of the ghastly experiences most if not all of them had had during the war to their advantage and profit."

"Six Rambos on the loose?"

Laura laughed for the first time that evening.

"Yes, I suppose you might say that. The first Rambo, that is, the one who takes the Vietnam War to that fly-blown place called Hope, of all names. Break what's trying to break you was a famous slogan of the nineteen sixties."

"Then there was the trifling matter of the treasure trove," Ignace said. "They had left that in the cave."

"Yes. Well, since none of them knew anything about the others' whereabouts and could not even be certain that anybody else of the group had survived the war, each and every one of them must have gone on a pilgrimage to Sark first thing. Strangely enough, they didn't bump into one another over there."

"They probably kept a very low profile. Besides, there must have been German POW's around plus their British guards. And communications between the islands and the Continent weren't all that smooth again yet. But let me guess: the treasure trove had gone."

"That's right. They all came away empty-handed, or so it seemed. There would be rumours, of course. Some lucky local could have found and...appropriated the knapsack. A fisherman, for instance, or kids playing in the caves."

"Or maybe a German who had deserted shortly before the capitulation and hidden in the cave till the coast was clear, as it were."

Laura shook her head.

"Unlikely. Despite their desperate situation, it took the Germans quite some time to resign themselves to the idea of capitulation. Nobody would have lasted that long in the cave, I don't think. The German Feldjäger or MP's were all over the place towards the end of the war, shooting or hanging alleged deserters by the score."

"Then there is only one solution left."

"Which would be?"

"One of the six must have taken the treasure with him then, the moment they split."

"And who, in your valued opinion, is most likely to have done so, dear Watson?"

"My money would be on Lamont."

"How so? He was the first to leave, under the eyes of all the others."

"Yes. But do you know exactly where he went?"

"Sir Lucas and I didn't have time enough to discuss that. And, to be quite honest, I had somehow lost interest. It all seemed so desperately insignificant, so far away and long ago, if you see what I mean."

"Yes, I believe I do. But what if he just bided his time and waited in hiding somewhere till he could be sure that no-one was left in the cave? The way Ronny characterizes him, he seems to have had a proper cool-hand Luke approach, alright. When his mates had left the nest, he flew back and grabbed the cookie jar."

"But why? He had to count on getting caught by the Germans. In which case the treasure would have been gone irretrievably. Plus, it would presumably have got him into even deeper trouble with the Germans. What was his plan?"

"Let's presume he hid the knapsack somewhere else, at a place henceforth only known to him. Then, he handed himself in. Just like that. The Germans would give him a thorough beating, torture him, interrogate him, whatever. But before they hanged or shot him, he may have traded the cookie jar against his being spared."

"You mean he bought his way out in very much the same manner as the surviving German soldier had done hours before? How would he have managed that? The Germans would simply have taken the treasure and then shot him without so much as a thank you for the trouble."

"We mustn't underestimate Lamont. Maybe it went down something like this: he may have cajoled the officer in charge on Sark into taking him to Guernsey in exchange for the treasure or, more likely, parts of it. You take me there, pretending to hand me over to the Gestapo and, once there, I'll let you know where I hid the goodies. Something like that, anyway. Thus, the German had a reasonable guarantee Lamont wouldn't just disappear in the woods. Lamont, for his part, would rely on the fact that the German would find it difficult to explain to his superiors what Lamont was doing on Guernsey and what the treasure was all about."

"I don't know, sounds far-fetched. But let's assume it went down more or less like you just depicted it. That would beg the question why he would bother to round up the Yarmouth Six again after the war, instead of doing everything to avoid them."

Ignace shrugged his shoulders.

"I could think of at least two reasons. To begin with, he probably hated the thought of having to look over his shoulder for the rest of his natural life. He had to count on one or the other of his erstwhile mates finding him and asking awkward questions.

Second, it seems he was embarking on the career of a professional criminal and knew from experience that keeping your options
open as long as possible is a principle worthwhile adhering to in
all walks of life. And, whatever his precise plans, he was going to
need reliable accomplices, associates. They are hard to come by
in a normal business environment, I guess, but all the more difficult in a criminal setting thriving on dastardliness and betrayal.
Looking at things from that angle, his five ex-companions must
have headed the short list easily: young but experienced, totally
without scruples, and specialised in most of the relevant fields."

"But he still had to be afraid one or the other of his mates might
cut his throat at some inconspicuous moment when his defences
were down for once."

"Not necessarily. By killing him, they had nothing to win
except the satisfaction of having taken their revenge. That you
can't live on, can you? Besides, you told me yourself you were
impressed by his personal charm and powers of manipulation.
Even now, at his age! He may not have been born with that silver spoon in his mouth, but he seems to have a silver tongue
alright. And, don't forget, he possessed the necessary will-power
and intelligence, as he demonstrated during the crisis situation
caused by the drowning Gooey. In short, he encapsulated all the
necessary ingredients of a natural born leader in his person. His
mates must have sensed this already during their raid on Sark
and known that, with him around, they would make headway in
the world. If the Yarmouth Six were to make crime their bread-
winning pursuit, and what else was there, after all, for someone
wishing to get rich before old age caught up with him, Lamont
would be their man."

Laura nodded.

"Yes, that seems to make sense. And is borne out by Ronny's
protocol of what must have been their first meeting after the war.
Where do I have it again, now?"

Laura put on her glasses and searched for the text. Meanwhile,
she had learned to live with Ronny's appalling handwriting.

"Here it is. Listen to this:

We met in a pub practically in the shadow of Tower Bridge. The Fox and Ferret, that's what it was called. The owner was a Jamaican, who had probably never seen either a fox or a ferret. Notwithstanding, the pub would become one of our several haunts during the years immediately following. The Duke thought it wise not to meet in one place all the time, but to spread our interest, as it were, not to make it too easy for the cops to track us. When I entered, welcomed by some soft Reggae music that worked wonders on my nervous system, I immediately saw the Duke. Not much change, there. He was sitting with his back to a wall, next to another door that led to a back exit, as I was to learn soon after. He looked at me like an innocent new-born babe, but couldn't fool me. I was sure he kept a gun under the table, its barrel pointing at yours truly. I moved very slowly, always keeping my hand in the Duke's full sight, not to provoke a rash reaction on his part.

For a brief spell there, I had feared he would get up and give me the Judas pecker. But that didn't happen. I looked around a little apprehensively. He noticed that, of course, and seemed insulted I didn't trust him. I would have a lot more occasions to watch and admire the Duke read a public location full of people in no time, check it for vermin, as he used to put it. His instincts could always be relied on. If and when you saw him sitting or standing somewhere, inside or out in the open, all you needed to do was watch the collar of his jacket or coat. If the collar was down, the coast was clear. If it was up, you had better make yourself scarce, fast. But that was later. Now, he was just sitting there, smiling blithely and, with his free left hand, inviting me to join him at the table. I hung my coat and sat down, ordering a Guinness from the Jamaican waitress who packed a cleavage the likes of which I hadn't seen for a very long time and smelled of papayas. I didn't know that then, of course, never had set eyes on papayas, but the smell makes me randy even today.

The ensuing conversation between the Duke and myself belongs to some of the strangest I ever experienced before or after. We were both under considerable tension, I take it. I certainly was and I think I sensed a definite uneasiness with him as well. I had prepared for this meeting and formulated a number of questions I was going to ask him. But as we sat there, I realized he must have pre-empted those questions and prepared all the appropriate answers. Might as well forget about it, I thought. And so, instead of discussing or quarrelling, we just chatted as if we had separated the day before yesterday or maybe a week ago and were exchanging news about what stupid little things had happened in this or that quarter meanwhile. Unreal is the only word that comes to mind when describing the situation. But he did have this kind of soothing effect on people's minds.

The next one to arrive at the pub was Hooch. I almost hadn't recognized him, emaciated and worn down as he looked. It was only when he opened his mouth and let fly I was sure it was him and not some twin brother Hooch had not told us about. He, too, had hardly shoved a chair to our table and sat down, when he joined the chorus and let us have a fresh selection of Irish jokes into the bargain. I started feeling like I had ended up in a colony of baboons in full swing with their grooming routine. It was as if all three of us took utmost care not to touch on the subject of the past. As if we had concluded a moratorium on things past. What more can I say. The four others who arrived shortly after, one by one, tuned in to the melody. I am convinced that, had one of us suddenly mentioned, say, the cave or the dinghy episode, let alone the treasure, the others would have looked piqued, as if hearing the bloke fart, and gone on with the conversation. Of course, this wasn't entirely due to the Duke's calming influence either. We all had experienced atrocities that had lain beyond the horizon of our imagination. Things that had changed our respective ways of looking at life, I guess. We weren't here to revel in the bloody past but to look towards the future. The Duke may have been a rat, for all we knew, but one who had an idea of where the cheese was to be found.

Looking at my mates one by one, I was suddenly reminded of my co-prisoners at Sylt during what our guards would call breakfast. These boys didn't look much better, for the time being, skinny and grey, marked by what they had gone through. But not only did they have teeth, albeit not their own, but their eyes weren't dead either. Sad, yes, melancholy, if you will, but not totally void of this occasional spark of hope. Somehow, we must have felt that, if we had a future, it would be as the Yarmouth Six. Had we fallen out for good there and then, we would have lost it, all of us, so....

Strangely enough, there never was any talk of the treasure trove either. Why would there be? He didn't broach the subject, understandably. We somehow knew the Duke had taken it. But since he showed no signs of extraordinary material well-being, whatever he had done with the treasure, it hadn't made him a rich man. Presumably, we felt he had invested it for us and would, sooner or later, gratify us with the incurred interest. Which, seen in the wider context, wasn't even that far off the mark.

Yes, he had managed to work his magic on us that night. What may have helped him was the total absence of any system of moral coordinates. If you want to judge right and wrong, you need moral coordinates to move along. The Nazis had lost the war, it is true, but had managed to prove to all and sundry the relative weakness and fragility of humanitarian values thought to have been universal and basically inviolable till then. Nobody, absolutely nobody, survives all-out warfare without either betraying or being betrayed. Like in that Orwellian nursery rhyme: under the spreading chestnut tree, I sold you and you sold me. That decline of values was amply demonstrated by the paradoxical ambiguity of the Nuremberg trials. Their ghostly unreal nature did not rest so much in the obstinate refusal of the surviving Nazi leaders to admit to the deeply criminal and immoral character of their actions. Much rather, it lay in the frightful realization that, as Hermann Goering put it, I believe, rightly: it would have taken very little for the dock and the judges' bench to have been inverted. Not a question of White Queen takes out Black Tower, of right beating wrong. A few more German tanks and another Waffen-SS regiment on the heights of Normandy, and the Nuremberg trials would have looked that little bit different. The roles of those in the dock and those in the judges' chairs would have been reversed. If this was so, why then would we pick up a rock each and throw it at the

Duke? It would only have brought forth the vermin hidden under the stones. At the time, in the Fox and bloody Ferret, I would not have been able to formulate this as lucidly as I do now, I guess. But my gut feeling was the same then as now. Hitler and his companions had held up a mirror to more or less the whole world, and what we saw wasn't pretty. So that, when he shot himself in the end, he may have derived a last bit of satisfaction from the knowledge that the consequences of his ideology and actions would last the thousand years that their Reich had lamentably failed to.

It was on that memorable evening too that we planned our first heist. The time seemed more than ripe for it. Everywhere in London, people were cleaning up the mess, removing the rubble, trying to make a living. Everything seemed in motion, in a totally disorderly kind of way. People were looking for their next of kin or for something to eat or both. The old structures had crumbled, the new ones not in place yet. One of the few things that worked, though, was the banking system. Some of the major banks had survived the war more or less unscathed and the English pound sterling's status of a globally accepted gilt-edged standard had been confirmed, Bretton Woods still being a few years away. On the flip side, the general traffic chaos risked seriously hampering our logistics. The access and escape routes had to be planned very carefully, with all sorts of alternative options. It wouldn't do to get stranded in some blind alley after having zig-zagged across half of the City in an attempt to avoid piles of rubble, long queues forming literally everywhere, women and kids pulling overloaded carts, trucks without gas or overturned cars –not to forget the fuzz. Just thinking back to some of those hot pursuits through all kinds of back yards and deserted industrial sites makes me feel a hundred years younger. Here and there, the garlicky smell of gas escaping through punctured tubes would signal that a shoot-out might bring a whole block of hitherto intact houses down, killing many innocent people in the process, no doubt. Such were the crazy foundation years of the Yarmouth Six in their new look of a gang of heavies. With money came status. To all practical purposes, we became shareholders of a flourishing concern with multiple interests. Diversification is what they came to call it later. The Yarmouth Six Inc. was led by the Duke as our managing director.

Some of our gatherings, which grew more and more rare and had as their principal objective a sort of half-yearly inventory, felt like shareholders coming together to hear the accounts of the board. Doors that would have been locked in a jiffy at the mere sight of the likes of us approaching would now be thrown open invitingly. People who would at best have kicked us in the crotch years ago would now practically lick our balls. Nothing is so successful as success, isn't that what they say? Well, they are damn right.

During operations in the field, as we used to call it, we started off by working together all six of us. Over the years, however, we went asymmetric. At times, three of us would mount a robbery, at others, two of us break into a jeweller's and so on. The proceeds always went into our common kitty. That worked surprisingly smoothly. No complaints to speak of, none of that childish 'I did more footwork than you and request to be paid more accordingly'. For that, our group was just too mature, too professional, and the booty too voluptuous. There was enough for everyone, in other words. Whenever someone could claim an extraordinary expense, that would be reimbursed as a matter of course. If someone got caught, a bevy of legal eagles would descend on the police and the DA and dig their beaks into whatever sorry excuse of evidence the fuzz thought they had against us. In the very rare cases where even that failed, we did everything we could to render the inmates' usually short stay in jail as pleasant as possible. Any next of kin would be taken care of, meanwhile, so the mate in prison had nothing to worry about on that score either.

"All fine and dandy," Ignace said when Laura had finished.

"But what's it to us with regard to the murders? Where's the black hole you mentioned on the telephone?" Laura smiled.

"I didn't say I had identified the black hole. I said we found the orbital anomaly. Meanwhile, I've had time to think. If the black hole is not on the list, it's got to be on the back of it. And it's got a name. It's called Gooey."

EIGHTH CHAPTER

1. The Deal

"Gooey? You mean Peter Collins? What gives you that idea? He drowned during Operation Sea Leopard."

The retired Chief Superintendent was quite obviously puzzled. Laura took it as an indication of the Yard's ignorance of the precise circumstances of Gooey's death. Neither Lamont nor his five companions had apparently breathed a word about it all those years. The real question was how the Boxer had got wind of the true story. How? And, almost as important, why so late? Those were questions only he could answer. Always assuming he would be caught alive, which wasn't guaranteed by any means.

"Let me remind you. If you know more than we do, you have to tell us. If you don't, you're committing what we call obstruction of justice. That's a felony you can go to jail for."

Laura laughed rather maliciously.

"Yeah, that'll be the day. I have been on this case for…what, a month, now, and know what I know. The Metropolitan, for its part, has been sitting on the case for several decades, on and off. Time enough to come up with some palpable results, one should think. Which begs the question whether the Yard may perhaps not have paid the Yarmouth Seven the kind of attention they deserve. Not surprising, then, that you seem to have dragged your feet somewhat with your investigations, with due respect. So, don't try to steal the thunder from a rank beginner such as myself. And don't try to scare me. Other, much more scary people have found that the instrument of their own undoing."

For an ominous moment, there was silence at the other end. Then the Chief started rowing back.

"Okay, Laura. I think you are being a little too strict with us. Notwithstanding, I offer my excuses for my stern admonition. All the more so, as I am retired and, hence, have no business scolding you. Just one of those nasty habits you acquire in the years of service. To get back to Mr Collins, Gooey, that is. You're right in assuming we never paid him much attention. Why should we have, under the circumstances?"

"Yes, I understand that. Dr Watson, I mean Ignace and myself, we started off by ignoring him, as well. Until that moment he suddenly caused an inexplicable blip on our Doppler radar. That's when we changed course and applied Sherlock's famous method of elimination. If none of the descendants of the Yarmouth Six that appeared on the list could possibly have anything to do with the killer, it had to be someone who, even though he wasn't on the list, threw a long shadow on it all the time. Had we bothered to look in that direction a little earlier…But that's how it is. You may seek consolation in the fact that probably only a pedantic person such as myself would have thought of that. Besides, God knows we may still be on the wrong track. Which reminds me. Have you any idea whether or not this Mr Collins had any children of his own? I mean, children already existing or in the making at the moment of his own death?"

"Vaguely. I think the latter applies. His widow received…Yes, now that you mention it, I remember. His widow was pregnant at the time Operation Sea Leopard went down. She was only weeks away from giving birth, in fact. A tragedy. During peace time, it would have been all over the papers. But in war, you know, there were thousands of such sad stories about. Collins had apparently had a relationship with a woman somewhat older than himself, something he wouldn't brag about. She probably planned the child behind his back, as they say. Happens in the best of families. Personally, I have never quite understood…Never mind that now. At the time, the women had no way of knowing whether or not their husbands or lovers would return after waving them goodbye at the end of their most recent leave. And in Gooey's case, if the lady in question wanted a child from him, she seemed to have made the right decision. That's what it looked like to us."

"What happened to the child?"

"Like I said, he was born only weeks after Collins' death. A boy, if my memory serves me right."

"Any idea what became of him?"

"Both mother and child were killed in an accident some years later, I think. I'll check that again for you, if you wish. But I'm pretty sure. For us, it was an additional reason to side-step the Gooey track. He was dead, his family had been wiped out, and so…. What are you hoping to gain by digging his corpse up now?"

Laura reflected for a moment.

"Between the two of us, Harry? Not a bloody thing," she lied.

"If it had been for me, I would have buried the whole thing long time ago. Now, that I have other cats to skin, lots of them, as it were. But Ignace has been all over me these last few weeks. And as long as we haven't turned even the smallest stones lying by the wayside, he won't let up. In a way, I admire his doggedness. But there have been moments when I rather cursed it, quite frankly. Which is why I'm begging you: do try and unearth a few more files. In London, you have all sorts of means at your fingertips. I would appreciate that no end."

Laura thought she could hear the flattered Chief purr at the other end of the line.

"Will do, Laura, will do. I feel I owe you one. You okay for the rest?"

"Oh, absolutely. Never been more okay than at present. My loan has been lost in a blocked pipeline, it seems, the audit bill is overdue and, yes, all's swell."

"Good luck then, is all I say. I'll report back as soon as I have any news."

Laura thanked him and hung up. Then she called Marquardt.

"What's it look like, Heinz?"

Marquardt appeared uncharacteristically pessimistic.

"I'll say this. One more week, and the dice are down."

"The chips, you mean."

"Whatever. The Chinese are hoovering the market. And if they can't make it, the Arabs will. Or the bloody Russians. And our hands are tied behind our backs."

"That bad, eh? Listen. I'll go for another heart to heart with Lamont, on the phone, this time. I have one more card up my sleeve. No ace, no queen, just a measly seven of the hearts. Lamont doesn't know this, though. It's worth a try. If he calls my bluff, I'm done for. Even you can't help me then. But thanks a lot for your unflinching loyalty. You did what you could. Now it's up to me to let my pants down."

Marquardt laughed.

"I'd rather be present when that happens."

"You should be so lucky."

Few minutes later, she asked Brigitte, her secretary, to be good enough to get her Lamont on the phone. As far as she knew, he had left Jersey and returned to sunny Puerto bloody Rico.

It took a while till the connection seemed stable. Probably, Lamont's assistant, maybe Harold, in fact, tried to fob Brigitte off. He wouldn't know, of course, that Laura had picked Brigitte years ago after a murderous casting and a short probation period, not least because of her leech-like qualities. To lose Brigitte was harder than losing the scabies.

Finally, the call came through. Harold must have seen the futility of his efforts. Laura heard a mumbling of men's voices in the background. Then, Lamont picked up the phone.

"Mrs Forster, I hope you have something to offer that fully justifies your dragging me out of my siesta dreams."

Laura looked at her watch. On Puerto Rico, it must be close to high noon.

"Last I heard was old people don't need much sleep."

"That may be as it is. I think what counts is not so much the mere quantity in absolute terms but the spread over the day, you see."

"Ever tried nights? Some people swear by them." Laura remembered her nightly perambulations all over Lamont's Jersey manor.

"Yeah, I find them largely overrated. What can I do for you? Or better even, what can you promise to do for me?"

"Well, my impression is you're something of a gambling man, Sir Lucas, aren't you."

Laura wasn't sure of that, at all, but she knew men liked to be called gamblers. It flattered their male vanity, God knows why. As for herself, Laura couldn't think of a more stupid way of losing your money than to lay it down on a gambling table. Robert had never touched cards either, and he had probably known why not.

"What if I were?" Lamont replied.

"I'd like to propose a kind of wager, one that concerns the person you used to call Gooey."

There was silence. Had to be. Lamont had just opened a cupboard and found a skeleton had fallen into his arms. He needed time to digest the situation.

"You mean, Peter…Collins? Yes, just to be sure we're talking of the same man. Well, he's been resting on the bottom of the sea these, what, seventy years. Not much left of him, if you ask me. With any luck, I'll meet his ghost in the other world that nobody has ever seen but almost everybody seems convinced that they know what it looks like."

Laura laughed. Not a jolly laugh, more one of the aggressive sort, the one that bodes evil for her respective opposite party.

"I wouldn't count on it if I were you. I'm guessing here, but the image of Gooey slowly sinking to the bottom must have been haunting you all these decades. Maybe that's why you prefer sleeping it off during daytime. Because with darkness come the spectres of the past. And you got some heavy traffic going in that department, I bet." Again, there was silence. Then Lamont coughed.

"You still haven't told me what it is you want."

"Well, let's assume Gooey's ghost paid me a visit, as well, and whispered some worrying tidings in my ear, you know, Hamlet-like. News about the true circumstances of his unfortunate drowning. Instead of pulling him up to the surface, he claimed you actually pushed him down to the bottom. A delicate point where your narrative deviates more than just an iota from his."

"Maybe so. And to tell me this you have me woken up and called me to the phone? I ask your forgiveness, but who says Gooey's ghost's version is the right one? Spectres have been known to lie through their teeth, too. What motive should I have had to kill him off?"

"Let's say, the one justifiable reason to drown him you might put forward is bound to be phoney. He was shouting too loud? The

Germans wouldn't have heard him if he had played the trumpet. No, you killed him, because you are a naturally greedy person. Six people dividing the treasure trove among them fare better than seven. The fewer men knew of the knapsack's contents, the smaller the risk of someone talking too much. In short, there were many reasons to pick from." Lamont was breathing more and more heavily.

"Okay, Laura Forster, just to humour you, let's assume you are right with what you're saying. So, what? In a court of law, it would be your word against mine. The word of a German national, a descendant of the people who occupied the islands and deported many and killed not so few their inhabitants. A descendant of the people who built four concentration camps on Alderney alone. Her word against that of a British war hero and social benefactor of high standing. Whose favour do you think the jury's verdict would sooner come down to?"

Laura swallowed. She knew he was right there. That was part of the trouble with the Anglo-Saxon jury system. If you were guilty, you stood to gain. If you were innocent, however, a jury was more than likely to be your undoing. The concept of twelve good men and true but selected arbitrarily, she felt, had always been precarious at best and open to all kinds of manipulation, at worst. Plus, it turned what should be sober legal proceedings into theatrical events where lawyers turned into ham actors. People who notoriously fell victim to the most blatant rubbish they were told by their politicians could hardly be expected to differentiate between substance and hogwash in a court. Besides, the law and people's innate sense of justice seldom ever form a happy marriage.

"And even if, contrary to all expectations, you were to carry the day, what would you personally stand to gain from it?" Lamont continued.

"You don't give me the impression of a passionate idealist but rather that of a smart business woman who knows full well on which side her toast is buttered."

Laura was about to lose her patience.

"I rest my case for now. Even though I seem to remember that, in the English penal system, crimes such as manslaughter do not fall under the statute of limitations, ever. My personal interest? Well, the profession of a barrister would have been my second choice if my father hadn't insisted on my taking over the firm one day. Maybe, he was right. Black robe and white wig just wouldn't look good on me, I'm afraid. But since you've addressed yourself to the businesswoman. I guess you know that I asked my bank for a sizeable loan some weeks ago to finance a major takeover operation. But even though I was able to balance the bank's prospective claims with all-round surety, the loan sum in question has so far been blocked. The alleged reason: differences in the evaluation of some of our immobile assets. Which is pure, unmitigated bull. My guess is the loan transaction got stuck due to the successful wheelings and dealings of a competing company that belongs to your conglomerate."

Lamont laughed. The change of subject seemed to work wonders. Corporate machinations would be right up his alley.

"Well, ain't that a shame. But that's business, I guess. What's it got to do with me?"

"A word or two from you dropped in the right place at the right moment could work wonders here."

Lamont chuckled.

"I'm flattered, but also afraid you overestimate my powers of persuasion. A figurehead isn't the ship's captain, not even the first mate. But even if I were to intervene in your favour and supposedly be heard in the circles that count, why would I do you that favour? I hope you have more to offer me than threaten to drag me to court or denounce me publicly. I'm not one of your pathetic concentration camp guards suddenly smoked out of their cosy little hiding places they managed to dig for themselves after the war with the help of generous state pensions."

Laura hesitated. Now she had to four them or shut up forever, as far as that aspect of things was concerned.

"First, I got to know whether or not you are recording this conversation of ours."

Now it was up to Lamont to hesitate.

"Why on earth would I do that?"

"Sheer habit, maybe?"

"No, I can assure you, no recordings. I would give you my word on it if I didn't know you don't give a damn for it."

"Alright. Like I said before, I have a deal to propose. As you also know, together with my son Ignace, I have been hard on the heels of the person who killed Solveig and is responsible for the deaths of many of your next of kin. Do I still have your full attention?"

"Absolutely."

"Okay. Thanks to some more recent disclosures in this matter, I am firmly convinced that I will be able to corner the killer, soon. Now, if I assess the penal system right – yours, ours, anybody's – he might get off with a few years in a mental institution and a serious reprimand. I guess you would hate that. I wouldn't like it either. Hence, I might be willing and ready to serve you his head on a silver platter, figuratively speaking."

Lamont coughed again.

"How figuratively are we speaking?"

"You'll get the address at which you can have him picked up. The rest I don't even want to know. If he resists arrest and gets killed, his head will be considered as delivered."

"In a word, he'll be mine, dead or alive."

"Precisely."

"You know of course that, in view of the large sum of money I put on his head, already, there's a whole army of bounty hunters out there eager to lay their hands on him. So, once again, what makes you think you'll be more successful than them?"

"Professional secret, none of your business. No magician worth his money ever unveils his tricks. Do we have a deal or don't we?"

"Oh, yes, we do, absolutely. You know, it brings back memories. Every now and again, we would discuss the question of accepting a woman in our exquisite freemasonic circle of the Yarmouth Six. Emancipation, political correctness, and female quotas were still decades away then. No, but for us it would have been fun, I guess."

"So, why didn't you?"

"Easy: we found no candidates that would fit the job description. Had we come across a certain Laura Forster at the time…."

"…you would soon have had to yield control over your operations to a woman smarter than any of the six of you."

Lamont laughed.

"Yeah, I guess, all things considered, we were lucky there. Bring me the killer's head, Laura. I prefer to face him while he's still alive. But dead will do just as well. And you'll get your loan, I'll see to that."

2. Calypso's Bridal Den

Laura hung up. Her stomach was turning and churning like a concrete-mixer's drum. What was it that gave her the unshakable confidence to be able to nail the Boxer in the very near future? The deal with Lamont had been a shot in the dark, properly speaking. What she needed now was to dodge any possible ricochets and find a suitable bait for the killer to bite.

Late in the afternoon, Colestron was on the phone again.

"That was cool running, Chief. I'm impressed."

"Don't be. It's not much, but I thought I let you have it, anyway. For starters, I was right about the mother's and son's death in that car accident. As for Gooey's body, it was never found. Which, in those waters round the islands, is not surprising."

He paused.

"Well, like you said, it isn't much. But I thank you for taking the trouble, anyway."

"Patience, Desdemona, I haven't finished yet. As you can imagine, the strange succession of accidents that killed off the Yarmouth Six with the notable exception of Sir Lucas gave the Yard a headache or two. We investigated the matter but found nothing to go by in the way of possible foul play. Some of the objects we collected as possible evidence remained in our boxes on the basement shelves, so to speak. A fig leaf, if you will. Essentially, we felt the five hoodlums' deaths was good riddance, but just in case...Anyway, among many other items, there were personal belongings of the Collinses, you know, brushes, toys, odds and ends. Nobody feeling responsible for it, nobody touched the stuff for decades. During the nineteen eighties and nineties, the techniques of DNA comparison took a steady upswing, as you know. The colleagues in the laboratories needed a lot of different material to test all sorts of hypotheses. One of them being the question how far you could go back and still discover DNA material fit for reliable analysis. Hence, the scientists began rummaging in our stocks for evidence that had been collected ages ago and would, in all likelihood not be needed ever again, so they could tamper with it to their hearts' delight. In so doing, they must have come across a hairbrush or comb of the fifties, one that had belonged to Gooey's lover. Since not only the lady in question, but also Gooey himself had used that brush, which was later used on Gooey's son as well, apparently, all three of them had left material that could be analysed. Which it was."

He fell silent again.

"Yes? So, what? Gooey wasn't the biological father, is that it?".

Colestron laughed.

"Funny that that possibility should be the first you think of. Always a favourite with the sexes, I suspect. But no, or rather yes, he was the father alright. The point I'm making is a totally different one. At the scene of one of the more recent murders, the ones on the Wily Minx, that is, the colleagues found skin cells whose DNA they could attribute neither to any of the four victims, nor to any of the two salvagers of the yacht. So they uploaded the DNA bar code into the computer screening system, just like that, at random, as it were. And, you won't believe it, they had one of the most bizarre matches ever."

Again, he paused. Laura felt she was losing her mind.

"Yes, then what? Spit it out, Chief, spit it out."

But Colstron was determined not to sell his little triumph under par.

"The DNA match allowed, or rather imposed the conclusion that Gooey's long defunct son must at some stage have been on board that yacht."

"You're having me on."

"No, I'm not. Furthermore, since the yacht is brand new, only two years old and the skin cells rather fresh, he must have been aboard at or around the time of the murder. Which probably means, he's the killer."

Laura felt like she didn't understand anything any more and tried to let it sink in.

"Can't be. How's that possible?" she asked at long last.

"Surely, someone must have made a mistake, mixed up the samples or something?"

Colestron drew a deep breath.

"That's what our colleagues in the Yard say too. So, they had all tests repeated. The net result was the same. The scientists insist the DNA doesn't lie. On the other hand, there have been remarkable cases of blatant errors.

"Yes, like the nationwide search for a mysterious woman who was supposed to have committed no end of crimes of totally different nature and severity all over Germany: one day a murder, the next a break into an allotment garden or shop lifting, totally against all practical experience, according to which perpetrators tend to stick to their category of crime. In the end, it turned out the police had used Q-tips contaminated with the DNA of a female worker in the company that produced the stuff."

"Exactly. Such things have happened and will happen. In our case, what traces there are seem to lead nowhere. To a grave, if you prefer." Laura reflected.

"Speaking of which. Gooey's body was never found, you said. As far as I know, the sea, as a rule, returns its victims at some stage. Unless they happen to come to rest at a depth of more than seventy meters, say, in a wreck of some sort. Those will never come up again. Question of pressure, I suppose. Hence, a fisherman should have had Gooey's mortal remains in his net some time or other. Or he should have been washed up on a shore.

"Not necessarily. Not in the Bay of St. Malo. What are you driving at?"

"Sherlock again. What if the killer, our Boxer, was a descendant of Gooey, as hilarious as it may sound? He would have to have begot him long time after his death, wouldn't he? Not the easiest of exercises, once you are in a coffin. Yet if we continue on this track, there is but one logical conclusion: Gooey did not drown. Gooey survived."

"But Lamont saw him die."

"Lamont saw him sink to the bottom. That's not the same as saying he saw him die. If we go along with the thesis that he didn't die, the next question would be where and in what physical condition did the sea spit him out again?"

"Somewhere around the coasts of Sark, I should think. Like his mates. They were all on the same tide, as it were. Since he was closer to the bottom than to the surface, the current that took him may have followed a slightly different route alright. But essentially, he should have ended up not far from his mates."

"And, hence, never have left Sark?"

"That we don't know, do we? The state he was in after having spent quite some time under water, he must have stayed on the island for weeks if not months to recover, that's for sure. What do you think?"

"The cave. Lamont told me about another cave on the western side of the cape, on whose rocks his six mates had landed. The other cave would remain dry even during high water, he told me. They had been about to move in there but didn't because they were afraid some locals might show up there sooner or later and feel tempted to report them to the Germans. Let's presume, then, they were right and a local came down there hours later, out of curiosity or for whatever other reason, and found Gooey lying there half dead."

"In that case, he or she would probably have felt obliged to tell the Germans about it. If only to take pressure off the locals."

"Exactly. Except that's obviously not what happened. Whoever found Gooey must have had a heart soft enough not to hand him over but to take him home, somehow, hide him, and nurse him. At some considerable risk for him- or herself."

"I think we're talking of a woman, here, no doubt. To begin with, after the second wave of deportations, there weren't that many men left on Sark anyway. Besides, girls and women regularly searched the accessible, unmined parts of the shore for firewood or something to eat. Caves were their favourites, one should think. Limpets, mussels, cockles, crab, the odd lobster dying of old age, whatever."

"And one of those Sark ladies happened to find her Prince Charming there. Heart-warming theory, that."

"The only one possible, if you ask me."

"Why then didn't Gooey manifest himself afterwards, I mean, after the war and all that? He must have seen his comrades return in search of the treasure, at least some of them. They would have to come right by his window in such a small place as Little Sark."

"Well, if we take it he had been under the surface for quite a while, he may have sustained serious brain damage for lack of oxygen. Damage that may either have been irreversible or gradually compensated by other regions of the brain over a long period of time. Amnesia is a real possibility. Or maybe his merciful Calypso led him, reduced to a simpleton as he may have been, to believe the war was still on long after it had actually ended, so that he had better stay with her, in hiding. Not to lose him, I mean."

"And even if he had come away with his brain fully intact, which is unlikely, he had had the sad experience that Lamont had tried to kill him. If the Duke was to realize that his first attempt had failed, he might have given it another go to complete the job."

"My compliments, Laura, you should have become a detective."

"Well, who says I won't be. My present job having become a real pain in the butt, lately…."

"What next?"

"I guess I'll have to pay that little island a visit, after all. It all starts there and might find its climax there, too."

"In that case, shouldn't I rather come with you? Alone, you might be on a suicide mission."

Laura didn't answer right away. If she was to come across the Boxer on Sark, Colestron would be in the way. He would never allow her to put the killer's head on ice and send it to Sir Lucas, Puerto Rico post restante. On the other hand, she would have a hard time trying to persuade the Chief to lay off and stay at home. And even if, eventually, he didn't come himself, he might drop a few words at the Yard so that, before she knew it, she would have a whole SWAT team parachuting down on Sark. So better bite the bullet and have him accompany her. Or them. Ignace would want to come too, without doubt. She would refuse but feared that, this time, short of dripping ketamine in his tea.

"Okay. Be ready for take-off then. I'll be coming for you. Don't know how, don't know when, but you'll learn in good time. And do bring a weapon. I can watch one man's back, but not two."

The Chief laughed.

"You seem to forget I was with the Sweeney for ten long years and had to shoot the odd gangster who wouldn't give in. You're not the only one with notches on the handle of her gun."

"Okay, we'll see."

Laura ended the talk and stretched her legs. She hadn't counted on things taking quite that kind of turn. She had no idea what Sark would have in store for her, if anything. One thing was clear, though. If the Boxer was using the island as his hole in the wall refuge, her visit there would rustle him up. And maybe cause him to commit his first real mistake.

"Who was it on the phone?"

Ignace had been sitting in his room plunged in noisy video games that re-enacted the destruction of the Planet of Death or the annihilation of Rommel's Africa corps. Now, he came ambling down the staircase, probably to have a go at the fridge. Feeling a second difficult conversation coming her way, literally, Laura heaved a deep sigh.

"Harry Colestron. He's hell-bent on accompanying me to Sark."

"To Sark? Why?"

Laura gave him a short account of the gist of her conversation with the Chief.

"Wow! I'm in. When do we leave?"

"We don't leave at all. Things seem to be hotting up to a degree that only experienced cooks should remain in the kitchen. I didn't go through all the formalities of adopting you and the indescribable pains of bringing you up decently only to see you return to Hamburg in a body bag, see."

"I can handle a gun like the next man. Or woman. They taught me all about it in Florida."

"Oh, did they really? Well, without underestimating the Florida academy of gator shooting, let me tell you it's one thing to take a shot a cardboard target, moving or not, at a funfair and quite another to shoot at a human being, one that risks shooting back too. There's that excellent Western movie starring Burt Lancaster as an aging but tough lawman or marshal, as we would probably say nowadays. His job is to bring wanted individuals to justice, catch them dead or alive, that's his simple remit. One night, as he is about to make camp out there in the Arizona wilderness, he is joined by a young would-be gunman who claims to be faster on the draw than anyone else, certainly faster than old Mr Lancaster. Yeah, the marshal goes. So were many of those I had to kill and take home lying across a horse's back. And he explains why that is so. To begin with, he represents the law, which gives him a psychological advantage. More important, he may be that bit slower, but his hand doesn't tremble, 'cause when he shoots, he shoots to kill. Solveig's murderer, the Boxer, is a chip off that kind of hardwood block. Hence his predilection for the one-bullet kill. He is no murderer. In his world of moral values, he is an executioner. That's what makes him really dangerous. His hand never trembles either. Yours will, trust me. He acts with a heart of ice, you risk becoming the victim of your emotions. I've been there."

Ignace let that sink in for a while. Had she managed to convince him? Solitaire would have been better at the job. Or maybe not. Sol was a natural born killer who had never been in need of a learning process. How then would she be able to pass her experience on to someone like Ignace?

"You're forgetting my genes, mom. May I remind you my father was one of the most dreaded killers of the Caribbean. You don't escape that altogether, ever. See, when that Texan lout insulted me at the Golf club, I was putting my act together to hit him so hard he might never get up again. If Solveig hadn't stepped in, I might have killed hum with my bare fists. And I guarantee you, my hands wouldn't have trembled for a moment."

Laura fell silent. Her son's plea had been as passionate as might have been expected. And convincing, to be honest. She pulled a last string.

"I think Solveig would have expected you to live on in her spirit, not to die in her memory."

Ignace dropped his hands in his lap. She had found a soft spot and hit hard.

"Yes, maybe you're right. In fact, I'm sure you are. But she intervened instinctively when she felt it was necessary. Some things you don't even discuss, you just do them. And to set your mind at rest, I have absolutely no death wish."

Laura sighed.

"Okay, William Bonney. Let's see you do it then."

She stood up and crossed the room. Ignace had sat down at the table. Laura took her scarf and wrapped it round the young man's brows, so he was blindfolded.

"Wait a second, don't move."

Then she went to the cupboard on the far side of the room, opened a drawer and took a gun out which she lay down on the table.

"There's a pistol lying in front of you. It's loaded with live ammunition. I always keep it ready to deal with any burglars who might be stupid enough to break in while I'm at home. I'd like you to take the gun apart and put it together again. Tell me what brand it is, what calibre the bullets are and how many shots. I'll be timing you. On three."

Ignace had hardly made five movements when Laura had already realized that he had not exaggerated when claiming he knew about guns. Maybe those gator-shooting soggy-pant rednecks in Florida did know what they were doing, after all.

"Two and a half minutes, not bad. So?"

"Easy. A Walther PPK nine mill, semi-automatic, six slugs in the magazine, one in the chamber. Loaded and secured."

Laura was impressed.

"Okay, Billy, welcome to the posse. But don't forget what I told you. Speed isn't everything in life. Not if it isn't matched by steely determination."

Ignace took off the scarf.

"No, maybe not. But without speed, it all comes to nothing, I guess."

3. Each to their Own

Laura looked at her wristwatch and suffered a sudden panic attack. According to schedule, the Prince of Wales would slip her moorings in less than an hour. She had made haste, accordingly, and packed whatever she felt were absolute musts in the way of clothing and documents. Not half of it fitted into the tiny, old-fashioned kid's suitcase that seemed to be the only thing at her disposal, strangely enough. So, she had to leave behind much of what had constituted her life so far.

After having closed the lid with some difficulty by sitting on it, spreading her legs and hammering at the two locks with her fists, she jumped down the staircase and rushed outside.

The running, shoving, and pushing in the few narrow streets and alleys of the little harbour town had reached a point at which you could speak of proper bedlam. That's roughly what the Warsaw ghetto must have looked like shortly before the upheaval.

Everyone was trying desperately to reach St. Sampson harbour quay on the other side of the basin, where the Prince of Wales was moored. A worn-down tramp ship the British government had chartered for the occasion. Her possible loss due to a stray German torpedo could easily be written off as collateral damage. Its hawsers were hanging loose, so that her hull could be lifted by the incoming tide inch by inch without her mooring lines breaking under the growing strain.

Wedged in between two families with kith and kin, everybody using their elbows to make some place left, right and centre, Laura was shoved towards the harbour basin more than she walked, her feet sometimes clean off the ground, it seemed. Like a huge flock of sheep hearing a wolf pack howl from the near-by edge of the woods, Laura thought, as she, too, resorted to kicking and elbowing so as not to stumble and fall over her own legs. Anyone falling down risked getting trampled to death by the hooves of the herd. Most of the others were carrying small, old-fashioned suitcases not unlike Laura's. Some didn't even have that and carried their stuff in sheets or blankets slung over their shoulders like so many Fathers Xmases on Boxing Day. The bane of modern nomad perambulations, the trolley bag noisily hopping over the cobblestones, hadn't yet made its appearance, or so it would seem. Nobody that she saw around looked in the least prepared for long trips or voyages, that was for sure.

Why would they? The locals would leave their respective island only grudgingly and for brief spells at a time. A subject the Doc and herself had once discussed on the Saintes, she remembered. Of course, this wasn't the Caribbean, but a certain mental dwarfing, as the Doc had called it then, was conspicuous enough here too. Even the neighbouring island of the same archipelago would be regarded as a planet belonging to another galaxy: different dialect, different topography, different agricultural and "industrial" set-up, different mentality, and, if at all practicable, a totally different and even more whimsical legal-constitutional order than that practiced at home.

Having been moved to one side of the road by the crowd of people hitting out, shouting aloud and pressing on more or less blindly, Laura risked getting squashed against the façades of the houses facing the harbour basin. So, she finally squeezed herself through a pub door standing ajar and sat down on a vacant bar stool, dropping her suitcase to the floor and resting her elbows on the counter. One of the two locks of her cute little suitcase had given up and deserted. The other, now bearing the responsible for the entire load, wouldn't last much longer, either, she feared.

"Nothing like a well-organized evacuation, is there," a thin, sarcastic man's voice to the right of her said in an English tainted by the faintest of German accents.

Laura stared into the darker part of the pub that she had presumed empty. It took her a little while to discern a man in the black uniform characteristic of the SS. He was sitting on another stool sipping beer. With his left hand, he was holding the glass, whose volume rested in that typically British no-man's-land between half and full metric litre called a pint. Probably an officer, maybe a colonel. Next to his right hand lay his cap with the metallic skull emblem ominously staring at Laura. What was missing to complete the pirate's impression, were the crossed thigh bones. He seemed to be begging the question what use the evacuation would be, seen the Germans were already here? The officer seemed to read her mind.

"I'm a member of a discrete vanguard," he said, almost apologetically.

Now, that her eyes had adapted, she was able to take a closer look at the man. His physiognomy appeared to have a striking resemblance to that of Heinrich Himmler, whose face she had seen on blurred black-and-white photos and jittery old feature footage. The same brow, the smooth hair combed back as if dry-blown by a starting jet plane's booster, with brutally clean-shaved temples. The same half-ironic, but always watchful eyes behind wiry glasses above the mere hint of a moustache. Had he grown a beard, he might easily have passed himself off as Leo Trotsky, on a dark night, she thought. Did totalitarian ideologies attract men with notorious insignificant or vaguely ridiculous physiognomies? Or were such physiognomies shaped under the influence of unrestricted power fantasies? Compared to the rustic Stalin, the Nazis, with their bits of moustachios always looking like a dicky slipped out of position during a moment of heated rhetoric, had a vaguely shy, inhibited air about them. As if they didn't quite believe in their own luck: blond like Adolf, slender like Goering, with eagle's eyes like Himmler, who was it had said that?

"Quite. I....think I should be going now. My boat...."

Laura didn't quite know how to extricate herself out of the awkward situation before she had even really got into it.

"Why do you want to leave the island at all? Now, that it's about to get real interesting?" the SS officer asked.

"You are obviously an Aryan woman, by the look of it."

He chuckled like a little boy in class who had just cracked a joke at the expense of the generally despised maths teacher. Laura felt more and more uneasy and wished to get out.

"I...have next of kin in Britain," she stammered.

"I had only come visiting here on Guernsey. That's why...."

The man looked at his watch and stroked his hair.

"Hm. I haven't introduced myself. Von Achenbüttel, colonel of the Waffen SS. You?"

Laura told him her name.

"A pleasure, I'm sure, Frau Forster. May I invite you to a glass or two before you dash off again? One for the road, as they say? I mustn't stay too long myself either, you know. I'm on my way East. Just thought I might as well pass by the islands, since they seem so close to the Fuehrer's heart. Personally, no disrespect, I find them rather tepid, I must say."

"So you're on your way to…the Eastern front?"

The colonel smiled ruefully.

"Would I were, would I were. But, you see, the Fuehrer thought it wise to keep me close to his orbit. That said, ever since we took over Germany, the front is literally everywhere, don't you think. I am bound for Poznan, where my boss, Heinrich Himmler is supposed to give a speech. Not his cup of tea, really."

"What isn't, Poznan? The Poles?"

"No, delivering speeches. We usually leave that to Josef."

"You mean…Stalin?"

The colonel was taken aback a second, then laughed and slapped his thighs.

"That's a damn good one, got to pass it by Heinrich tonight. No, our very own Prop Min Joe Goebbels, is who I meant. Strange name, don't you think?"

"Prop Min? I thought it was just an abbreviation for minister of propaganda."

"Goebbels, Frau Forster, Goe-be-be-bels."

He drew out the name like chewing gum, as if he was relishing each self-created syllable.

"Personally, I smell something uncouth there, don't you? I mean, good old German names are the ones derived from craftsmen such as Miller, Baker, Farmer, Forester or…."

"….Hitler?" Laura ended the sentence for him.

"Come to think of it, though, what exactly is a Hitler? I mean, what kind of craftsman? Who would call for a Hitler? To have what done?"

Achenbüttel shook the index finger of his right hand at her.

"Watch it, young lady, you're moving onto thin ice there. Hitler is Austrian, of course. What it means and whether it ever meant anything at all, only God and the Austrians know. Hitler, Huetler, Hitteler, all the same family, I guess. Anyway, Adolf Schicklgruber wouldn't have worked, now, would it? Heil Schicklgruber? Would have rocked the ghetto, I bet. No, no. But Goebbels. What's that? Where does it come from? Palestine? My experience so far: if only you dig deep enough, you hit Jewish ancestors sooner or later."

Well, you're bloody bound to, Laura thought. He who diggeth deep enough, landeth himself on the Ararat. More Jewish than Noah, you die."

"Thanks for your kind offer, Colonel Aschenputtel…"

"Achenbüttel. Lieutenant Colonel, to be precise. What offer?"

"So sorry, Achenbüttel. But I really have to get going now."

Achenbüttel had come closer and closer to her in the course of their conversation. Now he seized her arm.

"The common Jew is a wily individual. Wily and insidious," he continued, disregarding her.

"Disguises his true identity behind a front of anti-Semitic attitudes, sometimes. Can you think of a better kind of camouflage than open anti-Semitism? I can't. But he's not fooling me, the halting little devil, not me. Himmler hates his guts. Says he takes himself for someone better even than the Fuehrer himself."

Laura was beginning to be desperate. Her ship was to push off in about half an hour and her talk with Aschenputtel was clearly degenerating rapidly. She slid off the stool, grabbed her suitcase and made for the exit.

"Goeb-bels…" was the last she heard before the battle for the survival of the fittest had her back. She felt she should jump on a barrel or dustbin and shout out loud that all this running and shoving and fighting was to no avail since the Germans were already in town. But she might just as well have tried to tell a flock of sheep there was no more need to run since the wolves had miraculously turned into vegan vegetarians overnight. And so, she moved with the flow, fell on her knees, got up again, hit out with her suitcase until the second lock kissed the rest goodbye and the contents were spread all over the place. No point in trying to recover them either. Hundreds of feet trod one part of her belongings literally into the pavement, while scattering the other, lighter half to the four winds.

Laura let go of the suitcase, now suddenly as useless as a third tit and rushed on, with only a measly fifty yards separating her from the gangway. The crowd suddenly came to a jerky halt in fits and starts. That was almost more ominous than its pressing on. At the beginning of the gangway, people had to squeeze through the eye of the needle. Or rather be squeezed by the guards brandishing their gun butts and landing them indiscriminately on the backs and in the sides of all and sundry. The elderly and weak, women and kids. fell to the ground and were trampled upon and beaten simultaneously. If the dark rim of heads with or without headgear at the railings of all three decks was anything to go by, the Prince of Wales must already be way over and above its nominal payload.

Yet that didn't seem to bother anyone. Laura briefly remembered the terrible accidents of hopelessly overloaded ferries. Mostly, such dramas happened in some obscure sounds and fjords of the Philippines, alright. But that was no guarantee of it not happening here and now as well.

Finally, she had cleared the gangway and was aboard. But there was no time to catch her breath or maybe sit down and rest for a moment. Instead, she was immediately chased down several companionways with handrails shining from the touch of hundreds of hands. Here, people stood so close to one another that nobody could have fallen down, not even in a state of unconsciousness. The stink of sweat, urine and faeces was overpowering and mingled with a sweetish scent Laura could not identify at first. Then she recognized what it was: beer. Until some recent point in time, the Prince of Wales must have shipped beer barrels.

Down in the hold, Laura fought her way to the side of the hull which was almost as wet from the inside as from the outside because of the condensing breath and sweat of all those unfortunate passengers. But she hardly even felt that. Huddled against some crates, she could at least steady herself and take the weight off her legs and hurting feet for a moment.

Suddenly, the steel behind her started to quiver like the armour of some primeval dinosaur waking from its thousand-year-long hibernation to look for a suitable female to mate with before falling into a thousand-year stupor, again. The Prince of Wales seemed to be getting under way.

How long the passage had lasted, Laura couldn't tell. While she had been listening to the sea's rushing and splashing against the hull and had tried to suppress her urge to vomit, she must have dozed off and slept a while. When she woke up now with a jolt, the ship appeared to have moored again at her port of destination already. Laura's coat was gone. So was her wristwatch. She cursed herself for not having paid better attention by staying awake

As if to crown her misery, it started raining through the wide-open hatch of the hold. Laura trembled from the humid cold. She was very thirsty but hurried after the crowd that was beginning to climb up the companionways like so many chickens scrambling up a ladder.

Back on deck, still feeling cold and thirsty, and dirty and dishevelled to boot, she looked around with some consternation. The crew that had organised the embarkation with some difficulty at St. Sampson's had been replaced by heavily armed German MP's who would obviously be in charge of operations as of now. Even though it kept raining incessantly, with thin curtain-like clouds of fog or haze slowly wafting across treeless hills, it was pretty obvious to Laura that this wasn't part of the Southern coast of Britain but rather one of the less attractive corners of some other island. The harbour looked decidedly smaller and way more primitive than St. Sampson's. It seemed to consist of a crude basin surrounded by solid if ungainly blocks of concrete and protected from the sea by a seemingly never-ending breakwater that protruded far out, parallel to the coast. With the kind of brutal force that only nature appears capable of mustering, Atlantic rollers kept hammering against this wall, hardly higher than a tall man.

The gangway was well-nigh level at present. Which meant that the short period of the mid-tide had set in. Hence, the whole passage could only have lasted some three hours, tops. Not long enough, in other words, for the Prince of Wales to have reached Weymouth, Portsmouth, Southampton or any other port along the English South coast. Especially when considering that this old vessel would not be able to do more than ten, eleven knots without inadvertently disintegrating. Nor did this panorama evoke Cherbourg, which Laura was fairly familiar with. Yet before she had time to address herself to one of the locals standing on the quay, watching this spectacle with gaping mouths, she was again wedged in by the steady stream of people rudely herded off the ship by the MP's. Everybody had to fall in to form four long rows altogether, irrespective of age or sex: men, women, kids with or without parents, old-timers, the lot. The smaller children and babies were carried and comforted by their mothers, some by their fathers. Most if not all of them were as thirsty as herself, Laura suspected. Many probably had to relieve themselves after the passage, but there was no toilet of any kind in sight anywhere around. What in God's name was that bizarre hostility between the Nazis and toilets?

Or was it a deliberate ploy levelled at increasing the humiliation of being deported, trans-shipped, and herded together?

On the harbour basin's land side, the intimidated and disorientated men and women were advised in no uncertain terms to drop whatever luggage they had on the ground there and then and follow all instructions of the MP's without a moment's hesitation. Then, they were divided into four large groups. With amazing rapidity, the groups gathered round the four tall soldiers who held up cardboard signs in different colours, very much like cruise-ship passengers rallying round the guides who are to take them round the major sights of today's illustrious stop-over port. Without her glasses, which were stuck in the pocket of her coat now warming some thief's shoulders, Laura was barely capable of reading the black writing on the yellow sign that belonged to her group. It appeared to her, though, as if it said something like S-Y-L-T.

Once all groups were ready to go, people were chased up a rather steep, wet, and, hence, slippery hillock covered with long grass that hadn't been cut for ages. The sharp-edged blades would get trampled down to form an even more slippery natural carpet. Men, women, and kids would lose their foothold, slide, fall and tumble down half the hill like so many Sisyphus rocks, knocking others off their feet, too, and pulling them down with them. On arriving at the bottom, they would try and climb up again, spurred on by the cursing guards constantly shouting abuse at them. Others got stuck in patches of mud and were herded on before they could free their shoes or boots stuck in the ground and, hence, had to continue in socks or on bare feet. Everybody looked and smelled more or less like they had just been pulled out of a putrid cesspool.

Soaking wet hair was hanging down people's faces and necks. Dripping wet clothes stuck to people's emaciated bodies like some sticky second skin. Whoever still had shoes on their feet would feel black, earthy water well up from them with every step they took. On the bright side, the toilet problem was solved in that everybody just let go, because under those conditions, it was generally felt that it did not make much difference.

Laura's group seemed privileged. Instead of being chased up the hill like all the rest of the passengers, its members were hauled onto a freight train. Which Laura saw as a good sign. Any train covering only a short distance or meant to transport goods on the premises of a large industrial site would have presented itself as a narrow-gauge variety of railroad. What she noticed here, though, was normal-gauge rails as deployed in ordinary British Rail traffic.

Alas, for once, her reasoning proved erroneous. The sliding doors of the carriages had hardly been slammed shut and the train started when it came to a halt again after what could have been no more than two or three miles. And the fact that Laura, despite the din inside the carriage, had never stopped hearing the clamour of the sea must mean that they had done no more than roll along the coast. Which confirmed her impression that this was an island.

The sliding doors were slammed open. They all had to jump out and form two long rows. Laura's right-hand neighbour had dressed unusually warm for the time of year. Probably, to have an excess number of pockets in which he could carry whatever belongings he had managed to take with him that far on his person. He plucked at her sleeve and asked her something she didn't understand. She assumed he had no idea where he was and was looking for her to get some more information.

"Alderney," she replied at random. Had she said Auschwitz, instead, the man could hardly have looked more horrified than he did.

Laura was at a loss, to put it mildly. Had she got on the wrong vessel at St. Sampson's? Possibly. There had been several rusty cargo ships of more or less the same make and general state of neglect moored on the quay. And, contrary to her habit, she had allowed herself to just follow the crowd, instead of checking whether or not she had been heading for the right boat. Mass psychosis is what they called it. But at present, it was a little late to be speculating about that, anyway.

Again, the caravan of despair set itself in motion. Now that she had no coat any more, Laura felt the wind whistle through her ribcage, as it were. Her shoes got stuck in the first mudhole she came across so that she had to cover the rest of the way barefoot as well. Cursing her bad luck and stupidity, she kept stumbling on. Was this exodus ever going to stop?

After what felt like an eternity, they seemed to have reached their goal. A rusty stretch of barbed wire emerged from the fog. The caravan did a right turn and, for a while, followed that malicious wire, always paying great attention not to get hooked by its rusty barbs sticking out like thorns from a rosebush. Finally, they found themselves standing in front of a primitive wooden archway that must have been knocked up by some rather untalented or careless men that had taken no particular pride in their piece of handicraft.

"Welcome to camp Sylt," a fairly delicate voice Laura thought she recognized shouted out over their heads.

"Our slogan here is Each to their Own. I hope you'll find yours with us, is all I wish to add at this stage. You'll be given time enough to search for it, I think I can promise you that."

Again, the group set itself in motion. When Laura arrived at the gateway, she saw Aschenputtel, her acquaintance from the pub at St. Sampson's, standing there, watching the sheep scurry into the fold. He was wearing a coat now and had donned his cap, but the metal-rimmed glasses, slightly misted up from the rain were unmistakable. For his part, he seemed to have recognized her, too, amidst the slowly moving crowd and stopped her, grabbing her by the arm as he had done in the pub.

"I thought I had advised you to stay on Guernsey, now, hadn't I?" he said with a reproachful overtone.

"Each to their Own?" Laura asked.

The SS colonel waved his arm as if clearing a table.

"One of Heydrich's screwy ideas. Eerie fellow, Heydrich. Between you and me, I wasn't at all aggrieved when he bit the dust in Prague. Nor was Himmler, I gather. This guy Heydrich had collected compromising material on all Nazi leaders. And sneaked up to Goebbels. Foul play? Maybe. Anyway, a much less cynical slogan than Work sets you Free, I should think. Freedom's just another word for nothing left to lose, don't you think? Society, the state, will only let go of you if and when you're down and out. Looked at it from that angle, for a common mortal, the microcosm of a concentration camp is not much worse than a mirror of the world at large. More brutal, yes, and more realistic. But a notorious misfit and loser will be whittled down to nothing by our everyday madness just as reliably as the inmate of a concentration camp. More slowly, more politically correctly and socially compatible, if you like, but just as inescapably. Think about it while you enjoy the Sylt set-up."

While Laura was trying hard to think of arguments apt to denounce the man's ridiculous thesis, someone was vigorously shaking her shoulder. Again and again, presumably, to make her move on instead of blocking the whole procedure. Unwillingly, she opened her eyes. Ignace was standing over her, probably after having tried to wake her up for quite a while already.

"Sorry, I must have dozed off there for a minute or two," she murmured and sat up with the help of Ignace.

"More like half an hour, but who's timing it? Marquardt, your loyal servant, called to say he chartered a plane for us. Take-off is foreseen for eight a.m. We'll pick up the Chief at London City Airport and fly on to St. Peter Port."

"In what? A Messerschmitt?"

"No, they were fully booked. So were the Heinkels. Hence, we'll have to make shift with a twin-engine Piper Seminole. That should do the trick. At St. Peter Port, we'll take the ferry to Creux Harbour. My things are packed already. So don't try to pull one over on me and leave me behind."

Laura shrugged her shoulders.

"Of course not. Would I ever stoop that low now?"

"No offence, mom, but I wouldn't put it past you altogether."

"Shame on you. You ought to know your mother better than that. William Bonney. I'll see you in the a.m., bushy-tailed as ever."

NINTH CHAPTER

1. The Seventh Little Indian

"You're kidding me. Goering? We're flying with Hermann Goering at the stick?"

Laura looked at Ignace with manifest disbelief.

"No, not Hermann, Rudolph. Rudolph Goering, that's what the man said. Not so rare a name as it may seem then."

"Could he be...I mean, did the other Goering have any offspring?"

Laura had addressed herself to the Chief this time. Colestron shrugged his shoulders.

"I shouldn't think so, never heard of a son or daughter anyway. Besides, even he would now have to be way past flying age, wouldn't he?"

Laura was about to get up and look for herself whether she would detect any likeness in the pilot's features. But she thought better of it. To begin with, the poor man must have been through a multitude of jokes referring to his name. And besides, the Seminole was losing height and preparing for touchdown. Not the best of moments to divert the pilot's attention.

To be looking down on the Bay of St. Malo from the plane had had its charm. Till that moment when Laura had suddenly remembered the collision of two private propeller planes in the airspace above Grandville. A single-engine Piper had crashed into the side of a twin-engine Cessna. A weird collision that had taken place on a sunshiny day, best of weather conditions with one hundred pro visibility. Not surprisingly, it had taken the relevant French authorities quite some time to identify the probable causes of the accident. As their investigations brought to light, the Piper had, with the Grandville tower's permission, deviated from its original course, because the pilot, a French businessman alone on board his plane, had wished to take a look at some sort of Naval parade that was in full swing down in the

Bay. He had veered to his left, at some stage, tipping the plane in the process. The specific lay-out of his cockpit was such, that his downward-forward vision, always a bit of a problem, had been partially blocked, altogether for just a few seconds. Long enough for his plane to bump into the right side of the Cessna, whose pilot hadn't seen the Piper on a collision course because it had practically come from behind. The Cessna not being provided with an outside rear mirror, the accident had been the logical consequence. Well, a professional pilot by the name of Goering probably wouldn't make that kind of mistake.

"No offence, people, but with Sol watching my back I would feel a lot better."

Laura said that as an afterthought an hour or so later when they were sitting on the deck of the little Travel Trident passenger ferry to Creux Harbour. In those calm conditions, practically no wind and a sea smooth as a mirror's surface, the boat needed just about an hour to get there. After all the turbulence they had had to undergo because of the constant change of land and sea, this short voyage was pure bliss, Laura felt.

"What's your plan, then?" asked the Chief after a while, dragging her out of her little chrysalis.

"Play it by ear, basically," she replied.

"We'll step ashore and try to find the Boxer's mother. If she's still alive. We'll drill her for any information on her son that she is ready and able to part with. I mean, she might be demented and not remember she even has a son. Maybe we're lucky and he's paying her a visit, back from Helgoland or Norderney or wherever he carried out his most recent killing. Then we squish him. No, seriously, I think we ought to tackle this from two sides simultaneously: one secular, the other more…clerical, so to speak."

Having said that, she started renewing her lip gloss, leaving her two listeners somewhat in limbo.

"My suggestion," she continued after a while," would be for Harry to take a walk to the Seigneurie and get what information on the Gooey family they may have in store there. Don't hesitate to pull what weight you can, brandishing your title about and all. They won't know you're nothing but a retired cop and there's no need to let them into the secret right from the start, is there? These people don't get visitors from the Yard every week or even every month now, I suspect. So, they may yet be impressionable."

Colestron nodded.

"Okay, I'll see what I can do. Would the Seigneurie be the secular or rather the clerical side of things, then?"

"As you wish, Harry, as you wish. Of course, it would have helped to make an appointment with the Seigneur himself, but the Almighty didn't answer the phone. Be that as it may, Ignace and myself, we'll hang about the chapel and scan the churchyard if necessary. If you want to learn about the living, you had better start looking among the dead – especially when dealing with small communities such as this one."

"German saying?"

"No, Laura Forster's Collected Aphorisms, Volume One, Early Days. We'll stay in touch over the phone and as soon as one of us has any news, we'll discuss the next step."

The Chief nodded again.

"Sounds like the sketch of a draft of a plan alright."

Then he became more formal again.

"The two of you don't know your way around Sark. A word of warning, therefore. Don't allow yourself to be taken in by the generally Hobbit-like atmosphere of the place. It may look like a Garden of Eden, but there's more than meets the eye. If it's any help, think of it in terms of the pirates' stronghold it once was, and be on your guard at all times. You're both packing guns, I suppose?"

Laura and Ignace nodded.

"Make sure to watch your own step," Laura answered.

"I have Ignace covering my back. You'll be on your own."

The Chief smiled.

"I appreciate your being worried about me. But, let me assure you, I have been on the job long enough to weigh up my risks and defend myself whenever necessary. I just hope the killer has no supporters in the local population. That might complicate matters considerably."

The Travel Trident breezed into Creux Harbour and lay moored only seconds later. Looking over the railing, Laura could see the bottom, so clear was the water and so shallow the harbour. They waited for a handful of other tourists to get off the ferry and then stepped ashore, all three of them. As they passed the short tunnel which formed the harbour's only access, Laura instinctively ducked forward, even though, as a medium-sized person, she could easily have walked upright without bumping her head on the rocks above her. Then, she followed the others onto Harbour Hill Road leading towards St. Peter's church, whose steeple was already visible above the trees.

Now Laura understood what the Chief had meant with his warning. Looking around, she felt like a female Ulysses shipwrecked and washed up on the island of the Phaeacians, whose exact localisation was a bone of contention among historians, archaeologists, and botanists, in fact. That quarrel could now be declared over, Laura felt. Not Corfu, but Sark, the island of rosy-fingered dawn, had to be the home of the hospitable, friendly, hedonist Phaeacians. Wherever she looked, her eyes would capture a Paradise blossoming in all the colours of the rainbow. Not one house without a well-kempt little garden and a diligently pruned hedgerow. Crime must be unheard of here, where no harsh words were ever spoken.

"Have I promised too much?" Colestron asked under his breath.

"Not at all. A proper Garden of Eden. But then, even there, things went FUBAR at some stage, or so we are told…."

"Precisely. So better keep your eyes peeled."

Laura could hardly restrain herself.

"It reminds me of the lush flora of the Caribbean. Except that the Caribbean air is spicier, more humid. And the scenery not quite as orderly. But it would be sufficient, I suspect, to let a class four hurricane pass over Sark, for once, and it might come out somewhat more ruffled too." ,

The Chief agreed.

"Yes, and what with global warming, that may not even be such a remote possibility any longer."

After a brisk walk of only a few minutes, they had reached the church of St. Peter's. An Anglican dream dressed in Victorian Gothic, erected with reddish and grey granite. As was still quite easily discernible, this had originally been a rather plain rectangular building with a surface area of roughly sixty feet by thirty, with a height of maybe twenty. Not the most ambitious dimensions for a church calling itself a cathedral, but rather comparable to those of the numerous gingerbread churches of Antigua that housed an impressive array of sects. The steeple had obviously been added later but was now nestling to the nave with a great sense of proportion. During the first years of its existence, the steeple had fulfilled the dual function of calling the community members either to mass or to a shipwreck.

"This is where we split," Laura said.

"Let's synchronize our watches. I don't know that it makes any practical difference, but it sounds more professional. Harry, we'll talk in two hours at the latest. Ignace, fall back a little, melt into the décor, to the utmost extent possible. Don't ever lose me out of sight, son, hear? My life might depend on it. So pull yourself together and don't go catching butterflies."

And so, whilst Colestron strode on towards the Seigneurie, Laura opened the screeching iron door and stepped onto the gravelled churchyard path, here and there overgrown by stubborn weeds. Slowly, she strolled along the rows of graves, some of them very old, others of more recent date, like the Queen trooping the colours on her official birthday. Some of the gravestones displayed a slant that Laura would have considered dangerous. Back home in Hamburg, this sort of thing wouldn't be allowed. Kids playing among the graves could all too easily be smashed by one of those slabs of granite losing it. Suddenly, she heard steps behind her.

"I thought I had asked you to keep...."

Turning round while speaking, she realized this wasn't Ignace, as she had thought, but a stranger. A clergyman. More precisely, an Anglican reverend, it would seem. At a first superficial glance, he could also have been a Protestant, had it not been for the

"Papal" violet kind of vest he wore under his black jacket. It lent a touch of vivacity to what otherwise would have been a rather dead-pan assembly of undertaker clothing. Without, on the other hand, going over the top and displaying a degree of fashion-consciousness that might have looked oddly out of place here.

"Can I help you in any way? It would seem you are in search of a specific grave? If you give me a name, I might..."

The man's voice was pleasantly mellifluous, almost silken. He was a good head taller than Laura who had to look up to him, something she instinctively hated to do. Age fifty-five or thereabouts, he gave her the impression of someone of affable politeness and the emphatic aloofness characteristic of men of his profession – the clerical version of the proverbial stiff upper lip. If anything was brushing that pleasant physiognomy up the wrong way, as it were, it was his rather massive nose and the strange husky's eyes that seemed to have the power of some X-ray unit and made Laura feel uneasy.

At his age, his black hair must have been dyed. Which betrayed a touch of vanity that would not normally stand a clergyman in good stead, she thought.

"Hello....Reverend, I take it?" Laura wasn't quite sure how to address the man and handle the situation. Who would have thought that, with a church to her right and a churchyard to her left, she might risk bumping into a clergyman, silly.

"I'm just looking around," she said, as if the Reverend was selling lady's underwear at Harrod's and had asked her for her preferred bra colour.

"Well, I hope you'll find something to your liking. If not, we have another little plot further down the road...I think, many of us feel the everlasting presence of death in the midst of life and try to get a foretaste of things to come. Like children on Boxing Day, unwilling to wait for the handing out of presents and peeping through the keyhole instead. I can understand that. Even though we have to remember that the mortal remains assembled here do not represent the essence of our being and yield no evidence of the true nature of life hereafter."

"Amen," Laura couldn't help herself.

"That was well put, if I may say so. As for myself, now, I guess I prefer to linger on this side of paradise for a few decades longer, if it pleases the Almighty to let me, eh, Reverend."

"Deacon, I'm the local PD. Brown's the name."

Laura gave him a winning smile.

"Brown? Seriously? I'll be…eh, my name is Forster, Laura Forster. What's a PD then?" Laura asked, painfully aware that, in France, this treacherous abbreviation would make him the local paedophile on duty, as it were.

"Enchanté, Mrs Forster," the deacon replied and squeezed her outstretched hand.

"PD stands for Permanent Deacon, a matter of internal cuisine in the Anglican church, without bothering you with any details. You're German, then, I take it?"

Laura nodded. In places formerly under German occupation, she always hesitated to give away her nationality. You never knew what kind of reaction you would get. Trouble was, though, that, by and large, German occupation had covered nearly the whole of Europe.

"Hm, that's interesting. You see, there was a time when Germans would drop in here in droves, so to speak. Ex-Wehrmacht or their offspring who wished to visit or re-visit the scene of the crime, as it were. Not so many as have been drawn to the coasts of Normandy, of course. Did you know there are villages and towns on that part of the French coast that still live at least in part on that kind of war tourism? Places like Arrowmanche, Caen, Bayeux, and so on. Well, they have the advantage of attracting not only Germans, but Americans and Brits, as well. Personally, I like it calm and quiet. Imagine Sark to be literally flooded by thousands of tourists during the summer holidays. The island would never recover."

"Hence, you prefer the much more discrete invasion of letter-box companies…?"

The PD laughed.

"Touché. You don't see them, smell them, or hear from them. Are you here to establish an offshore corporation yourself?"

Laura shook her head.

"No, I would hardly have come here if I were, would I? Unless St. Peter's is really a secret HSCB branch office. No, I'm an independent journalist working on a series of articles, maybe a book, on the German occupation of the Channel Islands."

"Hasn't that lame horse been flogged to death yet?"

"In Britain perhaps, but not in Germany it hasn't. I suspect a lot of Germans have never even heard of the islands and many more have no idea they had been occupied by the Nazis. You see, they say that when the first German soldiers arrived here, they mistook the Channel Islands for the African coast, due to the mild climate and rather exotic flora. And irrespective of our modern forms of travelling, this basic ignorance hasn't changed. For many Germans, the archipelago of the Seychelles is probably nearer to their hearts and minds than the Channel Islands. The only German really infatuated with them was Adolf the Fuehrer Hitler, I guess."

"I see. And you have made it your mission to remedy that situation. What particular aspects of Sark will your book be focussing on?"

"Well, I need a peg to personify, to individualize things, that's basic technique for us journalists. Individualize, then gradually generalize, from the concrete to the abstract, that's how we work. In the course of my investigations, I came across a British military operation of stupefying pointlessness, a kind of raid that must have taken place around the critical year 1943, here, on Sark. I thought that might be my peg."

At that very moment, the church's single bell started tolling so loud, Laura didn't hear what she was saying, any more. PD Brown took her by the arm and led her a few steps away from the offending steeple.

"I'm sorry. I'm sure that wasn't deliberate. The bell was formed from the metal of two melted-down six-pounders, by the way. I guess that's why it sometimes manifests acertain aggressiveness, like just now, for example."

"Six-pounders? Sounds like the heck of a cheeseburger to me. With loads of relish, mind. The kind I could do with right now."

The PD smiled. "Yes, it does, doesn't it? Well, in the old days before the invention of rifled barrels, cannon used to be classified according to the weight of the iron balls they could hurl at the enemy. This was then replaced by the calibre during the nineteenth century, when balls were replaced by grenades that flew further and wrought death and destruction not just by the force of their kinetic energy but by their explosive power. Anyway, I'm digressing…You mentioned a military operation of sorts here on Sark? Pointless, you say? Without professing myself a specialist in the field, I think it could safely be said that the history of warfare from antiquity to modern times literally abounds with pointless operations costing the lives of hundreds of thousands of soldiers. Which begs the question who is ultimately responsible, misguided military strategy or brick-faced politicians? What do you think?"

Laura shrugged her shoulders.

"My money would be on the latter category, to be honest. But be that as it may, the operation I'm talking about was carried out by a handful of young men, the so-called Yarmouth Six. Ring a bell at all?"

Laura had pronounced the name after a wee pause in mid-sentence to watch for a reaction on the part of the Deacon. But there was none. The husky's eyes didn't even blink.

"Six men, you say? How many managed to survive?"

"That's where the opinions start parting company. According to my research so far, it wasn't six, really, but seven. And all but one survived, or so it seems."

"Seems? It shouldn't be that difficult to find out, now, should it?"

"Well, like I say, in the case of six of them, yes, there's no doubt. As for the seventh…little Indian, no disrespect, there are different versions to choose between. Some say he drowned. Others claim he didn't but was washed ashore without his mates being aware of it. In which latter case, he would probably have been given asylum on Sark by a person or persons unknown."

"Hm. Fascinating stuff. Got any names?"

"Yes. The seventh little Indian was called Peter Collins, nicknamed Gooey."

Again, Laura had inserted a little pause before dropping the names like dumplings into a pot of soup, but again no visible reaction from the Deacon.

"Collins, like the dictionary?"

Laura nodded. Either the man really didn't know, or he would have made a good actor.

"Quite. Like I say, his nickname was Gooey. A born Guernsey man, grew up in London, though."

Deacon Brown seemed to be reflecting intensely.

"Hm. I must admit neither the name nor the nickname ring a bell with me. But while you were speaking, I remembered an old local story almost everybody around here must have heard at some stage. Certainly the members of the older generation."

"And what story would that be?"

"Sark being tiny and its five hundred official inhabitants having the reputation of being rather inquisitive and busy-bodies, that sort of thing will circulate no matter what, I guess. Some years, no, decades ago, there was talk of a lady living on Little Sark, the Southern part, that is, having hidden a British soldier in her house during the last years of the war. The man was said to be mentally handicapped to some extent and suffering from amnesia. Sad story this. Now that you mention it, I think there was even talk of a child they had between the two of them."

Laura felt her hands tremble. She was getting closer and closer to the solution, that was for sure.

"And why, indeed, shouldn't they? As long as the man's mental handicap had no genetic causes but had been acquired by dint of certain dreadful events he had had to live through."

"Do you know what became of the woman in question?"

"You happen to be resting your right foot on her grave."

Laura started and quickly moved a step to the right. At her feet, a small gravestone of reddish granite seemed to grow out of the ground like a finger stuck up by the grave's owner to remind the world that here lay the mortal remains of a certain Rose McAllister.

"Rose…Mrs McAllister?"

"Precisely. That's her. Used to be nicknamed the Rose of Sark, in analogy to the Jersey Lily, I guess. If you wish to learn more, we shall have to take a look at our registers, I'm afraid."

"And where would they be?"

The Deacon pointed over his shoulder.

"In the church. The Seigneurie keeps asking us to transfer the documents there, but so far, we managed to hold our own. It's all in there, if you're interested."

"Absolutely, it's more than I could have hoped for. Please, point me to them."

"Alright, please follow me then. The registers are locked away in a kind of safe with only the respective Deacon, me, in other words, carrying the key on his person at all times, or almost."

He turned and went ahead, rummaging in his pockets, at the same time.

Laura's hunting fever had reached such worrying heights that her attention lapsed for a moment. While talking to the Deacon, she had, from the corner of her eye, noticed a gardener busy cleaning a grave some rows further on but had attributed no particular importance to that observation. What's more natural than a gardener doing his job in a churchyard. It was only now, walking behind the Deacon who, she noticed, was dragging his right leg ever so imperceptibly, that she remembered a word of caution Solitaire had once handed her. In a crisis situation, don't expect to be attacked by green men from outer space. Watch out for the ordinary, run-of-the-mill kind of scenery: dustmen a little too ostentatiously busy emptying the bins, postmen popping mail into rows of letter boxes they seem none too familiar with, craftsmen on the job, gardeners trimming hedges, that sort of thing. One or the other of those will make the move.

From the corner of her eye, again, Laura now noticed the gardener had disappeared. The Deacon, for his part, seemed to find his encounter with this charming German lady invigorating enough to start humming a tune aloud, as if wanting to compete with the chorus of birds in the trees merrily chirping away. None of them, though, neither blackbird nor starling or bullfinch would have managed to happily fall in with the Deacon's hummed song that Laura knew only too well, the one that told of pocketfuls of marbles such are promises.

2. Rose of Sark

Laura opened her eyes and heaved a deep sigh. She was lying on the cold slabs of stone that formed the floor of a kind of humid vault. Her hands and feet were tied. The small, round, windowless den of a place was lit by only one fat candle someone had stood on a footstool like a lamp on a night table. Waves of blunt pain were pulsating through her head. The ropes on her feet and hands bit into her flesh. Fortunately, she had not been gagged. Anything impairing her respiration tended to cause her panic attacks. Plus, some kidnaping victims had died a slow and horrible death by suffocation because, by gagging their victims, the kidnapers had effectively blocked nose and mouth with duct-tape.

What the blazes had happened? The moment the would-be Deacon had given himself away by humming the tune of the Boxer, Laura had hesitated a second or two. Perhaps because the mere idea of a serial killer impersonating an Anglican Deacon had seemed a little too preposterous. And when she had finally gone for her Redhawk, she had been that split second too late. Someone, presumably the gardener, had pressed a cotton swab drenched with chloroform on her nose from behind while pressing her arms to her torso with a very firm, vice-like grip. Then she had lost consciousness.

What the hell had happened to Ignace? Had he lost visual contact with her despite her stern admonishments? If so, the boy was no good for operations of this delicate nature, where you had to be able to trust your mate or associate at all times.

On the bright side: she was still alive, which was more than most of the people who had ever made the Boxer's fleeting acquaintance could say for themselves. Had he twigged her from the very beginning? That would be a moot point now. By wandering around the churchyard, Laura now realized, she had given the killer an excellent opportunity of disposing of her. One corpse more or less in a grave hastily closed....True, Laura presumably didn't figure on his to-do list, but neither had Solveig or the uninvolved couple on the Wily Minx. And now that she had seen him and would be able to testify against him in court, he practically couldn't afford to let her live. Yes, all things considered, she had been lucky. Remained to be seen how far her lucky streak would go.

Behind her and outside her field of vision, a big key was heard turning in what seemed a very old and rusty lock. A creaking door opened and a torch directed its beam of light into the vault. Laura turned her head even further so as not to be blinded by the sudden inrush of light. Someone came up to her and cut her loose, so she could sit up and turn towards her attacker.

"Sorry for treating you that rough, Mrs. Forster. Joe, the gardener, who sometimes helps me with little jobs such as this one, is a man of little squeamishness. Pious and God-fearing, yes, I'll give him that. But squeamish, no. Given that his customers, as a rule, are dead as the proverbial dodo, I guess he must be forgiven for that little shortcoming of his. Here, let me help you."

He bent down and took Laura's arm to help her get on her feet.

"Let go of me, you freak," she shouted, vigorously pulling her arm away from him. Then she rubbed her legs and stretched her arms to let the blood circulate more freely.

"How come you knew me? And where am I?"

"For reasons both of us know, anyone manifesting an unusually lively interest in Sir Lucas Lamont or the Yarmouth Six can be assured of my special attention. So, I enquired about you, had you tailed, watched your movements, you know, the usual programme. Where are we? Well, we are at present in a secret subterranean vault of St. Peter's. Multifunctional, we would probably call it in our day and age. In the days of yore, people used to hide all sorts of private little treasures here – jewellery, coins, those sorts of things in the most unlikely places. The pirates haunting these islands were pretty long-lived, as it were. Not least, because they were tolerated by the Crown, the respective monarchs skimming a hefty percentage off the top of their spoils. Letterboxes hadn't been invented yet. Public finances were always ailing enough both in Paris and London to justify an occasional shot in the arm."

"What's to happen next?" Laura interrupted him before he was off to Hastings and all the rest of it.

The Boxer gone clergyman coughed a nervous little cough.

"That depends very largely on yourself, I'd say."

"How so?"

The Boxer hesitated.

"Well, let me put it like this. I didn't ask you to come here and could have done a little longer without your intrusion, no offence. But since you are here, you might as well make yourself useful, see."

"None taken. Useful? In what sense? You need your fancy deacon's uniform freshly ironed or your balls tickled or what?"

"Neither, I assure you. I'd like you to be my….executor."

"With pleasure. Just let me have my gun back."

"No, not my executioner, my executor. I want you to administer my legacy, my last will and testament, as it were."

"That's quaint. I was just trying to adapt to the idea that I was the one who had better think of her last will and testament, not you."

"Not if you play your hand right. You see, there's no end of studies on the frame of mind of serial killers, right? One of the more current theories say that, after an initial period of euphoria, people like me will be up against fits of depression and dejection at ever more shortening intervals. In the end, we almost beg to be caught, albeit by a rather run-of-the-mill kind of cop or private eye. The Raskolnikov-syndrome is what they call it. I will not comment on that. Much less so as my personal case is somewhat special. I know they all say that, but…, anyway. When I became a multiple murderer, term I prefer to the one of a serial killer, I was following a certain logic with deadly consistency, you might say. I obeyed a higher moral obligation, if I so may say, by violating another, lesser one. A matter of weighing up the options. Whatever I did or did not do, my principal objective has always been the honourable Sir Lucas Lamont. But since I could not touch him, so far, I resigned myself to reducing his clan, hoping he would give up and face me like a man one day. That was probably naive. I should have foreseen that men such as Sir Lucas don't give a hoot for their next of kin and couldn't care less if they are to be the last men standing, figuratively speaking, of course."

Laura was breathing heavily. Not from any hardly controllable excitement but from manifest lack of oxygen in this crazy clergymen's den.

"Yes. I think I understood how long time ago. What I'm still trying to wrap my mind around is why? Whence this unfathomable irreconcilability, this deep and dark hatred? And, incidentally, did you kill my friend Gillian?"

The Boxer pulled a small thermos from his jacket pocket, unscrewed the lid, turned it and used it as a small cup. He poured some hot tea from the thermos and offered it to Laura, who shrank away from it.

The Boxer smiled and drank a sip of tea himself.

"Have no fear. What sense would it make for me to put my executor out of action by poisoning or anaesthetising her?

He poured again. This time, Laura accepted and drank the tea.

"Did I kill Gillian Donovan? I take it you are speaking of the Gibraltar real estate agent? No, I did not, scout's word of honour. If I had done, you would have known. I have no idea what happened to her after your encounter at the marina restaurant, and that's a fact. Where was I? Sir Lucas, yes, Luke the Duke. My respect for your investigations, by the way. You seem more insistent than a Dobermann, once you get your teeth into a case. You are right. The man who his mates used to call Gooey didn't drown at the time. He survived. How and why, God knows. It would seem Death has his soft spots too. I am no medical man, but took the trouble, over the years, to read up on drowning. You know why small children drown almost instantly when falling into a pool or pond? Because they haven't learned to hold their breath yet. They keep breathing and instantly fill their lungs with water. On the other end of the scale, children as well as grown-ups who broke through the ice-cover and fell into a frozen over lake managed to survive for fifteen minutes or more. Question of the sudden cold blocking your normal bodily functions, whatever.

But, more often than not, there's a price to pay. A brain not sufficiently provided with oxygen will start shutting certain less vital functions down. Peripheral first, central at the very end. Like a computer whose semi-conductors go dead, one by one. Now, the water in the Bay of St. Malo must have been pretty cold that day. Maybe that's what saved him. When Rose McAllister found him, she, too, thought he was dead, for sure. Remember, it was the period when the bodies of Charybdis crew-members were being washed ashore all over the place. The commando raid mounted by the Yarmouth Six – or rather Seven – had passed Rose by, not least because she was stone deaf.

"What was she doing on the beach? The whole coast had been mined, it seems."

"True. That's why she didn't go to the beach but to the cave. From long experience, she had a knack of hopping over the cliffs where you can't easily hide a mine. She had been searching for lobster, mussels and the lot, when she came across Gooey lying there spread-eagled as if fallen from the sky. When she noticed that the man's heart was still beating, she pulled him further up the rocks and considered for a while what to do with the man. Saving him may not even have been uppermost in her mind at first. You see, dealing with castaways has a long and not entirely untainted history along the more dangerous bits of Northern European coasts. Such unfortunate victims of shipwrecks possibly induced by notorious beachcombers luring ships onto the rocks at night with fake lights would normally be frisked for any valuables and the returned to the sea. If a castaway happened to have survived the shipwreck and not been smashed to pieces by the hammering of the waves on the anvil of the cliffs, they would unceremoniously be killed by a merciless knock on the head. Since the local males tended to be at sea fishing, this task used to fall preponderantly to the women. Elderly bitches hardened by their existence on an iron coast where a life didn't count much anyway. For the purposes of prompt dispatch, such ladies would carry small hatchets not unlike those of the Red Indians on their belts. Only the bitches weren't out for scalps but for valuables."

Laura was breathing more and more heavily. The air in the vault was getting more and more stifling. At long last, even the Boxer seemed to become aware of that.

"I know, oxygen doesn't easily find its way here, but what I have to say won't take long. Hence, God knows what went through Rose's head that day she happened to come across Gooey. But since he had already been robbed of his knapsack, presumably there was next to nothing Gooey was carrying on his body that Rose could have made use of. Then she must have realized that her treasure trove was the man himself, so to speak. That he was a British soldier involved in some operation or other, she is bound to have noticed from his combat fatigues and the bullet wound in his shoulder. Normally, she would have reported Gooey to the Germans, if only to avoid reprisals. That had become a conditioned reflex by 1943. But somewhere in the furthest recesses of her brain, a plan of quite a different nature must gradually and vaguely have taken shape. Rose was a young widow of twenty-four. Born on Guernsey, she had followed her husband Bill McAllister to Sark, a major sacrifice on her part, one might say. One that she wasn't rewarded for, however. Shortly after their move to Sark, Bill had set out on his daily Channel fishing cruise and not returned. Happened a lot at the time, in fog. Fishing luggers or trawlers in the process of hauling in their heavy nets are lame ducks, have absolutely no chance of avoiding a cargo ship on collision course. If they got hit, they were gone. The big boys frequently wouldn't even notice they had rammed and sunk something out there. Ever since that, Rose would have been sitting high and dry on Sark where she didn't know anybody, Bill's folks having moved to Weymouth years before the accident. As you probably can imagine, a young widow's odds for making the acquaintance of a man suitable for wedlock were slim, especially during the war years."

He paused and poured the last drops of tea.

"Wedlock. I don't like that word. Makes you almost hear the cuffs click and the prison door slam shut behind you, doesn't it? To Rose, it may have had a different appeal. Anyway, why not take a chance and get this half-dead soldier back to her home and house-break him? Rose had no experience with first-aid measures in general but how to resuscitate victims of near-drowning was something she had picked up from watching more competent members of the Sark community do it along the island's beaches after this or that shipwreck or bathing accident. And so, she grabbed the man and folded him over her bent thigh and knee, face downwards, like a teacher about to give an unruly pupil a thorough spanking. Then she kind of let her leg bob up and down till poor Gooey retched his guts out, thus getting rid of all the surplus water inside his body. The man must have wondered what in the hell was happening to him, although….but I'll get to that...."

"How did she manage to take him home unnoticed too?"

The Boxer nodded.

"Yes, that would have been her first and most difficult problem. Obviously, she had to wait until dark. And she would have needed transport of sorts. Of rather sturdy build, she might have been able to lift skinny Gooey over her shoulders and carry him a few hundred yards like you would a sack of cement. But her little place was more than a mile away."

Laura accepted the tea and drank the last swig. Breathing was as difficult as ever.

"Hence, she draped Gooey on the rocks as best she could, so that he would not be snatched away by the next high water and hurried home to borrow her neighbour's wheelbarrow."

"Like Molly Malone."

"Quite. Bigger carts were few and far between on the island. Besides, a bigger one was likely to arouse curiosity if not suspicion. At the dead of night, she took the wheelbarrow to the cave where Gooey was still lying, wondering where he was and whether or not he was alive. Rose pulled his heavy body with the soaked clothing up to the road and dumped it in the barrow, whose wheels threatened to fall off any minute under the unusual load. If she had run into the Germans with a wounded British soldier on her barrow, she would have had a lot of explaining to do. Hence, she undressed Gooey, who probably slipped in and out consciousness, and folded the man's limbs in such a manner that he fitted the barrow like it had been tailor-made for him. To boot, she covered him with a tarpaulin that had belonged to Bill's, her late husband's fishing vessel. Then, she rumbled home with him through the starry night."

Laura heaved a sigh.

"I'm sorry to break the spell, but I need some fresh air lest I pass out at your feet in a moment."

The Boxer paused and shrugged his shoulders.

"Alright. If you promise not to budge, I'll go upstairs and see what I can do so that some more oxygen gets down here."

Laura smiled thankfully.

"That would be splendid. I have no more appointments today that I know of. Hence, you'll probably find me here on your return."

The Boxer disappeared through the creaky door, locking it behind him. Laura heard him climb up what was probably a granite staircase. A prolonged silence ensued. If only he had left his torch behind, she thought. The candle had gone out long ago, so that now, she was crouching in a dark vault, listening to her thumping heart like the protagonist of some freaky tale by E.A. Poe, the master of the unexpected.

"Nevermore," she murmured, as she suddenly heard the staircase coming to life again. This time, it wasn't measured steps but a curious mixture of stumbling, falling, and rolling, as if someone really drunk was coming down topsy-turvy somehow.

The door didn't just open but was almost kicked in and a torch beamed its light on the floor and walls, as if someone wanted to familiarise himself with the location quickly. Father Brown aka the Boxer fell into the vault and slid all the way to the footstool that Laura sat on. His forehead was bleeding from a gashing wound across the right eyebrow. Behind him, the face, distorted with rage, of Ignace emerged from the dark. He must have hit the Boxer over the brow and more or less kicked him down the stairs and into the vault. The glaring light from the torch blinded Laura so she covered her eyes with her hands.

"Hello Mom, are you alright?"

Ignace' voice sounded strained.

Laura shook her head.

"Fair to middling. But polite commonplaces apart, please do tell me which parts of don't ever let me out of your sight did you found hard to understand?"

3. Enter Mr. Goodfellow

"I honestly hadn't counted on your showing up here in the company of your son. My mistake. May I ask what your real interest in my case is? I mean, you might have made an excellent journalist, or even actress, but…"

The Boxer was sitting on the floor, leaning slightly forward and mopping up the blood from his forehead with a handkerchief Laura handed him. Ignace, still furious, kept his gun levelled at him while Laura was checking her Ruger revolver that she had taken back from the killer.

"You know what I do for a living. My interest is of a highly personal nature. Among your numerous victims, there's a young lady my son was rather infatuated with. You have to excuse his somewhat impetuous ways and lack of manners. He has Carib blood pulsating in his veins, as you may know. Cannibal blood, ultimately. His father was a much-dreaded professional killer in the Lesser West Indies. All of this to advise you that you had better weigh your words if you want to leave this vault in one piece."

The Boxer seemed to be taken aback for a moment.

"What's the young lady's name again? The one I'm supposed to have slain?"

"Solveig, you sorry son of a bitch," Ignace literally squeezed the words through his clenched teeth.

"Solveig? Oh, I understand. You're talking of the……."

He stopped dead in mid-sentence. Perhaps, because he instinctively felt that his life was hanging by a very thin thread at this very moment.

"Yes, I am inconsolable. The…young lady, of whose presence in the manor I had no idea, suddenly barged into the room so that I reacted instinctively, as it were. I am very sorry, indeed, all the more so, since she was no relation of Lamont's, as it would seem. She was just paying a friend a visit on Herm, of all places. Such collateral damage will happen, I'm afraid. As it did on Barbuda, when…."

"Yes, do go on while you're at it. That's interesting," Laura interrupted him.

"How did you manage to dispatch the four crew of the Wily Minx so elegantly?"

The Boxer shrugged his shoulders as if to say there was nothing much to it.

"Strictly speaking, my target person was the skipper, a certain Brian Hillman. The three others…well, like I say."

"But how did you get aboard and away from the island after the killing?"

"I had learned that this guy Hillman was going to transfer the recently sold Wily Minx from Sark to Antigua, together with his wife and an acquainted couple. At Falmouth Harbour, Antigua, the yacht would be handed over to her new owner. That was all part of the deal. And a risky business, because the hurricane season seems to be starting just that little bit earlier every year. And so, I flew to Antigua and waited for them to arrive. I enjoyed it despite the passage of the first cyclone that year. They had avoided it by choosing an extremely southerly course, almost touching upon the northern coast of Brazil. Which is not without risk either, because of the piratical activities of Brazilian would-be fishermen. Anyway, the new owner, for his part, had been a day late. Maybe the passage of the hurricane had given him second thoughts, who knows? That gave me an opportunity to impersonate him upon the yacht's arrival. On the pretext of requesting a test drive with the boat, as it were, I managed to convince Hillman to take me up to Barbuda, destroyed and deserted at that time. They found that a little eerie and would probably have found it downright spooky had they known who they had taken aboard. We were to spend the night there riding at anchor and then return to Falmouth Harbour."

"Did you know one of the two women you shot had made it ashore, where she was found by two blacks. If it hadn't been for her, they might not have discovered the Wily Minx and never have put me, us, on your track."

"Yes, I heard about that later. But what's it got to do with you and me?"

"The Boxer. It was the only thing she was capable of saying before she died. I would have thought her to have been referring to an ex-boxer. It was my son who directed my attention to the Paul Simon song, your favourite tune, as it seems."

"I see. Clever. Yes, you're right, it is my favourite tune, one that crops up almost automatically in all sorts of situations. Seems hard to control or suppress."

"How did you get off the island?"

"Ah yes, I forgot. Well, plan A foresaw my return alone on board the Wily Minx. But fate usually provides us with a plan B, does it not. I had noticed the two looters you just mentioned come to the island in a primitive, open kind of fishing vessel. I counted on them finding and searching the yacht at some stage. Which they did. While they were busy looting, I nicked their boat and took it all the way back to Antigua, where I dumped it in some remote bay. Quite an experience, I can tell you. The thing only had an outboard and...well, never mind that now."

Laura hated the man but could not help feeling a certain admiration for his cleverness and power of improvisation.

"And now what? You're going to have your pound of flesh and shoot me?"

"What if we were? You, of all people, would have to show a certain quantum of understanding if not sympathy for any such step. Actually, however, I promised Sir Lucas to deliver you to him free domicile in exchange for a service he declared himself ready to provide. And, incidentally, the deal says dead or alive. Your call. Whatever happened to the gardener?" she suddenly turned on Ignace." The lad shook his head.

"Don't you worry about him. He's not going to disturb us."

"Surely, you didn't...?"

"No, just knocked him out, tied him up and gagged him and dragged him into the church, where he is taking a nap in the pulpit, a little closer to the Lord."

"Good. He'll like it there. Back to our business," she turned to the Boxer again.

"So you see your life is worth nothing to me. But before throwing you to the wolves, I feel it's only fair to give you a last chance to free your conscience and bring what you call your legacy to an end. You were saying that Rose McAllister took the collapsed naked Gooey home, isn't that so?"

The Boxer ran his hands over his hair. A gesture of embarrassment, Laura concluded.

"Well, what more can I say. Rose hid the Brit in her house and did all she was capable of to nurse the man back to relative physical health. That was easy and difficult at the same time. Easy, because Gooey had fallen victim to amnesia, presumably caused by the prolonged interruption of oxygen supply to the brain. Rose, on her part, was not a genius, but no fool either. As soon as she had realized what state of mind Gooey was in, she started belabouring him into believing that he was her husband, had always been her man and never lived anywhere else but on Sark. I don't know how pronounced his amnesia was, but I suspect there were moments of doubt. But, on balance, Gooey offered no resistance and didn't do much to search for his true past, whose motley, disorderly episodes he must have seen like through a dense veil of fog."

He wiped a few drops of sweat off his brow. The presence of a third person, Ignace, made the air in the vault seem even closer than before. Except that now, Laura appeared to mind that much less.

"The more difficult part had to do with the fact that Gooey found it difficult to even remember the simplest things. Thus, even though she had inculcated it in him not to leave the house during daytime, he would simply forget and step outside, every now and again. Well, she couldn't watch him twenty-four seven, now, could she? Yet, as they say, fools have an extra guardian angel.

He didn't run into a German, fortunately enough. To satisfy the curiosity of the locals, who had obviously soon begun to notice the sudden addition to their small community, she had prepared a cock-and-bull story of a remote male relative of her late husband's, who she claimed had been wounded during a battle and had now made a surprise appearance on her doorstep. So, what could she do but take good care of him, albeit in the cherished memory of her husband, Bill. There must have been the odd eyebrow going up, but the war, so much had percolated through even to Sark by then, the war gave rise to an infinite number of stories of this or like nature. So why be distrustful of what Rose told them? And if she seemed to bloom and blossom of late, why, all the better for her."

"When and where do you come in?"

"Years later. Rose is my mother, as I believe you will have guessed by now. For quite some time, she wasn't sure whether she could have perfectly healthy and sound kids with a man as sick as Gooey. But she gradually realized that the British Army, despite its man-power shortages, would not have sent a mentally handicapped person on a commando raid to Sark. Hence, Gooey's present unfortunate state must have been caused by circumstances alone. Circumstances that would not be passed on genetically to any offspring. And so, she decided to take the leap before she would get too old to have children. And she was lucky one more time. I was delivered a perfectly healthy child."

"That being a point we might wish to contest," Laura interrupted him.

"Normally, I would probably have led a calm and quiet life on Sark as a gardener, fisherman, or who knows, a true deacon. That's how it all began for me too. My most important person of reference was Rose, my mother, of course. My father was there like the sofa and the stove were there. He didn't bother anyone but had no real part in things either. I guess there is no tea left, is there?"

Laura shook her head and pointed at the empty thermos lying on the floor.

"During my childhood on Sark, I was often joshed and bullied because of my father, which didn't exactly endear him to me, I must admit. Unfair, I know, but kids can be cruel. Becoming an outsider because of something manifestly not under your control makes you doubt the justness of the order of things at a very early age. I started venting my rage and frustration on whatever was at hand, objects as well as animals. There were moments when I even seriously considered killing my father. Shove him down the Coupée, for instance, or drown him a second time in the sea. Once he was gone, all our problems would cease to exist. Mine, anyway. Maybe he felt that somehow, because he didn't like to be in the room with me alone. He would get up and leave the room under some pretext or other."

He fell silent, obviously not taking much pride in this part of his life story.

"The turning point came with my tenth birthday. At long last, I could leave Sark's one-room schoolhouse and attend the school at St. Peter Port, where no-one knew my father. St. Peter Port looked like a real big city to me then. A place of sin, a true Babylon. I befriended a classmate from Guernsey, whose father apparently cut some considerable weight with the local freemasons. For all I know, he may have been their Grand Master. The man had taken a liking to me and often enquired about the circumstances of my life on Sark, my mother and father, and so on. He also used to ask me what my plans were for the future and all. For lack of a more concrete idea, I said I wanted to become a lawyer, a barrister. I had once watched the Witness for the Prosecution with Charles Laughton as a master barrister, which had deeply impressed me. Obviously, with my background, justice was my first and foremost pursuit. He nodded gravely and described the long and arduous path that lay ahead of me if I really wanted to put my plans into practice. His repeated questions and comments on the subject of my father aroused my own interest in the question how he had become that apathetic vegetable that he was. I mean, you know how it is. As a child and teenager, you tend to be preoccupied with yourself and have no time or enough motivation to delve into your parents' past. And when, finally, you think the moment has come for you to do so, it's usually too late already."

That didn't fall much short of her own experience, Laura thought and remembered those days in the Caribbean when the Doc had started to open her eyes with regard to her own past and that of her father and mother. The Boxer drew a sigh as if overpowered by the images of the past he evoked.

"Mr Goodfellow, that was the freemason's name, I kid you not, took me by the hand and made it possible for me to first attend the same expensive public school his son frequented and later saw to it I had the wherewithal and connections to take up and finish my law studies at Oxford University. With his help and occasional coup de pouce, as the French say, I managed to get called to the Bar. In short, I had put my plans into practice, indeed."

"So, you're not a Reverend, but a barrister. How does a servant of the law turn into a serial killer?"

"Multiple murderer, if you please. Serial killing always implies a sexual element lacking in my…exploits. Generally speaking, my turnaround is not as paradoxical as it may seem. Face to face with crime on an everyday basis, you get your nose rubbed in the moral relativity of law and justice. I don't know how familiar you are with our system of judicature. Thing is that, at the beginning of their career, English barristers as a rule don't earn very much money at all. That's an irritating left-over from the old days, when barristers were supposed to serve the law in the abstract, as it were, free of charge. Thus, it would be ascertained they had no immediate financial interest in the case. Maybe you noticed the little pocket barristers have at the back of their robe. That's where clients were invited to slip whatever sums of money they could afford, allegedly without the barrister taking note of it, as it were. Obviously, those days are over, but, like I say, at the beginning of your career, you have to fall back on your own private assets – if you have any. Besides, you're not only dealing with powdered wigs and black gowns smelling of mothballs, but also with all sorts of pigtailed mummies, figuratively speaking, that could only hide deep down in a hopelessly old-fashioned legal system such as ours. And when it comes to your clients, from petty thieves to child molesters and the occasional murderer, most of them with impressive criminal records, already, well, it's not all fun in the sun either. Most of the time, you don't believe what you hear yourself putting forward in the defence of despicable scum that, on a dark might, you might not hesitate to dispatch with your own hands. And so, one day, when a man from MI5 approached me with an indecent offer, I didn't think twice but accepted it."

"Despite your little…handicap?"

"You mean the limp? Happened during a game of rugger. A classmate of rather more solid build fell on my right knee and very nearly crushed it. The doctors did what was in their powers, but the limp remained. Anyway, maybe the ubiquitous Mr Goodfellow had had a finger in that pie too, I don't know. Be that as it may, the position I came to hold in MI5 soon made me feel that, perhaps a little prematurely hopping out of the frying pan, I had landed myself in the fire. Of course, I was making a lot more money now. But the day-to-day slog as such was a depressing disappointment. Everything there comes to you piecemeal. As a barrister, you're in a way the master of ceremonies. Normally, the solicitors will have gone through all of the files and feed you with the salient aspects of the case: pieces of incriminating evidence, protocols of interrogations, witness statements, expert opinions, the lot. When working for the secret service, on the other hand, you are on a need-to-know informational diet. You only learn what agents of your salary bracket are entitled to know to contribute their little stone to the overall mosaic. For weeks, you ass-tail a person of interest, as the saying goes. Why and how, you don't know. And when it finally comes to putting the cuffs on them, it will be done by other agents from a different service. Notwithstanding, I was able to not only defray my own living expenses but could send money home. Plus I learned a lot of useful new tricks."

"Such as handling firearms, I take it," Laura said.

"Quite. Guns and anything that can, at a pinch, be turned into a weapon. Apart from that, with increasing responsibilities came more and more legroom, so to speak. Not least in respect of access to records. Most of my colleagues had grown used to this piecemeal kind of work and literally had come to hate having to deal with stacks of files on rare occasions. What with my professional background, I didn't really mind. On the contrary. I wasn't married, had no kids or pets, not even an aspidistra to look after, so that I could work deep into the wee hours and pass many of my weekends studying files. Everything comes to him who knows the files, let me tell you. The more useless details you have at your fingertips, the more easily you can put one over on your colleagues and leave them behind in the rat race for this or that post. Plus, your superiors start being vaguely afraid of you, because they know or suspect you might make them look silly or uninformed in the eyes of their superiors, see. I became the Reinhard Heydrich of MI5."

"What was your relation to the Yarmouth Six then?"

"I was just getting there. During one of my more or less trivial MI5 pursuits, I happened to come across that gang calling itself the Yarmouth Six. My first reflex was to shove the file back into the cleared stack. Then, it set me a-thinking. What business did the secret service have with a bunch of hoodlums, albeit clever hoodlums? If the MI5 powers that were had found it useful, at some stage, to deal with the Yarmouth Six, they must have had a good reason."

Again, he wiped the pearly sweat off his brow.

"Well, it turned out they did. The context soon became clear to me. Over the years, and we're talking many years, decades, really, our secret services had regularly received morsels of intelligence from a mysterious source that went by the code name Pluto. How this person had come by his information, the files obviously wouldn't reveal. What did stare me in the face, however, was the fact that MI5 returned the favour by regularly providing Pluto with salient tidings of the results of current police investigations into all sorts of illegal operations carried out by none other than the said Yarmouth Six. Which, in turn, went to show that this man Pluto, if it was a man, was himself closely linked with this notorious gang.

From there, it was only a small step for me to unveil Pluto's likely identity – Sir Lucas Lamont. Such forms of clandestine co-operation in the lee of law and order have been on the secret services' agenda since the beginning of time. Which is why I considered this particular example of conspiration a mere side-show ultimately going back to the chaotic post-war years. Water under

the bridge, in other words. Till the moment I came across a mi-
nuscule handwritten note in the margins, one that made mention
of a certain Gooey. Now, my father had had a way of sitting on
the sofa, sipping his tea and munching his biscuits while mumbling low key, so that you wouldn't know was he talking to you,
to himself, or to some imaginary third person whose presence
only he would notice. I never did pay much attention but had
frequently overheard that word Gooey. I had always thought it
was his way of appreciating the biscuits and not realized, it was
actually somebody's bizarre nickname. When I bumped into it in
the MI5 files on that memorable occasion, it did dawn upon me I
was dealing with a person my father may have known or heard
of. Some obscure memory of a putrefying past, like the bits of
song from a distant siren. It was only years later, after thumbing
through lots more files, that I realized Gooey had been the nickname of none other than my father himself, given to him by the
Yarmouth Six, who had originally been a Yarmouth Seven."

He slowly took off his jacket and opened his violet waistcoat.
Laura was wondering which of them was more phoney, the fake
deacon Brown or the amateur detective Forster.

"For the first time, my hunting instincts had been aroused.
Digging in the more recent past, I felt a bit like an archaeologist, a
latter-day Arthur Evans, if you will, uncovering layer after layer
of another one of those horrid secrets that had been buried under the ruins and rubble of World War II. That's how I managed
to reconstruct the course of events that had led to my father's
near-drowning, or should I say, his near-assassination, and eventual rescue by our local nymph, the wonderful Rose of Sark. I
also noticed that, uncharacteristically, neither MI5, nor the Duke
aka Pluto had the least idea of my father's survival."

"Why was the Duke ever made a life peer, for God's sake?"

"Well, you know that cynical saying by Billy Wilder, don't
you?"

"Awards are like hemorrhoids...?"

"Precisely. Same thing applies to peerages. At least, if you belong to a certain class of people. And in Lamont's case, there was

the added reason that he was said to have rendered his country immense service during and after the war. On the flip side, the practical use of a peerage is limited. As nice as it will look on your visiting cards, no banks will grant you an extra credit line for it, no Tiffanies give you special rates."

"What special services had he rendered his country?"

"All and sundry. One of them being to rid England of the awkward legacy of war called the Yarmouth Six."

"What are you talking about?"

"Well, the records allowed for the assumption that the series of accidents which befell the Yarmouth Six during the nineteen eighties and killed five of them had not been the result of Fate's wilful blunderings, but man's foul play. My respective thesis would be that MI5, or somebody close to them, felt the Yarmouth Six had outlasted their usefulness and were due for permanent retirement. Who would they turn to if not to Sir Lucas, whose liability, it was probably felt, the other Yarmouth Five were. If this was the reasoning, it must have coincided with Lamont's own interests at the time. He was now on top of the world and probably thought he had better get rid of the people who had not only witnessed his career but largely contributed to it, in fact. From now on, they risked denouncing Lamont's own little fake narrative of his arduous path to the summit and, hence, had better go. So, he countersigned his ex-associates' death warrants. I have no idea who played the henchmen. Suffice to say that, without the help of some state agency or other, it would have been difficult, nay, impossible, to cover it all up so snugly."

"I get it. You had realized Sir Lucas was responsible not only for your father's deplorable state, and, at least indirectly, for the humiliations you had lived through during your childhood, but also for the deaths of five of his ex-mates. And decided play judge and jury, for once, to sign his death warrant, in turn."

"Yes, I suppose one might summarize it like that. Lamont had been a life-long double-talking egotistic son of a bitch, changing alliances as he saw fit and selling down the river whoever threatened to thwart his plans. A ruthless, merciless traitor playing the

English as he had played the Germans. All he was ever after was his own survival and well-being. His career had taken off here on Sark. I don't know how he did it, but, somehow, he must have nicked the knapsack with the treasure – the diamonds, jewellery, and counterfeit pound notes. He probably used the lot to sell himself to the Germans, I suspect. In the following years, he probably worked for them in Britain. Shortly before the war was over, I guess he changed sides and became a British spy in post-war Germany, itself a hotbed of clandestine operations of all and sundry in preparation for a World War Three, which seemed imminent then. So many ex-Nazis still circulated in practically all the key authorities of the newly-born Federal Republic, matched by a like number of ex-Nazis turned Stalinist hardliners in East Germany. With that set-up, you never knew which way that divided country was going once let off the leash of close Allied supervision. Somehow, I envy Lamont this time of chaos and frenzy, must have been a paradise for double agents."

"That's all very well, I suppose. But why did your reaction take such as long time to come?"

"Many of the more important records became accessible to me only few years ago. Everything has its shelf-life, you know. I had to wait till the last pieces of the puzzle had fallen into place, simple as that."

"Hm. I'm, trying to understand. But I cannot for the life of me see how any of that should have given you the right to…."

"Murder innocent people indiscriminately, is that it? Well, with due respect, I'd retort by calling that a naïve question. Who was it said life as we lead it is punished by death as we deserve it? Maybe I just made it up. You don't have to believe in God to realize that the concepts of man and innocence exclude each other. And, on the more practical side, Lamont knew how to make himself unassailable, legally as well as materially. Not just by dint of his small army of bodyguards, but also with the help of MI5, which still holds its protective hand over his head. I suspect they would have loved to see him dead and buried with his five accomplices, but feared he had hidden some highly compromising material somewhere safe.

So they rigged a sham road accident in which he was supposed to sustain some minor injuries, only, so that, henceforth, he would be considered a lucky devil having escaped the Grim Reaper's scythe. The irony of it: due to a technical hitch with the car, the crash was a lot harder than expected and put him in the wheelchair."

"But that wouldn't satisfy you as a punishment?"

"Certainly not. It would by no means be commensurate with the sum total of his wrongdoings, nor with the consequences of his evil acts for the unfortunate people concerned."

"And so, you went for the next best solution and killed off selected next of kin of Lamont's...."

"So I did. I just couldn't help myself, had to vent my wrath and frustration, somehow. Innocence? After so many years in the service, my moral scruples had been blunted, as it were. Ironically, what I had not counted on, but sure as hell should have, was that the moral conceptions of an individual such as Lamont would have eroded over time even more than mine, so that he would not give a hoot for what I did to his folks."

"And why this change of heart now?"

"I'm not sure that's the right term. Let's just say I am resigned to the manifest pointlessness of my mission and would like to end it, one way or another. Certainly not by exposing myself to Sir Lucas and his Puerto-Rican butchers, though. Hence, with all due respect, I'd much rather..."

He didn't finish the sentence but jumped up and swirled round on his heels with surprising agility all of a sudden. Before Ignace even knew it, he had been separated from his Browning, whose barrel was now levelled at his head instead of that of Father Brown's.

"I'm sorry, but if and when I surrender, I'd like it to be on my terms. Put down your Ruger, or your son dies, and so will you."

Laura did as she was told.

"Thank you. You made a mistake, son," he addressed himself to Ignace.

"One that may have cost you your life just now. Remember this: when pointing a gun at someone, you either pull the trigger or keep a distance of at least three yards from your opponent, if you can. You allowed your attention to sag and came too close to me, so I could jump you. Try and avoid that next time you approach a hardened professional, lest your detective career be nipped in the bud. Having said that, I must ask to be excused for now. Like the man said, you will probably remember this day as the one you almost caught the Boxer. Each to his own, I suppose."

With that, he backed up to the door that still stood wide open, left the vault, slammed the door shut and locked it from outside.

Laura waited till his steps on the stairs had faded and finally died away altogether.

"See what I mean?" she addressed herself to Ignace.

"That wouldn't have happened to a person imbued with the absolute determination to kill if necessary."

"I'm sorry, mom. I don't know what…"

"Don't be. I'd much rather make my peace with a son who thinks twice at the wrong moment than one who kills without a moment's hesitation. It's just that you have to be aware of that weakness, or else…"

"What now?"

"What now? I think that should be pretty obvious. We'll wait for the cavalry to arrive and then go after the freak in the frock."

"Fine. Except we will first have to find out where he's gone."

"Don't worry about that, son, he was kind enough to leave us his address."

TENTH CHAPTER

1.Gilbert and Sullivan

Gazing absent-mindedly through the windows of the Sword and Crown, St. Anne's oldest and still most popular public house, the late-afternoon shift of patrons was observing, through eyes at least as coated as the panes, a small fishing logger gracefully glide through the Swinge, Alderney's narrowest and most dreaded race, and then gently veer to the North.

"Like an ineptly placed suppository," was the publican's dismissive comment. Some patrons chuckled; others had apparently heard the quip before and shrugged their shoulders. Rupert had a reputation to defend. His caustic comments were feared the island over. Which, if the truth be told, wasn't much of a feat given Alderney's modest size and sparse population.

As it would seem, the logger's skipper was going to fish for scallops further up the Channel during the night. Fishing vessels were not allowed to hamper the passage of ships on the lanes of the Channel TSS, but were free to use the central dividing zone, which, in turn, was off-limits to the other users of the TSS. The English scallop season having not yet begun, this lad either had special authorization, which didn't seem likely, or he was out poaching. The patrons of the Sword and Crown nodded emphatically. Come what may, you couldn't just leave the stuff to the Frogs, on whose side of the Channel the fattest scallops apparently felt more at home than on the English side, God knows why. The lugger had hardly passed the islet of Burhou, however, when thick black smoke suddenly billowed forth from the vessel's exhaust and, drifting east on a light breeze, was dispelled in thin grey and blue wafts.

With a semi-automatic movement that gave away the addicted eavesdropper in him, Rupert, the red-nosed reindeer, as they called him when he wasn't there, switched on his radio on the pre-set emergency channel sixteen. If the skipper had a mechanical problem he might not be able to mend himself, he would very soon now emit a pan-pan call. Mayday would have been even better because Rupert would then start calculating possible salvage fees, but pan-pan would mean the island's only mechanic could only hope for a modest sum of money rolling in, at any rate. This time, channel sixteen remained silent, however. While the patrons were exchanging more or less learned opinions as to the causes of the engine trouble as evidenced by the colour of the smoke, the lugger, with a huff and a puff, slowly entered the harbour.

So the skipper seemed convinced he could repair the engine himself. Which, all things considered, was just as well, because the island mechanic was out for the day, paying his weekly visit to Cherbourg city, where he would shop, sup, and grab some pussy to go, as he put it.

The breakwater that offered its protection to the lugger led into a harbour basin that bore all the hallmarks of the high expectations that, for reasons unknown, it had never been able to live up to. Originally, a prestigious project of Victorian hauteur, some would call arrogance, Braye Harbour had been destined to become the final piece of a long chain of British ports and harbours along the Channel coasts. As such, it had been a spin-off of the first industrial revolution, when the global exchange of goods of any sort could safely be expected to take its first really dizzying upswing.

The preponderant part of those goods would, of course, be transported on ships that needed an elaborate coastal infrastructure targeted at their various functional requirements. The centrepiece of Braye Harbour was its monstrous breakwater. An architectural showpiece for whose construction and frequent maintenance works the engineers responsible had even laid on a normal-gauge railroad track on top of the breakwater to take the necessary granite, cement, and whatever else material was needed to the respective building site at the breakwater's moving target of an end.

Hydraulic engineering of such a complex and critical nature needed knowhow and experience. Both would be found preferably in Scotland, where some of the most treacherous North

Atlantic rocks are situated so far offshore, nobody would expect them there if it weren't for the lighthouses, literally standing in the water.

Most of those rocks being under water at least half of the day, workers would have to be ferried out there, get to it during low water, and be ferried back again hours later. Blocks of granite would have to be shipped out there and craned off at just the right stage of the tide or, if they missed it, to come back the next day. Gales would not only interrupt the works but frequently dismantle again what had been put together so far. Such were the conditions under which the male members of the Scottish Stevenson family would have to operate. The experience acquired being passed on from one generation to the next, the Stevensons became the household name of lighthouse-building. Ironically enough, the only Stevenson whose name would be famous the world over, however – Robert Louis, that is – never shared his family's passion for the bubble level or trowel.

What then was wrong with Braye Harbour? The Stevenson's would have foreseen the trouble its breakwater would come to cause, and the cost almost continuous repair and maintenance works would incur. Lighthouses such as, say, the Irish Fastnet, weren't just set up on top of a rock in very much the same manner as you might mount a pillar on a plinth. Instead, it would be embedded in the rock in such a way as to let the rock, and not the tower, bear the brunt of the highly destructive kinetic energy of the masses of water we call waves. Besides, the blocks that formed the lighthouse towers would be irregularly dove-tailed to increase their structural resilience. None of all this applies to breakwaters in general, certainly not to the one at Braye Harbour. That was just a wall, massive, it is true, but, compared to the forces that knock at its doors day in, day out, not much more than a Japanese paper wall.

Arriving at the harbour basin's inner end, the fishing logger's skipper, who appeared to be alone on board, picked up a mooring buoy with his boat hook and fastened the line on his forward starboard cleat. While the last of the ominous black clouds from the exhaust were wafting up the island's major hill, the skipper opened an aft hatch, waited till the engine room was free of smoke, and climbed down to look for the cause of the engine trouble.

When darkness had fallen, and the Quesnard lighthouse had gone into its fully automated routine, only the hard-core patrons remained in the pub. And they were much too nazzy to have noticed the three figures that came climbing out of the lugger's hold with manifestly stiff legs.

On deck, Laura stretched herself and moved her limbs to regain control over her extremities that had gone numb during the long wait in the hold.

Then, she looked at her watch. Five full hours was what she had passed in the logger's belly together with Ignace and the Chief. Normally, the hold would be bursting with of tons of fish, shellfish, or mussels. But even in its present empty state, the hold would have impregnated their clothing with its stink. Despite such obvious drawbacks, Laura had thought it wiser to remain invisible on the arrival of the lugger they had chartered at Creux Harbour, where they had happened to have run into Graeme, the logger's owner. So, now that darkness had fallen, they could go ashore without attracting anybody's attention. Or so she hoped.

If the Boxer had sought refuge here on the island, as Laura was convinced he had, he was likely to keep a close watch on any new arrivals in the harbour. There was a bit of an airstrip, too, but going back to Guernsey first and then waiting to get clearance for a take-off to Alderney – always provided its airstrip was long enough for the twin-engine Seminole, would have taken much too long. Hence, the faked engine trouble, the staging of which Graeme, the Scottish owner of the Guernsey Lily had managed to perfection. Just how he had done it without actually damaging the engine in earnest, Laura had no idea. She just hoped it wouldn't stand in the way of their return voyage to Guernsey.

Without Chief Colestron's prompt intervention, they would not have been here by a long chalk. He had been to the Seigneurie, without however meeting anyone even mildly competent. So, he had backtracked and started looking for Laura and Ignace, neither of whom had answered his repeated calls on the mobile. According to his account, he must even have run into Father Brown at the church, without of course having any idea of the man's true role and identity. Nothing more normal than a Reverend coming out of a church, after all. Colestron had asked him whether he had seen Laura or Ignace, but the clergyman had seemed in a hurry and not stopped to chat with the Chief. Instead, he had just muttered something in the negative and rushed on. The Chief had found that strange, but not to an extent that would have aroused true suspicion. He had entered the church and heard the gardener hammer his feet against the inside of the pulpit. He had untied him and "convinced" him to give away the location of the vault, where Colestron had finally found Laura and Ignace.

So that was alright, except for the fact that the Boxer had taken Ignace's gun with him. Which meant that, for the time being, and in view of what was likely to become the all-important end game, only the Chief and Laura were armed. That could be a critical drawback, Laura thought, as Graeme was putting them ashore in the dinghy. The risk of someone watching the Guernsey Lily with a pair of binoculars at this late hour was negligible. All afternoon, Graeme had ostensibly worked in the engine room, swearing every now and again and only coming up for a cigarette or a bottle of beer. Several times, he had started the engine, stalled it, started it again, and so on. Even the most distrustful of individuals must have concluded that this skipper was as much for real as his engine trouble.

Now, all was quiet. Even the ever-restless Atlantic Ocean seemed to respect the island's nightly serenity. The lighthouse lamp kept its rhythm and stuck to its slow circular movement with the light beam sticking out like a finger in search of any objects out at sea. Further east, above the Cotentin peninsula, a thunderstorm was brewing. Flashes of lightning illuminated the eerie scenery of the Cap de la Hague nuclear power station for fractions of a second at a time. Following the main direction of the wind, the storm would probably not come closer but move along the Franco-Belgian coast.

Graeme's recommendation had been to try the Sword and Crown for size. St. Anne itself seemed largely deserted. Here and there, flickering TV sets behind flimsy curtains and small, almost opaque windows transformed seemingly small living rooms into faltering spaceship cockpits. Laura's feet hurt. Once again, she was wearing the wrong kind of shoes. Fortunately, this island with its two and a half by one and a half miles probably wasn't big enough for her to grow blisters.

Two questions were uppermost in her mind. Was the Boxer really here on Alderney or had he held up a red herring? If he was here, where exactly would he lie in ambush? During their long wait in the hold of the logger, she had, time and time again, run the Boxer's final words by her own memory. Each to his Own was the Nazi slogan looming large over camp Sylt. It couldn't possibly mean anything else, not the way he had uttered it, totally out of context. If it was the hint she thought it was, he might well be waiting for them somewhere around the area where the camp had once been.

How had he got here? At Laura's request, Graeme had mustered the boats gently bobbing up and down in Braye Harbour's basin with the critical eye of the professional but hadn't been able to identify any yacht that might have had Creux Harbour as its albeit nominal port of register. Which didn't necessarily mean very much. To drop your anchor somewhere along the coastline of Alderney would have been well-nigh impossible. The nasty tidal currents would argue against that. Notwithstanding, the Boxer might have had himself ferried here by some friend or acquaintance who had put him ashore and headed back to Sark or Guernsey right away.

Laura was hoping to learn more about the Boxer's possible hideouts in the pub. But they would have to tread with great care so as not to appear much too interested in his person and raise suspicion with men who might know him and warn him.

As Laura stopped for a moment to catch her breath and looked back on the nocturnal scenery behind her, she came to admire the manner in which the yachts' mooring lights were dancing on the oily surface of the harbour basin. But a measly imitation of the starry sky, it is true, yet beautiful, nonetheless.

Considering this was a normal work day, the pub hosted a fair number of patrons. The old-fashioned telly hanging from the ceiling was broadcasting some Premier League football match that didn't seem to attract much attention here but rather served as an acoustic backdrop of sorts.

The arrival of the strangers did raise a few eyebrows, not least because of Ignace's mildly alien appearance. Caribbean Chabins weren't spotted all that frequently in places such as Alderney. Although, given the stupendous number of clerical toponyms such St. Peter Port, St. Anne, St. Sampson, Saint this and Saint that, a native Caribbean might feel pretty much at home here. And why shouldn't they: an isolated geographical position and the occasional havoc-wreaking tempests were common features of archipelagos that made their inhabitants resort to, and seek protection from, heavenly mediation.

Colestron discovered three lucky vacancies at a table which was already occupied by two locals in thick, weatherproof jerseys. When the Chief asked whether the three of them might be allowed to join the resident twosome, the one just threw them a dark glance that no-one in his right mind could possibly have interpreted as an invitation. The other one, however, gave them a friendly nod, looking them over with unconcealed curiosity.

"It's a free country now, ain't it?" he said. Then he turned his attention to his bad-mannered friend again.

The Chief went up to the counter and came back with three glasses of the good stuff. Laura, who preferred to keep all her senses about her that night, thanked him politely but didn't touch the beer.

From the corner of her eye, she looked at the patrons at the counter. A group of five people dressed in oilies probably came from one of the yachts down in the harbour. Presumably, they had crossed over from Weymouth, Cowes, or some such place, and would be heading back tomorrow. The locals were easy to identify by their leisure wear, hardly fit for a spree on the sea.

They conversed in a sort of French-tainted English that seemed to give Norman patois words and phrases a certain preference.

On these islands, the influx of both English and Irish workers as well as British holiday-makers and pensioners had ultimately tipped the linguistic scales in favour of the language of Shakespeare, alright. That said, the original French fire was still smouldering under the surface, as even the most superficial of glances at a chart of the area will reveal.

It didn't take long for the ill-tempered local to get up and leave. The glass of his kind friend being only half empty, the man would probably sit with them for a while longer, Laura suspected. Why not try him for some more information, the kind they badly wanted.

"And what wind blew you onto our little island?" the man asked, as soon as he had noticed a lull in the conversation of his three opposite numbers.

"We're here in search of a person, a deacon, in fact. Name's Brown, as in Father Brown. But that's only one of many. Could also be McAllister, in fact."

The man laughed.

"Yes, as is the habit of the men of God these days. Although, come to think of it, our local reverend only has one name. And, believe it or not, I couldn't for the life of me remember which it is. But it's probably not the one you're looking for, anyway, I guess."

Laura shook her head.

"Certainly not. The man I'm talking about is somewhat taller than I am, has dark hair, presumably dyed, and drags his right leg."

"I see. That kind of narrows it down dramatically. Tell you what, I'll ask Rupert, he knows everyone round here…"

He turned towards the bar counter but before he could holler the name across the whole pub, Laura stopped him dead in his tracks.

"No, no. It isn't all that important, you know. No need to bother the publican."

"Talking of names. Mine is Gilbert," he introduced himself.

"In that case, I'll be Sullivan," the Chief laughed.

It was a lame joke alright. At best ill-mannered, at worst an insulting insinuation of doubt or even suspicion. But Gilbert, if that really was his name, seemed to take it in his stride. It couldn't have been the first time he had heard the quip, anyway. So, Laura and the two men introduced themselves as well.

Gilbert must have been in his mid-forties, Laura guessed. His greyish curls made him look younger and lent him the vague air of an eternal scallywag, forever looking for trouble, and frequently finding it too.

His blue eyes were set close to one another which, if one were to believe in popular superstitions, could signify a certain stinginess and narrow-mindedness.

Somehow, somewhere, these eyes seemed to have lost their original sparkle. Now, they had a slightly sarcastic and, at the same time, sad look to them that betrayed the disillusioned idealist. In glaring contrast to most of the other patrons, he was clean-shaven and wore no moustache either. The deep furrows on his forehead found their counterparts in the vertical clefts that ran down his cheeks like canyons cut into the landscape by millennia of torrential rains.

"How do you make a living on Alderney?" Laura asked. Not because she was in the least interested but because she wished to keep this conversation alive."

Gilbert smiled.

"You don't. If you look around you during daytime, you will notice that most of us have already passed the timberline of whatever professional occupation may come to mind. Most of us are enjoying their retirement, Alderney being the Florida of Brits who hate or can't afford the Côte d'Azur."

Laura laughed.

"A little rougher than Miami or the Palm Beaches, it would seem."

Gilbert nodded and leaned over the table as if he was going to let Laura into a well-kept secret.

"Yes, no doubt. On the other hand, though, no Americans either. Or almost. And no hurricanes, as yet. That's how we're getting even. What do you do for a living then?"

Laura hesitated.

"I'm a journalist. Harry is my boss and Ignace carries the luggage and brews the tea. The three of us have come here to shoot a film on the island, a kind of docudrama, if you see what I mean. This deacon Brown was recommended to us as a first useful contact person."

"Well, you found me, that's almost as good, I bet. What's so interesting about Alderney?"

Before Laura had time to answer, the Chief and Ignace got up.

"I'm sorry," the Chief said, "but I have to answer a call of nature. And so does our young friend here, it would seem. I always thought young men's bladders to have a larger capacity. Another anatomic myth going down the drain. Follow me, Master Ignace.

When the unlikely couple had disappeared in the corridor apparently leading to the toilets, Gilbert leant across the table again and looked Laura straight in the eyes.

"Journalist? Really? Has anyone ever let you know you're a terribly bad liar, Lara?"

"Laura. And yes, words to that effect have reached me from time to time. I'm working on it is all I can say."

"Well, a piece of advice from a notorious liar: stay with the truth whenever discussing small fry. It will work in your favour by establishing trust. Thus, you can lie through your teeth whenever it's about really important matters. Believe me, I do it regularly. Maybe with less success than I had reckoned, given my two divorces. Anyway, you're packing a calibre .44 revolver and the man you call your boss another big-game piece; it sets me wondering what kind of docudrama yours is going to be. Furthermore, I smell trouble for Father Brown."

"Are we really that obvious?

"Maybe not to an uninformed observer. For me, however, the answer would have to be yes. You have that man-eater's glint in your eyes which struck me right away. And the company you keep means business as well, I bet. Welcome to Dodge City."

2. Daphne's Realm

"And you are dead certain the Boxer, as you call him, is identical with the deacon? Or vice versa? Gilbert asked, after Laura had, in the presence of the Chief and Ignace, given him a very short synopsis of what kind of killer they were up against. Gilbert, for his part, had presented himself as a retired British officer. Laura's surprised remark, he could not possibly be pushing sixty yet, had caused him to smile indulgently.

"All according to where and how they used to be deployed, Civil servants may retire earlier. In some cases, they even have to. Same applies to the armed forces. I served in the SAS, you know, an elite troop where the years of service don't count double, but triple. Many of my mates never get anywhere near their retirement age, boohoo."

He added that he came from Liverpool originally. He had first heard of the Yarmouth Six on settling on Alderney, after his retirement, he said.

"Why here, of all places?" the Chief asked him.

"Good question. I guess Alderney in all its bleakness reminds me of the Falklands. I took part in the fight against the Argentines as a very young man not unlike your son Ignace, I daresay. What I saw there left a deep mark on me and tainted the rest of my life, both private and professional."

He rolled down the collar of his turtleneck jersey, thus baring a long scar underneath his right ear.

"Shrapnel. I was lucky. A little further to the left and I wouldn't be sitting here. There's more of those, invisible ones."

Laura recalled some reports she had read on the so-called Falklands War, a gory armed conflict which, essentially, had served no better purpose than to cover up certain unpleasant things at home – such as the brutal scrapping of the erstwhile powerful mining unions. Economically speaking, England had needed the Falklands like Lady Thatcher had needed the clap. All the more disgusting, the war, like any war, had cost the lives of hopeful young men.

"You know what I think," Gilbert was musing, "I think that without the history of the Channel Islands' let-down, in 1940, the war over the Falklands forty-odd years later would never have taken place."

Laura nodded.

"You mean they couldn't afford that sort of betrayal a second time round? That may be so. The rest of the world just shook their heads in disbelief about the seemingly narrow-mindedness of the so-called Iron Lady. As if petty obstinacy was a value in itself. Well, maybe for the Brits it is, stiff upper lip and all that. An attitude that seems to have worked in the war against the Germans, but also produced resounding military debacles such as the war leading to the independence of the American colonies, the Crimean disaster, the Gallipoli shambles, or the Dunkirk cataclysm. But to get back to the Boxer...."

"...my guess would be he is familiar with the most salient features of Alderney's topography, above and below ground. Why else would he be seeking asylum in a little place like this, where he risks standing out like a sore thumb? He may even be in the possession of the original German plans showing the multi-branched network of bunkers and tunnels the Nazis left behind. Not that he would need them any longer, probably has it all at his fingertips, by now."

"If he was working with MI5, as he claims, he may have procured himself such documentation there."

"Yes, well, I'm thinking...Rupert here," he pointed at the publican over his shoulder, "once told us about a kind of local historian, I mean, he wasn't local, the history was. Is said to have walked across the island from one end to the other and back again with all sorts of gear, like an archaeologist, and burrowed and furrowed in Alderney's every nook and cranny. Hey, I say, Rupert!"

The publican looked across his counter, obviously expecting a new round of beer to be ordered.

"Do you remember this historian's name, you know, the guy who used to sniff around here some years ago? The one you told us about."

Rupert set himself to thinking. That took a while.

"Mc…something or other. I had taken him for a Scot, actually, but turned out he wasn't, at all."

"McAllister?" Laura called.

"Yes, maybe. Can't be sure, though, sorry. Why you asking?"

"Just so, no special reason," Laura replied.

"Do you remember any characteristic features?"

Rupert again went into meditation mode.

"Not that I recall. Or yes, wait a second. He had very piercing eyes, I think, husky-like. And a funny limp, dragged his left leg. Or was it the right one? Caught my attention because he managed to walk pretty fast all the same."

"Compensation reflex," Gilbert commented.

"I had an SAS colleague who had stepped on a mine during his service in the Middle East. Lost a leg. Whenever he would throw in an appearance at our annual reunions, he would be on crutches and yet always be the first to reach the buffet. You really had to watch it to get some salmon, roast beef or lamb chops when he was around. Name's Brunner, Brunner the Runner, we used to call him. Died some years ago, boohoo."

"Where did this limping historian live during his stay on the island?" Laura asked.

"In a shack not far from the lighthouse. Kind 'a cabin, very rudimentary. Shortly after his return to wherever it was he had come from, the thing was washed away by the sea during an extraordinarily springy son of a bitch of a tide. Lucky for him. A day or two later, and he would have been washed away with it."

"How many hotels are there on the island?" the Chief asked.

Gilbert reflected for a short while, then came up with a handful.

"Braye Beach, Harbour Lights, Victoria, couple more. Not as few as might be suspected."

The Chief looked at Laura, who had guessed his intention.

"It's worth a try, maybe. But I'll have to keep a low profile, else we'll have the Yard on our tails by tomorrow. And I'll need a phone list."

"I'll get you one. Must have one at home, I think."

"Personally, I don't believe he checked into a hotel. I rather imagine him sitting somewhere in the centre of this maze of old and new underground fortifications, calmly waiting for things to unfold. That's what I'd do."

"In that case, we may have to smoke him out," Gilbert said with the mien of a man who has some experience with such operations.

"But what's he waiting for? I mean, he could be anywhere by now, enjoying the New Zealand sun if he wanted."

Laura nodded.

"Could be but isn't. If and when you hunt a person long enough, you'll end up thinking and feeling like he does. You kind of become the person. The Boxer has been a loner and outsider for years. It's not for nothing that he loves Paul Simon's song. He is fully aware of how and when it's all going to end. He won't be able to reach his ultimate goal of killing Lamont. Certainly not now that we've seen his face. That's why he formulated what he calls his legacy. For some reason, he believes we might be able to achieve what he couldn't. Indirectly, that is, he seems to be making us his accomplices. This is the Boxer's last round. He's sitting there in his corner, waiting for that bell."

"Hm. You do seem to have learned to read the guy. But, with all respect, we may need the cavalry to come in."

"What cavalry? And what's that with we? You already fought a war that wasn't yours. Why would you wish to get involved in another?"

"Well, why don't you leave that to me? You'll need all the help you can get, underestimating, as I think you are, the enormity of the task you're setting yourself. Alderney isn't just any old rabbit warren, you know. You're thinking of throwing a couple of smoke bombs with the odd teargas grenade for good measure, and your man will come out with his hands stuck in the air? Forget it. If and when the Nazis started going at it, they would mean business. You're standing on a network of subterranean fortifications and service routes the extent of which you wouldn't believe. The OT, or Organisation Todt, needed thousands of workers, volunteers and forced labourers, on the island, plus millions of tons of building material. Where do you think all that has gone? Many of the installations they created are now situated on private allotments, whose undermined houses could at any time be swallowed up, disappear in holes the size of half a football ground. You know the phenomenon from your own abandoned coal mines back home, I imagine, whose pits and galleries run in all directions without anyone having precise plans any more. The Boxer is probably one of the few people left who has an inkling of the shape and size of that crazy maze of corridors, tunnels, magazines, batteries, command posts, soldiers' quarters, kitchens, sick bays, workshops and what have you. He's like a mole you will only find if he wants to be found. We need more staff to enter from more directions simultaneously. And we need someone, a sniper, to cover most of the exits from an appropriate vantage point to take him out as soon as he shows his mug."

Laura heaved a sigh.

"Thanks for trying to encourage us…."

Gilbert laughed.

"I'm trying to be realistic, that's all. You ain't seen nothing yet. Many hundreds of meters haven't even been secured by giving them a lick of concrete, so that they were even risky in '43. Today… When metal of any description was in short supply after the war, people started pulling, breaking, digging, and sawing iron, steel as well as non-ferrous materials from wherever they would find it, thereby weakening some critical structures beyond repair over here. And, saying that, we haven't yet talked about mines, booby traps, crates of old and unstable ammunition left behind and all the rest of it. Who knows what intricate system of explosives the Boxer has managed to establish for his own protection meanwhile? The local youths who don't as a rule stay on the island a minute longer than they have to regularly organise big bunker parties at least once a year, in the course of which they accept such risks by way of extra kicks. You shouldn't make that mistake."

"And your cavalry, what would that consist of?"

Gilbert passed the palms of his hands over his reddish curls.

"Let me put it like this. I happen not to be the only ex-soldier passing his retirement on Alderney. I can think of three or four mates nursing a variety of ailments, both physical and mental, who might be willing and able to participate in a manhunt like that. Men who don't really know what to do with themselves. For years, they've been waiting for that trunk call from the centre of special ops saying, terribly sorry, but we don't seem to be able to get along without you. We need you urgently in the Middle East. A helicopter with Arnie and Sylvester is already on its way to pick you up.

"I understand what you mean," the Chief said.

"Yea, you would, wouldn't you? Anyway, if I mobilize my powers of persuasion…A pity we don't have more time. I'm sure I could have raised a small army from across the Channel."

"But they wouldn't be familiar with the local conditions, would they?"

"Yes and no. The SAS used to mount manoeuvres on these is-lands with a certain regularity. Parachuting behind enemy lines, approach by stealth, feints, camouflages, the whole programme. That used to lead to heart-rending protests on the part of the is-landers, many of them fearing for their gardens, hothouses, or daughters. The SAS would offer their excuses, go someplace else, like the bloody Shetlands or windy Orkneys, only to come back to these islands in autumn once the climate up there in the North would get really shitty."

Laura tried to bring some order into all this.

"We would of course appreciate any help you might be able to offer. Do you happen to have any plans of subterranean Alder-ney? Sketches, descriptions, anything at all?"

"Negative. The Germans must have had a whole collection, for sure. The OT was famous for its pedantic bureaucracy. But where all these plans ended up, nobody seems to know. Hard to imagine the Brits, once they deigned to re-possess the islands, should have forgotten to ask for the plans not only of the minefields, but also of the underground installations. My guess would be someone in London or elsewhere is sitting on them, guarding them as a

Doberman pinscher would watch its feeding bowl. The Boxer may have found them, befriended the Doberman and snatched the stuff from under its nose when it wasn't looking."

"And, during all these years, nobody should have thought of establishing a new survey?"

"What for? Who but some marginal freaks would be interested in the Alderney underworld? If there were some Nazi treasures to be found, sensational files, Doctor Mengele's secret laboratory, anything, well, that would of course make a difference. But as it is…Such surveys are time-consuming and don't come cheap either. Hence, the few surveyors who got here gave up after a short while. Others…"

"Others, what?"

"Well, there has been talk of hearing voices, cries of tortured prisoners, suchlike. Hogwash, if you ask me. But enough to scare all but the most daring off, I suppose. With present-day technical options, it would presumably be possible to establish sketches from outside, without even setting foot in the maze. But, like I say, what for? Maybe the local sort of granite is impregnable even to infrared and other radiation. One way or another, a waste of time and taxpayer's money."

"I understand. Well, if you could convince some of your local colleagues, I'd suggest we meet at the harbour tomorrow morning."

Gilbert shook his locks.

"Nonsense. You are, of course, invited to my home. It may be getting a little crowded, and you may have to put up with my Winnie-the-Pooh pyjamas, but I'm sure Daphne, too, would be delighted to have you. Besides, with all respect, you want to lose that fishy smell of yours lest the Boxer sniffs you out before you even get anywhere near him."

Laura hesitated. She didn't want to importune the man. But the prospect of a shower and a night in a soft, snug bed in lieu of an ill-smelling bunk aboard the fishing lugger was something she found hard to withstand. Her two men didn't need a second invitation, anyway. The pleasure of a one on one with his wife or girlfriend Daphne worked as an added incentive. So she agreed.

"How far is it to your house?"

"Ten minutes flat. The whole island is no longer than two and half miles, as the crow flies. If you are really ambitious and clamber over the hills, an hour and a half from cape to cape. Underground, though, it will seem like an eternity, I bet."

The Chief and Ignace emptied their glasses and followed Gilbert, who was polite enough to open the pub door for Laura. Outside, Laura took a deep breath. The iodine-loaded air with its humid, salty aromatic overtones worked like a tonic on her system. The cloud cover further east had dissipated. Way yonder, some isolated flashes of lightning kept darting about undecidedly. Meanwhile, the starry sky above Alderney was unleashing its formidable splendour.

"What's this over there?" Laura asked, pointing at some dark, flat rocky island to the North.

"That's Burhou, an uninhabited and totally uninhabitable islet. You passed it by on your way up here. But then you were down in the hold, of course. There used to be some kind of cabin, for castaways to dry out, as it were. The Germans used it for their target practice. Some apostle of the simple life tried to breed sheep there later. Didn't work. There's no drinking water to be had and during high water springs, the whole thing gets flooded. You would have to be an extraordinarily patient and resilient breed of sheep to be able to stand that for any length of time."

Shortly after, they had reached Gilbert's cottage. Looking at it from this angle, it seemed to duck under the permanent onslaught of the South-Westerlies.

Gilbert had hardly inserted the key in the lock when something big inside the gingerbread house started barking with a dark, booming kind of voice. The door flew open and a cinnamon-coloured Labrador bitch came running towards her master and his guests.

"May I introduce you? This is Daphne, my domestic tyrant."

3. Jack in the Box

"Blackbird from Bullfinch. Blackbird from Bullfinch, what's your twenty? Blackbird please come in."

Laura, who had Ignace hard on her heels, had just been about to enter one of the humid, mouldy-smelling bunkers of what apparently used to be Moltke Battery. When she heard the call over her VHF device, she stopped to listen to the continuation of this ornithologically inspired exchange. In a moment's time, she would be surrounded by thick concrete walls that would effectively frustrate all further radio contact. From then on, she would have to stick to the agreed plan with great discipline and accuracy, lest Operation Minotaur went FUBAR, as Gilbert had put it in military terms – fucked up beyond recovery.

Neither Laura nor Ignace had had the foggiest idea what military radio speak was all about, so that Harry and Gilbert had been obliged to give them a crash course. The basic idea, Laura had distilled from what she had been told, consisted in communicating with your own people without letting on either your present position or your plans for the immediate future to possible eavesdropping enemies. Which is why all dramatis personae as well as all topographical hallmarks and rendezvous points convened would be identified by their respective codenames only.

The Bullfinch, for example, was none other than Gilbert asking Blackbird, aka Colestron, to give him his present position, coded, of course. It all sounded like something out of Dad's Army to Laura, but she was sure it served a purpose. At the end of the day, yesterday, Gilbert had managed to mobilize only one of his ex-SAS mates on the island. Not much, but, as they say, every little helps.

In their camouflage-coloured combat fatigues and blackened faces, the two of them would have scared the living daylights out of "Charly", let alone the Boxer. Himself a stern defender of the single-shot postulate, he probably had little or no experience in subterranean warfare and hand-to-hand combat, Gilbert had tried to set his troopers' minds at ease. Both Laura and Ignace had timidly ventured the opinion that the khaki-coloured fatigues would have made Bullfinch and Blackbird well-nigh invisible in the Gobi desert alright. Here, on the greenish black Alderney surface, it made them stick out like sore thumbs. But once inside the maze, such nuances would anyway be levelled by the generally weak and dim lighting, if any.

"Like two heavily armed giant rabbits re-possessing their warren," Ignace's caustic comment had made Laura laugh.

"Men will be men," was her only reply.

Harry Colestron, aka Blackbird, had given Gilbert's friend, a certain Bertie Fernside, the codename Robin, because robins, or so it seemed, were the bullfinches' best friends.

Laura thought she had heard enough and stepped inside the bunker. Before her eyes had had time to adapt, she heard a noise that she knew all too well. She turned round and shook her head reproachfully at Ignace, who had just cocked the replacement revolver he had been given by Gilbert. The boy was nervous alright, but Laura hated the thought of accidentally getting shot in the butt by her own son. Ignace let the cock of his gun slide back ever so gently and nodded. He had obviously understood.

Laura herself was packing her Ruger Redhawk, obviously. Automatic firearms would have been clearly out of place here, given the multitude of deadly ricochets they were bound to produce. Laura hoped they wouldn't get into an OK-Corral-like situation anyway. In this kind of labyrinth, you didn't really know what it was you were shooting at and risked falling victim to friendly fire.

With the help of Gilbert's list, the Chief had called all of the island's hotels that were open at this time of year and, presenting himself as a Yard man, had enquired about recent newcomers. There had been none. Most of the hotels were almost empty, anyway, so that any johnnies-come-lately would not have gone unnoticed. Which made it official: if the Boxer was here, he must have gone underground.

If Laura had understood "Blackbird's" reply on the VHF, he was in the process of squeezing himself through the exit hole, half hidden by weeds and bushes, of a tunnel that ended on the beach not far from the spot where camp Sylt used to be. That was in perfect keeping with the admittedly somewhat coarse strategy of entering the system from three sides simultaneously. Instead of sneaking up on the enemy, they would produce as much noise as possible in the hope of unnerving the Boxer and encouraging him to get out of the maze and, possibly off the island altogether. That would then be a mistake the man wouldn't have time to regret. Bertie, aka Robin, an experienced sniper, had taken up position in the old observation tower overlooking most parts of the island and a good deal of the Channel as well. From up there, he would provide cover for them with his old precision HK G 28 and pick up the Boxer as soon as he showed his face.

That was the plan, anyway. Its success or failure depended on a number of factors. For instance – had the Boxer protected his lair with booby traps that would be very difficult to detect, let alone defuse, in the twilight of the tunnels and bunkers? What if, contrary to their expectations, he would not hesitate to engage in a shoot-out? Or maybe he had placed explosives everywhere, so that, if he deemed it necessary, he could blow up the entire warren in one big whopper of a detonation that would produce a firestorm that would rage through the galleries, killing everything in its way? Unlikely, given the amount of TNT, Semtex or whatever else he possibly had at his disposal. In this day and age, any acquisition of large amounts of explosives by private customers, even if staggered over several months, would have alerted all anti-terrorist intelligence units in Britain and France.

In the bunker, a whole cloud of evil funk wrapped them up and rendered breathing difficult. Impossible for a human nose to identify them all, but some of the ingredients were pretty obvious: wet cement, mildew, rat shit, human urine, turpentine, waste oil and stale sweat. It smelled and felt as if a group of OT workers had dropped their tools only minutes ago and left for their damp and cold quarters. Was it possible for the Boxer to repair particularly decrepit bits and pieces of the structures to prevent them from crumbling, for his own safety? Hard to imagine, since his transporting all sorts of building materials here would certainly cause a stir or two.

The gallery they entered after leaving the bunker was so narrow and low, a soldier with his equipment and rifle in hand would have got stuck, for sure. Which probably meant that the men stationed here would be in charge of logistics and the operation of the batteries, flak, and MG's. They may have carried pistols and gas masks for their own protection, but not much more than that. Lamps covered by small metal cages sat on the ceiling at regular intervals. Laura wondered whether they would still function, once the power supply system had been repaired and made to function again.

For Laura and Ignace, pushing on in the quivering light of their torches, the gallery's height was just about as it should be. But not having worked in a coal mine for the larger part of her life, the half-crouched locomotion they adopted instinctively put a considerable strain on her thighs and back, Laura soon found out.

She kept holding the cone of light down on the ground, all the time, to be able to detect any booby traps or mines early enough and not to step on any rats accidentally. That being said, she was under no illusions as to the odds. If they so much as touched an IED with any part of their anatomy, that could be the end of it. Gilbert had warned them not to pick up anything from the floor, never mind how tempting it might look at first sight: money, documents, anything at all. It used to be "Charly's" booby-trap favourite back in the Vietnam days.

Ignace was shining his torch over Laura's shoulder and suddenly grabbed her by her arm hard. Laura didn't understand at first what he was on about but froze in mid-motion. It was only when he pointed at a very thin, almost totally transparent end of a fishing line that she realized what catastrophe she, they, had narrowly escaped. The plastic line was connected to two oval hand grenades of American make, one fixed on either side of the tunnel with some Plasticine-like material. One step further, and it would have been game over. She stood completely still squeezing Ignace' hand. Thank God his eyes were a good deal better than hers.

This was probably an older booby trap dating from some time back, Laura thought. Be that as it may, it looked recent enough to have become the instrument of their destruction, had they touched the line. Now, they had three options: turn round and backtrack, defuse the trap, or pass under the line without triggering the mechanism. After a very short whispered discussion, they both came out in favour of the latter option. Laura lay on her back and crawled under the fishing line illumined by Ignace. As soon as she had reached the other side, she took the torch and directed its beam of light on the line while Ignace slid underneath it.

There was no more radio contact with either Harry or Gilbert, no way they could have warned the men of this trap. How quickly you could lose all sense of orientation when moving in a closed-circuit kind of environment without any visual contact to the outside world, Laura had more recently experienced in the old and empty, derelict wooden Greek orphanage on Büyük Ada island off Istanbul. Together with Solitaire and her husband Jeremy, Laura had managed to free Ignace from the hands of the ill-famed Snake. So, this here was no entirely new sensation for her, but difficult to get used to, nevertheless. She thought she heard whistling and thudding from somewhere to her left. Probably the two men acting as beaters were trying to drive their prey into the muzzles of the hunters' guns.

She stopped short and handed Ignace her police-type whistle. Gilbert had found three of those in his house and distributed them among the members of the posse. Ignace tested it with a sound that almost split Laura's eardrums. If this went on much longer, she thought, they would all leave the maze empty-handed but deaf as doorposts for their troubles.

She felt sweat streaming down her face and backside. Why was it so stifling hot in here as if a central heating of sorts was at work? Breathing heavily, she got rid of her jersey with the help of Ignace. Then she tied its sleeves round her hips and pressed on. There was no telling how far they had penetrated into the maze by now. Presumably less deep than it seemed to them, but far enough to effectively shut out the daylight for good. Gasping for air, Laura stood still once again and placed her right index finger on her lips. A sudden accidental encounter with the Boxer and his nervous trigger finger was the last thing they wanted now. To her left, someone kept on whistling, to her right she thought she had heard someone shouting. The multiple echoes added to the confusing overall picture.

Suddenly, terribly loud music made the tunnel walls vibrate. Although she had immediately pressed both hands against her ears, her drums were still hurting. They had thought of many useful things but forgotten earmuffs. Laura knew the music. In fact, in Germany almost everyone knew it, had heard it at least once in this or that feature or film dealing with the Second World War. It was the so-called Russian Fanfare, which used to introduce special announcements by the Oberkommando Wehrmacht, the Supreme Command of the German Army. Laura had always assumed it was something out of the gargantuan works of Richard Wagner, so popular with the Nazis, whereas, in fact, it had been taken from a musical piece by Franz Liszt.

They should have thought of that. If he so wished, the Boxer could repay their idiotic whistling and shouting with hours of head-splitting music like this and effectively chase them out of his realm that way.

Finally, the Fanfare broke off; the Boxer had made his point. Laura and Ignace took their hands off their ears. What would Solitaire have done in a similar situation? Stuck her revolver in her belt and relied on her hearing alone, maybe. And kept her hunting knife ready, for sure.

An option that wasn't available to Laura. Much as she had learned to handle firearms, knives weren't her thing, at all. She was briefly wondering what Bertie aka Robin would make of all this. The precision optics of his HK M 28 would hopefully allow him to separate friend from foe, just in case things were going to heat up and several persons came out into the open simultaneously.

Some minutes later, they reached a crossroads in the gallery, with tunnel sections branching off to both sides. Right in front of them, on the tunnel wall, someone had drawn a primitive sort of swastika with blood-red paint. Laura turned right, but then stopped again. There was something not right with the thing. Then she saw what it was. It had been drawn the wrong way round. Whatever else it was supposed to represent, surely, the swastika was a kind of runic wheel that, when hit by a gust of wind, would have turned clockwise This swastika, however, would have turned anti-clockwise, instead. It could have been the error of some moderately talented graffiti artist not really being aware of what he was doing there in the dark. Or else it could be a deliberate hint. If so, what kind of message did it wish to convey?

Laura remembered something Ronny had written in his notes. Shortly before a blast, the guards on Alderney would sometimes point in this or that direction. Trouble was that, if you didn't understand what they were hollering, you didn't know whether they were indicating where the blast would happen or where you had better run to escape it. This thing here was begging a similar question.

"It's probably better for us to split at this stage," she said to Ignace and pointed to her right. He nodded.

"If that part of the tunnel proves a dead end, you whistle twice. It means we'll be meeting here again. I'll go left. Do take care, son, hear? No unnecessary risks. Now, you may cock your gun, incidentally. You might have to fire it."

Ignace pulled out his Browning calibre .38 Magnum, cocked it, and disappeared to the right.

When all was said and done, Laura would have preferred Ignace to stay by her side, but that wouldn't have furthered their mission a bit. And so, she quickly chased her dark thoughts away and crawled to the left, practically on all fours now. Dripping with sweat, she felt like she was going to disintegrate any moment now. Had the Germans deployed only dwarves in here? Or maybe kids, like they had done at the home front, shortly before it all imploded? Hardly. All along the Atlantic Wall, you probably came across installations such as this one. No way could they have found enough miners or dwarves to man all of those. There were the submarines too, which preferred small-size crew.

Then she thought she had noticed a few measly beams of daylight, all of a sudden, dead ahead. She crawled towards them and soon found herself in a relatively large bunker again. The daylight that had attracted her attention entered by a narrow observation slit. It looked like a former MG nest. When she had adapted to the glaring daylight, she moved closer to the slit and took a look outside. From this position, you could control a sizeable portion of the beach and become an important factor during an invasion attempt. She was sure that the bunker would be practically invisible from the sea.

With a sigh of relief, she pressed her lips against the slit and breathed in the fresh salty air. As she looked around, it seemed to her that at least four soldiers must have been stationed here. The iron bunk frames were gone, of course, but their rusty mountings were still there, firmly embedded in the concrete.

What must it have been like to spend years in here, doubly isolated from the outside world? Some used condoms lying on the floor bore witness to the fact that the local youth were occasionally using this bunker as a rendezvous point guaranteeing a maximum of privacy. And why not, Laura thought. That way, the bunker, which had never been put to the test at times of war, at least fulfilled a useful function in times of peace.

She wouldn't have minded staying on a little longer to rest and massage her aching knees, but a passing rat cast something of a dark spell on the otherwise well-nigh idyllic location. So, Laura got up and left the bunker. After a few more yards of crawling, she noticed with some relief that the gallery was widening somewhat and growing in height, as well. On the other hand, it seemed to lead uphill. She definitely could have done without that, she thought, when a sound right above her head caused her to startle. Not a whistle, nor a shot, but something lower and duller, as if caused by something or someone thumping or stomping on the ground.

What was it? Your guess is as good as mine, she told her alter ego. One thing was for sure – she didn't like it. Maybe one of the hunters had stumbled over something and fallen. In that case, she would probably have heard a half-muffled cry or someone swearing aloud. No, that sounded more like someone moving something heavy, like, say, a sofa, briefly lifting it and then dumping it again, maybe to hide behind it.

Slowly, cautiously, she went on, now standing almost upright. The bunker with the MG nest must by now have been almost fifty yards or so behind her. Nevertheless, the quality of the air she breathed seemed to remain very much the same. That could mean there was a duct of sorts somewhere around that provided this part of the underground maze with the necessary oxygen. Which, in turn, only made sense if there was a room, or hall-like structure that would have been frequented by a larger number of people, an operational centre, or something of the kind. But where exactly was it? As if to answer her question, a rusty ladder, again embedded into the concrete, emerged on her right. Laura let the light beam wander up and down the contraption. The narrow Jacob's ladder was firmly fixed to the right wall of the tunnel in such a manner that you had to take a rather large straddling first step to get your foot on the lowest rung. A complication that wasn't insurmountable, but whose practical sense escaped her.

Not exactly what you might call easily accessible, she murmured as she looked above her to see where the ladder ended.

Funny enough, it seemed to pass right through the ceiling. How, was hard to tell from where she stood.

So, she pocketed her Ruger, took the torch between her teeth and stepped on the ladder with a big leap, holding herself on the handrails. After a few rungs, she hit her head against the ceiling. That couldn't be right. Clutching the handrail with her left, she ran her right hand across the ceiling as if in search of a magic button. There was none. What she could feel, though, was some sort of fissure that seemed to run round a kind of metallic trap door. The moment she exerted a little more pressure on it, the door started to give and finally swung open. Since it had been painted in the same greenish colour as the rest of the ceiling, it had been practically invisible at even the shortest of distances.

She let the trap door opening upwards fall backwards on its hinges like the lid of a tea box. Then she squeezed herself through and stepped onto the ground of the floor above her. She had hardly closed the door again when she heard a series of shots in quick succession, shots from guns of different calibre, as even a layman would have noticed. A lively gunfight with slugs drilling themselves into the cement with a thud or recoiling from metal structures with a sickly high singing sound. Laura wasn't quite sure, but thought she could discern Ignace' Browning from a calibre nine mill gun. Because of the different degree of gas-confinement, the discharge of a revolver firing has a blasting kind of sound markedly different from that of a more discrete pistol, largely irrespective of the respective calibre. If that was Ignace, what was he doing on this side of the system? She hadn't heard his whistle and, hence, assumed he had continued to the right.

Laura moved on, bent slightly forward, her Ruger ready to be fired. The upper gallery suddenly grew so wide it would have let a horse and carriage pass.

Again, the gallery hit a T-crossing. The shots kept on coming from the right, so that would be the direction to avoid. Before she had collected her wits to turn left into a part of the tunnel she could not easily peep into beforehand, the shooting stopped. A few last shells dingle-dangled across the concrete, then all was ominous silence again. Breathing in what gun smoke was wafting towards her through the gallery, she instinctively knew that the moment of truth had come.

"Is that you, Mrs. Forster?" she heard the Boxer's voice call. Acoustic impressions in this kind of environment could be deceiving, she knew, but here she was sure the man had to be somewhere to the right of her. She stopped dead in her tracks. Several thoughts ran through her head simultaneously. Possibly, the Boxer had her over the barrel of his gun right now, so that any rash movement on her part could mean her death. Yet, since he knew her perfectly well, his question only made sense if he thought he had heard her from behind his cover and could not see her. Notwithstanding, he might have brought Ignace under his control and be pointing his gun at him this very minute. One way or another, the situation was unclear enough not to make matters worse by brandishing her Ruger about.

She raised her hands and turned without haste.

"Who's that wants to know?"

The Boxer coughed. Had Ignace hit him? What was the boy at?

"I think you know the answer to that one pretty well. If, on the other hand, you are asking yourself where Ignace is, well, he's right here with me, wounded, but alive, I might add."

"Where's here?"

"In what used to be the underground operating theatre cum emergency room. You have to walk on a little further in the direction you seem to be heading at present. Wait, I'll provide some more light."

Laura saw a bright line of electric light right in front of her that came from underneath a door that swung lightly, noiselessly, on its hinges. She walked towards it and flung the swing door open.

Again, the light was too strong for her to be able to discern much at first. It came from an array of strong lamps either fixed to the ceiling or else encapsulated by a swivelling round mirror-like device OT's use to be provided with. Even though the room may never have been used according to its intended purpose, it actually smelled of camphor, iodine, and all sorts of other disinfectants. In the case of an Allied invasion of the island, any wounded Germans would have been taken here to undergo what surgery they needed.

To the extent that her aching eyes became adapted to the light, she started identifying details of the furnishings There was a small round table with two chairs, a primitive two-flame burner probably operated by propane or butane, a sink filled with plates and knives and forks, and another rectangular table that might have served the Boxer as a desk. Ignace was lying on a sofa in the far corner, apparently bleeding from a wound to his right shoulder. True to style, the Boxer must have put the boy out of action with one single shot – not in the head, this time, but in the gun-shoulder.

The Boxer was standing in the middle of the room, his arms hanging from his sides, a sign of resignation. He carried no weapons. On his forehead, blood trickled from the wound he had sustained on Sark, when Ignace had pushed him down the staircase. The man seemed to have aged disproportionately quickly during the past forty-eight hours so that now, he looked the sixty years of age Laura had attributed to him when first setting eyes on him at St. Peter's church. A reasonably well-off pensioner who might as well have spent his retirement in some Mediterranean or Caribbean setting, instead of furrowing through the obscure maze of underground Alderney. Laura also noticed he was standing somehow uneasily, unnaturally, as if he had stepped on a rat and dared neither lift his foot lest the rat got away, nor put his foot firmly down to squish the animal.

"Snug little place you got yourself here," Laura commented.

"I'm glad you like it. A little spartan alright, but far from the madding crowd. I spent many happy hours here, reading up on files or revelling in memories of my own. The spaces we move in determine much of our thinking, have you noticed? In these rooms and tunnels, bunkers, batteries and quarters, of course, it's all memories of the war that somehow shunned the island. Same thing at Gibraltar. A similar system of intricate underground fortifications never put to use. Well, you must have seen it when you were there to talk to…Gillian."

"What happened to Ignace?" The Boxer shrugged his shoulders.

"We exchanged a few shots and one of my bullets must have lodged itself in his right shoulder. I'm confident he'll live."

Laura wasn't sure how to deal with the situation. It didn't come near any of the scenarios she had tried to prepare herself for. She raised her right arm with the gun in her hand.

"What now?"

"Whatever you do, make sure you don't pull that trigger."

This sudden word of warning came from Gilbert, who had entered the OT noiselessly and was standing right behind Laura at present. She lowered her arm and, without letting the Boxer out of her sight for so much as a second, waited for an explanation.

"Might I draw your attention to the Boxer's right foot. You see that object under the sole of his boot? I don't think it's an empty can of beans. BFM?"

That latter quizzical question was addressed at the Boxer, who just gave the slightest of nods.

"What are you talking about?" Laura asked.

"He's standing on what they call a bouncing fragmentation mine or BFM. If you shoot the man, his foot will release it, so that it will bounce to about the height of your navel and spit out thousands of pieces of shrapnel at high velocity, shredding everything and everyone in this room and the adjacent ones. I've seen it happen on the Falklands. To identify our mortal remains, of which there would be next to none, they would have to scratch tissue samples from the walls. I have seen victims of this dreadful weapon and prefer not to die that way, so better go easy on that trigger."

The Boxer nodded again.

"If I had wanted you dead, I would have had ample opportunity on Sark. But I was hoping to have convinced you I'm no Hannibal Lecter. I am more like a pedant, working off a hit list, that's all. And your name never figured on it."

Laura didn't answer but, with a movement of her head, pointed at Ignace.

"The boy? Oh, he's just passed out. You take him with you as you go. Like I say, he'll live, unless, of course, you send us all to the high heavens. He should learn to control his emotions or stay out of trouble, preferably both."

Laura let the cock of her gun sink back into its bed with a soft click and put the Redhawk away.

"And what's it with this mine of yours? I mean, how do you reckon to get out of here alive?"

The Boxer smiled.

"I don't, frankly. The moment you step on the BFM, it is armed and ready. Whatever you do from then on, it'll be faster and bound to get you."

"Hell of a way to go, though."

"There are worse. Getting mangled and eaten by a croc, for instance. Like with divorce, there aren't any really good role models, never mind what people will tell you. It all has to end sometime, one way or another. I offer my sincere excuses for this bit of pathos and drama, but the idea of going out with a big bang appealed to me, I guess. Incidentally, when the boy comes round again, do tell him that Solveig's death was an unfortunate accident which I sincerely regret, but which, unfortunately, I cannot make undone."

He held his peace for a moment as if wanting to observe a minute of silence in Solveig's memory.

"What are you doing to do with the body of intel I gave you?"

"Intelligence on Sir Lucas? You really want me to execute your legacy?"

"I'd be honoured and die a happier man. Well, in a curious sort of way. Speaking of which, I almost forgot."

He reached into his pocket and pulled out a stick which he threw at Laura's feet.

"If you need more convincing, read those files, please! They concern the wheelings and dealings of Lamont, aka Pluto. You'll be surprised what he has to answer for. Someone ought to confront him with it and insist he pays what is due – to me, to society, to the nation at large. Lamont trusts you more than anyone, I think. That's the Shakespearean flaw you have to home in on. Or not, as the case may be, it's your call."

Laura picked up the stick.

"Well, I don't as yet know how to go about it. But I think I can give you my word, Sir Lucas will have to answer for his actions, and the answer had better be a good one."

The Boxer nodded.

"Your word is good enough for me. And now, in your own best interest, I'd ask you to leave me in something of a hurry. My right leg is beginning to develop cramp. Funny it should be a pathetic pop song that would give me away."

"We all make mistakes, why would criminals be the exception to the rule? Farewell, Mr Brown or McAllister or whatever your real name may be. I can't say it was a pleasure knowing you, but all told, I've been exposed to worse individuals."

"Thanks, I'll take that as a compliment. And, believe it or not, Brown is my real or official name. I always found McAllister too Scottish for the region and Collins too learned, as it were."

The Boxer smiled absent-mindedly. The merciless light of the surgical lamps made him appear thinner than he was and gave his physiognomy a satanic touch his character probably didn't justify.

Laura and Gilbert went across the room and picked up Ignace from the sofa. He was just coming round and found it difficult to focus. Besides, he was hurting from his injured shoulder.

His right arm round the Chief, and his left supported by Laura, the three of them left the OK Corral. Before the door swung back for the last time, Laura took a good look back over her shoulder. The song line came to her mind: On the clearing stands the Boxer, in his anger and his shame...."

1. Pluto's Moons

From the porch of his villa aptly placed on a hillock roughly in the middle of his vast Puerto-Rican estate, Sir Lucas Lamont enjoyed a gorgeous view over land and sea. Situated few miles southeast of San Juan, his Haziende del Suerte, a former sugar cane plantation, reached almost all the way to the beach, from which it was only separated by the heavily solicited coastal free-way, one of the island's major traffic arteries.

The abolition of slavery and the frequent passage of devastating hurricanes, as well as, and probably more so, the massive cultivation of sugar beet everywhere in Europe had tolled the death knell for local sugar production long time ago already. Many members of the Puerto-Rican sugar-cane nobility, who traced their families all the way back to the Spanish conquistadors, had had to sell their land at give-away prices to newly-rich parvenus such as Sir Lucas, leave the island and seek paths to new fortunes elsewhere.

Lamont's estate not being used for either land cultivation or cattle breeding, the entire area was dominated by his villa in post-colonial style, which he had had erected to his own plans after having had the original planter's palace torn down. The adjoining stable complex, which had also housed a fair number of slaves, at some stage, he had left in its original position and shape. Since the present landlord had long since given up all hope of one day being able to mount a horse again and to the extent that the number of his potential successors was being reduced almost by the week, the interior of the stables had been converted into rooms for his army of mostly local bodyguards. These men would watch over the estate in shifts at all times. What facilitated their task was the fact that the entire rolling country-side Sir Lamont had bought up was nearly treeless and figured only few bushes high and large enough to offer an intruder cover.

Everything looked very thoroughly thought through, planned and executed to the point without, on the other hand, appearing pretentious. The one overriding principle dwarfing any aesthetic considerations was to ensure the owner's personal safety.

Word in the bars and whorehouses of the San Juan harbour area was that large parts of the estate had been mined for good measure. But those were rumours, so far unconfirmed by either the owner himself, any of his guards, or by some otherwise inexplicable nightly detonation followed by the sudden disappearance of this or that local thug who might conceivably have been foolish enough to venture onto Lamont's land.

"Harold, the binoculars, if you please."

The butler, as always scurrying about his master, obliged him without so much as a second's hesitation. Lamont pointed the binoculars north, in the general direction of the port area. His attention had been caught by a pink SUV of unknown make that had left the freeway and seemed at present to be heading for the Lamont estate. Two more measly miles, and it would reach the large cast-iron gate of the Hacienda del Suerte. Proceeding at a sustained pace, the vehicle drew a long triangular cloud of dry dust behind it and, hopping and skipping over the odd bump on the beaten path, seemed a little like a pink pebble skimming across the smooth surface of a lake.

"Would we be in for some visitors, Sir Lucas?" Harold asked in a soft murmuring voice.

"Not that I know of."

"Is it possible you forgot to mention an important meeting to me this morning?" Harold drove in the nail. Not many people in Sir Lucas' surroundings could afford to address themselves to the landlord in such almost jovial terms.

"I just told you I have no idea who that is. I never forget appointments, you know that. And if I did, you would be there to remind me. I'm wondering who might be brave enough to approach my place in a pink vehicle. You?"

"Indeed, no," Harold replied and shook his head disapprovingly.

"Wouldn't be surprised if whoever drives that thing is dressed in a shell suit. Pity we don't have a gun to take that tasteless bastard off the road before he even reaches the gate."

"I'll add it to tomorrow's shopping list," Harold tuned in.

"Any preferences as for make, calibre, or range? I hear Bofors are thinking of ridding themselves of some shelf huggers at affordable prices."

"Don't try to be funny, Harold. It's highly unbecoming in a serious butler such as yourself. That said, you see me puzzled, a state of mind I abhor. I didn't pass any invitations that I know, and…hold on there a minute!"

He seemed to have recognized someone, maybe the driver, and now that the SUV had reached the gate, picked up his mobile.

"Diga me, compañero. Quién? Mrs. Forster accompanied by whom? Vale. Yes, yes, let them in, for God's sake. But be sure to check whether they're packing."

He handed Harold the mobile and looked at his watch.

"I hear it's Mrs. Forster accompanied by none other than her son and sister. Ever met her sister? Good for you, neither have I. A nasty piece of work is what I hear. The result of a scorpion mating with a rattler. Anyway, let's prepare something for their welcome, a poisoned tequila sunrise or something, with olives, tapas, small parasols, the usual spiel. I have a feeling they won't be staying for long."

"No dinner then?"

Lamont gave it a thought, then decided against it.

"No dinner. That's what you get for surprise visits. I hate that. Let's play it by ear, shall we."

Harold disappeared into the house. Sir Lucas grabbed the binoculars again and followed the pink spot moving across the landscape and growing bigger fast. Finally, it came to a halt with screeching tyres right in front of the porch. Sir Lucas got up from his wheelchair, seized his cane and made an effort to meet his uninvited guests at the step of the porch. This gave him the fleeting satisfaction of looking down on the three people walking towards him.

Harold, who had performed a magic re-appearance act, rolled the wheelchair so it picked up the small figure of Lamont almost like a forklift will snatch a pallet off the ground. Somewhat unceremonious treatment Sir Lucas seemed accustomed to.

"Hello Laura, pleased to see you again. You must be Ignace, and you…"

"My sister Solitaire. Sol, this is Sir Lucas Lamont, who I have told you so much about."

"Don't believe a word," Sir Lucas cried.

"But do come in. I'm delighted to welcome you in my modest home. I believe Harold prepared a few drinks and stuff. You must be hungry. When did you arrive on Prico?"

"On what?"

"Puerto Rico. I call it Prico for short."

While he was chatting away, Sir Lucas secretly kept looking Solitaire over. It was more than obvious he had heard a lot about her, scandalous things that he was trying to find traces of in her physiognomy.

For quite a while, Laura had been in two minds about springing this raid-like visit on Sir Lucas. On the one hand, this kind of procedure was cavalier, to say the least. On the other, hers was no mere duty call either. Not by a long chalk. Considering what she was going to confront the man with, the surprise element would probably work very much in her advantage.

The big bang with which the Boxer had taken leave from the world at large only days before still rang in Laura's ears. Without the trap door she had discovered, they might not have escaped the jack-in-the-box of a fragmentation mine.

The idea to ask Solitaire to accompany her to "Prico" had already been born on Alderney. A little egotistic, perhaps, but not knowing how Sir Lucas would react to her initiative, Sol with all her combat experience would be a kind of life insurance for her. Besides which, Sol's Caribbean connections included quite a few shady characters from the seedy San Juan periphery, hoodlums who might be willing to lend a helping hand if and when someone like Solitaire alerted them, borrowing Tarzan's staging cry. And, last but not least, they hadn't seen each other for a long time and Laura had absolutely no intention of inviting a torrent of abuse from her sister because she had not profited from her visit to the Caribbean by coming by to see her.

"And how are you these days, Sir Lucas?" she smiled at the man disarmingly as they sat down at the round table in the parlour, where Harold had served the drinks and snacks.

"Each to their Own. Really, now?"

Laura was referring to the Sylt camp motto Sir Lucas had had imprinted on the archway of the hacienda gate. Laura had noticed it with some pangs of virtual memory. Was it the expression of pure cynicism or the tasteless sentimentality of a half-demented old-timer?

Remembering the body search she had had to undergo on Jersey, Laura had insisted on everyone leaving their guns at home. Their practical usefulness would have been limited to increasing Lamont's natural caginess even further. Solitaire's and her own shooting prowess notwithstanding, they would not have been able to fight Lamont's entire army. It had taken Solitaire a little while to see the logic of that kind of reasoning, but then she had agreed, much against her will. Knowing her sister all too well, Laura suspected her of having mobilized a gang of local cutthroats that were waiting for her call somewhere in the wings. In the US, many men and some women carry firearms. On Puerto Rico, a turnstile of Caribbean drug trafficking, nobody leaves home without one. Hence, to raise a small posse of men able and willing to hunt, harrow, and kill, was an easy exercise – provided you had the necessary loose change.

"Why not? Each to their Own is the liberal answer to the Socialist merit principle. It's been preached ever since antiquity, if you take the trouble of reading up on some of the classics…."

Ignace had shaken Lamont's right hand with his own left, because he carried his right arm in a sling to protect his healing shoulder. Gilbert had seen after the gun wound shortly after they had exited from the underground maze, a considerable part of which would now be lying in ruins. Gilbert was no physician, of course, but his experience with gun wounds was such as to render him more competent than any general island practitioner who, for his part, had perhaps never seen anything like that at close range. As long as there was no bullet to be removed or broken bone to be put in splints....

"Fascinating woman, your sister," Lamont murmured to Laura. "You are the same age, I believe?"

"Very much so. We're twins, dizygotic ones. With very different characters, I can assure you. Solitaire is more spontaneous, impetuous, even. Must be her hi-carb diet, I suspect. Back on Dominica, she hunts down and eats members of the indigenous population. I don't think you would be on her menu, but better not turn your back on her unnecessarily. I thought I had better mention that beforehand, you know, so there would be no complaints..."

Lamont laughed, but didn't seem sure to what extent Laura was really joking. .

"We haven't been in contact for a while, so I thought I might as well bring her, since I was going to visit the Caribbean, anyway."

Lamont turned to Solitaire.

"Dominica, eh? I guess you're still in the midst of clearing up after the last hurricane?"

Solitaire looked at him and gave him a cool nod.

"Your sister understands our language, does she?" Lamont enquired of Laura.

"Yes, if you speak slowly enough and not use too many hard words. I hate to admit it, but she's not the brightest of sisters I could have imagined. Oooh!"

That latter sound was caused by a kick on the shins she had received from Solitaire.

Laura knew full well that her sister's taciturn attitude was at least partially provoked by her habit of "reading" both the room and everyone in it. According to...Ronny, was it, she shared that habit with Lamont.

If matters came to a head, which they well might, Solitaire would know how to react. Hopefully.

"I hope you had a pleasant flight, although, personally speaking, I'm not even sure such a thing as a pleasant, comfortable flight does exist. I always find flying a pain. Thanks for the drinks and stuff, Harold. Here's to your good health. Speaking of which, you must forgive my drinking only water. My liver's in limbo, I hear…"

They all raised their glasses.

"Terribly sorry to be barging in on you and thank you for receiving us, nonetheless."

Lamont put his glass down and tried one of the canapés.

"Well, I guess you haven't come all the way from….Hamburg, was it, to admire my Hazienda del Suerte? So, why don't you tell me what's on your mind. If it has anything to do with our deal, you shouldn't have taken the trouble to get on a plane. I would have preferred to lay my hands on the killer, but knowing him dead will do it for me just as well. They tell me he was a son of Gooey's. I still cannot believe the man hadn't drowned. I mean, I looked him in the eyes as he sank to the bottom and would have sworn any old oath he had that dead expression on his face that I had first seen on the German soldiers we had killed on Sark."

He paused and snatched another canapé from the tray Harold held under his nose.

"Hard to believe, is all I say. Why didn't the man ever manifest himself to us, his ex-brothers in arms? Anyway, let the dead look after the dead is what I say. Water under the bridge. Our deal said dead or alive, so, I complied with it and honoured my obligations before you even got here. Your firm should be thriving from now on."

"Actually, it had been thriving before. But thank you, Sir Lucas, I appreciate you're as good as your word."

"No problem. If you're thinking in terms of going public, stock market, and all, I can recommend a broker's of some standing. I think we ought to drink to that. I see Harold's chosen a bottle of '98 Veuve Cliquot. Excellent bubbly. To be sipped with awe."

Harold re-filled everybody's glasses but Lamont's, and they all looked at Laura to bring out the next toast.

"I'll drink to another motto of historic connotations: My Honour is Loyalty."

As she said this, she was watching Lamont's facial expression with great attention. The old man seemed to freeze for the briefest of moments but didn't twitch an eyelid. Presumably, he would have been able to cheat any polygraph.

"You do know, though, what neck of the woods that comes from, don't you?"

Laura nodded.

„Yes, I do. One of those sudden intuitions seemed somehow appropriate."

Nobody else taking issue, they drank and put down their glasses.

"Why this sudden change of atmosphere, those sombre countenances? I had expected a bit more joy, seeing the generally gratifying tidings we were discussing just now," Lamont said, while Harold was placing the bottle into the ice bucket.

"Maybe we should try and not go over the top yet. No reason to get carried away. After all, we're talking of a human being ending his days…."

"…in a bunker on Alderney, by blowing himself up, yes, I know. But I fail to feel any sympathy or commiseration. What goes round…."

"Definitely. Before going down that road, though, the Boxer, as we have come to call him, asked me to promise him something I'd rather like to honour. In fact, honouring it is my ultimate motive for coming here. In business as in all other walks of life, you ought to be true to your word, right?"

"Absolutely. And what exactly did you promise him, then?"

Laura fell silent for a moment. She had prepared her text during their flight across the Atlantic almost word for word, only to find that now, when the show was on, she stalled and felt somehow empty. The jury was getting edgy, the judge impatient. Pull yourself together, for God's sake. Solitaire, who had instinctively fathomed her sister's momentary blackout, kicked her on the shins again. That helped Laura to focus.

"I'll be coming to that in a jiffy. First things first, though. As it would seem, and I'm weighing my words, you…interpreted the saga of the Yarmouth Six a little one-sidedly when we last discussed it in your Jersey manor. I realized that when studying some of the authentic records and protocols left by your…brothers in arms, as you called them. There were important differences in detail. You might retort that these men's memories might be as defective as yours. Trouble is, their versions happen to tally a lot better with what the Boxer told me on Sark than with what you told me on Jersey. And truth being largely a matter of statistics, I would be inclined to believe them rather than you."

Lamont took it in his stride.

"You're free to believe who and whatever you please. But do consider this. When you met the…Boxer, he was already at the end of his tether. To wrap it all up in a manner satisfactory enough for him, for his conscience, he needed to spin a yarn that, short of whitewashing him, at least seemed to make part of his actions seem mildly justifiable. Serial killers are like alcoholics or junkies in that they will always find fault with someone else – you, me, society at large – that they can blame for their addiction. But I'm racing ahead here. Do go on. Maybe you can shed some more light on the man's motivation." Laura nodded.

"I think I can. The overall impression he gave me was that he hated to see the truth accompany him to the grave, so to speak. If he couldn't get at you physically, the least he could try to do was unveil the truth about you, or whatever, in all fairness, he took for the truth in that impenetrable maze of lies, intrigues, and machinations."

"The truth about me? Or about the Yarmouth Six? What would that look like? Why did he even bother, after all those years?"

"The truth about you, Sir Lucas, about you, personally, and none other than you. And about your role in that farce."

"Well then, let's hear it, by all means. We might all learn something from it and I myself might not die an ignorant ass."

Laura leaned back in her chair, trying to remember the very words of the Boxer, making him her prompter.

"When you had saved your skin on the coast of Sark that fateful foggy morning, Peter Collins, the seventh dwarf of your commando, the man you called Gooey, had drowned despite all your efforts to save him, or so it would seem. That's correct so far, isn't it, Sir Lucas?"

Lamont nodded consent.

"Yes, I had told you all that myself. In spite of my attempts at pulling him to the surface, Gooey sank to the bottom. I just couldn't hold him, heavy like a whale and slippery like an eel as he was."

"Right, well, it's here, at that critical stage, that we stumble across the first contradictions. In his...well, let's call them memoirs, shall we, Ron Goldsmith, for instance, claims to have watched you not so much trying to save Gooey as pushing him under. Collins probably lost conscience and was carried away by the tidal current. Minutes later, he re-emerged, more dead than alive, it is true. You didn't see it happen, because it went down on the western side of the cape on whose eastern side the rest of you had crawled ashore, see. He was lucky enough to end up in a cave that was relatively dry at all states of the tide. But most if not all of this you will probably already have surmised."

If he had, Lamont didn't show it.

"I always thought I would recognize a dead person when I'd see one. That aspect of things apart, Ronny must have either seen or remembered wrongly. The fog of time that fuzzies our recollections must, in his case, have matched the fog we had on the day. We were all physically down and out. Plus, we still had residues of Pervitin and stuff in our veins, some more than others. Under such circumstances, the brain will play all sorts of tricks on you. I wouldn't be surprised if he had sworn an oath he had seen me strangle his mother into the bargain."

Laura swallowed. He was right. In a court of law, Ronny's testimony would not have pulled much weight.

"Cui bono? Why would Ronny try to throw those sorts of serious aspersions on your person? No, I think he was motivated by the same urge as was the Boxer – to help the truth to come out.

Goldsmith was the last surviving member of the Yarmouth Six, barring Gooey and yourself, of course. But you don't count in that context. And Ron may have felt his own end wasn't all that far away either. That makes two men speaking out in a situation where you don't normally lie any longer, not face to face with the Grim Reaper, that is. Both Ron's and the Boxer's testimonies were Alknomooks."

"They were…what?"

"Alknomooks. That's what some redskins call the death chant they will break into when feeling their end approach."

This explanation came from Solitaire. Since this was the first time she opened her mouth since their arrival at Lamont's porch, her hoarse voice now held sway. It may have been an exaggerated view, but somehow, Laura at least felt for a moment there that Death herself had sat down among them for a serious chat. Why not, she thought, since this was the day of uninvited visits, anyway.

Lamont was the first to shake off any such premonitions, if he had had them in the first place.

"Well, bugger it. Yes, I pushed him under, had to do it. With his whining, Gooey could have put the Germans on our tracks. It was an act of self-defence."

"Maybe," Laura half-conceded.

"But had it become known at the time or even years later, it would have left a nasty dent on your war-hero bodywork, wouldn't it?"

"Perhaps, who knows? Would that be all? Again, if it is, you shouldn't have come all the way to confront me with it. You may not believe this, but I am sincerely sorry for what I did to Gooey. His pale greenish face sinking to the bottom has followed me about almost every night for more than half a century now. That's punishment enough for something no court in the world would send me to jail for."

"No, that wasn't all. Aren't you interested in what became of Gooey? Why he never manifested himself to you or any others of his brothers in arms?"

"You want an honest answer? No, I couldn't care less. But, at the same time, I have that nagging feeling you're going to tell us, anyway, depriving me as you do of my well-deserved siesta. Have you no pity at all with an old man?"

"Not much, Sir Lucas. But we, too, are in something of a hurry and yes, there's a lot more to bring up to set the picture right. I'll try and be short, but I can't make any promises. Incidentally, a glass of water might oil my throat and accelerate matters."

Harold, whose presence was noticed but not remarked upon, immediately withdrew and came back with a carafe filled with ice cubes and water. He poured Laura a glass, which she emptied in one swig.

"Gooey was found by a local lady called Rose McAllister. She nursed him and took care of him. His brain had sustained irreparable damage because of the prolonged stay under water."

In few but inspired words, Laura told Gooey's story as well as that of the Boxer, according to what she had heard and learned from both, both directly or indirectly. Every now and again, she interrupted her narrative flow, drank some water and looked at Solitaire as if she needed her sister's moral support. Solitaire kept nodding at her encouragingly.

"Gooey was the man who never was. When he died in the nineteen eighties, Rose buried him. To this day, nobody knows exactly where his grave might be. Not even his son. Rose took that secret with her to her own grave. Which, incidentally, is in the churchyard of St. Peter's, on Sark. Thus, the weeds of oblivion would have pushed up and covered up all memory of Rose and Gooey, had it not been for the Boxer. And even he would hardly have been able to clear the ground and dig in his father's past, if it hadn't been for a certain Mr. Goodfellow. It was he who saw to it that Gooey's son could go to public school and later attend university. Without that kind of educational background, the Boxer would not have been able to track one of the most skilled and most dangerous double agents of the war and immediate postwar years while at the same time pursue a personal vendetta. He was, of course, helped in this by the fact that both spectres of the past he pursued soon rolled into one. By putting the various pieces of the puzzle in place, the Boxer happened to unveil the true identity of that double agent bearing the code name Pluto. All depending on the respective political and military situation, Pluto would follow the ups and downs of contemporary history, working, now for the Germans, then for the British, or Americans, or whoever paid best. Frequently to the detriment of third parties, such as the French or the Russians. Which is why he ended up on the wanted lists of almost every secret service around the globe. The Boxer made it his mission in life to apprehend Pluto, at first. When he realized that couldn't be done because Pluto had too many moons out there protecting his orbit, the Boxer changed tactics and started taking out the man's next of kin, in the vain hope, Pluto might, at some stage, either kill himself or give up and get killed or go to jail, whatever."

She fell silent for a moment, collecting her thoughts.

"What are you calling his moons?"

Laura shrugged her shoulders.

"Well, like I said, many secret services the world over were looking for him at one stage or another. At the same time, however, the other services, those he happened to be working for, would protect him, circling around him to destroy any comets or other galactic debris that might otherwise have harmed or destroyed him."

Lamont had almost shrunk out of existence in his wheelchair. Irrespective of how high the war criminals of this world may have sat on their horses, Laura thought, once in the dock, they all dwindled to a pathetic bundle of rags. What would Hitler have looked like at the Nuremberg trials? And, more interesting, who would have been willing to act as his barrister?

"I rest my case, for the moment, and pass the floor to the defendant, Sir Lucas. Or should I say, Pluto?"

2. Hopscotch

"After having left your mates on Sark, you defected to the Germans and offered them your services as an agent. The fact that you managed, despite Hitler's Night-and-Fog decree, to avoid the execution squad is exemplary for your surprising ability to extricate yourself out of any predicament, against all odds. An extraordinary talent, I've got to hand it to you."

A cynical little smile lit up Lamont's face for a second or two.

"You're flattering me, Laura. Actually, I was close enough to death at the time to feel his foul breath in my face. Oh yes, believe me. I already thought that, to save bullets and get some exercise at the same time, the Germans were simply going to beat me to death. Wouldn't have taken much more of this and they would have done. Fortunately, there happened to be two SS men on Sark at that time. Looking back at it later, I came to the conclusion that, in any other constellation, those two would have dispatched me between breakfast and lunch. But in this particular situation, they became my saviours. That's life for you, all happenchance. Thing is the Wehrmacht couldn't pick their noses, let alone execute someone, without asking the SS for permission. Now, those two jokers looked me up and down like an extra-terrestrial and listened to my offer calmly and quietly, like humouring a demented old geezer. Why not? They were in no hurry, and I had no-one else to turn to."

He chuckled.

"Surely, they didn't just take your word. You must have had something substantial to offer them."

"Of course. Well, there was my knowledge about the locations and structures of special ops training camps such as the one we had been to near Yarmouth."

"Not a lot of bargaining power, if you ask me."

"No, I agree. But a beginning, a good-will gesture."

"You gave away your mate's hiding place?"

"Not immediately, as I may stress. I started off by pretending I was the only survivor of Operation Sea Leopard. Not as a heroic stance, I have to admit, but because I was afraid that, by the time they arrived there at the bloody cave, everyone would have been gone and the Germans would have come to the conclusion I was holding out on them. No, my ultimate object of barter was the treasure, of course. While I was licking the warm blood gushing forth from my various head injuries caused by their truncheons, I asked myself a simple question: how could I sell a treasure to the Germans that belonged to them in the first place? A stunt that would make the proverbial sale of a fridge to an Inuit family look like a practical joke. I had at all times tried hard not to lose my mind, despite the beatings, the pain, the loss of consciousness on and off and the catastrophic loss of blood. It paid off in that I noticed that, whatever they seemed to be blaming me for, from the assassination of Abel to that of Franz Ferdinand of Austria, they never even so much as mentioned the treasure. That could mean they had no idea of its existence. You have to remember that the German administrative structures were multi-faceted and implied a lot of ineffective duplicate work. There was the Wehrmacht hating the SS but depending on them in many ways. There was the civilian administration and the OT. And there was the local admin meant to take care of the island population. A duplicate, triplicate structure that, obviously, invites all sorts or of in-fighting for competences and authority. There has been much talk of the alleged German organisational genius. That's baloney. Look at the logistic shambles they made of the Russian campaign. I'll let you into a secret: had the German industrial complex been placed in one controlling hand and focussed on nothing but the production of war material, they would have won that war hands tied behind their backs. As it was, the competences were spread all over the place and much energy wasted on pulling the strings together. Nothing easier than playing one party of an administration off against another to the detriment of the whole. The more ramified a system, the less effective, you know that better than I do, presumably. Anyway, the officers stationed on Sark, off the mainstream, as it were, had tried to profit from their privileged position for a while. Now that the SS was there, the Wehrmacht had to tread way more softly lest they got their fingers rapped hard. There was more and more talk of losing the war and there was the build-up to the assassination attempt on Hitler. Back in Berlin, your Goerings, Goebbels, Himmlers, Bohrmanns and what have you, were all warming to the idea of replacing the wreck of a Fuehrer in the not-too-far future. Not without eliminating their worst competitors, of course. Not the kind of climate conducive to inspiring confidence and trust, wouldn't you say? This was the stage set by the forces that were and I was the magician ready to conjure up what truths were requested on the menu."

"What happened next?" Laura interrupted his flow. The man was unashamedly proud of his actions; he risked swaying the jury.

"They took me to Guernsey, first, where I underwent a new series of abuse and beatings in the torture chambers of the Gestapo. When the beating and kicking didn't seem to produce the desired results, they treated me with truth sera such as midazolam and drugs such as mescaline and various selected opiates, I trust. I have no idea what I told them during such sessions that seemed endless. One thing was certain, though: they knew about the existence of both the treasure and my brothers in arms. With reference to the latter, they had to weigh up two main options. They could have rounded up what remained of Operation Sea Leopard personnel, shoot everyone and be done with it.

If they wanted to deploy me as an agent, however, they had better not touch them to make it look as if I had not been caught either. I'm happy to say they plumped for the latter option. Five individuals roaming the island of Sark couldn't wreak enough havoc to make their seizure a top priority. On the contrary, I believe they even let the Wehrmacht know that, if any members of the commando were discovered, they should be left in peace, neither shot nor arrested. I don't know for sure. If that's what they did, it would have been a smart move. Suddenly, the beating and abuse stopped. I was getting medical help and, after some weeks, even made presentable. I lacked almost all my teeth by then, but the Germans had good dentists. Sadists, but competent ones, experimenting with implants, even then. They provided me not only with new teeth, but also with the narrative of a British war hero who had just fallen short of liberating the Channel Islands single-handedly. One good turn deserving another, I presented them with the free masons' treasure. Always assuming it was indeed theirs. On Sark, a few heads must have rolled in the aftermath of all that. But that was for the Germans to elucidate among one another. I was ferried across the Channel in a U-boat again, this time a German one. U93 commanded by Kapitänleutnant Achim Helmstedt. I still remember it as if it had gone down the day before yesterday. Let me tell you: if you need to go subsurface at sea, there's nothing like a German U-boat, take my word for it. Minus the Labskaus, which I personally abhor. Apart from the food, it was all much more comfortable and restful than that awful outward leg aboard the Sunfish. Anyway, they dumped me with a kayak close to the English coast. That part, I didn't like. I'm no bloody Eskimo and this kajak was going all over the place with me rather than vice versa, as it should have been. It wouldn't have surprised me if it had taken me all the way back to Alderney, just out of spite."

"And so? Did the Brits buy your story?"

"Buy it? The literally embraced it. A few young men had managed to cross the Channel in collapsible craft, rowing boats and suchlike precarious transport, before me. Not that often, of course, but every once in a while. So that part of the story was easy to sell. The Army was happy to be able to present an operation crowned by success, for once. No interest in digging deeper."

"Which means your war heroism is a cheap fake?"

"Well, you might put it that way. But if you stop to consider for a moment what the six or seven of us had suffered on Sark in the framework of Operation Sea Leopard and during the ensuing weeks, an honorary mention would be perfectly in place, I should think. It had no immediate effect on the course of the war. I'll give you that. But it did keep the Germans on their toes. Besides, most war heroics, once you put them to the acid test, are likely to turn out to be fakes. You need something to keep up morale and, since beggars apparently can't be choosers, you take what you get. Add to this the privileged treatment I received at the hands of the SS, and cheap is not the first adjective that comes to mind, I don't think."

"I'll concede that. So, as a war hero, you forged yourself a career with MI6?"

Lamont smiled his toothless smile.

"You would have made a useful addition to the Gestapo, Mrs Forster, no offence. The way I see it, you would have got to the bottom of things without even resorting to Mescaline and other stuff, no doubt, but just by making a pest of yourself."

"Were there any women in the SS?"

"No, that was probably the one good thing about it: off limits for women! You see, the SS were married to Hitler, in a manner of speaking, not totally unlike Catholic clergymen to the Almighty, or the Pope, by way of substitute. It wouldn't have gone down well if, say, a higher SS echelon would have refused to supervise the gassing of a batch of Jews because he had promised to take the kids to the zoo that self-same afternoon, if you see what I mean. There was something called the Retinue or Entourage. They essentially represented the logistic support and had a fair number of women among them. Women, who, incidentally, made more assiduous concentration camp guards than many men. In all fairness, it has to be said that quite a few young SS concentration camp guards asked to be relieved of their post or even committed suicide because they couldn't stomach the Shoa." Laura swallowed again. In a court of law, his clever rhetoric would have made him a formidable opponent for any prosecuting counsel.

"Our chief task was to feed the German secret service motley pieces of intelligence – sometimes true but hard to believe, most of the time false but plausible. My department focussed on the Channel Islands…."

"…though, strategically speaking, those were next to useless."

"I beg to differ. From an objective point of view, you're right, of course. But in war, objectivity is the second victim after truth. Competent Generals such as Rommel weren't dupable enough to believe the baloney we were trying to sell, obviously. Hitler, however, lived in a world of his own, a Nazi Wonderland abounding with Cheshire cats, Black Queens, and Humpty Dumpties. Almost childlike, he would stomp his foot when his generals told him that Tweedledum and Tweedledee didn't exist in the real world. Have you ever seen any footage of the Fuehrer perambulating on the terrace of his Obersalzberg mansion? It's uncanny, one of the strongest impressions of the man who was Hitler. Twice removed from the hear-say reality beyond those magic mountains, he looks like a retired banker who wouldn't either know or believe the real world to be at war. And so, like most creatures of poor intellect, he would all the more greedily embrace whatever conspiracy theory was coming his way."

He paused as if to let it sink in. If Laura didn't intervene, soon, she felt, he would succeed in converting them all to his creed of cynical egotism.

"To get back to the islands. Paradoxically, the more material we fed them showing that the Allies had absolutely no interest in the Channel Island archipelago, the more frantically Hitler would convert them into daunting fortresses. Try as you will, you can't fool a Hitler. Which tied up an enormous quantity of men and material for no earthly use whatsoever. Men and material that would have been desperately needed at other places, such as the heights of Normandy."

"And what did you feed the Brits?"

Lamont was in full swing now. Looking at him, he seemed to be shedding a year or two with every new chapter he broached.

"Material on first top-secret preparations for the Fuehrer's assassination. Fake, of course, transmitted to me by my newly-won friends from the SS. But that was small fry. My masterpiece, and I'm putting all false modesty aside, here, my masterpiece was Operation Hopscotch."

"Hopscotch? Sounds compelling."

"You bet. In a nutshell, it consisted of a series of fake plans, documents, aerial photographs and what have you, all insinuating that, in view of the Soviet's advance west after Stalingrad and Kursk, the Germans were seriously considering moving their Peenemuende rocket complex onto the Channel Islands. They would thus become the launch pads of the instruments of the Endsieg, the final victory, figuratively speaking. A major logistic effort, obviously, but hair-raising enough to be plausible. Everywhere in the Alpine regions, the Germans were busy digging whole underground railway lines, factories, offices, what have you. So why not dump the stuff on an island? Mine was true premium material with detailed time schedules, transport routes on land and at sea, the sketches of a new V5 model of such devastating force it would come close to a nuclear bomb minus the ensuing fall-out. At Whitehall, it must have impacted like an old V2. Churchill is said to have dropped his cigar in his whisky glass when he received first news of it."

He chuckled again.

Looking at, and listening to him, Laura couldn't help thinking of Graham Greene's Our Man in Havana, who, lacking more substantial intel, sends his people at home detailed sketches of blown-up vacuum cleaners' spare parts and sections masquerading as rockets with and without nuclear war heads.

"Hard to explain the degree of both chaos and hysteria rampant in those days to a modern audience, I'm afraid. And that applies to both sides. At home, MI6 and MI5 were watching each other with beady eyes, always afraid one might snatch functional responsibilities at the cost of the other. Both were united again in their shared hatred of the arrogant OAS agents and the Enigma eggheads at bloody Bletchley Park. Excesses of any kind tend to cause addiction, mutual distrust gone over the top not constituting an exception. And I was the born provider, your friendly red-nosed candy man."

"Win-win?"

"Exactly. As we know or always suspected, all parties involved hurriedly swept a lot of disreputable stuff under the carpet.

If someone had had the political guts to try and get to the bottom of things, men such as myself, double or triple agents, in other words, would soon have been burnt. But that was never on the cards. The obliteration of the rocket to a better future, or so public opinion was made to believe. Not surprisingly, under these circumstances, we were almost condemned to repeat the past. Had it not been for the nuclear deterrent, the Cold War would soon have heated up something awful."

"Hence, men like you were still in demand?"

"Are you kidding me? That's when the party really got under way. All I had to do was re-orient myself. Farewell to MI6 and the Germans, welcome to the Yankees and Ivans."

"How and why did you resuscitate your Yarmouth brotherhood?"

"A precautionary measure, originally. Sometime in the future, my past would presumably have caught up with me, and blow my cover – as always, at the least convenient moment."

"Distorted and disordered as it was, you would hardly have recognized it yourself, I suspect."

"Maybe. Then again, life is full of little surprises, as they say. Imagine me standing on the platform of some subway station, waiting for the train to arrive. Of a sudden, someone ticks me on the shoulder and calls out something like, Hey, Duke, old geezer, how's it hanging these days. I thought you had kicked the bucket long time ago, already, I honestly did. And so on. The voice of Hooch, or Haggis, or whoever. Wouldn't do, would it? Wouldn't do at all. I had to know where I had them, walk them on a short leash. Which, in turn, could only succeed if I gave them the perspective of rapid advancement by dint of a criminal career. What else was there for five young guys who had not exactly invented the wheel but knew how to use it to their benefit? Any other options would have taken too long. For them, crime was the silver bullet."

He spread his arms and heaved his shoulders.

"Like I said, I wasn't working with MI6 any longer. That said, I saw to it that my bridges to all secret services, those that mattered, I mean, remained intact. Hence, it wasn't exactly rocket science for me to raise one brother after another till the Yarmouth Six were assembled, once again. I convened the…constituent meeting of what was now to become our brotherhood of crime at a pub under the Tower Bridge, as it were. I trust you appreciate the symbolism: a get-together of a would-be legendary gang in the shadow of a legendary British dungeon. Talk of karma."

"Did it work out?"

"Absolutely. I had been prepared for all sorts of reproaches and accusations. They might have half a mind to shoot me, strangle me, tear me to pieces. But nothing of all that happened, though. You probably won't believe this, but they all remained calm and peaceful. Not one of your annual graduate reunions, of course. More like the routine meeting of the heads of department of a major company that had sustained a few unfortunate turnover setbacks more recently, caused by circumstances and events beyond their collective control. The share capital, viz. our precious treasure, was obviously lost. They all took that in their stride, not least, because they could see I had not enriched myself to their detriment. But there was more. Each and every one of them had a chip on his shoulder, had lived through so many tales of personal hardship and deprivations, they wished nothing more than to close that chapter and make a fresh start. And they felt that their best option would be to follow whatever route I would pick for them, as I had hoped they would. And so, in that crummy little pub called the Fox and Ferret, we decided to go hunting anew, this time according to our own Night-and-Fog law and for our very own profit."

"Even there, you managed never to sully your hands in a way that might mean your ultimate undoing."

"Correct. Can I be blamed for taking precautions? I saw to it that we adhered to the division-of-labour principle. That's what had made the industrial revolution a success, so, chances were, it would do it for us. I was the CEO, scouting out premium opportunities and promising victims. The brothers stood for the footwork and logistics, mostly: escape routes, hide-outs, faked papers, the entire programme. Very old-school, from a modern point of view. But those were post-war times. Thus, reasonably well organised, we began to rob, steal, and borrow to our heart's delight. We may not have managed the massive re-allocation of assets that the Socialists were always lathering about, but I daresay we came a pretty long way, all things considered. Our speciality was raids on…"

"Yes, thank you. We already heard most of that from the Chief Superintendent, who gave us a rough idea of your collective rap sheet."

"The Chief Superintendent, eh? Harry the Merry Coleman. How is he these days? Battling with the idea of retirement, I bet."

"Colestron, actually. He's fine. Wanted to come along and put a bullet or two in your chest. I only just managed to discourage him."

Lamont laughed.

"Speaking of which. Of course, we always packed firearms during our operations, but rarely ever used then for anything else but fireworks of intimidation. No police officer or civilian ever lost life or limb because of us. The public liked that. Juries like that. I guess we enjoyed a lot of sympathy with the population. A lot of envy, as well. The only ones to hate our guts were bank managers and insurance damage assessors. Never fire a shot in anger was our motto. Even later, when drug trafficking and fierce, gory fights for territory became the bane, the order of the day, we managed to stay aloof. We never wanted any part in it. Young louts who thought they could take a shortcut to glory and fortunes. Mostly ended up in ditches or refuse dumps. Others would float in the Thames on a chilly Monday morning. Having witnessed the effects and, in particular, the long-term side-effects of drugs such as Pervitin or cocaine, we wouldn't bother to get involved, which was largely accepted by the Lodge of London war lords of crime.

Laura nodded and gave Sir Lucas one of her steely looks that use to make her opponents cringe.

"That sounds very romantic, almost Robin Hood-like. What happened to the distribution of assets among the poor, though? But what I hear, all was not to the best of worlds, now, was it? I suppose you couldn't help yourself and took to double-crossing, again."

For the first time, Lamont seemed seriously taken aback, almost miffed.

"I'm afraid you must help me out there; I don't know what you're talking about."

"I think you do only too well. I'm talking about the ultimate liquidation of the Yarmouth Six Ltd. I imagine you would have vastly preferred to take this last chapter of the annals to your grave, but I'm afraid I can't allow that to happen. The truth will out or so they say. And this seems as good a day as any for it to do so."

The old man seemed to shrink and crumple again. The twenty or so years he had shed in the course of his passionate plea fell back on him fast and made him look his age again.

"If I may be frank, I am beginning to find your ways a little offensive. You come here, to my home, without even being invited, and keep interrogating me, nay, insulting me. You may consider yourself lucky I belong to the old school of gentlemen who will respect the rules of hospitality, no matter what. But, as the Greeks say, dhen mou lidhoris allos topos – beware of insulting me at any other place, one, that is, where my hands will not be bound by custom and etiquette. What is it really you want from me? A sweeping confession? And why do you make yourself the advocate of a serial killer?

'Cause that's what he is, a serial killer, in case you happened to forget in the course of your little crusade…."

Laura fell silent. The man wasn't entirely wrong with what he said. What was it she was she doing here? Why was she attending to the Boxer's unfinished business? There was no black and white in this matter of the Yarmouth Six. All depended on the perspective you chose to adopt. Maybe it would have been better to follow Solitaire's advice and let the past rest. Except that it wouldn't have been commensurate with Laura's natural disposition, which allowed for no loose ends. Somehow, this wasn't so much about right or wrong as about total chaos versus precarious order.

"Well, I told myself someone's got to do it lest the ballad of the Yarmouth Six ends on a false note. Which is why I must ask you for a few more minutes of your patience. Thank you very much, I appreciate it. Where was I? Ah yes. You knew, of course, that the criminal activities of the Yarmouth Six had to come to an end sometime. Even if the secret service continued throwing spanners in the works of police investigations. Strange, Harry and his colleagues would regularly arrive that little step too late. Stranger, even, that crucial pieces of evidence would disappear, or key witnesses have second thoughts, all of a sudden. Coincidence? Hardly. Must have been extremely frustrating for them."

She paused and studied the play of Lamont's facial features. If he lost it and made the wrong move, that could have meant curtains for all of them. So better tread softly.

"End of the nineteen sixties and beginning of the seventies, forensic science and modern investigation techniques such as profiling made rapid advances. This was of course largely due to profound social changes and the waking of the terrorist sleepers. Predictably, your brotherhood would implode. So, you sought the proximity of the relevant authorities and offered your services as liquidator. The arrest and subsequent exhaustive interrogation of your brothers in crime risked unveiling monstrosities not only you preferred to remain secret. You started plotting discrete final scenarios and saw to it they were put into practice. With the tacit permission of the secret services, if not with their active collaboration, you arranged a series of would-be accidents during the nineteen eighties which killed off your ex-mates one by one. It had to be you. Nobody else would have taken the trouble of lending that ironic touch of having them fall victim to the specialities in which they excelled during their lifetime, as it were: mountaineering, gun-handling, swimming, and so forth. That was a mistake prompted by arrogance."

"And what about my own accident? If I had arranged that too, I would probably have seen to it that I didn't sustain injuries that would tie me to a wheelchair, wouldn't I."

"Yes, I must admit that puzzled me a great deal. Till I learned from the Boxer that this, ironically enough, was in fact due to co-incidence. A stupid technical hitch that turned a simulated crash into a really violent one. Shit happens. On the flip side, it made for a lot more credibility. Who would go the length of putting himself in a wheelchair to conceal a series of crimes, manslaughters, he had committed? At the same time, it gave you the image of fragility and helplessness that you have thrived on to this day."

"I think that's perfectly merited, after all I've been through. And, to tell the truth, a wheelchair is quite comfy, once you grow accustomed to it. Should try it one day."

"On top of that, you received awards for your alleged social work, which, again, protected you from critical scrutiny. Not a bad move for a despicable creature such as yourself."

Lamont didn't react immediately. He sat still, petrified, as it seemed. Laura understood. The old man had wriggled his way out of so many predicaments and personal near-catastrophes, he just hadn't counted on his ever having to account for his acts. Certainly not now, at the end of his life. Of course, there was always the risk of the Boxer finally getting hold of him, despite all of his safety precautions. But that would have been a snap and a bang. This endlessly prolonged turning on the spit enacted by that idiot German woman must be extremely embarrassing and annoying for him.

"Alright then. Tell you what. Let's assume for a moment you are right in what you claim. So what? You want to take me to court, destroy my reputation, blackmail me, what? When all is said and done, what's your ultimate interest?"

"I'm trying to fulfil an aesthetic requirement. To be complete, a story needs an ending. I know there are other theories saying that stories never really do end but the narrators just stop telling. I don't know about that. I think the first and most basic requirements of any narrative are a beginning and an end. You don't judge a painting until the artist has applied his last stroke of the brush. And the Ballad of the Yarmouth Six deserves a particularly reverberating final chord, don't you think?

"One you will hardly be in a position to strike," Lamont wheezed. Laura saw Solitaire's hand grope for what had to be her mobile under the table. How she had smuggled it past the guards frisking them at the gate, Laura could not begin to imagine. One or two clicks of Sol's thumb, and the platoon of trigger-happy Puer-to-Ricans on impatient standby would mount the attack. Only to find they were too late, Laura feared, and, staring at her sister, tried to hypnotize her into standing down. It seemed to work. Solitaire's hand came back up on the table.

"You didn't seriously think I would let you off the hook just like that, with all you actually do or only think you know about me. If you did count on that, you've got another think coming, I'm afraid."

Laura straightened her back and stared both at Solitaire and Ignace as if to warn them not to lose their cool at this critical junction.

"So what happened to the laws of hospitality, all of a sudden? How would you suggest stopping me? Don't you think you left enough corpses by the roadside of your career?"

Laura tried to remain calm and composed, yet emphatic.

"Kill three people to keep hiding the nefariousness of your do-ings? To keep dissimulating the utter pointlessness of your mis-erable existence? That'll never do."

"You wanna bet? You seem to be forgetting where you are and who I am. You shouldn't have come here, you know. On Puerto Rico, the sudden disappearance of people is an everyday occur-rence nobody wastes too much thought on. Like the milk van not coming by one morning. This is the most important trans-ship-ment point for drugs in the Caribbean. Loads of money involved, lots of lives lost. Who do you think will give a hoot about the disappearance of a young man and two sisters, one of whom is a notorious killer wanted by many countries in the world? And all of that to revenge the death of a young little whore."

Laura was dumbfounded. That was the one thing not foreseen in her scenario, the one thing that should under no circumstanc-es have happened. She watched Ignace, sitting to her left, out of the corner of her eye. He twitched as if struck by a bullet, but didn't budge. Maybe he was old enough to understand that Lam-ont was playing his last card, upsetting his opponents to provoke them into doing something foolish.

When nobody moved, however, Lamont called for the butler, who appeared instantly, as always, and took up his position behind the wheelchair. What made a marked difference from his earlier appearances was the small revolver in his right hand, a kind of Midnight Ladyhawk that looked a trifle effeminate on him.

"I think our visitors wish to say goodbye. Do see to it they'll be leaving by air mail, will you."

Laura looked at Harold screwing a silencer on his Ladyhawk. Air mail she knew from Solitaire to be current slang for the disposal of persons, dead or alive, by throwing them from a plane cruising high above the sea."

Harold pointed the short barrel with the big silencer at Laura, who sat in her chair, immobile from shock and fear.

Before she had come to and could react in any way, Harold lowered the barrel and turned it to his left with the most discrete of movements. Then, he pulled the trigger. The small calibre bullet must have struck Lamont at the very spot where his spinal column made contact with his brain. His head fell forward on his chest. There was no exit wound and practically no blood. An uninformed observer would have thought Sir Lucas to have dozed off, as he was wont to round the midday hour.

"What the heck…?"

Laura had jumped up so vigorously, her chair toppled over, the back crashing onto the floor. The fact that Lamont had been shot by his butler didn't necessarily mean they were home and dry. Maybe he had planned his coup in a manner such as to make it look like an exchange of gun fire between Sir Lucas and his guests, with the deplorable result of both parties getting killed.

But Harold seemed unperturbed, almost business-like. He had already unscrewed the silencer again and put it away together with the Ladyhawk.

"Might I suggest we follow Sir Lucas' piece of advice and make ourselves scarce, before his bodyguards get suspicious."

Laura wasn't quite willing to let him off just like that.

"Who…are you, I mean, what are you?"

Harold smiled affably.

"What does it look like? I am a butler."

"Butler my foot. Why did you kill him and not us?"

"Let's just say, Sir Lucas had outstayed his welcome with the services he thought he had in the palm of his hand. Whatever knowledge of us he once possessed has become as useless as he himself. You, on the other hand, happen to have learned a lot about him, but next to nothing about us. So, why draw unnecessary fire by killing you too? But I really think we ought to be off."

"How do we get past the bodyguards," Solitaire asked, her mobile ready for use. Harold shook his head disapprovingly.

"Don't make that call. You'll cause unnecessary bloodshed. The guards are perfectly used to my accompanying guests of Sir Lucas' back to town. It's become a ritual."

"And you, what's going to happen to you?"

Harold shrugged his shoulders.

"Oh, don't you worry about me. I have my own means of transport. By tomorrow night, I hope to be back in London."

"Lamont?"

"Tends to take a prolonged siesta at about this time every day. Hates to be woken too. I'll take him upstairs. You know why Stalin died? He had had a stroke and for hours, nobody dared touch him, so that, when his doctor finally took heart and looked him over, it was way too late. Everybody will be tiptoeing till tomorrow morning so as not to wake the tyrant. Don't move, I'll be back in jiffy."

He rolled the wheelchair to the elevator Sir Lucas had had installed to facilitate his moving around the villa and went up to the first floor. Here, he would probably drape Sir Lucas on the bed or couch the way he used to lie. Thus endeth the ballad of the Yarmouth Six, Laura thought. Not quite the ending Laura had imagined, but then, life being no stage, it hardly ever was.

She took Ignace in her arms.

"I'm sorry, son. What Lamont said about Solveig, I'm sure he was lying through his teeth, just to get at you, at us."

"What do you mean? Oh, I get it, her little escort jobs on the side. I knew. She had told me about it that very night we met.

Take it or leave it, she had said, that's me, the whole package. She didn't have my kind of luck with a well-off parent supporting her studies, so…."

"So you have known that all along? I don't believe it."

"Sure. I see nothing disparaging in people making a living every which way they can, do you?"

By way of a reply, Laura stood on her toes and kissed her son on the forehead.

3. CRAWL

"That could have gone awfully wrong, sis. If it hadn't been for that creature Harold…Next time, when I tell you to let it be, you better do as I say."

Laura and Solitaire were sitting on the patio of the new wooden bungalow on the brink of a slope dropping into the cobalt blue Caribbean Sea a few hundred yards further down. The breath-taking landscape still bore the ugly scars of the most recent cyclone that had hit Dominica hard. Nothing ever being so bad that it wouldn't carry some seeds of good in it, the landslides and crushing of trees caused by the hurricane had created a whole new vista for Solitaire and her family. For the first time in years, they now looked straight at the sea and enjoyed it.

Jeremy and Ignace had taken the pickup to Roseau to fetch some more minor building materials. The works on the bungalow were still a long way from being finished. Fortunately, Jerry possessed most of the technical knowledge and skills necessary to build a new bungalow more or less from scratch. Bobby and Penny, Solitaire's and Jeremy's son and daughter being at play with some other kids in their grandparents' garden next door, the two sisters had some precious time for themselves.

"Yes, I'm sorry to have put you through this. I should 'ave known a creature like Lamont would not shy away from the thought of cold-blooded murder when it comes to eliminating someone a little too hard on his heels. Honestly, I don't know what I was thinking. Somehow, I felt like I was remotely controlled by the Boxer."

"What's the guy's real name, after all?"

Laura shrugged her shoulders.

"Dunno. Brown, McAllister, Collins, take your pick. Brown's what he preferred, apparently. To me, he'll always be the Boxer. Since almost everybody in this story went by their nicknames, it seems only fitting to leave it at that: Hooch, Haggis, Gooey, Lily, Brain, Duke, and the Boxer. And Ronny the Scarface, not to forget…"

Solitaire nodded.

"You could be right there. In the churchyard lies the Boxer, how's that for the beginning of a new last stanza? That said, are you really sure he's dead? I mean, all you heard was an explosion and there's bound to be no corpse. So maybe he just retired and had you finish his work."

Laura smiled.

"Yeah, I thought of that. To be on the safe side, you would have to scratch some tissue off…the walls, I was going to say. Except there probably are no more walls where he blew himself up. There may not be anything like the perfect murder, but maybe he committed the perfect mock-suicide. If so, he had better stay underground on Alderney, 'cause with those huskey eyes, he sticks out in any crowd."

"Terrible weapon, those BFM's. Mines in general. On the other hand, had he fallen into Lamont's hands, he would have kept him alive and cut a little piece off his anatomy every morning, I guess."

"Imagine I tried to keep the awful truth about Solveig from Ignace at all costs, and then it turns out this son of a b… had known all along. Makes me look pretty foolish, doesn't it?"

"Not really. Without your intervention, both the Boxer and Lamont would now be going strong for a while longer. More murders, more collateral. No, I think you did good to help wipe them out. Looking at it from that angle, Solveig didn't just die for nothing. What I don't get is why did it take the Boxer so long to start his vendetta? "

"A question of opening the archives. Particularly sensitive information is only released at a point of time when it can safely be assumed that everybody even remotely involved in the matter has kicked the bucket. No one left to shoulder the blame, pick up the ticket, take the drop. The official version speaks of considerations of national security. That's hogwash. The real motive is the protection of all agents involved. If that wasn't so, if everybody working for one more or less secret state agency or another had to fear getting dragged out of the undergrowth one day with his pants down, all intelligence agencies would be paralyzed, nobody would dare take the necessary decisions any longer. Follows its own logic alright, I guess. Some MI6 and MI5 archives of the fifties and sixties possibly remained classified material until very few years ago. Not only to outsiders, that is, but also to agents from other state services. It's all on a need-to-know basis. And so, it was only when they were thrown open to at least a small circle of privileged people rightfully claiming a legal interest, that the Boxer got half a chance to take a glimpse at the files and piece the threads together."

"Which means his motives were strictly personal?"

"Oh yes. The personal element was paramount, you might say. Even though the way such a person's brain works is a secret to even the majority of forensic psychologists. Frequently, it's a conglomerate of personal, ideological and even religious aspects and views. Sometimes, sheer lust to kill, I suppose. I suspect most serial killers have no idea what urges them to take other people's lives. Take the Boxer, for instance. Was he really deeply convinced that he was on a crusade with the objective of bringing down one of the biggest rascals of our time or did he only vent his own frustration about what had happened to him in the course of his life."

"Yeah, who knows? I don't envy psychologists their task. Having to plunge into the soul of child molesters, murderers, rapists, what have you. And, once familiarized with what unspeakable horrors they find, having to get out of the quagmire again unscathed."

"That's right. I often have to think of something Ti Martin said to me shortly before his death on Montserrat."

Solitaire raised her glass and gave her Caipirinha a couple of swirls.

"Here's to Ti Martin! May he rest in peace."

"Amen. To Ti Martin and the Doc! I hope the two of them are sitting on cloud thirteen, playing chess all day long."

Solitaire laughed.

"Ti Martin hated chess. Or rather, he hated losing at chess. Was a sore loser, anyway. When we were looking for the icon of the bullet-proof Madonna on Crete, Jeremy and myself, I mean, we happened to watch two locals playing tavli, backgammon, that is, in a kafeneion, at the table next to us. They bore a striking likeness to Ti Martin and the Doc, only a little wilder, less well-kempt, obviously. Still, it gave me the impression of the two Frenchmen having suffered a shipwreck and been washed up on the Cretan shore, you know, Ulysses-like. Strange, I can see them even now. It was one of those scenes that, even though you may only have caught it for a few seconds, will stay with you for the rest of your life like a photo engraved in your head. Ultimately, we seem to have little control over what our brain decides to retain and what it rather discards. Its logic doesn't always follow our algorithms."

Laura nodded.

"Yes, I remember your excursion into the Sfakia at the time. Some adventure that must have been."

"Another local, who knew sufficient English, told us that some of the feuds fought out there have been running on for so many decades that no-one alive even remembers the causes but from vague hearsay. What counts is you're born into a clan, a family and have a moral obligation to do something as immoral as commit murder. Makes precious little sense. And lowers life-expectancy in those regions dramatically, I should think."

For a while, the two of them silently kept walking down memory lane. Laura sipped her drink and stared at the sea, with her eyes turned inwards, as it were. That's how she had been sitting on Theo's lawn, when one of the letters she had found on board the Yellow Dancer revealed to her that Frederike wasn't really her biological mother and her late father a crook and drug trafficker. And that she had a twin sister called Eleni, but known and feared all over the Caribbean as Solitaire.

"And now, what new plans are you hatching?" Solitaire asked at long last.

"You mean professional ones?"

"You know what I mean."

Laura thought it over for a moment.

"What can I say? Now that Lamont liberated the loan a little prematurely, from his point of view, I can go back to Hamburg without being shot or stoned to death by the other ROLA share-holders. My problem: I seem to have strayed from the path of righteousness."

Solitaire laughed.

"What are you talking about? You wouldn't recognize right-eousness if it stared you in the face."

"Maybe not. Like I say, if it hadn't been for Ignace and Solveig....Anyway, to begin with, I kept focussing on the job and treated the murder caper like a sideshow. With time, however, the focus seems to have shifted."

"How do you mean?"

"Well, you know, what I always really wanted to be was a lawyer. I embarked on business administration to do my father a favour, follow in his footsteps and all that. Trouble is, the per-manent struggle for yield maximalization and expansion isn't my thing. I tried to convince myself it was, but hell, it isn't. I know that now. The more I heard and read about it, the legend of the Yarmouth Six got under my skin. I feel like I never was so much alive as on those occasions when we chased the Snake round Istanbul and now the Boxer round the Channel Islands. Pure adrenaline, Robert's genes, I suppose. He was really a pirate turned merchant. Well, I seem to be going back to the family's true origins."

"So, you want to become a Ma Baker? Now, when all seems to be falling into place."

Laura laughed.

"No time better suited to jump ship than the moment you are on top of the world, when all seems as good as it's ever going to get. Trouble is, most of us realize that only with hindsight. But then it's way too late. We can't muster enough courage to be true to ourselves and take the plunge."

"What plunge? You're not thinking of..."

"No, no. Just a figure of speech. I feel I rid myself of all obli-gations towards God and the world at large. Ignace will soon be forging his own life, founding a family, the way it goes. More children are not on the biological cards as far as I'm concerned.

Pets I don't have and don't need. Looks like I might start living my own life instead of heeding the legacies of others."

Solitaire nodded.

"I can see you've tasted blood. Sniffed adventure like others sniff meth. Now you find it difficult to return to your Hamburg bourgeois life-style with a solid income and all sorts of perks. Well, take a look around and don't expect any pity from the likes of Jerry and me."

"I don't. I respect what you're doing, I really do. Bringing up two kids and a husband is more than anyone can expect from a woman."

The both laughed.

"The company can do without me, I'm sure. Shareholder value, stock exchange, Dax, Dow Jones, Nasdaq, hedge funds, offshore banking and all that crap. Who needs it?"

Solitaire laughed.

"I'm sure I don't. Nor does Jerry. Theo might be the only person on the island who needs that. And he's welcome to it."

"Who's welcome to what? That was Jerry having returned from his shopping.

"I've told you a hundred times not to sneak up on people like that. One day, someone will put a nervous bullet in your head because they got startled by your sudden presence. Might even be me, actually.

Solitaire got up and took two huge paper bags off Jerry's hands. "What have you bought, chief? Did you remember Penny's muesli?" Jeremy nodded.

"'Course I did. Gluten free, sugar free, low carb. Makes you wonder why on earth she takes the trouble of eating it. Might as well hold her tongue out of the window, should yield about the same quantity of nutrients."

"Don't be ridiculous. Where's Ignace. You didn't forget him, now, did you?"

"No, he didn't," Ignace shouted as he turned the corner of the bungalow. His one arm still in a sling, he carried only one paper bag, which he put down on the patio."

"On our way back, we tossed a coin to see who's going to pre-pare supper, and guess what, Ignace lost." Jeremy said and ruf-fled his dreadlocks.

"May I see that coin," Solitaire replied.

"Suspicious as ever, that's how I love my wife. Forget it, we'll share the cooking. Any preferences?"

While the two men disappeared in the kitchen with their bags, Solitaire started preparing two more cocktails.

"So, what're you gonna do? I mean, if you go about it smart enough, you can get away with a golden handshake worth its name. And then what, dolce far niente? Cruises and cold drinks?"

"Give it a name. How about founding a private detective agency?"

"A what?"

"A detective agency, private eye office. Specialising in cold cases."

"You've lost your mind?"

Ignace, who had been eavesdropping by the wide-open kitch-en window, couldn't help interjecting.

"May I join?"

Laura shook her head.

"No way. This is strictly women's business. Both what con-cerns the staff and the nature of the cases. A Caribbean version of the Number One Ladies' Detective Agency with Laura Forster in the role of Mma Bots…whatever."

"Mma Ramotswe is who you mean," Ignace helped her out.

"You know, that boy's better than Wikipedia and Google rolled into one," Solitaire praised her nephew.

"Yes, I know. Maybe I'll take him on the team, after all. Some-body's got to brew the coffee. In the movies, detectives drink no end of coffee."

"From notoriously empty cups."

"And always carry empty bags. I find that annoying. You can see that, I mean everyone can see that. An empty bag in some-one's hand looks different from a loaded one. Escapes me why they don't put a couple of books in, anything. Would look a world better, more authentic."

"And where would this agency of yours be located?"

Laura didn't have to reflect long.

"Anywhere but in Hamburg. This is the age of the Internet, or so we're being told. One condition, though: the local communications infrastructure must be in running order – phone, WiFi, plane, train, that sort of thing. Without that, there's going to be no end of frustrations."

"Well, I know a skilful young man who could fly you to one of the other isles with direct connections to Europe or the US. Unless he's busy sneaking up on young women, that rascal. So why not open your agency on Dominica, at Crayfish River?"

"Why not indeed?"

Laura raised her glass.

"I'll drink to the CRAWL, then."

"To the what?"

Jeremy and Ignace had both come out on the porch and taken their glasses in hand.

"The Crayfish River Agency for Well Educated Ladies."

Solitaire looked sceptical.

"I dunno. Sounds kind a kinky. Like some premium escort service."

Laura laughed.

"Well, in that case, I guess we'll have to work on the name a little while longer."